Praise for Kasey Michaels

"Using wit and romance with a master's skill, Kasey Michaels aims for the heart and never misses."
—bestselling author Nora Roberts

The Butler Did It

"Witty dialogue peppers a plot full of delectable details exposing the foibles and follies of the age… The heroine is appealingly independent minded; the hero is refreshingly free of any mean-spirited machismo; and supporting characters have charm to spare…[a] playfully perfect Regency-era romp."
—*Publishers Weekly*

Shall We Dance?

"Brimming with historical details and characters ranging from royalty to spies, greedy servants to a jealous woman, this tale is told with panache and wit."
—*Romantic Times BOOKclub*

Kasey Michaels is a *New York Times* bestselling author of both historical and contemporary novels. She is also the winner of a number of prestigious awards.

Available from **Kasey Michaels** *and Mills & Boon*®

THE BUTLER DID IT

IN HIS LORDSHIP'S BED
(short story in the *The Wedding Chase*)

SHALL WE DANCE?

IMPETUOUS MISSES

MARRIAGEABLE MISSES

Kasey Michaels

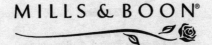

MILLS & BOON®

*First published in Great Britain 2006
by Harlequin Mills & Boon Limited,
Eton House, 18-24 Paradise Road, Richmond, Surrey TW9 1SR*

MARRIAGEABLE MISSES © Harlequin Books S.A. 2006

The publisher acknowledges the copyright holder
of the individual works as follows:

THE DUBIOUS MISS DALRYMPLE © Kathie Seidick 1990
THE CHAOTIC MISS CRISPINO © Kathie Seidick 1991

ISBN-13: 978 0 263 84958 5
ISBN-10: 0 263 84958 9

153-0906

*Printed and bound in Spain
by Litografia Rosés S.A., Barcelona*

CONTENTS

THE DUBIOUS
MISS DALRYMPLE

PROLOGUE

"HAVE YOU HEARD the news?"

Lord Blakestone lowered his newspaper to glare overtop it at the excited young man who had dared to intrude on his peace. Heaven knew he got precious little of it these days. "I *read* the news when I require an infusion of knowledge, Hopwood," he told the fellow in crushing tones meant to depress this increasing familiarity that was fast making Boodle's coffee room too common for words. "If I wished the day's happenings bellowed at me, I would sit in my own house and let my wife's dear, beloved mother natter me to death."

Hopwood was instantly cast down, but he was by no means to be counted out. He'd come directly from Bond Street, where tongues had been wagging nineteen to the dozen, and he'd be damned for a dolt if he was going to allow this chance to elevate his consequence here at Boodle's—a club he had stumbled into because of his parentage, and not his own standing or even inclination—to be stomped on by a pompous blowfish like Blakestone. "But—but I just heard. It's the most incredible thing! Lord Hythe is dead!"

Blakestone tossed his newspaper to the floor in an untidy heap, grumbling something about the servants being reminded to take better care when pressing the pages so that they would refold themselves automatically when the dratted thing was no longer required.

After venting his spleen on both the hapless newspaper and the overworked Boodle's servants (who were undoubtedly at that moment boiling coins somewhere in the bowels of the club so that the members should not have to smudge themselves by handling dirty money), he looked up at Hopwood and inquired shortly: "I don't believe it. Wythe? Wythe's dead?"

Hopwood shook his head vigorously. As audiences went, Blakestone appeared to be a poor choice. "No, no. Not Wythe. Hythe."

"Don't correct your betters, you miserable scamp. I say, Freddie!" Lord Blakestone called to Lord Godfrey, who had just entered the coffee room. "Have you heard the latest? Dreadful news. Wythe is dead."

"No!" Lord Godfrey ejaculated, pressing a hand to his chest, as if to be sure his own heart was still ticking along normally. He and Wythe were much of the same age. "How did it happen?"

Lord Blakestone waved an arm imperiously, summoning a servant and ordering another, freshly pressed, newspaper. "Damned if I know, old man. What do I look like, Freddie? A bleeding newsboy? Ask this puppy here. He seems to be hot to spread the gossip. Finally!" he groused, snapping the freshly pressed newspaper out of the servant's hand. "Took you twelve seconds too long, my fine fellow. You'll never get ahead in life lollygagging, y'know."

Lord Godfrey turned to Hopwood, who was leaning against a heavy mahogany table and most probably wondering what he had done to deserve membership to a snake pit such as Boodle's. "Corny says to ask you, whoever you are. So? Well, speak up, young man. What happened to

Wythe? I saw him just last week at Tatt's, full of piss and vinegar as ever. Dead, you say? How'd it happen? Apoplexy? He was getting on, wasn't he—at least ten years my senior, I'm sure.''

"Five your junior," Lord Blakestone corrected heartlessly, turning the page to check on the latest news of Napoleon Bonaparte's bloodletting on the Continent. "You're looking pale, Freddie. It's all that running about you do with that warbler from Covent Garden. Not seemly in a man your age—nor smart, now that I think about it. Best sit down before you join Wythe below ground.''

Hopwood felt an almost overwhelming urge to pull at his hair and scream, or possibly even throw something—Lord Blakestone's dusty wig was the first object that came to mind. "Not Wythe, sir—Hythe. He was young, in his prime. I was just taking the air on Bond Street when I heard the news. He was lost overboard from his yacht in a storm or something. Near Folkestone, I think.''

Lord Godfrey subsided into a burgundy leather wing chair, glaring impotently at Lord Blakestone, his agitated brain taking in information only as it pertained to him. "A yacht? I didn't know Wythe could afford to keep a yacht.'' As he couldn't show any real anger toward Lord Blakestone, whose social connections were considerably powerful, he directed his fury at a man who could no longer hurt him. "Y'know what—bloody stingy, that's what Wythe was. A yacht! Never took me up on the thing.''

Goaded, or so he felt, past all bearing, Hopwood opened his mouth and shouted—just as a half dozen worse-for-liquor gentlemen sitting in the dirty end of the room exploded in mirth over some joke or other: "Not Wythe, you feather-witted old nincompoops! *Hythe! Hythe!*''

While neither Lord Blakestone nor Lord Godfrey paid so

much as a jot of attention to the red-faced young man bellowing ridiculousness within four feet of their ears, they were attracted to the sounds of merriment across the room, and immediately longed to join in the fun. Looking back and forth to each other across the table that separated their matching burgundy leather wing chairs, the two lords scrambled to their feet, knowing their gossip would be a sure entry to the group.

As they walked toward the small gathering of gentlemen, they called out in unison, "Have you heard? It's all over town. It's the strangest thing. Wythe's dead!"

"Not Wythe, you paper-skulled asses. *Hythe!* Alastair Lowell, Fourteenth Earl of Hythe, and a damned fine gentleman." Hopwood pushed the discarded newspaper to the floor and collapsed into Lord Blakestone's abandoned chair, giving up the fight. "Oh, what does it matter anyway?" he soothed himself. "The fellow's still dead, ain't he?"

A MEMORIAL SERVICE was held three weeks later at Seashadow, the Hythe seat in Kent, with several of the late Earl's friends making the trip down from London in the fine spring weather to pay their respects—although it was rather awkward that there was no body to neatly inter in the family mausoleum.

"His bright light lies asleep with the fishes," the vicar had intoned gravely upon mounting the steps to the lectern, these depressing words heralding an hour-long sermon that went on to graphically describe the water fate of Alastair Lowell's earthly remains until a none too discreet cough from Miss Elinor Dalrymple—sister of the new Earl—caused the man to reel in his tongue just as he was about to utter the words "putrid flesh" for a seventh time.

The number of fashionable young ladies of quality (as

well as a colorful spattering of beautiful but not quite so eligible women) among the mourners would have cheered Alastair Lowell no end had he been privileged to see them—and so said his friends as they paid their respects to the new Earl and his solemn-faced sister before hastily departing the crepe-hung chapel for some decidedly more cheerful atmosphere.

"Made a muff of it," Leslie Dalrymple, the new Earl, said tragically, watching from the portico as the last traveling coach pulled out of the yard, leaving him to deal with a dining room piled to the chandeliers with uneaten food. "Ain't congenial, y'know. Never were."

"Nonsense, darling," Elinor Dalrymple consoled her brother, patting his thin cheek. "You were all that is gracious, and your eulogy, although understandably brief, as you had never met our cousin, was everything it could be. The late Earl, rest his soul, merely attracted those of his own, irresponsible ilk—considering that it is rumored our departed cousin was deep in his cups the night of his fatal accident. Doubtless they're all off now to carouse far into the night, toasting their fallen friend and otherwise debauching themselves."

Leslie shook his blonde, shaggy head, dismissing her assumption that he blamed himself for his guests' hasty departure. "Not me, Elly. You. You're the one routed them— what with your starchy ways. Scared them off, that's what you did. Besides, black does not become you. Don't understand it, as you're blonde and all, but there it is. I do wish you wouldn't persist in wearing such dark colors."

Elinor looked up at her brother, who, although three years her junior, stood a full foot higher than she. "Thank you, Leslie," she rejoined calmly, slipping her arm through his. "You have truly made my day. Now, would you be so kind as to join me in the dining room? I wouldn't wish for all that food to go to waste.''

The pair entered the house to see that the Biggs family, clad in their Sunday finery, was lined up at attention in the enormous three-story-high hall, obviously in preparation of meeting the late Earl's mourners.

Nine heads turned toward the doorway as Leslie and Elinor stepped across the threshold; nine necks craned forward to look past their masters for the horde of diners about to push their knees beneath the late Earl's table and eat their heads off; nine pairs of sky-blue eyes widened as Elinor closed the door firmly on the spring sunshine, and nine mouths split into wide, anticipatory grins as their new mistress announced that the Biggses would just have to discover some way to dispose of the bound-to-be-ample remnants of the funeral feast.

Billie Biggs shifted Baby Willie, her youngest, on her hip and took one step forward. ''Chased 'em off, did ya?'' she asked in her deep, booming voice that reached all the way up to the rafters. ''Good for you, missy. Never saw a sorrier-lookin' bunch in m'life. They'd have ate us out of house an' home before we knew which way to look. Come on, children—best get outta those duds afore ya ruin 'em.''

Each Biggs child obediently stepped forward in turn, to either bow or drop curtsies to the Dalrymples before leaving the hall.

Little Georgie, who helped his father in the kitchens (and the eldest at eighteen, though definitely not the brightest), tugged at his forelock and bowed his immense frame low, saying only, ''Daft sort of party,'' before shuffling toward the scullery—his mother's absentminded cuff across the top of his head hurrying him on his way.

Lily, sixteen, a very pretty girl who served as upstairs

maid, made an elaborate curtsey to Leslie—ignoring Elinor's presence—and headed for the staircase, her skirts twitching side to side as provocatively as she dared allow in her mother's presence.

Fifteen-year-old Harry, who worked in the stables, approached the Dalrymples and offered his condolences in a polite voice before passing behind them and through the front door, intent upon returning to the stable yard to check on a mare ready to drop her foal.

Elinor, whose new shoes were pinching her unmercifully, resigned herself to accepting the mumbled condolences of Iris, aged ten, Rosie, eight and one-half, and Bobby, a five-year-old cherub whose tumbling curls and intelligent eyes had, at first sight, prompted Elinor to believe Billie Biggs had played her husband, Big George, false at least once.

Finally, with Billie shooing the younger children in front of her with her immense white apron while reminding the Dalrymples to hurry to the table before the food got cold, the hall was emptied of all but Elinor and her brother.

"Lovely people," Leslie said, waving to Baby Willie as the child dangled backwards over his mother's shoulder, all ten fingers stuck in his wet mouth. "So kind, so caring."

Elinor looked at her brother askance. "Leslie," she intoned coldly, "the Biggses are not our house guests. They are the sum total of the late Earl's idea of a servant force on this estate—other than the farm laborers and such. Big George cooks because Billie can't boil water without burning it—although he told me the other day that it suits him fine anyway because she keeps a neat house and can make babies. Harry is a good worker, but Little George is a complete loss. Lily is ripe to seduce anything in long pants, while Rosie, Bobby, and Baby Willie are too young to do much more than eat their heads off and take up space—although I must admit Iris shows promise.''

Leslie was immediately apprehensive. ''You don't mean to turn them off, do you, Elly?''

Elinor shook her head and sighed. ''No, Leslie,'' she soothed wearily, ''I don't mean to turn them off. Truthfully, the estate was running quite smoothly when we arrived, so I see no need to change anything. It's just—it's just that it's so depressing. I have nothing to *do,* Leslie. That boisterous woman and her gaggle of children have made me totally superfluous!''

Leslie was immediately all concern—for himself. ''You—you wouldn't leave me, Elly, would you? I mean, I depend on you terribly—always have. Besides, you promised Papa you'd always take care of me.'' His green dreamer's eyes brightened as a thought hit him. ''Tell you what, Elly. You can be in charge of my studio. That should keep you busy. I promise to be as messy as possible.''

Elinor looked up at her brother, sure she could see a betraying tear in the corner of his left eye, and her heart softened. At three and twenty, she had long ago resigned herself to caring for her younger brother.

''Of course I would never leave you, darling,'' she assured him, patting his hand. ''Where would I go? I was just being silly—thinking only of myself. I should be jumping through hoops at our good fortune, not complaining that fate has made us wealthy and comfortable. Three weeks ago I didn't know where our next quarter's rent was coming from—and today you are the Fifteenth Earl of Hythe, and so deep in the pocket, we shall never have to concern ourselves about money again. I shall just have to educate myself in the pastimes of the idle rich, that's all.''

Leslie smiled, his fears banished. ''That's settled then,''

he pronounced happily, secure once more in the comfortable cotton wool his sister had kept him in for as long as he could remember. "Shall we go in to luncheon? I want to get back to my studio before the light leaves me." Walking three paces ahead of his sister, who only shook her head in resigned good humor as she brought up the rear, Leslie began to expound on his latest project—a painting of a spotted dog, as viewed by a flea—all thoughts of the late Earl and his flighty cronies forgotten.

VISITORS TO THE SEAPORT city of Folkestone, when not worried about Bonaparte's threats of imminent invasion from the French coastline that was so close it was often visible with the naked eye, could amuse themselves by taking walking tours along the Leas, a grassy expanse on the top of the cliff that looked upon the Strait of Dover, or, on less balmy days, by strolling the wooded paths on the face of the cliff and the Undercliffe.

Few people, however, chose to walk much beyond the quaint and irregular streets of the oldest section of town to the most remote, windswept beach, and the odd, derelict cottage that huddled against the base of the cliff. There were stories about this cottage—blood-chilling stories told late at night to visitors as they sat in cozy inn parlors, rubbing mugs of mulled ale between their hands.

It seemed that a giant lived in the cottage, an immense, growling ogre who—if anyone were ever so foolish as to approach him—would crack that poor unfortunate's skull like an eggshell with his great club as soon as look at him! The good people of Folkestone cut a wide path around the Ogre of the Undercliffe, and even the military, customs officers, revenue men, and smugglers showed no interest in routing the ogre from his lair.

The cottage was small, but with high ceilings—probably to better accommodate the ogre's great height—and was most likely composed of a single, irregularly shaped room that served as kitchen, sitting room, and bedroom. The ocean served as the ogre's privy. Although even the most modest cottages in Folkestone boasted milky-paned glass windows, the ogre's three small windows were hung with oiled rags and black paper, so that no one could even boast of actually having seen inside the darkened cottage. They only knew it was a place they would rather not ever find themselves near on a moonless night.

It was to this unnatural darkness that the man awoke, at first only for a few moments, his mind unclear, his body racked with pain and fever, before slipping once more into a merciful oblivion where the smell of dog and sweat and damp and old meat could not find him.

The man had dreams as he lay on the hard cot, dreams that included a gigantic, hovering beast who could only be the Gatekeeper of Hell; although why the Gatekeeper of Hell would be feeding him snail tea in barley water was for the moment past his power's of comprehension.

As time went on—be it hours or days or weeks, the man did not know—the most annoying thing about his current position was the grating sound of an unoiled wheel that seemed to be constantly in motion. In the end, it was just this sound that brought the man to full consciousness, and he propped his weak body up on one elbow to squint through the darkness in search of the source of the sound.

''That explains the smell of dog,'' he pronounced blankly, looking at last to the crooked fireplace and the antiquated dogspit that was cut into the wall beside the stones. As the dog ran inside the wheel, chasing a pitifully small marrow bone that hung suspended just out of reach, the spit in the fireplace turned, allowing the unrecognizable joint of meat to cook evenly over the fire, basting in its own juices.

The man sniffed at the air tentatively a time or two, trying to recognize the meat by its smell, then looked to the slowly trotting canine. "Not a close relative, I trust?" he asked the mutt facetiously before collapsing once more onto the hard cot.

He hurt like the very devil, from the top of his pounding head to the tip of his toes, but the pain told him that he was alive, and he supposed he should be grateful for small favors. He coughed, and that action brought on more pain in his chest and throat. "Dog sick," he said, not bothering to excuse himself to the mutt.

Lifting a hand to his face, he touched a considerable growth of beard, which told him that he had been in the cottage a long time—although how he had gotten here, he could not remember. As a matter of fact, the last thing he did remember was taking the air on the deck of his yacht, the *Lark,* as it lay at anchor just off Folkestone.

Before setting sail he had endured a rather boring, if profitable, evening onshore at cards, his three casually met companions having proved to be as dull-witted at faro as they were in the art of conversation, so that it had not bothered him overmuch that he had pushed away from the table the big winner, leaving the other gentlemen to commiserate with one another over their collective run of bad luck.

Walking to the rail as the yacht headed out to sea, he had spent a few idle moments trying to make out the mist-softened shoreline in the still dark sky of early morning before turning in—his reminiscences stopped there as the full realization of what had happened finally hit him.

"I was pushed!" he shouted—startling the underfed

hound into ceasing his endless walk on the wheel. "I was conked on the noggin like some wretch set upon by a press gang—and then tossed overboard as if I were so much garbage! I can even remember the feel of the water closing over my head! God's teeth, but I'd give half my fortune to know which one of the filthy bastards did it!"

He turned on the cot, forcing his bare feet to find purchase on the uneven packed-dirt floor of the cottage, and rose, nearly toppling backward as his physical weakness threatened to overcome his resolve to get himself back to civilization as fast as possible so that he could shoot somebody.

Only then did he realize that he was naked as a jaybird, with his clothing nowhere in sight. He stood in the dim light cast by the small fire, his rumpled blonde hair and fuzzy beard glowing golden in the glow, searching out the dim corners of the small cottage for any sign of his belongings.

A sense or urgency overcame him, giving him new strength. He had to be gone, had to seek help, had to discover who had pushed him—and why. Stumbling to one of the rag-covered windows, he ripped the material away and looked out across a rocky beach to where the surf was pounding against the shore. He looked back at the interior of the cottage, which hadn't been improved by the addition of a little daylight and fresh air.

Where was he? The place was a hovel; there was no other word for it. This was no Kentish farmer's cottage. It was too close to the sea, for one thing. Could some fisherman have plucked him from the Channel? No, there were no nets drying outside in the sun, no harbor from which to launch a boat. He swallowed hard. He had to be in a smuggler's hideaway. It was the only answer.

"Probably holding me for ransom," he thought aloud, the pounding in his head threatening to send him back to the cot to mewl like a wounded sheep. "I wonder how much an Earl brings on the open market these days. Damn your shaky legs, Alastair Lowell, you've got to find something to wear and get the blazes out of here before the baddies get back!"

Just as Alastair was becoming desperate enough to consider draping himself in the tattered blanket that had covered him, the door to the hovel burst open. A wide shaft of sunlight sliced through the cottage, nearly blinding him, to be followed by a sudden and nearly total eclipse as the doorway was filled with the largest man he had ever seen.

"Hell's Gatekeeper!" Alastair breathed incredulously, involuntarily backing up until the edge of the cot caught him behind the knees and he sat down, covering his nakedness with the blanket. He knew he hadn't led the most exemplary of lives, but had he really merited this?

The giant advanced into the room, his huge head tipped inquisitively to one side as he looked at his guest, before his attention was distracted by something near the fireplace. He turned slowly toward the fireplace and growled deep in his throat. The dog, which had been curled up asleep at the bottom of the wheel, leapt to his feet and began running as fast as he could, the singed joint on the spit spinning about so rapidly that hot meat juice flew off it to sizzle against the stones of the hearth.

The giant grumbled in satisfaction, turning his attention once more to his guest. Advancing toward Alastair, he reached into his pocket and withdrew a greasy piece of much-folded paper and extended it to the smaller man.

"For me?" Alastair asked, hating the slight tremor in his voice. "You want me to read this?" The ogre nodded. "All right,'' the Earl said, gingerly accepting the scrap of paper. He looked up into the larger man's face, searching for some sign of intelligence. "I'm going to have to get up now, and move closer to the window to get some light. Is that all right with you? Good."

Alastair, the tattered blanket wrapped about his muscular frame like a toga, moved slowly toward the small window—doing his utmost not to make any disaster-causing sudden movements. "I'm Alastair Lowell, by the by," he said, making what he hoped was idle conversation as he unfolded the paper. "I'm the Earl of Hythe—which should not be too far from here, unless I somehow ended up on the wrong side of the Channel. *Parlez vous français,* friend ogre? No? Well, that's some small relief. All right, let me see what this says."

He read for a few moments, then looked up at the giant, who was hovering just a mite too close for comfort. "Hugo, is it?"

The giant nodded vigorously, a large smile cracking his face to expose a childish, gap-toothed grin. He slammed one hamlike fist against his barrel chest and growled low in his throat as if repeating his name.

"Uh-huh," Alastair said dryly. "Obviously Hugo. And this letter was written by your mother—dictated from her deathbed, actually, to someone who wrote it for her. How touching." He lowered his head to read the remainder of the short note. "Good God!" he exclaimed, looking up at Hugo, then down at the note once more. "Cut out your tongue? I can't believe it. Why in bloody hell would anybody want to—"

Hugo's left hand came down heavily on Alastair's shoulder, nearly buckling the Earl's knees. *"Aaarrgh,"* the giant groaned, opening his cavernous mouth to let Alastair view the damage for himself.

"Yes, indeed," the Earl concluded quickly, trying not to gag, "it's gone, all right. My condolences. Your mother says you're a good boy, Hugo, and that I should be nice to you. You're seven feet tall if you're an inch, old man. I'd like to meet the fellow who wouldn't be nice to you. Besides, unless I miss my guess, you saved my life."

Nodding his head several times, Hugo stepped back to begin an elaborate pantomime Alastair believed was meant to depict Hugo's daring rescue at sea. As the performance took some time, and the Earl was beginning to feel slightly giddy from being on his feet so long, it wasn't too many minutes before Alastair could feel the small room begin to swirl in front of his eyes.

The giant, apparently sensing Alastair's imminent collapse, broke off his performance to scoop the smaller man into his arms and lay him gently on the cot. His movements swift and economical, he had a meal of meat, thin broth, and boiled potatoes in front of Alastair before another ten minutes had passed, and he fed this to the patient from his own spoon, grumbling compliments for every bite of stringy meat Alastair swallowed.

Later, after watching Hugo wash the plates in a bucket of seawater he had carried into the cottage, and while the spit dog hungrily wolfed down the remnants of the meal, Alastair, his strength at last beginning to return, began a fact-finding conversation with his nurse-savior.

"How long have I been here, Hugo?" he asked as the giant unearthed the Earl's clothing from a small chest near the hearth.

Hugo held up three fingers.

"Three days? No, my beard is too long for that. Three

weeks?'' Hugo nodded his head in agreement. ''Good God—the whole world must think me dead! Hugo—do you have a newspaper?''

The giant looked puzzled for a moment, then removed one gigantic wooden clog and pulled out the folded layers of newspaper that served as a cushion for his feet. Alastair accepted it gingerly, unfolding it with the tips of his fingers to see that the newspaper was six months out-of-date.

''Thank you, friend, but I fear I need something more recent than this,'' he said politely, quickly returning the paper, which Hugo replaced inside the clog. ''We'll need money. Did I have any money with me? I should have—I was a big winner, as I recall, and hadn't as yet gone to my cabin to change out of my evening dress. But no, doubtless the man who hit me made sure to empty my pockets before dumping me overboard—why else would he bother with the exercise at all? I should have known that at least one of them would prove to be a poor loser. Good Lord, Hugo, I think I'm babbling.''

Within moments Hugo had laid a considerable sum of money in Alastair's lap, amazing the Earl with his honesty. The man couldn't have spent so much as a single copper on himself the whole time the Earl was unconscious. But, relieved as he was to see the money, it also seemed to eliminate his disgruntled gambling companions as possible suspects in his ''murder.''

Counting out a hundred pounds, Alastair handed it to Hugo, who refused to take it. ''Here, here, man, don't be silly. I owe you my life. Besides, I want you to go into the nearest town and buy every newspaper you can find. Where am I anyway, Hugo? East or west of Folkestone? West? Good. That means I can't be more than a stone's toss from Hythe—and Seashadow. That fits my plan exactly—did I fail to mention that I have a small plan building in my head? Tell me, my large friend, would you like to be a part of it?''

''Aaarrgh!'' Hugo agreed, clapping his hands.

"Good for you, Hugo, and welcome aboard! All right, let's get down to cases. I'll need some clothes—nothing too fancy, just a shirt and breeches, and perhaps a vest and hat. Oh, yes, I'll need smallclothes and shoes as well. The salt water has made my own clothes unwearable, even if you were so kind as to wash them. Do you think you can take care of that for me? Of course you can. You're very intelligent, aren't you, Hugo? Your mother said you are.''

Hugo's gap-toothed grin was curiously touching.

"I'll need paper, and pen and ink, of course," Alastair added, thinking aloud. "I should think I'll want to get word to that Captain Wiggins fellow in the War Office that I'm still alive. He may prove useful. But I don't think I would wish the knowledge of my survival to go beyond him for the moment." He looked across the room at Hugo, then smiled. "Not much fear of that, is there?" he joked darkly, and Hugo's grin appeared once more.

"Yes," Alastair said, smiling genuinely for the first time since waking to find himself in the cottage, "this could prove to be extremely interesting.''

CHAPTER ONE

THE KENTISH COAST had long been considered the gateway to England, an island empire whose six thousand miles of coastline were its best defense as well as its greatest weakness.

The Romans had landed along the Kentish coast, followed by the Germanic tribes that were united under Egbert, the "First King of the English." Alfred the Great, England's first great patron of learning, was sandwiched somewhere between Egbert and William the Conqueror, followed by the Plantagenets, the Tudors, the Stuarts, the terrible, tiresome, homegrown Cromwell, and finally, the House of Hanover and its current monarch, George III.

The king, blind and most decidedly mad, was not aware that his profligate, pleasure-seeking son had been named Regent, which was probably a good thing, for the knowledge just might have proven to be the death of poor "Farmer George"—but that is another story. More important was the fact that another adventurous soul was once again contemplating the Kentish coast with hungry eyes.

Napoleon Bonaparte, ruler of all Europe, had amassed the Grande Armée, his forces surpassing the ancient armies of Alexander, Caesar, Darius, and even Attila. He had set his greedy sights on England early in his campaign to conquer the world, although pressing matters on the Peninsula and to the east (where the Russians and their beastly winter had proved disastrous to the Little Colonel) had kept him tolerably busy and unable to launch his ships across the Channel. This did not mean that the English became complacent, believing themselves invincible to attack from the French coast.

Quite the contrary.

Martello Towers, an ambitious string of lookout posts built on high ground from Hythe to Eastbourne, were still kept munitioned and manned by vigilant soldiers of His Majesty's forces. Dressed in their fine red jackets, the soldiers stood at the high, slitted windows of the grey stone cylindrical towers, their glasses trained on the sea twenty-four stupefying hours a day. In their zeal to protect their shores, the English had even dug the Royal Military Canal between Rye and Appledore, optimistically believing that it would give them an extra line of defense from the Froggies.

Five great seaports—called the Cinque Ports—lined the southeast coast, at Hastings, Dover, Sandwich, Romney, and Hythe, with the towns of Rye and Winchelsea vying with them for prominence, and these too had garrisons of soldiers at the ready.

All this vigilance, all this preparedness, the Peninsula Campaign, and the Russian winter—added to the fact that the Strait of Dover, also referred to as "England's Moat," was not known for its easy navigability—had proved sufficient in keeping Bonaparte from launching his soldiers from Boulogne or Calais.

It was not, alas, sufficient in preventing inventive English smugglers from accumulating small fortunes plying their trade from Margate to Bournemouth, almost without intervention.

Using long-forgotten sea lanes, the smugglers, known as

the "Gentlemen," did a roaring trade in untaxed medicine, rope, spices, brass nails, bridal ribbons, brandy, silk—even tennis balls. So widespread was the smuggling, and so accomplished were the Gentlemen, that even the Comptroller of the Foreign Post Office sanctioned the practice, as it brought French newspapers and war intelligence reports to the island with greater speed and reliability than any other, more conventional methods.

But, the Comptroller's protestations to one side, there were the Customs House officers to be considered. The smugglers may have been helping the war effort in some backhanded way, but they were also making the customs and revenue officers a redundant laughingstock, as the flow of contraband into England was fast outstripping the amount of legal, taxable cargo landed on the docks.

Many customs officers, loyal and hardworking, employed the King's men in forays against the smugglers. Many more did not. A few slit throats, a few bludgeoned heads—these were ample inducement for most customs officers to keep their noses tucked safely in their ale mugs on moonless nights, when the Gentlemen were apt to be out and about. Besides enhancing the possibility of living to a ripe old age, turning one's head was a good way for customs officers to increase their meager salaries, for the smugglers were known to be extremely generous to those who were good to them.

Popular sentiment as well was on the side of the Gentlemen, whose daring at sea demanded admiration—and supplied the locals with a wide variety of necessities and luxuries without the bother of the recipients having to pay tax on the goods.

As late as July of 1805, Lord Holland, during a Parliamentary Debate, conceded that: "It is impossible to prevent smuggling.... All that the Legislature can do is to compromise with a crime which, whatever laws may be made to constitute it a high offence, the mind of man can never conceive as at all equalling in turpitude those acts which are breaches of clear, moral virtues.''

All in all, it would be easy to believe that a, for the most part, comfortable bargain had been struck between the Gentlemen and the rest of the populate, but that was not the case. As the war dragged along, the unpaid taxes on contraband goods were, by their very absence, depleting the national treasury and war coffers, making the customs officers the butt of scathing lectures from their superiors in London.

The coastal forces, made up mostly of young men who had joined the military for the fun—the ''dash'' of the thing—only to be denied the clash of battle with the French, were itching to do battle with anyone. The Gentlemen and their nocturnal escapades were just the thing to liven up the soldiers' humdrum existence.

But most important, the Gentlemen, who were extremely profit-oriented, were lamentably not the most loyal of the King's subjects. Contraband was contraband, and money was money, no matter whose hand had held it last. Along with the spices and brandy and silk, there was many a French spy transported across England's Moat, carrying secrets that could conceivably bring down the empire.

All this had served to complicate the Gentlemen's position, and by 1813 the many small dabblers in the art of smuggling had called it a day, and the majority of the contraband was brought to the shores by highly organized, extremely unlovely gangs of cutthroats, villains, and sundry other souls not averse to committing crimes "equalling in turpitude those acts which are breaches of clear, moral virtues."

THERE WAS A LONG, uncomfortable silence in the main drawing room of Seashadow, broken only by the light snoring of the napping Mrs. Biggs, whose impressed services as vigilant chaperone of Elinor Dalrymple's reputation left much to be desired.

"That was a most edifying dissertation, Lieutenant Fishbourne—even if the bits about Cromwell and the Regent did not necessarily relate to the Kentish coast. But it begs me now that you have concluded—you have concluded, haven't you?—to ask how all this pertains to me," Elinor Dalrymple inquired wearily as she poured the young man a second cup of tea—for his lengthy, dry-as-dust dissertation on the history of England and smuggling must surely have caused him to become quite parched. "Or should I say—how does all of this pertain to Seashadow? Surely you haven't had reports of smuggling or spying along our beaches?"

Lieutenant Jason Fishbourne, attached to the Preventive Service by the Admiralty and stationed these past eighteen months in the port of Hythe, leaned forward across the low serving table to utter confidentially, "Have you ever heard of the Hawkhurst Gang, Miss Dalrymple?"

Elly's voice lowered as well, one slim white hand going to her throat protectively, as if she expected it to be sliced from ear to ear at any moment. "The Hawkhurst Gang? But they are located near Rye, aren't they—if, indeed, that terrible gang is still in existence."

The Lieutenant sat back, smiling, as he was convinced he had made his point. "There are *many* gangs about, Miss Dalrymple," he intoned gravely. "Each one more bloodthirsty and ruthless than the next, I'm afraid. And yes, madam, I do suspect that one of them is operating in this area—very much so in this area.''

Elly swallowed hard. Smugglers operating near Seashadow? Spies? And she had been walking the beach every day—sometimes even at dusk. Why, she could have stumbled upon a clutch of them at any time!

''What—what do you wish for us to do?'' she asked the Lieutenant, who now commanded her complete attention. ''We have only been here a few weeks, since just before the memorial service for the late Earl, as a matter of fact, but we intend to be contributing members of the community. I, in fact, have been searching for a project to occupy my time. Could I serve as a lookout of sorts, do you suppose?''

''Indeed, no, madam, I should not dream of putting you in any danger.'' Lieutenant Fishbourne rose to his not inconsiderable height, smoothing down his uniform over his trim, fit body before donning his gloves. ''I ask nothing of you—your King asks nothing of you—save that you report any strangers to the area and any goings on that appear peculiar. You and the Earl are not to involve yourselves directly in any way, of course. I only felt it fair to warn you about the shore, so that neither of you is inadvertently taken as one of the Gentlemen by my men, who on occasion will be, with your kind permission, patrolling the area at night.''

''I would not think to take on the daunting project of trying to capture an entire band of smugglers, Lieutenant. But if, as you suggest, there could be a spy—or even spies—operating near Seashadow, it would be my duty to do my utmost to capture him—or them!''

''Miss Dalrymple,'' the Lieutenant reiterated, ''we have

everything well in hand. Please, ma'am, do not involve yourself. If anything should happen to you because of my visit, I should never forgive myself. If you see anyone acting suspiciously, just have one of your servants summon me.''

Reluctantly nodding her agreement, Elly escorted the Lieutenant to the door, past Lily, who was making a great fuss out of dusting a gleaming brass candlestick as she watched the handsome tall, blonde officer.

Before the man could retrieve his hat from the table, the young girl had snatched it up, dusting it thoroughly before handing it to him with a smile and a wink. ''There you go, you lovely man,'' Lily cooed sweetly. ''Oh, you are a tall one, aren't you? Drop in any time,'' she added with a wink before Elly pointedly cleared her throat and the young girl scooted for the safety of the kitchens.

''She belonged to the late Earl,'' Elly explained, only to amend hastily, ''That is, she was a servant in the household when my brother and I came to Seashadow. She's been given her head too much, I daresay, and I have not as yet had time to instruct her in the proper behavior of staff.''

The Lieutenant shook his head. ''There's no need to explain, madam. I've heard the late Earl was a bit of a runabout, but I'm sure you and the current Earl will set it all to rights.'' He looked around the large foyer, his faded green eyes taking on a hint that could almost be termed envy. ''This is a lovely establishment. It would be a grievous sin to have it less than perfect.'' He brightened, smiling down at Elly. ''But if your brother the Earl is anything like his gracious sister, I'm sure there is no worry of Seashadow succumbing to the vagaries of poor husbandry.''

Knowing that her younger brother was at that moment in the west wing billiard room, blocking out a mural depicting the evolution of an apple from first juicy bite to bared core, Elly smiled enigmatically, allowing the Lieutenant to comfort himself with his own visions of the new Earl, and waved the man on his way.

Once the door was closed behind him, Elly stood staring sightlessly at the heavy crystal chandelier that hung over the flower arrangement atop the large round table in the middle of the spacious foyer. "Smugglers and spies," she intoned gravely, her curiously slanted brown eyes narrowing. "Carrying intelligence to Bonaparte so that he can kill more of our young men. Young men like my poor love, Robert—cut down before they've had a chance to live, to marry, to have sons." She raised her chin in determination. "Well, they won't be doing it from Seashadow. Not if I have anything to say about it!"

ALASTAIR LOWELL stood lost in a pleasant daydream on the small hill, gazing across the rocks and sand toward his ancestral home, watching as the sun danced on the mellow pink brick and reflected against the mullioned windows.

Seashadow was particularly lovely in the spring of the year. It was almost as lovely as it was in the summer, or the fall, or the winter. "Face it, man, you're in danger of becoming dotty about the place. Being near to death—not to mention the weeks spent in friend Hugo's airless hovel—have given you a new appreciation for those things you have taken for granted much too long."

He turned toward the water, smiling indulgently as he watched Hugo at play on the shore, chasing a painted lady—one of the thousands of butterflies that spanned the Mediterranean to cross the Channel each spring and make landfall on the edge of Kent. Dear Hugo. Whatever would he have done without him?

"I would have been breakfast for some sea creature, that's what I would have done," he reminded himself, his grey eyes narrowed and taking on hints of polished steel. "I mustn't allow my joy in being alive to distract me from the reason behind that joy—my near murder."

He turned back toward Seashadow, rubbing a hand reflectively across his bearded chin. He still found it difficult to believe that a new Earl had been installed in his family home, a fact he had discovered during his first clandestine meeting with Billie Biggs—once that devoted woman had finished thoroughly dampening his shirtfront with tears of joy over his lucky escape from drowning. His eyes narrowed. "So now I have a logical suspect. I hope you're enjoying yourself, Leslie Dalrymple, Earl of Hythe, eating my food and drinking my wine—for if Wiggins's and my plan goes well, you are very soon going to be booted out of my house and then hung up by your murdering neck!"

"Eeeeek!"

"Aaaarrgh!"

What a commotion! What a to-do! What high-pitched, unbridled hysteria!

"What in bloody hell? Hugo!" It all happened so quickly that Alastair was taken off guard, his hand automatically moving to his waist, and the sword that wasn't there. All he had was his cane, and he raised the thing over his head menacingly, vowing to do his best with the tools at hand, for obviously there was murder taking place just out of sight along the beach.

Cursing under his breath, he began to run down the hill toward the shore, the shifting sands beneath his feet nearly bringing him to grief more than once before he cannoned into Hugo—who had been running toward him at full tilt—

and was thrown violently backward against the ground, his wind knocked out of him, his senses rattled.

Air returned painfully to his starving lungs and he took it in in deep, hurtful gulps. There were several painted ladies hovering over him, swirling about in circles like bright yellow stars. No, they were stars, brilliant five-pointed objects that hurt his eyes. But that was impossible, for it was just past noon. There couldn't be any stars.

He shook his head, trying to clear it, slowly becoming aware of a shadow that had fallen over the land. Hugo. The man's enormous head blocked out the sun, the butterflies, and the circling stars.

"Aaarrgh," Hugo moaned, his hamlike hands inspecting Alastair from head to foot for signs of damage.

Suddenly a parasol, built more for beauty than for combat, came crashing down on Hugo's back, once, twice, three times, before splintering into a mass of painted sticks, pink satin, and lace.

"Unhand that man, you brute!" a woman's raised voice demanded imperiously. "Isn't it enough that you accost helpless females—must you now compound your villainy by trying to pick this poor fellow's pockets? Away with you, you cad, or it will be much the worst for you!"

Alastair struggled to sit up, trying his best not to succumb to the near fit of hilarity brought on by both Hugo's frantic expression and the outrageousness of the unknown female's accusations. This proved extremely difficult, as Hugo, who was obviously thoroughly cowed, had buried his face against the Earl's chest, seeking sanctuary. "I say, Hugo, leave off, do, else you're going to crush the life out of me," Alastair pleaded, trying to push the man to one side.

"You—you know this brute?" the woman asked, dropping the ruined parasol onto the sand, clearly astonished.

"I came upon him as I rounded the small cliff over there. I thought he was a smuggler going to…but *he* must actually have been afraid of *me*…which is above everything silly, for he is four times my size…and then I took him for a robber when he was only trying to help you? This is all most confusing. I don't understand."

"That makes the two of us a matched set, madam, for I am likewise confused," Alastair replied, prudently reaching for his cane before attempting to rise and get his first good look at the woman who had so daringly defended him against Hugo.

She was a young woman of medium height, slightly built in her rather spinsterish grey gown, her fair hair scraped back ruthlessly beneath her bonnet so that she looked, to his eyes, like drawings he'd seen of recently scalped colonials. Her huge brown eyes were curiously slanted—probably a result of her skin-stretching hairstyle. She looked, and acted, like somebody's keeper, and he immediately pitied her "keepee."

"When last I saw friend Hugo here, for that is his name," Alastair continued, "he was amusing himself chasing a painted lady."

"I beg your pardon," the female said crushingly. "I have not insulted you, sirrah! Just because I am on the beach without a chaperone is no reason to—"

Alastair hastened to correct her misinterpretation. "A painted lady is but another name for a butterfly, madam— the two-winged variety, that is," he said, rising to his knees as Hugo put a hand under each of his arms and hauled his master ungainly to his feet. "Ah, there we are, almost as good as new. Thank you, Hugo," he said, having been righted satisfactorily. "Now, perhaps we might try to make some sense out of these past few minutes."

"I knew that," the woman said in a small voice.

"You knew what?" he asked, bemused by the slight blush that had crept, unwanted, onto her cheeks.

"I knew about painted ladies—that is, about butterflies," she stammered, looking at him as if she had never seen a man up close before. "Are you sure you are quite all right? That was quite a blow you took." Her voice trailed off as a humanizing grin softened her features. "You—you must have bounced at least three times," she added, belatedly trying to disguise the grin with one gloved hand. "Oh, I'm sorry! I shouldn't see any levity in this, should I?"

Alastair made to push the kneeling, still-quavering Hugo—who reminded him of an elephant cowering in fear of a mouse—away from his leg. "Oh, I don't know, madam. If we can't discover the levity in this scene, I should think we are beyond redemption." He held out his hand. "I am John Bates, by the way."

She looked at his outstretched hand, then pointedly ignored it, all her starch back in her posture. "I am Elinor Dalrymple, sister of Leslie Dalrymple, Earl of Hythe—on whose lands you, Mr. Bates, are trespassing. May I ask your business at Seashadow?"

"*Aargg, ummff, aaah!*"

"Yes, yes, Hugo, I quite agree with you. I shall tell the lady. Don't excite yourself," Alastair soothed, patting the giant's head as he tried desperately to gather his thoughts, and control his anger. Who was this unlovely chit to dare ask his business upon his own land?

Why, the only reason she was still here rather than rotting in some damp jail—her and her miserable, conniving brother—was due to his charity in not demanding they be arrested the moment he'd first learned of their usurpation of his lands and title. No, he corrected himself, that wasn't quite true. It had been Geoffrey Wiggins's idea (conveyed in a hurried meeting between the two men) to continue the deception Alastair had first planned while still recuperating in Hugo's hovel—and the romance of the thing was fast losing its allure.

"You know what he's saying?" Elly asked, clearly surprised, as she peeped around Alastair to get a better look at Hugo.

"By and large, Miss Dalrymple, by and large. Hugo doesn't plague one with a lot of idle chitchat, having lost his tongue in some way too terrible to tell. However, if you should wish for him to show you the wound, I'm sure he would be delighted to satisfy your—"

"That won't be necessary," Elly cut in quickly. "But you—you understand him, poor fellow?"

"Now who are you calling a poor fellow, I wonder? But never mind. I shall answer your question the best I can. Yes, Hugo and I have, by way of his most articulate grunts and some acting out of intent, learned some basic communication. For instance, I am sure Hugo is devastated at having frightened you—nearly as devastated as he is by his fear of you. Please wave and smile to him, if you will. I should like for him to feel secure enough to leave go his death grip on my leg, for it is just regaining its strength from the wound it lately suffered on the Peninsula."

"You were on the Peninsula?" Elly asked, dutifully smiling and waving to Hugo before returning her gaze to Alastair. "I'm so sorry. I didn't know."

"And how should you, madam?" Alastair asked, intrigued by her quick about-face. She seemed almost caring. "Tell me, is your brother the Earl in residence? I wished to thank him for renting me the cottage, but all I have seen thus far, other than your delightful presence, of course, was a slightly vacuous-looking youth walking the beach earlier, collecting seaweed for only the good Lord knows what purpose.''

He watched as Miss Dalrymple blushed yet again, and had the uncomfortable feeling that he had just struck a nerve. ''That vacuous-looking youth, as you termed him, Mr. Bates'' —she shot at him in some heat— ''is the Earl of Hythe—and I should thank you to have the goodness to keep your boorish opinions to yourself.'' So saying, she turned on her heels, about to flounce off, he was sure, in high dudgeon.

She had taken only three steps when—again, as he was sure she would—she turned back, her slightly pointed chin thrust out, to exclaim, ''What do you mean, sir—you wish to thank my brother for the use of the cottage? What cottage? Where?''

As Hugo had been distracted by another gaily colored painted lady and was lumbering down the beach in pursuit of the gracefully gliding butterfly, Alastair felt free to spew the remainder of his lies just as he and Wiggins had practiced them. ''Why, madam, I thought you knew. After all, it was your brother who agreed to lend me the cottage on the estate while I recuperate from my wounds. It's the cottage just to the east of here—slightly inland, and with a lovely thatched roof. Hugo and I have been quite comfortable there for over a month now, although this is my first venture so far from my bed. But you still appear confused, Miss Dalrymple—and you shouldn't frown so, it will cause lines in your forehead.''

''Never mind my forehead, if you please!'' Elly shot back, bending down to retrieve her ruined parasol. ''Wait a minute!'' she said as she straightened. ''Over a month ago, you say? Why, that must have been the late Earl. Of course! You rented the cottage from the late Earl! That's why Leslie and I weren't aware of it.''

"The Earl is dead? I have been out of touch, haven't I?" Alastair bowed deeply from the waist. "My condolences on your loss, madam."

"None are required, Mr. Bates," Elly answered distractedly, clearly still trying to absorb his news. "I never knew the horrible man, I'm happy to say."

Alastair longed to take Elinor Dalrymple's slim throat in his hands and crush the life out of her. Smiling through gritted teeth, he responded, "Then may I offer my congratulations to your brother and yourself, for surely the two of you have fallen into one of the deepest gravy boats in all England. The late Earl was known, after all, for his great wealth."

"That's not all the late Earl was known for," Elly said, sniffing. "He was a profligate, useless drain on society, if half the stories I have heard are to be believed. If you wish to talk about painted ladies, you should have been here for his memorial service. There were more butterflies at Seashadow that day than this, if you take my meaning."

This time Alastair could not suppress a grin. "Lots of weeping and gnashing of teeth, was there? There's many a man who would relish such a send-off. Was there a redhead among them? I'd heard the late Earl had quite a ravishing redhead in keeping."

Elly's spine stiffened once more, most probably, Alastair supposed, more in self-censure at her own loose tongue than at his daring response to her indiscreet chatter. "Be that as it may be, if he leased a returning veteran a cottage in which to recuperate, he did at least one good deed in his wasted lifetime, and I shall not take this one vestige of goodness from his memory by refusing to honor his wishes."

"You are kindness itself, Miss Dalrymple," Alastair cooed, longing to throttle her.

"The sea air will doubtless be salutary to your wounds," she continued. "As a matter of fact—as a small way of showing you Seashadow's hospitality—may I tell my brother that you are to join us this evening for dinner?"

Alastair smiled, succeeding in splitting the three-week growth of beard so that his even white teeth sparkled in the sunlight. "Madam," he said sincerely, "I should be delighted!"

THE EVENING WAS comfortably cool, with a slight breeze coming off the sea as Elly stood just outside the French doors watching the sea birds as they circled the beach. Raising a hand to her throat, she adjusted the cameo that hung from a thin ivory ribbon, wondering if jewelry—even such simple jewelry—was proper during her supposed time of mourning for her cousin, the late Earl.

"Oh, pooh," she said, allowing her hand to drop to her side, where it found occupation smoothing the skirt of her silver-grey gown. "What does it matter anyway, now that you've been so stupid as to express your true feelings about the man to a relative stranger—a relative stranger you have invited to dinner, and then dressed yourself up like some man-hungry spinster at her last prayers?"

She should have invited Lieutenant Fishbourne to join them as well, considering the fact that his warning to her was the main reason she had invited John Bates to dine. "Report any strangers to the area and any goings-on that appear peculiar," the Lieutenant had cautioned her, and Elly had every intention of reporting John Bates and Hugo to the Lieutenant just as soon as she was sure if they were smugglers or spies. She only needed to squeeze a bit more pertinent information from Mr. John Bates so that she wouldn't disgrace herself by turning in an innocent man.

"John Bates couldn't be innocent," she told herself reassuringly, hearing the brass door knocker bang loudly in the foyer, announcing her dinner guest's arrival. "Nobody that handsome—or forward—could possibly be innocent."

Stepping into the drawing room, she looked around to see that Leslie, who had been dutifully sitting in the blue satin striped chair when she had left the room, was nowhere to be found. "Leslie?" she hissed, looking about desperately as she heard footsteps approaching the room. "Leslie! You promised! Where are you?"

"Lose something?" a voice inquired from behind her just as she was peeking through the fronds of a towering fern in hopes of discovering her brother hiding behind it.

Straightening, Elly pasted on a deliberate smile and turned to greet her guest. "Lose something?" she repeated blankly. "Why, yes, I seem to have misplaced, *um,* my knitting. Mrs. Biggs, our housekeeper, appears to delight in hiding it from me."

"You don't knit, Elly. Never could, without making a botch of the thing."

Elly swung about, to see Leslie down on all fours behind the settee. "Leslie!" she gritted under her breath. "Get up at once. What are you doing down there?"

Leslie Dalrymple, Earl of Hythe, rose clumsily to his feet, his pale blonde hair falling forward over his high forehead, his knees and hands dusty. "I was sitting quite nicely, just as you instructed, Elly, when a breeze from the doorway sent the loveliest dust bunny scurrying across the floor. See!" he demanded, holding up a greyish round ball of dust. "I think it's just the thing to complete my arrangement of Everyday Things, don't you?"

Elly didn't know whether to hit her brother or hug him. He looked so dear, standing there holding his dust bunny as if it were the greatest treasure on God's green earth, yet he was making the worst possible impression on John Bates. John Bates! Elly whirled to face her handsome guest, daring him with her eyes to say one word—one single, solitary word against her beloved brother.

Her fears, at least for the moment, proved groundless. John Bates, who had indeed witnessed all that had just transpired, only advanced across the width of the Aubusson carpet, his golden hair and beard glinting in the candlelight, his cane in his left hand as he favored his left leg, his right hand outstretched in greeting.

"My Lord Hythe, it is a distinct pleasure to meet you," he said, his tone earnest even to Elly's doubting ears. "I wish to thank you for agreeing to honor the rental arrangement made between the late Earl and myself. And, oh yes, please allow me to offer you condolences on your loss."

Leslie looked down on the dust bunny. "But I didn't lose it. See, I have it right here."

"Mr. Bates is referring to our libertine cousin Alastair's untimely death," Elly corrected sweetly even as she glared at John Bates. He already knew how she felt about her late cousin. Why was he persisting in bringing it up again and again? Anyone would think they had killed the stupid man, for pity's sake!

The dust bunny disappeared into Leslie's coat pocket as he took John's hand, wincing at the older man's firm grip. "A strong one, aren't you? Oh, you meant m'cousin, of course. Please excuse Elly. M'sister's taken a pet against him for some reason, ever since his mourners wouldn't stay to tea after the service, as a matter of fact. Rather poor sporting of her to my way of thinking, as the fellow's dead, ain't he—leaving the two of us as rich as Croesus into the bargain.''

"Leslie, please," Elly begged quietly, steering the two men toward the settee and seating herself in the blue satin chair.

But Leslie was oblivious to his sister's pleading. Seating himself comfortably, one long, skinny leg crossed over the other, he informed his guest, "I have been considering composing a picture to honor the late Earl and his accomplishments—only, I can't seem to find that he actually accomplished anything, except a few things best not remembered. I'm an artist, you understand."

"You wish to do a portrait?" Alastair asked, to Elly's mind, a bit intensely.

Leslie waved his thin, artistic hands dismissingly. "No, no. Never a portrait. That's so mundane—so ordinary. No, I wish to execute a chronicle of Alastair's life, with symbols. For instance," he expanded, thrilled to have found a new audience for his ideas, "if I were to do Henry the Eighth, I should include a bloody ax, a joint of meat, weeping angels, a view of the Tower—you understand?"

"What a unique concept, my lord," Alastair complimented, his eyes shifting so that he was looking straight at Elly, who shivered under his penetrating, assessing grey gaze.

What was he looking at? she wondered. And why did she have the uncomfortable feeling that John Bates could prove to be a very dangerous man?

CHAPTER TWO

HE WAS STARING at Elinor Dalrymple; he knew he was, but he couldn't help himself. Alastair had come to Seashadow to unmask the new Earl as his attacker. It had seemed so simple, so straight-forward—in a backhanded sort of way. But Leslie Dalrymple, bless his paper skull, wouldn't harm a fly—even if he knew how. Alastair wasn't so bent on revenge that he couldn't see that.

Unfortunately, he told himself as Mrs. Biggs called them to the dinner table, that left only the sister, Elinor, to take Leslie's place as suspect. Offering Elinor his arm to escort her in to dinner, and throwing a stern look at Mrs. Biggs, who so forgot herself as to begin a clumsy curtsey as he moved past (after she had done so well earlier when he had first arrived at the door), Alastair knew he had to rethink his deductions.

A man, after all, did not accuse another man of attempted murder without a wheelbarrow full of irrefutable evidence. Wasn't the desire to accumulate evidence what had brought him, under an assumed identity, to Seashadow in the first place? But a man—at least any man who considered himself to be a gentleman—never accused a lady of anything.

Once he had helped Elinor to her seat and taken his own chair across from her, Alastair resumed staring at her, knowing he was dangerously close to being indiscreet, but unable to help himself. A woman! It had never occurred to

him that his attacker could be a woman. Oh, certainly she
had employed someone to actually perform the dirty deed—
to conk him on the head and send him to a watery grave—
but that didn't make her any less guilty, did it?

This was going to take some getting used to, Alastair
decided, deliberately smiling at Elinor Dalrymple, as if en-
chanted by her spinsterish charms and idly wondering if her
small, shell-like ears really fit so snugly against the sides
of her head or if her ruthlessly pulled-back hair had anything to do with it. He watched her spine straighten as it
had on the beach and this time recognized the action as the
proud, stiff-necked posture of one who has had more than
a nodding acquaintance with poverty.

And with a brother like Leslie to support her, he considered thoughtfully, is it any wonder the two of them had
been purse-pinched? He doubted he had to look much further for a motive.

"Do I have a smut on my nose?"

Alastair blinked, his attention caught by the question in
Elinor's voice, although he hadn't quite comprehended
what she had said, his attention still concentrated on her
blonde hair as he tried to imagine her as she would look
with it soft and loose against her high-cheeked face. "I beg
your pardon?"

"You're staring, Mr. Bates," she pointed out needlessly.
"I wondered if there was something wrong with me that
has put you off your food. You haven't even touched your
meal, and Big George has really outdone himself with the
veal."

"Yes, indeed, I have—" Alastair had always relished
Big George's way with veal—so much so that he nearly
gave himself away, only catching himself in time to amend
his conversation by ending, "always enjoyed a veal. Big

George, you say? Is there also, perchance, a Little George running about somewhere?''

Leslie Dalrymple, his mouth full of veal, answered. ''Little Georgie, actually, even though he's past eighteen and fully grown. He doesn't cook, though—big George won't let him, at least, according to Mrs. Biggs, not since he set the capons on fire. Little Georgie just helps. Biggs is their name. You already met Mrs. Biggs, our housekeeper. Big George is her husband.''

''Making Little Georgie their son,'' Elinor completed hastily. ''It is as logical as it is boring, Leslie, my dear, and before you launch into a dissertation on all the other little Biggses running tame about Seashadow, I suggest a change of subject. Perhaps our guest would rather discuss something more worldly than our servant situation.'' Leaning forward slightly, she went on encouragingly, ''You served with Wellington perhaps, Mr. Bates? What battles were you in, exactly—and *when?*''

Alastair was amazed at the obvious intensity of her interest. He suddenly felt like a prisoner in the dock, undergoing a detailed cross-examination bent on exposing his guilt in some heinous crime. ''Well, actually, madam, I didn't see much action before—''

Leslie stuck out his bottom lip petulantly and interrupted, ''Who cares, Elly? I wanted to tell Mr. Bates about Rosie.'' He brightened slightly, looking to his sister. ''I'm going to paint her, you know.''

''Yes, dearest, I do know,'' Elinor said, reaching over to pat her brother's hand. ''Rosie will be a wonderful subject, once she cuts her second teeth. Now, why don't you try some of those lovely peas?''

Alastair watched, bemused, as Leslie obediently picked up his fork and began to eat. Oh yes, there was no question as to just who was in charge here. Elinor Dalrymple of the flat ears, scraped-back hair, and miserable disposition—sitting at her brother's right hand—was the real Earl of Hythe in all but name. Wait until he ran this one past Wiggins!

"Mr. Bates?"

Alastair looked across the table at Elinor, his grey eyes deliberately wide, his expression purposely guileless. If he had decided nothing else, he had decided that this woman was intelligent—which also made her dangerous. "Yes, Miss Dalrymple?"

"You were telling us about your time with Wellington," she prompted, accepting a small serving of candied yams from the hovering Mrs. Biggs. "From the left, Mrs. Biggs. You serve from the left."

"Do yer wants 'em or not, missy?" Mrs. Biggs challenged, glaring at Alastair as if begging his permission to dump the bowl on Elinor's head. "Right, left. What does it matter? I've got Baby Willie crying in the kitchen, afraid of that horsey-faced brute, Hugo, and that lazy, good-for-nothin' Lily nowheres ter be found."

"Baby Willie's crying?" Leslie exclaimed, hopping from his seat so quickly, the chair nearly toppled behind him. "We can't have that, Elly, now can we?" He reached up to pull the large linen serviette from his shirt collar, where he had obediently tucked it after dripping soup on his neckcloth. "I know. I'll make him a crow from this serviette—of course, it will be white rather than black, but then, that just adds to the romance of the thing, doesn't it? I can use these peas for eyes," he went on excitedly, filling his hand with the green vegetable before heading for the kitchens. "It will be famous, I vow it will! Here I come, Baby Willie! *Caw! Caw!*"

"Leslie, come back here—" Elinor began as Alastair hid

a grin behind his own serviette. "Oh, what's the use? It's like speaking to the wind."

His sense of the ridiculous overcoming his good manners, Alastair threw back his head and laughed aloud for a moment before sobering and apologizing almost meekly, "I'm sorry, Miss Dalrymple. I am but a lowly soldier sitting at an Earl's table. I really shall have to cultivate more elegance of mind. But you have to own it, Miss Dalrymple— your brother is most amusing."

Her brown eyes turned as black and forbidding as an angry sea. "You think he's an utter addlepate, don't you, Mr. Bates?" she accused hotly. "Well, perhaps he is, but Leslie is my addlepate, and I'll thank you to keep your thoughts to yourself!"

Alastair waved his hands in front of his face, as if to ward off her accusations. "No, no, Miss Dalrymple, please don't fly into the treetops. I meant nothing by it, really I didn't. Besides, you are wrong. Your brother is not an addlepate. He's rich, madam, which makes him a delightful eccentric. Only a poor man is an addlepate."

There was a commotion in the kitchens that reached into the dining room, turning the heads of both its occupants toward the baize door just as Hugo exploded into the room, Leslie on his arm. "Elly, look! A giant. A Titan! Isn't it above everything famous!"

Leslie turned delighted eyes to Alastair, who felt himself rapidly wilting beneath Elinor's white-hot glare. He had brought Hugo along with him because he couldn't feel right leaving him alone in the cottage. He'd had no idea the man's presence would cause either Baby Willie's tears or Leslie's euphoria.

"Is he really yours?" Leslie went on in accents of rapture. "Mrs. Biggs says he is. Do you think I could borrow him? I've just had the happy notion of painting him—for comparison, you understand—alongside of Baby Willie, if that poor dear will ever stop crying. Hugo's the loveliest thing I've ever seen!''

''*Aaahh,*'' Hugo crooned softly, accepting the compliment most graciously by picking Leslie up by the coat collar with one hand and placing a smacking wet kiss on his lordship's thin cheek.

Elinor leapt to her feet. ''You brute! You put my brother down this instant!''

''*Aaarrrggh!*''

Feeling as if he had just stepped unawares into a Covent Garden farce, Alastair rose as well, ordering, ''Don't growl, Hugo. It isn't polite. And put his lordship down; I think he's having a spot of trouble getting his breath.''

''Dear me!'' Leslie gulped, nervously smoothing his neckcloth as he gazed up at the giant. ''He is a strong fellow, isn't he? But not to worry, Elly, I'm convinced that Hugo and I will become fast friends. Won't we, Hugo?''

The giant grinned, showing the gap between his teeth—the sight of which immediately transported Leslie into another bout of ecstasy—and gently patted the young man's blonde head. ''Glugg, glugg,'' he crooned affectionately.

''That is *it!*'' Elinor exclaimed, the high pitch of her voice clearly indicating that she was about to fly into the boughs. Alastair privately commended her restraint, for he should surely have exploded long ago had he been so pressed. ''Leslie, excuse yourself,'' she ordered in a voice that brooked no opposition, and her brother meekly left the room, turning only once, to wave goodbye to Hugo.

She then turned to Alastair and said coldly, ''Mr. Bates, as you are living on the estate, we shall doubtless be forced to deal with each other from time to time—at least until I can have my brother's solicitor make other arrangements for you. But for the moment, sir, I ask nothing from you other than that you retrieve your cane, whistle this brute to heel, and remove yourself from these premises at once!''

Alastair, who had grown heartily sick of Hugo's attempts at the culinary arts over the past weeks, eyed the veal hungrily before giving in to the inevitable. The evening had been a shambles from odd beginning to even odder end. But, knowing that tomorrow was another day, he wisely motioned to Hugo, and the two of them headed for the door.

They had just stepped onto the porch—the heavy oak door slamming behind them, obviously propelled by the gentle hand of their hostess—when an insistent *"psst, psst"* came from the bushes.

''Who's there?'' Alastair whispered, looking about in the darkness as Hugo growled deep in his chest.

The bushes rustled behind them, and out stepped Lily Biggs, her hips undulating wildly as she approached, as if she were trying to navigate her way across a mound of feather pillows. ''G'evenin', yer lordship,'' she crooned, batting her eyelashes at her master. ''Mum told me yer was back, but I didn't believe it. She says I'm not ter say nuthin' about knowin' yer neither, or else I'll get my backside switched.''

''Your mother is a very wise woman, Lily,'' Alastair said, idly inspecting the impressive cleavage revealed by the snug white peasant blouse and wondering just when it was that the once angular young girl had developed the soft, enticing body of a woman. Had it really been that long since he'd visited his smallest, yet favorite, estate? ''You won't betray me, will you, my little darling?''

With a toss of her head, Lily's long, dark hair resettled itself on her snowy white shoulders as she stood toe to toe with Alastair, her firm young breasts pressed invitingly against his chest. Reaching up with both hands to smooth his neckcloth, she grinned and purred, "And what would be in it fer little Lily, d'yer suppose, iffen she was ter do as yer says? I love yer beard, yer lordship," she continued, lightly stroking his face. "It's so golden—like the sun or somethin'—and so fuzzy."

Now, here was a dilemma to tax the brain of the wise Solomon himself. Alastair had been without a willing woman for more than a month—quite possibly a new personal record he wouldn't wish bruited about among his acquaintances. It would be nice having an unattached, willing female so close to hand—although he supposed he could just as easily import one from the city if he so wished.

Besides, Alastair had known this child since her birth, and would never do anything to betray Billie Biggs's faith in him. But at the same time—could he trust this willful child to keep his secret if he insulted her by turning down what she was so obviously offering?

"Lily, I—" he began at last, not really knowing what he was going to say, just as the oak door swung open in a rush and he looked toward it, praying it was Mrs. Biggs come to his rescue.

But, alas, just as it had been with the veal he'd hoped to enjoy, he wasn't going to be that lucky.

"Here, Mr. Bates, you forgot your—oh, good Lord!" Elinor exclaimed, her arm halting in the action of tossing Alastair's curly-brimmed beaver at him. "Oh, this is beyond anything low!" The beaver came winging toward him, to be deftly snatched out of the air by Hugo, who then sat the undersized thing atop his own oversized head. "You lech! Let go of that poor, innocent girl this instant!"

"Miss Dalrymple," Alastair began hastily, silently cursing his continuing run of bad luck, "this isn't what you think. Let me endeavour to explain."

He turned toward the doorway, slapping Lily's greedy hands away as he tried to explain. "Leave go, Lily, for God's sake," he hissed angrily. "Don't make this any worse than it is." He looked up into his hostess's angry face. "Miss Dalrymple—please listen to me!"

"Listen to you? Listen to you!" Elinor exploded, grabbing hold of Lily's elbow and yanking her up the steps and into the foyer. "I have two eyes, don't I, Mr. Bates? There is nothing you can say that could possibly erase the evidence my own eyes have delivered. You may be a veteran, but you are no gentleman. Kindly keep to your cottage until I speak to my brother's solicitor—and don't try to approach this house or any of its inhabitants again. Do you hear me?"

"I should think they heard you in Dover, madam," Alastair replied tightly, his pride stung. "And once again, Miss Dalrymple, I bid you good night. It has truly been an experience." Feeling he had gotten in the last word, he then limped off into the night, Hugo, as Elinor Dalrymple had so imperiously ordered, at his heels.

"HERE THEY COME! I can see the bow of the boat hitting against the waves, turning them white. They're about to land."

"Quietly, your lordship, quietly," Captain Geoffrey Wiggins admonished in a fierce whisper. "There are three of us and twenty-five of them. I don't much like the odds."

Alastair pushed his prone frame more closely against the body-sized hollow he had dug in the sand, kicking out his left foot as some hungry insect feasted on his ankle bone.

"Then why in bloody hell didn't you bring more men? You told me you were almost certain the Gentlemen were landing here tonight. If I had known when you came to my cottage that all you wanted was for me to put lampblack all over my face and hands and burrow in the sand and watch, I could have stayed by my fire, dreaming about the veal I didn't get to eat while trying to down Hugo's swill—no offense, Hugo,'' he shot back over his shoulder to where Hugo was likewise lying half-buried in the sand. "What an evening I have had! I tell you, Geoffrey, the Dalrymple woman is mean; mean clear through to the bone.''

"*Shhhh!*'' Wiggins hissed, trying his best to bury his short, round body deeper in the sand. The Gentlemen were on the shore below them now, hastily unloading their cargo of brandy kegs, each gang member hoisting a barrel onto his shoulders before heading inland, the boat returning to the sea. "Count them,'' he whispered imperiously.

"Christ on a crutch, man,'' Alastair gritted back at him in exasperation, still itching to do combat with something other than the insects that continued to plague them, "you can bloody well count them yourself! What do I look like, a schoolboy at his sums?''

But, his protestations to one side, he did as the older man bid, dutifully counting kegs and gang members until the last of them trailed away over the hill to whatever hidey-hole they had chosen to stash their booty until it could be dispatched farther inland.

"It's just as I had thought, your lordship,'' Captain Wiggins said at last in quiet satisfaction, clambering to his feet and wiping his sandy palms briskly against each other.

"Don't look so pleased with yourself, Wiggins, or I might just do you an injury. Just as you thought about what?'' Alastair asked, turning over so that he could prop his sitting form against an outcrop of rock, his filthy hands dangling from atop his propped-up knees. "This may come as something of a shock to you, old man, but it wasn't what I thought at all. We came, we saw, we did nothing. No wonder you fellows at the War Office asked for my help. I'm bloody surprised old Boney ain't tripping down the dance at Almack's with Silence Jersey on his arm, nattering at him nineteen to the dozen, if this is the way you go about things. Hugo, stop threatening Captain Wiggins! I'll fight my own battles, thank you.''

The usually gentle giant, who had been eyeing Geoffrey Wiggins in a menacing way that had the squat, rotund man looking about himself as if planning a hasty retreat, growled low in his throat and moved off into the darkness.

Alastair waved Hugo on his way, his teeth flashing white in the faint light of the approaching dawn as he smiled at Wiggins's obvious relief. "And you worried about my safety, Wiggins," he said, shaking his head. "I hope your mind is set at ease now."

"In all my fifty years, your lordship," the Captain said, extracting a huge red handkerchief to wipe his sweaty brow, "I have never seen the like. How big is he, anyway?"

"Seven feet? Twenty-five stone? He is slightly smaller than Westminster Abbey, however," Alastair answered disinterestedly, rising so that he looked down at the older man, his hands on his hips. "Now, if we are done discussing the so estimable Hugo's dimensions, perhaps you can explain why we have partaken in this ridiculous, uncomfortable exercise."

"Ridiculous? How so, sir?"

Alastair shook his head in disgust at the question. "You came to my cottage at midnight—throwing those pebbles against the window was a tad dramatic, Geoffrey, by the by—promising me a sight of the smugglers you commissioned me to help ferret out for you. I'll say one thing for you—you didn't promise more than you delivered. We did see them, for all the sense it made. All we did was lie in the sand for three hours—I've been bitten badly, fleas I suppose—while we watched them land at Seashadow, and then counted them as they passed us. I could just as easily have taken your word for it, you know, and remained happily at home.''

Wiggins shook his head, his bushy grey side-whiskers serving as anchors as his chubby cheeks swung back and forth. ''Didn't you see, your lordship? There were twenty-five smugglers, and only twenty-four casks! Think, your lordship!''

Alastair shrugged, not comprehending. ''So? One of them is a lazy bugger. What of it?''

''Think again, please, sir. The Gentlemen never waste a motion. One of them,'' the Captain imparted importantly, ''wasn't a smuggler!''

The dawn broke, both literally and figuratively, as Lord Hythe snapped his fingers. ''A spy?''

Wiggins nodded emphatically. ''Precisely, my lord, very good. And I got a fairly good look at his face. I'm sure I'll recognize him when I see him again—as I can promise you I will. The brandy casks were only a diversion, probably a gift to the men who helped him cross the Channel. A truly dedicated group of the Gentlemen would have brought twice the booty—and no passengers. Twenty-four casks weren't worth the trouble of trying to get past Lieutenant Fishbourne and his men. Oh, yes, your lordship, we have found our man at long last!''

Alastair brightened even more. This was good news. ''Then there is no need to continue this masquerade! Actually you never needed me at all, Wiggins, now that I think on it, although I do appreciate that you thought to include me. I only wish I could have discovered all this myself, but I was conked on the head and thrown overboard before I could do more than plan my first moves against the men you thought were using Seashadow's beaches. Now it will be a simple matter of surrounding the beach with soldiers and apprehending the fellow. When do you think he'll be back? I'd like to be here, of course.''

The Captain sighed. This was the most difficult part of his job—dealing with civilians. War Office matters were best left to those in the service, those who understood tactics, maneuvers—the workings of the enemy mind. It certainly hadn't been Geoffrey Wiggins's idea to bring the Earl of Hythe in on this enterprise. ''Thy will be done,'' the Captain blasphemed, raising his eyes to the heavens and seeing his desk-bound, hide-bound superior in the War Office. He sighed again.

Alastair Lowell may have been young, and relatively inexperienced, but he knew when he had leapt to an incorrect conclusion. ''He's just a little fish, isn't he, Wiggins? You're after bigger fish.''

The Captain looked at the Earl with growing respect. ''Precisely, your lordship! The man we just saw is but a paid courier. I have men waiting along the roadway, ready to follow him to his final destination. We want to know who he is reporting to in London. We brought you into the exercise, your lordship, because we wished permission to operate freely from Seashadow, as we were convinced that the courier was using your portion of the coast. But then, when the attempt came on your life so soon after we had spoken to you, we feared that our plan to spring our trap had been found out.''

''But, as I keep telling you, Wiggins, I'm convinced that the attempt had nothing whatever to do with spies or es-

pionage. It couldn't have done. Why, you had only told me
about your suspicions a week earlier and I hadn't so much
as lifted a finger to do anything more than give you permission to set yourself up as John Bates in the cottage I'm
living in now. It's a good thing you hadn't as yet introduced
yourself around the area, so that everyone believes me to
be you. No,'' he concluded, his eyes narrowing as he conjured up a vision of Elinor as she had stood at his front
door accusing him of lechery, ''it's that miserable Dalrymple woman, Wiggins. She's the one behind the attempt on
my life! All that remains is to figure out whether she did it
for love of her brother or love of money.''

''Be that as it may be, your lordship,'' Wiggins said re-
signedly, ''I still think I should inform Lieutenant Fishbourne that you are one of us. He is, after all, in charge of
this area, and as hot to catch himself a clutch of smugglers
and spies as any man I have ever met. Very dedicated,
Lieutenant Fishbourne is, as well as eagerly looking out for
a chance to improve his standing with his superiors. I have
to return to London in at least a fortnight, you understand,
to set things in motion from that end, and it wouldn't do
to have the good Lieutenant arresting you on suspicion of
being the man we're after while I'm not here to identify
you, now would it, sir?''

Alastair shook his head at this argument, which he had
heard before from the Captain. ''We'll allow Lieutenant
Fishbourne to continue in his ignorance, Wiggins. But don't
worry, I'll handle him if it becomes necessary. Remember,
I was almost killed. Somebody wants me dead. If you are
right, and the Dalrymple woman is innocent—well, I simply
don't know who my friends are right now, Wiggins, and it
is an uncomfortable feeling. I don't mean to set your back
up with my stubbornness, but I'm chary of confiding in

anyone just now. Frankly, if it hadn't been that I needed the cottage to lend credence to the story we conjured up between us, even you still wouldn't know that the real Earl of Hythe is alive.''

"Good afternoon to you, my lord, madam.''

Elly stiffened, the lilt of good humor in John Bates's cultured voice cutting through her like a dull knife, and turned to face him as he carefully made his way down the incline onto the beach, his cane in his right hand.

Wait a moment! His right hand? She closed her eyes, trying to remember how he'd looked as he'd crossed the drawing room to greet her and Leslie the previous evening.

He'd looked handsome, and as dangerous as the devil, that she remembered clearly, although she kept telling herself to banish such debilitating thoughts from her mind. And he'd had the cane in his left hand as he favored his left leg. She was sure of it.

But this afternoon—ah, this afternoon—he was favoring his *right* leg. Wait until she told Lieutenant Fishbourne about this! If the Lieutenant wanted a spy, she couldn't think of a better candidate than the insufferable John Bates. But first she would have to be sure, and to be sure she would have to force herself to suffer the man's company at least one more time.

"Good afternoon to you, sir,'' she said with a forced air of cheerfulness, considering it safer to humor the man by pretending to forgive his boorishness of the previous evening until he could be clapped in irons. "Please allow me to apologize for my wretched behavior last evening. Mrs. Biggs graciously reminded me of Lily's predisposition to throwing herself at anything in—that is, I was made to understand that I was mistaken to blame you for Lily's, *um,* for Lily's—''

''Apology accepted, Miss Dalrymple, and the incident already forgotten,'' Alastair cut in, rescuing her from further embarrassment with his easy forgiveness while not sounding in the least penitent for his own misbehavior— and making her twice as angry with him as she had been the night before.

How dare he be so nice, so condescending, so easy to placate? She had thrown the man out of the house, then all but accused him of immorality, for heaven's sake! Didn't he have any pride, any feelings of self-worth? The man should be outraged!

The fact that he wasn't—or at least was pretending that he wasn't—was only further proof that he had some special, undoubtedly nefarious reason to want to stay at Seashadow.

Swallowing down hard on her anger, Elly simpered (oh, yes, she knew she was simpering, but she was doing it, after all, for King and country), ''How kind of you, Mr. Bates. Might I call you John, I wonder? We are to be neighbors, after all, aren't we?''

''And you are kindness and charity itself, Miss Dalrymple,'' he responded, bowing deeply—most probably, Elly assumed meanly, to hide his triumphant smile at her veiled admission that she was not about to throw him out of the cottage as she had threatened. This entire stilted exchange, she knew, was as if the two of them were performing some intricate dance, with each of them being extremely careful about not treading on the other's toes.

Leslie, who had been silent all this time, now piped up cheerfully, while simultaneously showing his main concern in the matter, ''Oh, good! I made a sad hash of my first social engagement as Earl—or so Elly told me at great length this morning—but everything seems to be settled most happily now.'' He turned to his sister, tugging on her arm like a small child begging for a treat. ''Elly, does this mean I shall be able to have Hugo pose for me after all? I have had the most splendid idea of painting his massive hands as they gently cradle a purple butterfly.''

''But, my lord, I believe the painted ladies are white, and yellow, and even black,'' John corrected pleasantly.

''Not to Leslie's eyes, John,'' Elly informed him, her tone daring him to laugh. ''Leslie sees things differently with his artist's eyes.''

''Precisely! Deep, pulsating purple—for the pulsating blue blood of royalty. The royal butterfly, gaudy and fragile, nestled in the strength of the great, callused hands of the masses.'' Leslie grabbed hold of Hugo's elbow. ''You understand, Hugo, don't you? You, my friend, are to represent all of loyal England. It's quite an honor, you know.''

''Indeed, yes,'' John agreed in earnest tones, earning himself a cutting look from Elinor, which he returned with a smile and a wink.

Leslie remained oblivious to the none-too-subtle undercurrents of animosity swirling about him. ''John,'' he piped up brightly, ''I'll tell you what. I should really like to study Hugo some more before I paint him. Do you think we cold take a walk, spend a pleasurable hour as I come to know his many faces, his many moods? But before you answer, I must warn you, John. If you say no, I am not sure I can regard it. I am set on this. The apple was beginning to bore me to distraction—not to mention the flies it was drawing.''

''The apple?'' John whispered in an amused aside to Elly as he smiled and nodded his approval of Leslie's scheme. ''Or would it be better if I didn't ask?''

''It would be immensely better if you didn't ask,'' she

told him quietly, wondering why she suddenly felt as if, at last, there was someone in her life with whom she might be able to talk without feeling she had been dropped feet first into Bedlam. How terrible it was that the man she felt she could talk with was a Bonapartist spy!

Leslie, not noticing the quiet exchange—as he noticed less than nothing if it did not involve him directly—took up Hugo's hand and began walking toward Seashadow, only to stop some twenty feet distant, whirl about, and call out loudly: "Did I bid you good day, John? I sometimes forget to do that—saying hallo and good day. Elly hates that, and I wouldn't want to put her in one of her pets."

"I don't have pets!" Elly growled softly as John's shoulders began to shake in obvious mirth. "I have only been trying to put it across to him that he shouldn't be surprised if he doesn't get along in society if he just walks away from people without saying goodbye—just because he's been struck by some grand, artistic inspiration."

"It's just that she says people in society won't like an Earl who doesn't say goodbye," Leslie shouted across the sand, confirming Elly's explanation. "Not that I should care for all the toing and froing of Polite Society. I like it here, actually, much more than half. Well, toodle-oo, John. I'll bring him back—I promise!"

Elly put a hand to her head and sighed.

"You have the headache now, I suppose," she heard John suggest, his words penetrating the dense fog of her embarrassment.

Looking up to see the amusement in his face, she heard herself reply, "You must think you have a most winning smile behind that horrid beard, as you grin all the time. Much as I wish not to do fatal damage to your sensibilities, John, I think you look quite terrible."

The moment the words were out, Elly regretted them. How was she supposed to get close to this man—this miserable Bonapartist spy—if she persisted in saying such horrid things? She was so enraged with herself that she just stood there, staring up at him, unable to think of a single thing to say that would heal their most recent breach.

But she shouldn't have worried. She should have known that John Bates's skin was too thick to be penetrated by her feeble female insults. Slipping her unprotesting hand through his elbow, he merely began walking them down the beach, in the opposite direction from that taken by Leslie and Hugo.

"Mad as fire, aren't you?" he said as calmly as if he were making everyday conversation. "Ah, madam, you have cut me to the quick. And here I had dared to dream that we were beginning to get on almost civilly. But there you are. Tell me, Miss Dalrymple. Are you aware that we are without a chaperone?"

CHAPTER THREE

SHE WAS BLUSHING. Good Lord above, she was blushing— just as if she were some silly, simpering miss lately escaped from the schoolroom! It was mortifying! How dare he bring such a lapse to her attention—and grin through those horrid golden whiskers as he did it? She should slap him silly, that's what she should do.

No! She should pull her hand from its strangely comfortable resting place through the crook of his elbow, turn on her heels, and march posthaste back to Seashadow, cutting him dead.

No! She should face him down, stab him with her cold, steely stare, then proceed to slice a few wide, painful strips off his splendidly put-together hide with a few well-chosen words meant to depress his absurd familiarity once and for all.

No! She should take his cane (as it was obviously useless to his two perfectly healthy legs) and hit him repeatedly over the—

"Cat got your tongue, Miss Dalrymple? I was only teasing, you know. After all, it's the middle of the afternoon, your brother the Earl is just down the beach, and we're in full sight of Seashadow. It isn't as if we are about to elope together to Gretna Green, is it?"

Oh, how she hated—how she *loathed*—this insufferable man! Why didn't he just come out and say it—she was an over-the-hill spinster who should have long since donned her caps and stopped embarrassing everyone by pretending she was still an eligible *parti*. She couldn't cause a scandal if she were alone with any man in the kingdom—save perhaps Prinny himself, who was known to like his women a little longer in the tooth.

"Miss Dalrymple?" John Bates stopped walking to step in front of her, tuck his cane under his arm, and take hold of both her elbows as he stared down into her face. "Oh, dear. I have put my foot in it, haven't I? Both feet, perhaps. You're thinking that I'm thinking that you are ugly or something—aren't you? I assure you, Miss Dalrymple, that thought never entered my head."

Elly finally found her voice. She didn't give a tinker's dam if he were King of the Smugglers, Emperor of the Spies, or both. She had had enough! "I think, Mr. Bates, you do protest too much. For an idea that never entered your head, it certainly found its way out of your mouth quickly enough. Now, please unhand me. I wish to return to my brother."

She made to withdraw herself from his hold, but he thwarted her, his hands clamping down onto her wrists. "Bristly as a prickly pear, aren't you, Miss Dalrymple? I imagine I shall have to own it—I have had occasion to consider your looks over the past few days." He tipped his head this way and that, as if giving her one last inspection before rendering his decision. "It's your hair, I think. I mean, your face is unexceptional—a bit finely drawn perhaps, with a hint of a pointed chin, and your strangely slanted brown eyes are by far your best, most entrancing feature—but your hair, Miss Dalrymple, is a disaster."

"Oh, that's *it!*" Elly shouted in exasperation, feeling as if she were about to become totally unhinged. She yanked herself free of his hands. "I may be destined to lead apes in hell through all eternity, Mr. Bates, but I see no reason I should *listen* to one of them babble while I'm still above ground."

She set off up the beach as fast as her jean half boots, her swirling muslin skirts, and the shifting sands allowed, knowing without seeing that he was close at her heels, his limp forgotten.

"But, Miss Dalrymple, you didn't let me finish. You have lovely hair—much the same color as mine, as a matter of fact. Isn't that a coincidence? But you yank it up on the top of your head like some tight-lipped schoolmistress about to deliver a stern lecture."

Elly stopped in her tracks. Just as he had hit her sore spot, her looks, he had just as unerringly struck her one soft spot—her hair. She had lovely hair? She had always thought so, privately, and could admit to herself that she spent more hours in front of her mirror brushing the heavy, waist-length locks than was absolutely necessary.

Once, she had worn it down. Once, she had brushed it over the curling stick and looped it gracefully atop her head, allowing it to wave softly at the sides of her face. Her fiancé, Robert, had always liked it best that way, saying it reminded him of molten gold mixed with silver. But once Robert had been lost to her, there had been no reason, no inclination, to fuss with her hair other than in the privacy of her chamber, away from the eyes of the world. Her bottom lip began to quiver.

"Miss Dalrymple?" John questioned, stepping in front of her. "Oh, blast it all, you're crying, aren't you? I've made you cry. I always did have a tongue that was hinged at both ends—and the horrible habit of speaking before thinking." He took her hands in his, squeezing her fingers comfortingly. "Please, Miss Dalrymple, forgive me. I'm the scum of the earth, I'm the lowest of the low."

Elly heard the self-condemnation in his tone. It was entirely believable. She also saw the sympathy in his grey eyes. It was the sympathy that stiffened her lip and brought her back to reality. She had always hated sympathy. It was so useless, almost as useless as her overreaction to his observations.

She had more important things to consider. John Bates *was* the lowest of the low, with the tact and manners of a mediocre dandy. That shouldn't have surprised her, because John Bates was, she was sure, also a smuggler—or a spy.

Either way, he was a dastardly creature, the sort of slimy, money-mad, disloyal cad Lieutenant Fishbourne had talked about, who sacrificed fine British lives like Robert Talmadge's for his own profit—and she was going to unmask him and see him punished for his crimes, if she had to put up with his crudity and insults every time they met.

But, if she was really set on her plan—and she knew deep in her heart of hearts that she was—*she* too was going to have to somehow develop a thicker skin. Considering their encounters to date, that skin, she supposed quietly, would also have to boast the repelling characteristics of battle-quality steel mesh.

"You're forgiven, Mr. Bates—John," she said at last, trying her best not to smile as he heaved a sigh of relief. Obviously it was important to his dastardly plans for him to remain in the cottage on the estate. "You have said nothing I have not heard before from Leslie. He compares the styling of my hair to that of a yellow onion. But, your apology rendered and accepted, John—do you think you could be so good as to once again allow me the use of my hands? I have decided to give in to impulse and take down my hair. This isn't London, after all, and I have been harboring the urge to wear it loose just once, to blow free in the breeze from the Channel. It's a silly notion, I must say, but one I should wish to indulge in just this single time. Do you mind?''

Her heart pounding, Elly raised her hands to the top of her head and removed the pins that held her hair in a tight bun. It was the touch of his hands on hers, of all things, that had decided her once and for all that she was obligated to forge ahead for King and country; the touch of his hands and her thought that he reminded her of a lower-class London dandy.

There were, she had discovered, absolutely *no* calluses on his palms! Leslie had spoken of the callused hands of the workers of England. Surely soldiers would similarly have hard workman's hands—Lieutenant Fishbourne did.

Yet John Bates had the smooth, well-groomed hands and nails of a London dandy—not that she had ever been to London herself, but she was sure those effete, pompous nodcocks used more creams on their hands than any beauty-proud debutante or aging matron.

If she was going to get to the bottom of this—if she was going to find any evidence concrete enough to take to Lieutenant Fishbourne—she would have to become close enough to John Bates, trusted enough by John Bates, that he allowed her inside his cottage, where she could discover the truth about him.

And in order to do that, she would have to first capture the man's interest.

WHAT IN BLOODY HELL was the absurd woman doing now? Alastair hadn't been this nonplussed since, since—why, he couldn't remember a single time in his life when he had been at such a total loss for words, for coherent thought. Standing there dumbly, as if he had been momentarily converted into marble, he watched as Elinor Dalrymple—thin, over-the-hill, pointy-chinned, stick-in-the-sand, possible attempted murderess Elinor Dalrymple—stuffed hairpin after hairpin into her skirt pocket, while using her other hand to hold on to the tight yellow twist of hair.

When the last of the pins was disposed of, she bowed her head so that her face was hidden from him, scrubbed at her freed hair with her fingers, and then flung her head back so that a river of silver and gold flowed from her forehead to her narrow waist.

And then—directly in front of his eyes, like a lowly caterpillar shedding its cocoon—Elinor Dalrymple metamorphosed into the most glorious painted lady Alastair Lowell had ever been privileged to see!

Her smooth cheeks flushed a becoming pink with exertion—could any of that lovely color have come from the knowledge that she was facing a man whose mouth was at half cock?—Elinor's features changed from pinched to petite, finely sculpted by the hand of a master. Her brown eyes danced with delicious mischief. Her hair, that unbelievable, unexpected curtain of glory, seemed to have taken on a life of its own, and he immediately longed to run his fingers through it, bury his face in it, wrap his naked skin in its warm fire.

Alastair could feel his body responding to the stimuli of Elly's appearance, to the sweet violet scent of her hair as it billowed in the breeze off the Channel, to the moist sweetness of her mouth as she smiled up at him with all the guileless invitation of a first-time strumpet.

Oh, yes, Alastair told himself, holding on to his composure with every ounce of will he could muster, he most certainly would have to rethink importing a woman from London, although his sudden aversion to redheaded women worried him more than he'd care to admit at this moment.

Her hands on her hips, her entire stance daring him to speak, he heard her say, "Ah, you cannot imagine how I have been longing to do that. Well, John, do you still believe we are in no need of a chaperone?"

The little tart! She was baiting him, deliberately urging him to commit an action that—if the woman in question was, at least as far as the world knew, the sister of an Earl—could be seen as nothing less than a marriage-mandatory compromise of her reputation. He'd like to slap her silly. He'd like to grab her by the shoulders and—and kiss her until she begged for mercy!

Good God, what was he thinking? Only a month earlier this woman had tried to have him murdered! If nothing else convinced him of that, her actions of the last few minutes had shown him that Elinor Dalrymple might have been trying to present herself as a little mouse, a loving sister, a drab nonentity of no importance—but her *real* self was quite a different matter.

A few subtle insults directed at her lack of beauty had been pointed enough to scratch off the dowdy exterior and reveal the real woman inside. He could see that she was champing at the bit to have the official year of mourning over so that she could go to London and take it by storm—probably leaving her paper-witted brother, Leslie, behind at Seashadow to paint the Biggs's children in all their "moods." The coldhearted harridan!

These thoughts flew through Alastair's mind like lightning bolts exploding against the unwary earth at the height of a summer storm, none of them lingering for more than a brief second for closer examination, but all of them doing tremendous damage to the areas they had struck.

With his conclusions drawn, Alastair had no hint of what to do next. He could hardly stand up straight, announce his true identity, and then accuse her of attempted murder. But, while they played the roles of devoted sister and injured veteran, he could not act on his greatest impulse—which was to pull her along with him to some secluded spot beneath the cliff and spend a pleasurable hour investigating her for other hidden areas of beauty.

Not only that, but he had to remain friendly toward her, so that he could get back into Seashadow and examine the half dozen volumes of Lowell family history for mention of the Dalrymples. He had honestly believed himself to be the last of his line, with his title to pass either to the crown or into eternity along with him if he died without issue, and could not rid himself of the nagging feeling that Elinor Dalrymple had stepped in before his body could even be found and somehow hoodwinked his solicitors into believing a false claim to the title.

Good God! She might even, if he were to stretch the point, be one of the spies Wiggins was hunting, and his own murder was the means her gang of cutthroats had employed to gain free access to Seashadow. The possibilities were limitless! He'd have to suggest this last thought to Wiggins once the man returned from London.

So how was he to remain on good terms with the woman—would she for the love of heaven stop looking at him that way!—and not insult her by refusing what it was so obvious she was offering?

Taking a deep breath, Alastair uttered the fatal words he had not thought to hear himself say to anyone for at least five more glorious, responsibility-free years: ''Miss Dalrymple, would it seem too forward, too optimistic on my part, if I were to believe I might be allowed to speak to your brother? I am not a rich man, but I come from a good, honest family...." He allowed his voice to die away, as he was actually beginning to feel physically ill.

He watched as a shiver—of surprise? of shock? of antic-ipation?—shook her slim body. "You wish to—to *court* me, John? This is so—so *unexpected*. I should never had let down my hair, but you were all but *daring* me to prove that—I *am* in mourning, you understand—"

Dropping the cane on the sand, he grabbed her hands and held them tight against his chest, feeling like an actor caught up in a bad play. "In mourning, yes—for a distant relation you loathed," Alastair reminded her, trying not to grit his teeth. "I am attracted to you—deeply attracted to you. Come, dear Elly," he prodded, daringly, "don't say that you aren't attracted to me. You let your hair down for me. Admit to our mutual attraction, and we can go on from there."

He let go of her hands, bent to retrieve the cane, and turned to limp away, his head bowed, his entire posture one of hurt, of defeat. "I have overstepped," he intoned sor-rowfully. "I am a Nothing, a Nobody—begging favors from the sister of an Earl. You are right to refuse me, Miss Dalrymple. Please disregard the happenings of these past minutes. I shall try to do likewise, although it will be the most difficult thing I have ever done—that I will ever do."

He felt her hand touch his shoulder and nearly laughed aloud in relief. She had actually believed him! He should try his talents on the boards; it was possible he was another, but more handsome, Edmund Kean!

"Please, John," he heard her say as she tugged at his shoulder, "don't feel hurt. I didn't mean to upset you. It's just…well, it's just that this is so sudden. One moment we were bickering and the next you were on the verge of declaring yourself. My head is spinning.''

She didn't mean to upset me? What did she think she was going to do to him by turning from spinster to Come-Hither-Incomparable in front of his eyes—leave him unmoved? He was supposedly recovering from a war wound—not fighting off senility!

And did he detect a small note of placation in her voice, a hint of deliberate cajoling? Was she really attracted to him or did she have another motive? It wasn't in her nature to be so nice to him—not if his previous encounters with her were to be used as a yardstick with which to measure her reaction now. Perhaps she thought to recruit him to her gang of spies?

Alastair's head was beginning to pound with all of his jumbled thinking. It was time to end this conversation, this tense moment that had already gone on too long. Turning about, he took her hand and began walking back down the beach, idly noting that Leslie and Hugo had disappeared somewhere or other and were no longer visible.

''I think we two should separate and privately reflect on what has passed between us this afternoon, Miss Dalrymple. Then, later, over dinner at Seashadow, perhaps—and with your brother the Earl present as vigilant chaperone—we can reevaluate our reactions.'' There—that hadn't sounded as if he had deliberately tried to wrangle another invitation to dinner.

She nodded vigorously, removing her hand from his so that she could begin to repin her hair—making Alastair feel as if the sun, which was still burning brightly high in the sky, had suddenly disappeared behind a cloud. ''I could not agree more, John,'' she told him briskly, her mouth full of hairpins as she struggled to fix the mass of tangled gold into a clumsy yet attractive topknot. "And, please, you called me Elly in the heat of the—that is, would you please continue to address me informally? Miss Dalrymple seems so needlessly stilted now."

Alastair put his hand lightly, unthreateningly, against her slim back as they walked in the direction of Seashadow, his cane punching small circles in the sand with every step. "You are too kind, Elly," he said, silently thanking whatever lucky star he was born under for her willingness to go along with his plan, no matter what her motives. "Are you aware, Elly, that Saltwood Castle is nearby?"

She didn't disappoint him, but readily accepted his giant leap of conversation from the extraordinary to the mundane. "No, I did not know. Wasn't that once used by the Archbishop of Canterbury?"

"And as the rendezvous of the murderers of poor Becket before they did the dastardly deed," Alastair confirmed, smiling down at her. She really was an intelligent puss— intelligent enough to be everything he supposed her to be and more. "Hythe, I have found since coming to Kent to nurse my wounds, is a treasure trove of history—and me with only a few books in the cottage. Perhaps you will allow me to run tame in Seashadow's library, so that I might try to increase my knowledge?" he put out hopefully.

"I should be honored. Seashadow has an extensive collection of histories," Elly replied, smiling up at him, allowing Alastair to smile openly at what he believed to be his brilliant ploy for getting himself a step closer to the Lowell family histories.

"Let me think of other things I have learned about this area. There is a church built much along the lines of Canterbury Cathedral that contains a crypt boasting a huge collection of bones and skulls of what the book called 'sketchy' origin,'' he went on encouragingly. ''And of course, there is also Studfall Castle, site of an ancient Roman camp…''

HE WAS SUCH a lovely man, this Leslie was; kind, and gentle. A lot like his ma, come to think on it. Only, his ma didn't smile so much—or talk so much without really saying anything.

Hugo's massive brow puckered as he pondered the differences between the Earl of Hythe and his deceased mother, but he couldn't think about it for very long, because Leslie was talking at him again and he knew he should listen.

''This promontory, Hugo, is where I should like to pose you with the butterfly,'' Leslie informed his companion, puffing slightly as Hugo, with his hands on his lordship's derriere, helped push the man up the remainder of the hill to the cliff.

''Thank you, Hugo. I hadn't realized it was such a climb. But here we are now, aren't we? With the trees to one side, and all God's infinity to the other, it is the perfect place for what I have in mind. Don't you think so, my friend?''

Hugo, having gained the top of the hill himself, looked about inquiringly, wondering just what a promontory might be and if he should recognize it when he spied it, then gurgled and nodded his agreement The Earl might be a mite strange, but Hugo, who had experienced too little friendship in his life, would have followed the man into the fires of Hell with a smile on his face.

''Of course,'' Leslie went on, excitement building in his voice, ''I shall have you—or should I say, your hands, for that is all of you that is necessary to this particular creation—several times the size of the trees. I think I shall use three trees. Yes, three trees exactly. I like working in threes, you understand.''

As Leslie talked, he walked, his thin arms flailing in the breeze as inspiration followed hard on inspiration. Hugo watched, entranced by the frail man in full creative spate, then looked down at his hard, callused hands, once more wondering what it could be that Leslie saw in them that had excited him so. After all, they were only hands, and dirty hands at that, with broken and chewed nails. He couldn't talk with them, could he? He'd give one of them up most happily if he could but be given a tongue in exchange.

Leslie was standing close to the end of the cliff, *his* tongue still going sixteen to the dozen about ''space'' and ''infinity'' and ''the great power of the sea.'' Hugo didn't understand more than every third word, but he certainly did enjoy hearing the sound of Leslie's cultured voice as it rose above the crash of surf against the rocks at the base of the cliff.

''Your hands, Hugo, will be floating somewhere toward the middle of the picture, the butterfly cupped in your joined palms, just so,'' Leslie continued, cupping his own hands as he demonstrated what he had in mind. ''I should like the sun coming over your left shoulder—not that your shoulder will be there, of course, but I'm speaking figuratively. Oh, dear, you're frowning. Am I confusing you again, my friend? Not to worry. You'll understand when you see it.''

Hugo doubted that, but he flashed his gap-toothed grin and nodded vigorously, his smile fading only as Leslie turned and took another step toward the edge of the cliff, his eyes on the horizon. *''Aaaarrgh,''* Hugo warned quietly, advancing toward the Earl before the man slipped and tumbled to his death.

"What's that, Hugo?" Leslie asked.

As Leslie hesitated, Hugo's keen eyes caught the glint of something shiny among the trees to his right. A half heartbeat later, as Leslie was turning to look at Hugo, a very large, very dangerous-looking knife came winging out of the trees, to sail harmlessly past the Earl's shoulder and arc gracefully into the sea.

Hugo squeezed his eyes shut and shook his head. Had he really seen what he thought he had seen? He opened his eyes once more to see that Leslie was standing in front of him, saying something about painting the sea full of frogs, to represent the threat from the French, while filling the trees with snakes, and carrion crows, to signify—well, they would signify something. He'd figure out precisely what as he went along. Not all art was the result of instant inspiration. "What do you think, Hugo?" The Earl ended, hands on hips.

Hugo didn't think. Hugo *couldn't* think—he was too terrified at the realization that he had almost been witness to the death of his new friend. But, most important of all, he couldn't *speak*. He couldn't communicate what he had seen other than by acting it out—and Leslie Dalrymple could be murdered three times over until he could make him understand that he was in danger.

Yes, Hugo knew he could only do one thing—and so he did it. He lifted the astonished Earl over his shoulder as if he were no heavier than a sackful of feathers and ran as fast as he could down the hill toward Alastair, his deep, booming voice—filled with unintelligible urgency—preceding him down the length of the beach.

ELLY ALLOWED John's hand to remain lightly at her waist as they walked back up the beach in companionable silence, content to concentrate on the satisfaction she would feel once he was exposed for what he was and clapped in irons. So lost was she in this pleasant daydream that it took several seconds for the unearthly wail to invade her mind, and by then John had already begun racing full tilt up the beach ahead of her, leaving his cane behind.

"Oh, good lord, John, what is that terrible caterwauling?" she called after him, hitching up her skirts and breaking into a run herself.

"It's Hugo!" John called over his shoulders as his long legs ate up the grounds. He all but flew over it, his coattails flapping behind him in the breeze. "Something's wrong!" He disappeared around an outcropping of rocks that marked a turn in the beach.

"*Leslie!*" Elly fairly screamed, her heart pounding hurtfully somewhere in her throat as she skidded to a halt on the soft sand, her feet suddenly incapable of further movement. Yes, she had noticed that John had given up his pretense of a limp, but for the moment that didn't matter a jot. Hugo was in trouble, and Leslie was with Hugo! There must have been an accident!

"Oh, please, God, let him be all right," she begged, wiping sudden tears from her cheeks with trembling fingers. "If you let him be all right, I promise not to let him out of my sight ever, ever again. If you let him be all right, I'll turn the information I've discovered over to Lieutenant Fishbourne and—and put on my caps and learn to knit properly! I'll do good works in all the local villages, Lord. I'll— oh, thank God, *Leslie!*"

"Elly!" the Earl piped up gaily, trotting toward her from around the rocks. "It was the oddest thing. One moment I was discussing my ideas with Hugo and the next he was lifting me on his shoulder and running with me down the beach—screeching like a banshee. Do you think it was some primitive expression of joy because I want to paint him? Ah well, it was exhilarating, to say the least.''

Leslie stopped in front of her to straighten his disheveled clothing before looking at his sister. "Good gracious, Elly, get a grip on yourself. You look as if you've seen a ghost. And I thought the sea air would put some color in your cheeks.''

She didn't know if she wanted to kiss him or box his ears. Not only had he scared her half to death, he was insulting her for looking as if she had just been frightened out of ten years of her life—which she had. Deciding it was better to distance herself from her brother for a few moments while she searched for composure, she walked past him to where John and Hugo were standing, deep in conversation.

At least John was conversing. Hugo was gesturing furiously, demonstrating by use of his entire massive body what had transpired that had brought him to lose himself to the point where he would manhandle an Earl.

"Yes, yes, I think I see what you mean," she heard John say as she approached. "You're a cliff, right? Good. Well, since you couldn't actually *be* a cliff, you must mean you were *on* a cliff.''

Hugo grunted, his massive arms flailing wildly as he began to prance back and forth across the sand. He appeared almost light-footed for all his hugeness as he continued to race up and down the beach, looking like a flightless bird or—to Elly's mind—a pachyderm attempting ballet.

"Correction," John continued with a noticeable hint of

humor in his voice, watching the giant's ungainly dance. "You *and the Earl* were on the cliff."

"Wretch," Elly said quietly, silently agreeing with John's deduction. If one could mentally deduct about two-thirds of Hugo's weight, he was Leslie to the life!

The giant nodded to John, then began performing in a way that looked to Elly as if he were attempting to demonstrate something between drawing a line in the air and his own rendition of the death scene in *Romeo and Juliet*.

"I have to own it, Hugo," she heard John say, "you have totally lost me on this one. I haven't the faintest idea what you're talking about. And why were you carrying the Earl when I found you?"

Elly felt a cold horror invade her chest. "Leslie was running about…full of himself and his new idea…and…and he nearly toppled over the cliff! Oh, of course, what else could it be?" She advanced on Hugo, intending to thank him for saving her brother, but the large man eluded her, shaking his head, becoming increasingly breathless as he continued to act out his explanation.

"Yes, yes, Hugo," she soothed, taking hold of his hand, "I understand completely. There's no need to exert yourself further. My brother must have frightened you extremely—so much so that you grabbed him up and ran back to us just as quickly as you could. Oh, Hugo, you are a hero!"

"Aaaarrrggh!" Hugo groaned, lifting his massive hands, palms up, before turning to John, as if begging for help.

"Don't be modest, my friend. I already have reason to know what a hero you are. I couldn't agree with Miss Dalrymple more, Hugo, and I think you behaved admirably," John answered before turning to Elly. "Have you ever considered keeping Leslie on leading strings, Elly? It might save everyone a lot of bother."

For once Elly didn't mind that someone had insulted her brother, because she agreed with John completely. This wasn't the first time since arriving at Seashadow that Leslie had escaped a near disaster. There had been the toadstools he'd purchased from some traveling merchant while out for a walk and nearly ingested before Big George could stop him—and the morning he had been walking on the beach near the cliff and a loose rock had fallen not two feet form his head.

"Now what is he about, do you suppose?"

Elly looked at John, to see that he was looking past her to Leslie—who was walking toward the path that led up to Seashadow, his arms waving wildly, deep in conversation with himself. He was off on another of his tangents, she was sure of it, leaving her to find her own way home. "There are times I could absolutely *choke* that boy!" she said feelingly.

"Really?"

"Don't be ridiculous." She didn't understand the tone of John's voice. It was almost as if he actually believed her capable of murder. Looking over her shoulder at him as she started after her brother, she said, "We'll expect you later this evening for dinner, John. And, oh, yes, I'm so glad to see that your leg is better." She watched as he looked down at his legs, then across the beach to where his cane lay, forgotten.

"Well, stap me if it isn't! I guess it was a miracle," Elly heard him say weakly as she walked away, already planning her next move meant to expose his real identity—all earlier pleas and promises to her Maker forgotten.

CHAPTER FOUR

ELLY WAS WELL pleased with the furnishings at Seashadow, handsome yet functional furniture that reflected the exemplary taste of the previous Earl—which was the *only* good thing she had been able to attribute to that man since she had first learned of his existence.

The Rudd's Reflecting Dressing Table in her own Dresden blue and white boudoir was, however, her particular favorite. The Hepplewhite piece had been meticulously designed with an abundance of intricately compartmented drawers to hold her meager supply of beauty aids. But for sheer genius of design, nothing could surpass the arrangement of not one, but two mirrors that could be adjusted to endless positions—obviously fashioned to provide milady with limitless views of her person.

And for the past fifteen minutes Elly had been doing just that—examining her reflection from every possible angle— while at the same time trying desperately to convince herself it mattered not a jot to her if her scalloped lace hem was dragging, or her ruched sleeves uneven, or her hair (which she had combed over the curling stick until it was turned into a mass of curls) was too high, or her cheeks were too pale.

The gown she had chosen for the evening, an incredibly soft butter-yellow silk, had not been worn since Robert's death three years previously and was most woefully out-of-date, even for her, but it was the best she could do. The best she wished to do. It had been Robert's favorite, and besides, it wasn't as if it would send her into a rapid decline if a certain Mister John Bates didn't swoon with ecstasy at the sight of the thing.

Yet, it was her complexion that bothered her most, if the truth were to be told. Leaning forward, and adjusting the small brace of candles that stood on the dressing table, she turned her face this way and that, wondering if she dared to touch her too pale cheeks with a discreet dusting of rouge. She wanted to keep John's interest, but she didn't want it to be too obvious that she was all but throwing herself at his head.

She leaned closer to the mirrors and compromised by pinching her cheeks tightly between thumbs and forefingers, the stinging pain immediately bringing tears to her eyes. The pain also brought her crashing back to reality. What in the name of all that she held dear was she doing?

"John Bates means nothing to me—*less* than nothing! I don't believe his protestations of affection for a moment. As if he had *really* been suddenly struck with love the moment I let my hair down on the beach. It sounds like something out of a silly novel. Well, he doesn't fool me. He only wishes to ingratiate himself at Seashadow so that he can carry on his nefarious exploits without fear that I—his besotted slave—will be capable of seeing past the tip of my own infatuated nose to discover what he is really about."

This said—and said with admirable conviction—Elly gave the twin mirrors a determined push, so that all they reflected was a view of the stuccoed ceiling, and turned her back on Mister Rudd's versatile dressing table.

She stiffened her spine and her resolve, determined not to succumb to charm, or fancy words, or even longing looks from hypnotic grey eyes—all of which she was convinced she was about to receive from the hardened seducer she had already kept waiting downstairs for well above fifteen minutes.

There was a knock at the door to the hallway, and Lily Biggs entered the boudoir before Elly could give permission for her to do so. Holding on to the doorknob with one hand while the other rested indolently on her thrust-out hip, the girl looked her mistress up and down in an openly assessing manner that had Elly wishing she had chosen the drab chimney-smoke muslin rather than the more daring yellow silk.

"Don't yer look as spiffy as the kitchen cat's whiskers?" Lily commented at last, her expression one Elly would have put down to pure female jealousy if the girl had been older than sixteen. "I bin sent ter fetch yer, missy. His lordship said fer me to tell yer he's waiting, and Da says the pigeons are gonna go straight to Hell fer sure iffen yer don't put yer feet under the table soon."

"Inform my brother that I shall be down directly, please, Lily," Elly said as calmly as she could while hastily readjusting the mirrors so that she could give one last assessing look at the rather low neckline of her gown.

"Him? And wot does *he* care when you—oh, yeah, right," the girl replied, backing from the room. "Yer brother. I'll tell him, too."

"And don't swear, Lily," Elly added absently, biting her lip as she leaned forward to see that, yes, there was just a hint of cleavage visible above the silk. It was too much. She wanted to entice John, and for reasons of his own he seemed willing to allow her to believe he had been enticed, but she didn't want him to think she was about to throw propriety to the winds just because he wished to court her.

After all, when this was over and he was being hauled

off to the local guardhouse, she also didn't want him to be able to find solace in the sure knowledge that, although he had failed in his spying mission, he had succeeded in making a complete fool out of a gullible spinster—who would most probably wear the willow for him to her grave.

So thinking, she ruthlessly rifled through her armoire until she found the ivory cashmere shawl that had been her last present from Robert. Draping it modestly about her shoulders, she took a deep, steadying breath and headed for the long staircase, knowing she was as ready as she would ever be to do battle with the handsome, infuriating John Bates.

ALASTAIR FOUGHT the urge to make a detour between the dining room and drawing room to visit the kitchens and plant a smacking kiss on Big George's cheek in appreciation of an excellent dinner. It had been, in fact, the first truly edible—or at least completely *identifiable*—meal he'd had since waking in Hugo's hovel.

Of course, the pigeons had been a mite overdone, he remembered as he straddled his favorite Sheraton conversation chair—an inspired, round-seated convenience with its abbreviated back serving as its front so that a gentleman could sit comfortably without crushing his coattails—and faced his host and hostess. But the trout Madère had more than made up for this single lapse.

His host and hostess, he saw, had already made themselves comfortable on the settee. What a diverse pair they were, these two Dalrymples, no matter that they were both blonde—which was, Alastair remembered uncomfortably, a Lowell family trait.

Not, he went on mentally as he watched Elly pour tea, that blondes were so scarce on the ground in England that

being blonde could be used as proof of their right to inherit
Seashadow. Besides, he knew it as a fact that a woman's
hair color was not always what it appeared to be. Her brows
and lashes were dark, after all. The next time dear Miss
Dalrymple took down her hair to play the coquette, he'd be
well advised to take a long peek at her roots.

"You don't care for tea, John?" Elly said as he waved
his hand to turn down her offer to pour a cup for him.

"Truth to tell, Elly," he said as brightly as possible, "I'd
much rather have a brandy—for medicinal purposes, of
course. My leg is paying me back for that run I took on
the beach today, although I've consigned my cane to the
corner at last." His eyes slid to the far corner of the drawing
room and the sideboard hiding a cellarette that, at least during his tenure at Seashadow, had contained no less than an
even dozen wine bottles at all times.

Leslie hopped to his feet. "Of course you do, John," he
agreed happily. "I should have thought of it m'self, except
that I don't really drink. Well, not that I don't know *how*
to drink, or get all silly or weepy when I do, but I never
really liked the taste of the stuff. Elly," he questioned, turning to his sister, "where do we keep the brandy?"

Elly looked at Alastair, her slanted brown eyes narrowed
speculatively. "John, do you want to show him, or shall
I?"

"Me?" Alastair exclaimed, silently cursing himself for
a dolt and his hostess for an all-seeing witch. "Oh, very
well," he agreed, rising as his agile brain quickly scrambled
for and found a reasonable explanation for his potentially
disastrous faux pas. "I must admit I had done a spot of
reconnoitering while waiting for you to join us for dinner.
I think there may be some brandy in this lovely piece over
here in the corner."

"That's true enough, Elly," Leslie supplied, unknowingly earning himself Alastair's grateful thanks. "You took dashed long answering the dinner bell, not that it wasn't worth the wait. You don't look half so bad in yellow as you do in black."

Alastair turned to the sideboard to hide his smile. Poor Miss Dalrymple. No wonder she had turned to a life of crime, if she would have otherwise had to depend on her brother for financial support. The youth was amusing, to say the least, but his talent for plain speech wasn't exactly marketable.

"Ah," he said, opening the japanned doors and sliding out the built-in cellarette that moved on well-oiled rollers, "here we are. Lord Hythe, would you care to join me in a snifter? Brandy is an acquired taste, after all, and you may just have given up before your palate learned to enjoy it."

"My brother does not drink," Elly declared coldly, and Alastair was instantly glad that it was he and not she who was standing at the sideboard which was, he knew, fully supplied with many things, including a fine set of very sharp knives.

She certainly was protective of her brother—either that or she was angry that they had spent the entire dinner talking of the weather, without a single mention of Alastair's intention to ask permission to court her.

No, that couldn't be it. She didn't really want him—he was convinced of that. She wanted something from him, but he couldn't bring himself to believe it was romance. Why, the way she looked at him when she thought he wasn't looking back made him believe she'd rather have his head on a pike than his ring on her finger.

"Brandy costs too much, for one thing," Leslie groused, shifting in his seat and unknowingly bringing Alastair's mind back to the present. "But, Elly, now that I'm rich, don't you think—"

"No, I don't think," Elly cut in quickly. Her voice lowered to a near whisper. "Remember Papa, Leslie?"

"Drank like a fish," Leslie observed, nodding his head and looking, to Alastair's eyes, more envious than crestfallen as Alastair settled himself once more on the conversation chair to warm the brandy by rubbing the snifter between his palms. "He was a lot of fun when he was in his cups," the young man went on, confirming Alastair's assumption. "Bought me a pony once—though we had to sell it a fortnight later to pay the butcher or some such thing. Excalibur. That's what I called him—the pony, not Papa. Papa thought it was a good name, didn't he Elly?"

"I don't think John is interested in hearing about our late father, Leslie," Elly said, a little tight-lipped, although her cheeks were glowing a becoming pink.

So, Alastair thought, looking at his quarry as he allowed the first of the brandy to sear the back of his throat, it would appear I have stumbled onto another sore point. Perhaps the late Mister Dalrymple bears further exploration.

Aloud, he said sympathetically, "You have lost your father and mother as well, haven't you, Elly—and now the late Earl. It's a terrible thing, isn't it, how tragedies seem to come in threes?"

"I like threes," Leslie piped up happily, before interesting himself in a loose thread on his shirt cuff.

"Three deaths over the course of twenty years could hardly be considered an unending run of tragedy, John," Elly said, her fingers pleating and repleating a section of her skirt as she looked at her brother. "Our mother died in childbirth many years ago, and our father expired five years ago. As for the late Earl—"

"Yes, yes, I know," Alastair cut in, knowing he was not going to be able to hear her disparage his memory another time without longing to take her over his knee and deliver a few hard whacks to her uncaring posterior, "you did not know him and have not liked anything you've learned about him."

"Well, I like him," Leslie put in staunchly, earning Alastair's at least momentary adoration. "He left us all his lovely money, and Seashadow, and at least two other, even larger estates—Elly knows more about that sort of thing than I do, of course—and all his furniture, and his townhouse in London...and the Biggses." Leslie's smile broadened as he rubbed his stomach reflectively. "I think I like the Biggses best of all, come to think on it."

"Big George does have quite a wonderful way in the kitchens," Alastair agreed, liking Leslie more than he knew he should. Perhaps it was because he knew the youth to be too hopelessly naive to be involved in any terrible conspiracy—or perhaps it was simply because Leslie Dalrymple, unlike his prickly sister, was just a very likable person.

Or maybe, Alastair considered briefly, it is because I have gone stark, staring mad! "I know Hugo was over the moon when I told him we'd be returning here for dinner tonight," he added, feeling he had to say something.

Leslie nodded emphatically. "Good food is essential to happiness, John—and to creativity. Why, I think I have had more inspiration from Big George's strawberry pancakes than I ever had from Nellie's cooking."

"Nellie?" Alastair interposed, raising one eyebrow as he looked at Elly. "You didn't bring your own servant with you to Seashadow? Perhaps she was older, and didn't wish to leave her home. Where was it that you said you were from, originally?"

"North," Elly answered without telling him anything. A toothdrawer wouldn't be able to get anything out of her!

"Nellie's been gone six months or more," Leslie explained as his sister's elbow dug deeply into his waist. "Ow, Elly, stop that, do. John was just asking a question. We couldn't afford her anymore, Elly said. Not that I miss her. I tell you, John, it was insupportable!"

"She stole from you?" Alastair asked idly, beginning to lose interest in the conversation that, he could tell, was not going in any helpful direction. He'd had more invigorating conversations at funerals.

"Exactly! She ate the fruit arrangement I was painting—with Napoleon's face hidden in the wicker basket and all the fruit shaped just like the countries he has conquered. Took a whacking huge bite from Egypt, she did. Egypt—it was the pear. There was no way to hide it, so I had to abandon the project."

"Have another cup of tea, darling," Elly gritted through clenched teeth, obviously trying another avenue meant to shut up her brother before he could drag out any more of their personal family laundry for Alastair's inspection.

Alastair took another deep sip of brandy, knowing this talk of sacked servants and strawberry pancakes and Napoleonic pears was the oddest after-dinner conversation he had ever had, and waited to see what would happen next.

To Alastair's amusement, Elly's two obvious bids to silence her brother were both immediate and dismal failures. Leslie, who seemed to have the bit firmly between his teeth, was not to be distracted by either physical attack or offers of refreshment.

"Nellie was the only real servant we ever had, you understand," Leslie reported, as if explaining himself to a schoolmaster. "Elly has taken care of us all for as long as

I can remember. Cheap as a clipped farthing, our Elly is, or so Papa always said.''

As he watched embarrassed color flood Elly's face, Alastair was hit with a sudden, entirely uncharacteristic urge to rescue her from her brother's indiscreet mouth—although why he should feel this compassion for the woman, he had no idea.

"Leslie," he broke in just as that man was about to open his mouth once more and say something most probably directed toward explaining his sister's cheese-paring ways, "I couldn't help but admire the large oil painting in the dining room as we sat at table. It's a truly glorious landscape of this area of Kent, don't you think?"

Leslie's thin nose wrinkled, just as if he had suddenly smelled something rotten. "You liked that, John? Yes, well," he went on blithely, "there's no accounting for tastes, is there?"

"What's wrong with it?" Alastair was stung into asking for he had commissioned the painting himself, and it was a particular favorite of his.

"It's too ordinary," Leslie answered, taking another sip of tea.

"But it's a landscape," Alastair persisted, the insult to his taste—which had been touted in London as being nothing short of exquisite—overriding his need for caution. "What did you want, man—pink leaves and red grass?"

"Pink leaves?" Leslie questioned softly, his thin, artistic face lighting with inspiration. "Pink leaves." He rose from the settee, his sister taking the teacup from him before it could slip from his hand, and left the room, muttering over and over, "Pink leaves. Yes, I can see them. Pink leaves."

Alastair and Elly watched him go, the former shaking his

head in wonderment, the latter wearing a look that could only be called long-suffering.

"I suppose you think he's insane and I should have had him put away years ago," Elly said at last, turning back to Alastair.

"I didn't mean to set him off, Elly," Alastair began apologetically, for the hurt in her eyes was doing something very disturbing to his resolve to unmask her as a criminal. As a matter of fact, the way he felt now, for two pins he'd throw the whole thing up, confess his true identity, and have done with this increasingly intricate madness.

"At least he stayed for tea. He doesn't usually last this long," she told him, not making him feel any better.

"And I didn't even get to speak to him about my intentions," he added, that thought suddenly striking him, for although he would have liked to forget the scene on the beach, he was likewise aware that he could not do so and retain any credibility in Elinor Dalrymple's too keen eyes.

"You mean you still wish to pay court to me?" Elly asked, one slim hand going to her hair. He knew he should have commented on its looser, more attractive style, just as he should have complimented her on her ridiculously out-of-date yet becoming gown, but he also was aware that he had left it too late.

"Why shouldn't I, Elly?" he asked, scrambling to recall what it was like to try to insinuate himself with an innocent female. The redhead, and her small legion of predecessors—who had made up the majority of his female acquaintance for the past several years—had left him woefully out of practice for dealing with the tedious game of lighthearted flirtation. For Alastair, the gift of a strand of pearls or a diamond brooch had taken the place of flirtation, and he hadn't been disappointed with the results—until now.

He had burst upon the scene in London the year after his father's death, a raw enough youth with no real social graces, although his fortune and pretty face had gone a long way in gaining him entry to any level of society he chose.

His interests, physical inclination, and athletic prowess had naturally drawn him to the Corinthian set, so that he had adopted that group's disdain for tame entertainments. Indeed, Alastair's quest to enliven boring *ton* functions, when combined with his audacious conversation, had more than once sent the more gentle ladies searching in their reticules for restoratives.

Strangely, as he sat in his own drawing room in Seashadow, he felt more embarrassed than comforted by his remembrance of his life in London.

Once he was back in the city, he'd have to curtail his visits to his clubs and pay more attention to Almack's and all those insipid balls he's shunned so disdainfully in favor of more robust entertainment. After all, he was seven and twenty now, and he really should try to cultivate some decorum.

Elinor Dalrymple's poor opinion of him had not been sharp enough to wound him (or so he tried to convince himself), but the sure knowledge that she was only voicing the sentiments of many of the more acceptable members of Polite Society did rankle more than he cared to admit.

He should have gone to Spain, he told himself, sipping at his brandy. Many of his friends had gone. And it wasn't as if he were a coward, afraid of spilling his claret for his King and country. He had wanted to go, to follow the drum. But the war was winding down—everyone had said so—and it had seemed that Wellington and the others had everything pretty much in hand.

Oh, yes, he had taken up his seat in Parliament, and had

fought mightily for better provisions and pay for the soldiers in the field—and why hadn't Elly heard of that and tempered her disdain with some compassion?—but it wasn't quite the same as actually *being* there, and Alastair knew it.

That was probably why he had leapt at the chance to help Wiggins when that man had approached him. Why else had he been on his yacht, with his course already set for Seashadow from Folkestone, when he was dumped overboard to drown? He might have allowed Wiggins to think he'd had no intention of taking an active part in apprehending the spy, but deep in his heart of hearts he knew he had wanted to be in on the kill.

"John? Are you all right?" he heard Elly ask in a voice that sounded muffled, as if he were hearing it from a distance. He shook his head, bringing his attention back to her as she continued, "I know Leslie is a bit peculiar, and I quite understand if you wish to rethink your decision to ask him if you might pay your addresses to me—"

"What does your brother have to do with the thing?" Alastair asked, for she was confusing him. Why was she carrying on about Leslie? Why was it that a woman always felt she had the obligation to talk a thing to death? He had already told her he thought Leslie was a good enough sort.

He watched as Elly lowered her head, so that the candlelight was caught in the soft curls that crowned her head. "At home, Leslie was spoken of as…as the resident freak."

Alastair was instantly irate. No wonder she was worrying the subject—she was harboring a great hurt. Poor girl! Poor Leslie!

"People can be so damnably cruel, Elly," he said savagely, stung by the vehemence in his voice. "Your brother is anything but a freak. As I told you before—he is an eccentric. As far as I can tell, this whole island is awash in them. Why, I myself had an uncle who thought he was Alexander the Great. He was always racing about, hot to conquer things. Yet, for all of that, he was a good man and I loved him dearly.''

''But—but there might be a *taint,* some sort of strain of eccentricity, as you call it, that runs through the entire family. My mother was a Lowell—which is how we came to be here—and she married my father, which just goes to prove that she had an odd way of looking at life.''

''Your mother was like Leslie?'' Alastair asked, beginning to feel real sympathy for Elly, and silently thanking his lucky stars that, if they were indeed related—which he was nearly convinced they were not—it was a distant relationship.

She bit her lip. ''In her own way. Mama wrote poetry— her favorite subject was the supernatural. She was convinced that there exists a parallel world full of ghosts and spirits and the like. Supposedly they move all around us, eating and sleeping and doing everything we do. It's just that we can't see them.''

Well, Alastair thought, that knocks my uncle out of the running for the strangest person this side of Bedlam. ''And your father?'' he asked weakly, not really sure he wished to know.

''My father, rest his soul, was a gambler. Oh, how I hate to say that word aloud. The man would invest in anything— including those horrid bubbles that everyone thought were going to make them rich. Leslie may call me cheap, but it was very difficult to run the household and still keep Papa out of the Fleet. Oh, why am I telling you all this?''

Alastair couldn't answer her, because he was as completely at sea as she admitted to being as to why she was revealing her past to him. He only knew that every word out of her mouth could only serve to further damn her in his eyes—if his belief that she was a money-grubbing opportunist was to be his guide.

All he could do was rise from his chair, place his now empty snifter on the table beside the teacups, seat himself on the settee, his arm placed tentatively but supportively across her shoulders, and listen to what she had to say.

"We were living most precariously on less than two hundred pounds a year," she went on, searching in her gown pocket for a small linen handkerchief with which to wipe at her eyes. Alastair deliberately looked straight ahead, knowing that her exotic brown eyes were awash with tears, and the sight of them might prompt him into doing something stupid, like kissing her.

"Even with Papa gone, his debts didn't disappear. A debt of honor must be paid, you know, and I couldn't allow Papa's memory to be besmirched by any rumor that he hadn't settled his gambling debts."

"Debts of honor can be the very devil," Alastair agreed sincerely, having paid a few of them himself over the years.

"You can't imagine the pucker we were in before the solicitor told us of Leslie's inheritance. Turning Nellie off was the last of our little economies. I had no idea where I was going to get the next quarter's rent."

"Why—why didn't you apply to the late Earl for assistance?" he asked dumbly, remembering too late that she hadn't known of his existence.

He felt her spine stiffen as pride, it would appear, suddenly came to her rescue. "I would never have thought of such a thing—even if I had known about him!" she asserted haughtily. "I have looked over his books, John, since coming to Seashadow. Why, his expenditures on candles alone would be enough to keep Leslie and me in comfort for a decade! What could a hey-go-mad spendthrift like that understand of our problems?''

Alastair's arm slipped to the back of the settee. What was ten times two hundred? Good Lord! He'd spent that much on candles? It was impossible! To spend that much on horses, or fine wine, or brandy—that was one thing. But to spend it on *candles?* He was pretty angry with the late Earl of Hythe himself! With spendthrift habits like that, why, it wouldn't be long before he was out on the street, begging passersby for stale crusts of bread!

"You've suffered, Elly, haven't you?" he commiserated feelingly, his arm once more draped across her shoulder. The cashmere shawl had shifted, and he liked the soft, silken feel of her bare shoulder. A man could do a lot worse than to get himself a wife who was such a sensible, economical housekeeper. After all, somebody had to keep a rein on expenses, and according to Leslie, Elly could squeeze a pennypiece until it yelped in pain.

She sat front, dislodging his arm. "It wasn't that bad, John," she said, blowing her nose before replacing the handkerchief in her pocket. "Besides, that is all behind us now, thanks to Alastair Lowell's drunkenness."

Alastair's ears pricked up—he could swear he felt them move. "His *drunkenness?*"

Elly nodded. "I had a missive from his solicitor this morning. The final ruling on his death was just what we all supposed—that he had been drunk and must have stumbled overboard. It seems that he was playing at cards until nearly dawn, and drinking with both hands. He died, John, as he had lived—and with nothing to show for his life."

She turned to face him and he did his best to close his mouth, which had dropped open as she spoke. "That is why

I am so glad that I am here to guide Leslie. He has a heavy responsibility as Earl—the first of which is to marry to ensure the line."

Drunk? The world thought he had been drunk? He hadn't been drunk—well, maybe a little well to go, but not drunk! Surely he hadn't been *drunk!*

"Which is why," she went on, her voice suddenly very low, "I must decline your suggestion that we entertain the thought that the two of us might suit. I cannot marry, even if you are willing to overlook a possible Lowell taint. I cannot leave Leslie now. But that doesn't mean that we can't be friends while you are here, does it. John? John, have you heard a single word I've said?"

She was turning him down! She thought he was a rakehell, the whole world and his wife thought he had drunkenly fallen overboard, he had never made a worthwhile contribution to mankind in all his twenty-seven years, he spent money on candles like a drunken lighthouse keeper on a spree—and a plainfaced, firmly on-the-shelf spinster who was kissing her last chance for marriage goodbye *was turning him down flat!*

Alastair needed a drink. He got up from the settee, caught up his snifter, and fairly stumbled to the sideboard to pour himself three fingers of brandy—which he tossed off in one long gulp.

"You're hurt, aren't you?" he heard Elly say, as if from a distance.

"Hurt?" he repeated, whirling about to stab her with his steely grey gaze—the brandy he had imbibed nearly causing him to lose his balance. He had to say one thing for the woman—she certainly did have an eye for the obvious. "Madam, you are mistaken," he declared, his voice dripping with venom.

"I am?"

"Yes, you am—I mean, you are. I am celebrating my lucky escape! I succumbed to a bit of moon madness today on the beach—or should we call that sun madness, to be precise about the thing? For we should be precise about the thing, shouldn't we? I mean, a woman like you—who takes down her long blonde hair in front of a wounded, isolated, woman-starved veteran—wouldn't wish for it to be bruited about that she was the flighty sort who would trifle with a man's affections…now, would she?"

Elly rose, drawing her ivory cashmere shawl tightly about her damnably soft, silky shoulders. "John," she said quietly, "I think you should leave. We are, after all, unchaperoned once more, and I think you are a little the worse for drink."

He poured another three fingers of brandy and tossed it off. "Oh, a little the worse for drink, am I? And we all know how you feel about that, don't we, Miss Dalrymple? But just think—what it cost you in your father, you got back a hundredfold in the late Earl."

"What do you care about the late Earl? I fail to understand your interest in the man. You seem to think I should be building a shrine to him or some such nonsense."

He ignored her, as his tongue had taken control of his abused senses. He was feeling sorry for himself, the maligned, rightful Earl of Hythe, and sorry for his other self, the turned-down suitor, John Bates. As a matter of fact, he felt like the sorriest beast in nature.

Stung, he went on the attack. "Of course you don't want me, madam. Try to fob me off with some farradiddle about tainted blood, will you? You've got Leslie and his lovely money so firmly under your thumb that *you'd* be the insane one—to marry a penniless veteran and bail out of the deepest gravy boat in all England! The only taint you have is greed—and you have a bellyful of it. Well, let me tell you, madam, I shall go down on my knees this night and thank God that you don't want me, for I sure as hell don't want you!''

''You're drunk, and you don't know what you're saying,'' Elly told him, backing slowly toward the door. ''Once again, I must ask you to leave.''

''Leave? Leave my own—leave my own *true love?*'' he amended prudently, for he was not so angry nor so bosky that he was going to give the game away now. Oh, no. He was going to play out the whole string now—right to the very end. And she, Elinor Dalrymple, was going to dance to his tune.

Slamming the snifter down on the sideboard, he crossed the room so swiftly that Elly had no chance to react—to run. And before he had a moment to consider the real reason behind his actions, Alastair grabbed her by the shoulders and ground his mouth against hers in a kiss that was meant to show her all that she would be missing now that she had turned him down.

When the kiss was over, even though the sweet scent and soft touch of her mouth would haunt him for the rest of the evening—perhaps for the rest of his life—Alastair turned for the door.

''Oh, yes—about his business of having Leslie married off,'' he said, turning back to her with a wide sweep of his arm, as if just recalling something he had wanted to say, ''as far as I can tell, the only person besides the Biggses to have taken the man's fancy seems to be Hugo—and let me tell you, madam, I shall refuse the banns!''

CHAPTER FIVE

ELLY SPENT the majority of the next two days in a veritable frenzy of housekeeping, trying her utmost to banish the memory of that disastrous evening with John Bates from her mind. Mostly she tried to erase the memory of his kiss, which had set her heart to pounding even as she realized that his gesture had been meant as more of an insult than an expression of passion.

She had never been so angry, so embarrassed, so frustrated—or so hurt—in her entire life. Try as she might to convince herself that she had no feelings for the man other than suspicion, she knew she had been hoping against hope that in truth he had found her attractive.

But, as she had thought, he had been only toying with her, just as she had been toying with him. Yet, she knew after spending two long, almost sleepless nights considering the thing, she could still harbor the dream that he was now feeling just as confused and letdown as she was at their angry parting.

How had she ever gotten herself involved in such a stupid, convoluted project?

"It all started with Lieutenant Fishbourne," she reminded herself rationally as she laid cedar chips in the drawers in Leslie's chamber. "If he hadn't filled my head with all those tales of spies and smugglers, I wouldn't have given John Bates's appearance at Seashadow a second thought.''

A mental picture of the blonde, colorless Jason Fishbourne as he had sat in Seashadow's drawing room, pompously and endlessly expounding on the history of the area, filled her mind. ''As a matter of fact, I believe I am quite out of charity with the man. To add to his sins, the Lieutenant is also the most *boring* man I have ever met!''

Slamming the drawer shut on Leslie's flannels, Elly strode over to his bed and straightened the already pristine coverlet. ''I'm not being fair,'' she admitted to the empty room. ''I would have been suspicious of John Bates whether the Lieutenant had warned me against strangers or not. The man has intrigued me ever since I first laid eyes on him. His sudden appearance, his reluctance to talk about himself, his feigned limp, his seeming familiarity with Seashadow—they simply don't fit his explanation for being here.''

She walked into the hallway, turning toward the narrow servants' stairs that led directly to the kitchens. ''And then there's Hugo,'' she groused as her uncooperative brain persisted in tormenting her even as she tried to clear her mind of everything save the efficient running of Seashadow.

''Why would a man keep a brute like that, if it weren't for protection? Good Lord, the man is the perfect guard dog. He can't even speak—to give away John's secrets. And, while I am on the subject, why am *I* speaking out loud—and to myself? If Mrs. Biggs were to hear me, she'd probably want to immediately dose me with salts or something. I really must exercise more caution.''

As she entered the kitchens in the hope of finding something mundane to do to occupy her time, Elly stopped, sighed, and asked with controlled calm, ''Leslie? You aren't bothering Big George again, are you? And get down from that table this instant. Can't you see Little George is trying to chop carrots?''

Leslie obediently hopped down from his perch, his pencils and drawing tablet tumbling to the stone floor. ''Now look what you made me do, Elly,'' he complained pettishly—for he could be pettish when his concentration was interrupted.

''I didn't make you do anything, dearest,'' she returned wearily. ''I never could, more's the pity, and I'll thank you not to remind me of my failure. But, if you will, Leslie, please satisfy my curiosity even as you accept my apology. What were you doing perched on the table?''

Leslie grinned, mollified. ''There was a spider weaving his web inside one of the pots up there,'' he told her, pointing to the string of brightly shining copper pots hanging above the heavy wooden chopping table, ''and I had nearly captured his expression before you distracted me.''

''Of course. I knew it would be a simple explanation. Little Georgie,'' Elly ordered sternly, for she was sorry she had asked the question, as she was in no mood to listen to her brother's foolishness, ''either dispatch the spider to its reward or remove it to some other, less dangerous place. I definitely do not wish to see its 'expression' looking up at me from my plate at luncheon.''

''Yes, ma'am, right away, ma'am,'' Little Georgie spluttered, taking down the pot and heading for the door to the kitchen garden.

Leslie followed after him, his sketch pad clutched to his thin chest, his pencils escaping his grasp to make a drunken path from table to door, muttering, ''I'll have to begin all over, you know. He won't look pensive anymore. He'll look

terrified—or angry.'' As he turned to retrieve a single pen-
cil, he pulled a face behind his sister's back.

"And don't stick out your tongue, Leslie,'' Elly cautioned without turning away from the dry sink she was inspecting for signs of mold. "You're too old for that sort of
nonsense, you know.''

"Yes, Elly—sorry,'' Leslie mumbled before bolting once
more for the door.

Elly pinched the bridge of her nose between her fingers,
knowing she would have to seek her brother out later and
apologize to him. Having learned long ago that she could
not change him, make him more responsible, she had
vowed that she would do her best never to lose patience
with him.

It was all John Bates's fault, she decided as her lips
clamped into a tight, straight line. If her brain weren't so
crammed full with thoughts of him, she wouldn't be so
liable to snap off everyone else's heads with her short temper.

"Would Master Bates be comin' ter dinner agin tonight,
missy?'' Mrs. Biggs asked, the large woman coming up
behind her so silently that Elly nearly dropped the egg she
had absently lifted from a wire basket containing two dozen
eggs just brought in from the henhouse.

John Bates, again! Was she to be allowed no peace, no
escape from the man? Carefully replacing the egg, she
counted to ten, then turned slowly about to look at the
housekeeper.

The woman was holding Baby Willie on one comfortably
wide hip, and the child once again had both hands stuck in
his mouth while a foot-long string of drool hung from his
left elbow.

"I thought Rosie was minding Baby Willie while you

oversaw Iris and Lily as they cleaned the silver," Elly remarked questioningly, sidestepping the issue of John Bates as she searched in her pockets for a handkerchief with which to wipe the cooing child's wet face.

"I sent Rosie ter her bed, Missy, as she was feelin' poorly," Mrs. Biggs answered, shifting Baby Willie to her other hip. "Could be measles."

"Measles!" Elly shrieked, rapidly reviewing her past to remember whether or not she and Leslie had ever had the measles. Yes, she'd had them, but she didn't think Leslie had. "Are you quite sure it's measles, Mrs. Biggs?" she asked, knowing that Leslie and Rosie had been skipping stones into the Channel together the other day. This was what came of having a gaggle of children in a house that should boast fully grown footmen and chambermaids and parlormaids—all of whom would most probably have already had the measles.

Mrs. Biggs shrugged. "I said it could be—mayhap it's nuthin' but somethin' she ate. She tossed her breakfast right back at me the minute she ate it. Besides, now that I think on it, Rose already had the measles."

"Then why did you say—oh, never mind. Please disregard the question," Elly said as mildly as she could, wondering why she continued to put up with the Biggses. After all, just because the late Earl had hired them was no reason for Leslie to keep the family on—even if he was enthralled by them.

Just as she was about to open her mouth and hint that the Biggses would have to find some way to staff the house and keep the younger children tucked away in their living quarters, Baby Willie stretched out his damp hands, grinned his babyish grin, and launched himself into Elly's arms.

"Baby Willie!" Mrs. Biggs scolded, grabbing at the

child's ankles while Elly staggered beneath the sudden weight of Baby Willie's sturdy young body. "My, my, missy, would yer look at that. He sure has taken a likin' ter yer, hasn't he? My Baby Willie doesn't go ter just anybody, yer know."

Knowing that Baby Willie's affection might have something to do with the fact that she had begun slipping him sweets when no one was looking, Elly suffered the child's embrace in silence, feeling her traitorous heart melting away her resolve to remake Seashadow's staff into something less reminiscent of a well-run haven for drooling children.

"I'm flattered, Mrs. Biggs" was all Elly could say, taking Baby Willie fully into her arms. "As a matter of fact, now that I have him, would you mind if we took a stroll outside? I have been cooped up much too long in this fine weather."

"That you have," Mrs. Biggs seconded with an audible sigh, and Elly immediately got the feeling that the woman would be more than grateful to have her new mistress out from under her feet so that she could run Seashadow the way she wanted without any interference. "But about Mr. Bates, missy—"

Elly's temporarily lifted spirits plummeted at the mention of the man's name. "Mr. Bates again. What about Mr. Bates, Mrs. Biggs?"

"Will he be comin' ter dinner agin any time soon, d'yer think? Big George was thinkin' of fixin' his favorite— stuffed capon."

Baby Willie squealed aloud as Elly's arms closed a little too tightly around his pudgy middle. "His favorite, Mrs. Biggs? You don't say. How would you know that?"

The housekeeper fumbled with her apron for a moment,

her blue eyes wide as saucers, then lifted her head and said brightly, "He told me so himself—just yesterday. He brought Hugo ter the kitchens ter see Baby Willie. Those two are getting' on like a house afire, missy."

Elly looked at the woman levelly. "Of course. I should have realized that," she answered, turning for the door. "No, Mr. Bates is not coming for dinner this evening. However, the Earl is also partial to stuffed capons, so they won't go to waste. I'll have Baby Willie back before luncheon, Mrs. Biggs. Please see that either Iris or Lily is available at that time to take him from me."

"Lily." Mrs. Biggs sniffed derisively as Elly turned to the door. "The smithy is visitin' down ter the stables, missy. We'll be lucky if we see that one afore dinner! Big George is goin' ter have ter go husband-huntin' for that one soon, afore he has to do it with his cleaver ter hand."

For the next hour, as she and Baby Willie played on the sand, Elly considered all the ways Mrs. Biggs could have known that John Bates's favorite dish was stuffed capons— for as surely as she knew she was beginning to fall in love with the odious man, she was just as certain that the housekeeper had been lying to her about his visit to the kitchens.

There were only two answers.

One was that John Bates and the Biggses had known each other a lot longer than they had let on, proving that John was in the area for some reason other than to recuperate from some vague war wound—most probably making himself at home at Seashadow until she and Leslie had arrived, and then removing himself to the nearby cottage.

But why would he have been living at Seashadow? Were the Biggses also smugglers—or spies? No, she couldn't picture the Biggses in either role. After all, what would they do with the children?

That left but one alternative. John Bates could be working for the government, in much the same way the so-boring Lieutenant Fishbourne was. Yet, if he was, why didn't the Lieutenant know about him? And why would he feel he had to keep his true reason for being at Seashadow a secret from the Earl and his sister?

She finally concluded, much as it pained her, that she was going to have to swallow her pride, bury her traitorous personal feelings for the man, and continue to see John Bates, if only to satisfy her curiosity.

Their argument of the other evening would make it very difficult, as would her growing knowledge that she was becoming more than a little fond of the man. "For all the good that will do me," she told a giggling Baby Willie as she tickled his bare stomach. "I hurt him badly when I turned him down—even if we both knew he hadn't really meant to court me—and I shall have his injured sensibilities to deal with before I have any chance of learning his secrets."

Walking down to the water's edge so that she and Willie could gather shells, she stopped in her tracks, suddenly realizing that there was a third, hitherto unthought-of possibility—another answer to why John Bates was so familiar with Seashadow.

But that other answer was too ridiculous, too insanely ludicrous, too farfetched, for her to even consider. Wasn't it?

ALASTAIR WATCHED as Elly, Baby Willie held high in her arms, ran toward the incoming waves, then retreated as they chased her, the pair's delighted giggles floating upward on the air to where he stood.

He felt abandoned, lonely, and envious of a small child

who could make Elly laugh, while all he could seem to do was make her angry—and suspicious.

He reached a hand into his pocket, to crush the missive from Wiggins that had arrived only that morning. The Dalrymples were the genuine heirs—Wiggins would stake his reputation on it. The Captain had had his sources in London check with the Hythe solicitors, and everything was in order, although the solicitors had been amazed when they had stumbled over the existence of the last of the Dalrymple family. If Alastair Lowell were to have actually perished at sea, his very distant cousin, Leslie Dalrymple, would truly be the Earl of Hythe.

"I always knew it," Alastair said aloud, happy no one could hear his blatant, face-saving lie.

What a fool he had been! Had he actually believed that Elinor Dalrymple could be a money-mad impostor, or a smuggler, or even a traitor to her country? Had he actually convinced himself that—if she was a legitimate relative— she would have stooped to killing him in order to set her brother up as Earl?

Yes. Yes, damn his eyes, he had.

But he hadn't needed Wiggins's missive explaining how the Lowell solicitors had had to track down Leslie and Elly and convince them of the rightness of their claim to the title to straighten him out.

He had known the truth from the moment he'd kissed her—possibly even from the moment she'd taken down her hair on the beach and smiled up at him.

Fighting down the urge to join her on the beach and apologize to her—on his knees if necessary—Alastair turned away from the shore and headed for Seashadow, intent on meeting with Leslie, barely noticing as Hugo stepped out from behind a tree to follow him.

At least Leslie liked him—or Alastair would like to think so. Perhaps through the brother he could find a way back to the sister.

"The sister who—thanks to my stupidity—believes that I am either a spy, a smuggler, or worse," he told himself as he passed by the small stable and waved to Harry Biggs—who seemed to be yelling at the man-hungry Lily, while she most happily had her back turned to him. "Wiggins's letter says that his man—Fishbait, or whatever his name is—called on Elly to warn her of smugglers and spies using Seashadow's beaches. Now everything is falling into place. The dratted woman thinks I'm a spy—me! the Earl of Hythe!—and she's out to single-handedly catch me at it! Lord, I think I love that woman!"

"Aaaarrggh! Aaah!"

"What?" Alastair exclaimed, nearly jumping out of his skin as he whirled about to see the giant lumbering along three paces behind him, a grin as wide as a cavern splitting his face. "Christ on a crutch, man, don't ever sneak up on me like that again! How can anything so big move so quietly? And why are you looking at me like that? Oh," he said, shamefaced, remembering what he had just confessed to the air, "you heard me, my friend, didn't you?"

The giant nodded vigorously, clasping his hamlike hands to his chest and closing his eyes, as if in ecstasy.

Alastair's mouth began to twitch as a grin threatened to overtake him. "Evil as this sounds, my friend, this is one time I am actually glad your tongue suffered that little accident. I don't think I could hear your sentiments on the subject without becoming completely unmanned. I'm having enough difficulty reconciling myself to my unexpected mad-for-love state as it is."

"Gluugg, gluugg," Hugo responded, patting Alastair's

shoulder with one large paw, as if to tell him he understood the mixed feelings of a man who has just discovered that he has met his match, and his carefree bachelorhood was all but behind him.

As the pair crossed the rolled and scythed lawns that ran like a green lake from the raised porch surrounding the rear of Seashadow, Hugo split away from Alastair to head in the direction of the kitchens, his hand gestures conveying to his friend that he was on the hunt for a handout from Big George.

"If he has strawberry tarts, be sure to snaffle one for me as well," Alastair called after him as he mounted the stone steps to the wide flagstone porch and walked toward the French doors that stood open to the billiards room.

"Knock, knock! Is anyone home?" he called out cheerily as he entered the room, then ejaculated in sudden horror, "*Good God!* What in blazes happened in here? It looks like a Tothill tavern after a brawl. And what's that god-awful smell?"

There was a slight rustling in one corner of the jumbled room before Leslie Dalrymple's face rose above the back of Alastair's favorite leather sofa, and pulling an unfolded sheet of newspaper from its resting place atop his head, he exclaimed, "John! I thought I heard someone call. I was just meditating—contemplating my next work. This is my studio, you understand."

Alastair took another three steps into the room, scarcely recognizing it for what it had been when he had been the Earl—a snug retreat where a man could drink or play billiards with his chums without danger of being interrupted. "Where's the billiard table, Leslie?" he asked quietly, not knowing whether he felt closer to mayhem or to tears.

"The billiards table?" Leslie repeated blankly, uncurling

his skinny frame and rising to look about the room inquiringly. "Oh, of course. You must mean this thing," he said, walking across the debris-strewn carpet to point to a large rectangular object covered end to end with paint pots, sketch pads, one half (the bottom half) of a suit of armor, glass jars filled with a variety of insects, several pieces of fruit in various stages of decay—which accounted for the sickly sweet odor Alastair had noticed—and a cannonball-sized lump that must have been Leslie's string collection. "Isn't it a perfectly wonderful worktable? It has these lovely deep, knitted pockets in all the corners—see? I use them to hold my best brushes."

"That—that's my—that's the billiards table?" Alastair squeaked, feeling physically ill as he belatedly recognized the piece of furniture for what it was. He also recognized several of the paint and brush pots—for they were a small portion of his very select, very rare china collection. "Oh, I've got to put a stop to this madness once and for all, before this chucklehead lays ruin to the whole place!"

"What's that you say, John?" Leslie asked, for he had been busily wadding a piece of newspaper before looking at it, as if trying to decide what to do with it, shrugging, and throwing it to the floor to join a half dozen others just like it. "Uh-oh. You have that same pinched look Elly gets every time she comes in here. Don't you like my studio?"

"No, Leslie," Alastair bit out from between clenched teeth. "As a matter of fact, I don't think I do."

Leslie shrugged once more. "Well, no matter. I do." He spread his arms and turned about slowly, as if inviting inspection of his rumpled person as an alternative. "Maybe you'll like m'suit? It just came from the city. Elly has the dressing of me, you understand, ever since I ordered three yellow and black waistcoats from a man who came through our village a few years ago—she said I looked like an underfed bumblebee.''

Alastair wasn't listening. He was too busy looking at the once flawless green felt tabletop that was now damaged beyond repair, beyond any hope of redemption. He lifted a Sèvres vase, trying to chip away some of the hardened paint with his thumbnail before putting it down very carefully—so that he wouldn't give in to the temptation to throw the thing at Leslie's head.

''Your sister allows this—this desecration?'' he asked at last, lifting a stuffed owl from one of the chairs and sitting himself down before he fell down. ''I thought Mrs. Biggs had assured me—had told me Elly was a stickler for good housekeeping.''

Leslie nodded vigorously. ''Oh, she is, she is. Elly's a real crackerjack. But I found the key, you understand, so I can keep her locked out most of the time. She'd have a spasm if she could see how my studio looks right now. You won't tell her, will you, John? We can keep it our secret.''

Alastair was about to point out that locking the door to the rest of the house didn't mean much when one left the doors to the porch wide open for anyone to enter, but he didn't think he was up to the task. Instead, he said, ''I promise, Leslie. It will be our secret.''

''You! What are you doing here?''

Alastair turned to see Elly standing in the doorway, Baby Willie in her arms, the hem of her pink gown wet with sand, her tiny face a study in confused hostility.

He wanted to run to her, to kiss her, to clasp her hard against his chest forever—for she looked so dear, so appealing, with her glorious hair having escaped its pins to tumble over her shoulders.

Not only that, but after spending so much time with only

the wordless Hugo, the eccentric Leslie, and the war-mad Wiggins for company, he suddenly felt her to be the only sane person left in the world save himself—and he feared that he was fast losing his grip on that sanity.

He couldn't tell her any of this, of course—at least, not until he revealed who he really was. Besides, his tender feelings for her might just be a temporary aberration— brought on by his circumstances, the ruined felt, the paint pots, or the pickled insects—although he seriously doubted it. To cover his own confusion, he leapt to his feet, to respond to her rather rude greeting.

"Yes, yes, it is he!" he shouted, resorting to humor, flinging his arms dramatically wide. "Barricade the doors— the windows! That terrible John is back!" Then he sat at his ease, placed one elbow on the arm of the chair and his chin in his palm, smiled, waggled his eyebrows mischievously, and proclaimed gaily, "And how are you this fine afternoon, Miss Dalrymple? Feeling especially maternal today, are you?" He turned to Leslie. "What do you think, my friend? Is that a picture to inspire your muse, or isn't it?"

Elly advanced into the room to stand beside the chair and stare down at him. "Are you all right?" she asked, and he thought he heard a trace of real concern in her voice.

No, he wasn't. He had never felt less "right" in his life. But he was not about to tell Elinor Dalrymple that! Instead, he grinned up at her, knowing he should be on his feet while she was standing, but doggedly refusing to rise. "I am enjoying my usual good health—having fully recovered from my wounds—but thank you *so* much for asking, Miss Dalrymple."

He didn't add that he could tell even more precisely that he was in his usual good health because he felt so much better today than he had all the previous day, when he had been nursing a bruising hangover from the brandy he'd imbibed the last time the two of them had met.

She looked down at him for a long time—a lifetime during which Alastair thought of and discarded a dozen ways to tell her who he really was, knowing the truth had to be told while at the same time understanding that she would be devastated to learn that she and her brother were once more penniless.

Just as he thought he would have to either confess his identity or burst, Elly looked away to address her brother. "I shall deliver Baby Willie to the kitchens and take something to settle my stomach—for I believe the smell in here must be what is making it queasy—before returning here with Iris in order to attempt to make some sense of this chaos you have created, Leslie. I suggest you walk on the beach while we work, as I refuse to fight with you over the practicality of disposing of most of this mess."

Both men watched as Elly left through the French doors, then Leslie groaned aloud. "Elly's taken one of her pets again. This isn't the first time I've given her the stomachache—although why she should be so upset, I'll never understand, as it is *my* studio and I never asked her to live in it. She'll destroy everything, you know, John, trying to put it in order. I really thought she would leave me alone in this studio—as she doesn't care a whit for billiards, and the light is quite good—but Elly needs must put everything to order. I think it's a sickness."

"She is a good housekeeper, then?" Alastair asked, glad to hear it from another source. He couldn't love a poor housekeeper.

"Good? She's top o' the trees when it comes to housekeeping. She has even hung a list of rules in the kitchens.

Mrs. Biggs told me about it, but that dear lady only thinks it's funny."

Alastair nodded, not surprised to hear of Mrs. Biggs's easy acceptance of the list—as he full well knew that none of the Biggses could read more than their own names. "Your sister would have been horrified to see how the previous Earl used this place early in his salad days—not that it wasn't always kept scrupulously clean, for the Earl too loved order in his everyday life. But, if what I heard in the village the other day is true, the man wasn't above riding his favorite horse straight up the steps and into the drawing room one night when he was particularly full of frisk."

"You don't say!" Leslie commented, his smile lighting his formerly wan features. "I rather like that. You know, John, I've just had the happy notion that it might behoove me to rethink attempting an oil rendering of the man—for I do owe him a lot. If he hadn't died, I don't know where Elly and I would be now. Do you think there's a likeness of him about somewhere? This may be the family seat, but it isn't the largest Lowell estate and doesn't have a portrait gallery. But no, I suppose I shouldn't consider it, knowing how Elly feels about the man."

Alastair was past caring whether or not Leslie managed to dig up a likeness of him somewhere in Seashadow. He was past trying to satisfy his curiosity by searching the Lowell family histories for traces of Dalrymples—for he believed Wiggins's information that Elly and Leslie were legitimate.

Mostly he was past continuing this stupid, ill-conceived deception. The moment, the very moment, he had awakened in Hugo's hovel, he should have summoned his solicitors and informed them of his lucky escape, and all the misunderstandings, all the suspicions, all the ridiculous fencing between Elly and himself, could have been avoided.

"Because I would never have met her!" Alastair whispered hoarsely, the impact of his mental revelations succeeding in banishing any lingering remains of caution, any reticence keeping him from doing what he had come to Seashadow today to do—tell Elly the truth. "My God," he exclaimed, forgetting he had an audience, "what a tragedy that would have been! I have to go to her, at once!"

Leslie laid a hand on Alastair's arm, sympathetic but completely misunderstanding. "Oh, I am sorry, John. Don't take on so, though it's dashed good of you to want to come to my defense. It's not a tragedy—remember, it's only a picture. What does it matter if Elly dislikes it?"

"What?" Alastair asked uncomprehendingly. He looked down at the younger man—the man who thought he was the Fifteenth Earl of Hythe—and got an idea. He wouldn't go directly to Elly. He'd tell Leslie first, assure him that everything would be fine—considering that the Fourteenth Earl wished to marry his sister—and then the two of them would go to Elly together. That way, Alastair might just have a chance to explain everything without being tossed out of his own home on his ear!

"Leslie," Alastair crooned, putting his arm around the man's shoulders, "walk with me on the porch awhile, will you? I have something to tell you, and I'd rather do it away from the smell of overripe fruit."

"Elly said to walk on the beach," Leslie pointed out, then grinned. "Not that I don't like the beach, you understand. Both Elly and I had never seen the sea until we came to Seashadow. As a matter of fact, that's why we came here first, rather than to any of the other estates. But I'm the Earl, aren't I? I can do what I want—even if I want to commission another three yellow and black waistcoats. It has taken me some time to get the hang of it, John, but I have to own it—I do enjoy being an Earl.''

"I rather wished you hadn't shared that particular revelation with me, Leslie, old son," Alastair said, wincing.

Leslie, as usual ignoring all but his own feelings, slipped an arm about Alastair's waist. "Yes, John, let us walk on the porch," he agreed happily as the two of them stepped out onto the flagstones.

Ping! The sudden sound of metal hitting brick, following hard on the muffled sound of a distant shot, had Alastair unceremoniously throwing Leslie and himself forward onto the flagstones. He lay there behind the low stone wall lining the edge of the porch, his head raised slightly as he searched the tree line for a hint of a gun barrel glinting in the sunlight, but he didn't see anything.

After a moment he turned his body about to look at the mellow pink brick that was head-high next to the open doorway. Yes, there was a raw scar in the mortar and—he saw a moment later—a ball embedded in the wall.

"What—what happened?" Leslie croaked at last, rubbing at his bruised shoulder. "Was that a shot, John?"

"It was," Alastair answered, helping Leslie to his feet and back into the billiards room, "but I don't think there will be another one."

"No, there never has been before," Leslie answered absently, brushing off his pants.

Alastair, who still had his eyes trained on the trees, whirled about to face Leslie. No, it was impossible! It didn't make any sense. *He* had been the one targeted for murder, hadn't he? If somehow someone had discovered that Hugo had saved him, it stood to reason that the bullet had been another attempt, meant for him. It was the only thing that made sense. "Before?" he questioned softly. "What do you mean, Leslie? Has this happened before?"

Leslie nodded. "You won't tell Elly about this, will you, John? Elly won't let me out of her sight if she hears about it. After all, it's only stray bullets from hunters, or poachers, isn't it? Just like the toadstools were an accident—and the rock that fell near me on the beach. But you know women—she'll probably start reading all sorts of nonsense into a few coincidences if you get upset now too. Elly does that sort of thing most especially well."

Alastair's head was reeling. He had been concentrating for so long on believing the Dalrymples to be guilty that he had refused to believe Wiggins's theory that someone—either spies or smugglers or both—had wanted the Earl out of the way so that they had free access to Seashadow.

As he had only changed his mind about the Dalrymples this morning, he had yet to think up another theory as to who could be behind his near drowning. Now it looked as if Geoffrey Wiggins had been right all along.

Alastair was supposed to be dead. Perhaps—as he had believed himself—the murderers had thought the title would revert to the crown once the last Earl of Hythe was dead—leaving Seashadow to be run by a skeleton staff, its beaches fair game to anyone who wished to set up housekeeping there. Who was to stop them—the Biggses? Hardly.

But Alastair hadn't been the end of the line. There had been Leslie, and Elly, both of them walked the beach daily.

And now the murderers were after Leslie!

Alastair opened his mouth to tell Leslie what he thought, caught a glimpse of the shambles that was once his billiards table, and thought better of it. It would be like talking to the wind to even attempt to explain this convoluted intrigue to Leslie Dalrymple.

He would just have to assign Hugo to guard the man until he could lay everything out in front of Elly, call in Wiggins, who was still in London trying to tie things up at that end, and locate the person or persons who were trying to eradicate the residents of Seashadow!

Ordering Leslie—who was already most happily engaged in adding a coat of paint to a canvas boasting the rendering of a single blade of grass—to stay put until Hugo could join him, Alastair headed for the kitchens, hoping to locate Elly.

"Missy's up in her room, your lordship," Mrs. Biggs told him a few moments later, clucking her tongue. "I think she's come down with what Rosie's got—or at least she came inter the kitchens lookin' as green as Rosie did a while ago, though Rosie's settin' up and sippin' soup now, tryin' her best ter fill up her empty belly. It comes on sudden, and leaves just as quick. I suppose I'll have 'em all down with it afore too long. Do you want me to send Iris upstairs ter ask Missy ter come down?"

Alastair rubbed a weary hand across his forehead. His confession—as well as his suspicion that her brother's life was in danger—would have to wait for another day. "No, Billie, don't disturb her. Just have Harry get some of the farm laborers to help him stand guard all around Seashadow tonight, and send someone to fetch me tomorrow as soon as Miss Dalrymple is up to seeing visitors. Hugo will be staying with Mr. Dalrymple."

"Is somethin' goin' on, yer lordship?" Mrs. Biggs asked. "Somethin's goin' on, ain't it? Are we goin' ter be able ter stop this playactin' soon?"

"Soon, Billie, very soon," Alastair assured her, scooping

up two still warm strawberry tarts as he headed for the door, before stopping to tell the woman mournfully, "Believe me, I like this even less than you. Have you seen what he's done to my billiards room, Billie?"

"It's a cryin' shame, your lordship," the housekeeper commiserated, shaking her head. "But yer'll set it all ter rights soon, yer lordship, and so say we all."

Alastair's shoulders shook in wry mirth as he walked back out through the kitchen garden. "Poor Billie," he said aloud. "Wait until she finds out that Leslie Dalrymple is to become a permanent fixture at Seashadow. The whole lot of them will probably hand in their notices."

CHAPTER SIX

ELLY STARED INTO the mirror in the drawing room, a hand to her cheek, appalled at the sight of the white face that looked back at her.

"Good afternoon, Miss Dalrymple."

She whirled about—the quick movement reminding her of the still-not-quite-settled state of her stomach—to see Lieutenant Jason Fishbourne standing beside the open doors leading from the patio.

"Lieu-Lieutenant!" she exclaimed unsteadily, before her rising temper hardened her tone. How did he walk in on her, unannounced? "Have you lost your way? The front door—and the knocker—are on quite the opposite side of the house."

The man appeared impervious to insult. He bowed deeply from the waist, saying only, "We have pressing matters to discuss, madam, *privately,*" before walking more fully into the room.

"We do? *Indeed?*" Elly countered, wondering if all men were so rude, or if blonde men, like John Bates and the Lieutenant—and even her beloved brother Leslie—had some taint in their blood that predisposed them to riding roughshod over the formalities. "And what would those matters be, sir?"

She walked over to the settee, motioning for the Lieutenant to sit across from her, and sat down, for her legs still weren't too steady twenty-four hours after her brief but violent relationship with whatever stomach upset was fast laying low nearly every Biggs at Seashadow. Mrs. Biggs, Big and Little Georgie, Iris, Harry, and even Baby Willie had all fallen victim to the same illness during the night—which undoubtedly had made it easier for Fishbourne to make his way into the house unchallenged.

She watched as the Lieutenant sat back at his ease, crossing one long leg over the other. "You have a guest on the estate, madam, I believe?" he asked without further preamble. "One Mr. John Bates?"

Elly's heart began pounding hurtfully in her chest. "I do," she answered, knowing her chin was tilting at an aggressive angle. "Does that present a problem to you, Lieutenant?"

Fishbourne searched in his pocket for a small copybook, holding it in front of him as he read what was written there. "Name, John Bates. Occupation, retired soldier in His Majesty's service. Personal history, none. Companion, a hulking deaf and dumb brute named Hugo."

"Only dumb," Elly corrected, feeling her hackles beginning to rise anew. "Although I must say I dislike that description intensely, as it implies that Hugo is stupid as well as speechless. Nothing could be further from the truth. As a matter of fact, Hugo's intelligent action saved my brother from a nasty fall just the other day."

The Lieutenant looked up from the pages of the copybook, directed a level, assessing stare at Elly, and then returned his eyes to the page. "I stand corrected, Miss Dalrymple. I shall, of course, adjust my notes accordingly once I am back at headquarters. Dumb, but not deaf. Now, if I might proceed?"

Doubting that she could stop him without resorting to physical violence, Elly motioned for the man to continue.

"The aforementioned Mr. Bates," Fishbourne went on, still consulting his notes, "is a stranger to the area who somehow came into possession of a cottage on this estate for an indefinite term—paying no rent, by the way— through application to the Fourteenth Earl, your brother's predecessor."

"Obviously a patriotic act of thanks to a man who had been injured fighting Napoleon," Elly said wearily, for it appeared the man was going to prolong his introduction into whatever matters he felt they had to "discuss."

"Alastair Lowell—*patriotic?* Surely, Miss Dalrymple, you jest. Yes, of course you do. I am much amused." As if to prove his amusement, Lieutenant Fishbourne laughed aloud, a short, barklike laugh that had the hairs on the back of Elly's neck standing at attention. "The man was a useless wastrel, as I believe you yourself said."

Whether it was because of her growing dislike for the Lieutenant or due to her own feelings of vulnerability about her initial opinion of the late Earl, Elly heard herself springing to the dead man's defense.

"I have been reading some of the late Earl's private papers, sir," she said, her voice cool, "and I believe you to be in error. He was very active in Parliament on behalf of our soldiers in the field. As the last of his line—or so his solicitors have told me the man believed—and without issue, he had every reason not to endanger the Hythe succession by crossing the Channel to spill his blood on foreign soil. Someone, my dear Lieutenant, had to stay behind to help run the country. Have you, Lieutenant," she ended, hoping to change the subject, for she felt curiously uncomfortable in the role of defender of Alastair Lowell, "served anywhere other than along the relative safety of these well-defended shores?''

His cold, faded green eyes raked her from head to foot as Elly mentally added the term "dangerous" to those she had already assigned to the man: pompous, boring, and rude. "That is not germane, Miss Dalrymple," was all he answered as she involuntarily squirmed in her seat. "We seem to have digressed. We were, I believe, discussing Mr. John Bates.''

"What about him?" Elly asked pugnaciously, for ill as she still felt, she knew she was about to order this insufferable martinet out of her house.

The Lieutenant referred once more to his notes, tempting Elly to snatch the copybook from his hands and rip the offensive thing to shreds. "The man is not what he appears, Miss Dalrymple. There is no record of a John Bates serving anywhere in His Majesty's army, in any capacity.''

Elly shrugged, hopefully appearing to be unimpressed by the Lieutenant's shattering news. "So? Perhaps he served in His Majesty's navy. I think your information is incomplete.''

Fishbourne smiled at her. "He said he had served in the army, Miss Dalrymple. I saw no reason to investigate further.''

Anxious not to draw out the interview, which was becoming increasingly painful to endure, Elly asked, "Have you confronted Mr. Bates with your findings, Lieutenant?''

He ignored her question, his attention once more on his copious notes. "You—and your brother the Earl, of course—have been seen conversing with this Mr. John Bates, and he has partaken of his meals at Seashadow on several occasions.''

"Two occasions, Lieutenant," Elly inserted through

clenched teeth. Yes, she would definitely like to rip up that copybook—and stuff the pieces one by one down Fishbourne's throat. "I hadn't known that my brother and I were under surveillance, sir."

"No one is totally above suspicion, Miss Dalrymple, when the safety of our beloved country is at stake," Fishbourne informed her authoritatively, snapping the copybook shut at last. "Not that I believe you and the Earl could possibly be involved in any traitorous activity."

"How terribly condescending of you, Lieutenant," Elly purred with heavy sarcasm, rising to cross over to the bellpull, knowing that none of the Biggses were in any condition to come to her rescue.

Fishbourne rose as well, tucking the copybook back inside the jacket of his uniform. "My question, madam, is simply this: Why, when you said you would do all in your power to help your government, did you not report the existence of Mr. John Bates to me as soon as you discovered his presence on Seashadow property?"

It was a good question, Elly knew, and one she had racked her brain to answer on more than one occasion. After all, she had promised to report any suspicious person or persons, hadn't she?

Lieutenant Fishbourne considered John Bates to be suspicious, and he didn't even know about either the feigned limp or John's disquieting familiarity with Seashadow.

She opened her mouth to tell the man these things, then closed it again. She wasn't going to reveal her own discoveries about John Bates. She had never really planned to tell him—not deep in her heart of hearts. She was going to be stupid and foolish and protect John Bates from Lieutenant Fishbourne—behaving just like any at-her-last-prayers spinster who needs desperately to believe every man who so much as compliments her is in love with her.

She tugged once more on the bellpull, hoping her brother—whom she had last seen in the kitchens, creating some muddy-looking concoction he called "prunes and prisms gruel" for his luncheon—would come to her rescue. Where was Leslie when she needed him? Silly question. Where had he *ever* been when she needed him—nowhere to be found!

"Miss Dalrymple?" The Lieutenant had somehow come up beside her, and his voice made her flinch. "I sense some discomfort in your manner. He hasn't threatened you, this John Bates, has he?"

Of course John had threatened her. He threatened her peace, her supposedly well-ordered life, her traitorous heart that she had believed would always belong to Robert. She turned to face the Lieutenant, her smile as brilliant as she could make it. Elly closed her eyes, watching her figurative bridges burning into ashes behind her eyelids. "Threatened me, Lieutenant?" she repeated, then giggled. Lord, how she abhorred giggles! "Why, sir, I don't think so—unless you consider a proposal of marriage a threat."

Fishbourne took a single step back. "He—he proposed *marriage?*"

Well, Elly thought meanly, the man didn't have to sound so surprised. She knew she wasn't looking her best—what with her face still pinched from being ill and her hair pulled so unattractively atop her head—but he didn't have to make it seem as if John would have to be the most desperate, or least discriminating, creature on earth to have proposed to her.

Her chin lifted. "And what do you *think* he proposed,

sirrah!'' she asked archly. "I think, Lieutenant, that you overreach yourself.''

For once she seemed to have penetrated Lieutenant Fishbourne's thick hide. "I—I didn't mean to infer—that is, I certainly was not implying that—''

Elly took his arm and steered him toward the door. "Of course you didn't, my dear Lieutenant,'' she said soothingly. "Just as I may have overreacted to your questions about my dearest John. You do understand how shocked I was to hear that you thought my betrothed could ever be involved with anything nefarious.''

"Still,'' the Lieutenant persisted as Elly led him through the foyer, "I think I should stop by the cottage to meet your fiancé. Perhaps he has seen something unusual in the area?''

No! He couldn't see John—at least not until she could see him herself and tell him what she had just done! Giggling girlishly again, and hating herself twice as much for it, Elly trilled, "Oh, pray do not trouble yourself, Lieutenant. Mr. Bates has gone to visit his doctor somewhere or other today, and will not be back in his cottage until very late this evening. Perhaps you will accept an invitation to dine with all of us tomorrow night—giving me, *um*, giving my fiancé, that is, time to recuperate from his trip?''

Elly stood at the open front door, watching as the Lieutenant strode away, willing her pulse to return to its usual slow, steady beat. Now what had she done? Wasn't it bad enough that she had protected John Bates from the law? Had she really been forced to claim him as her fiancé as well? Now she had no choice but to go to John as soon as possible and convince him that her lies had been in his own best interests.

"Ah, there you are, Elly. I've been looking high and low for you. Now, let me think, what was it that I wanted?"

"Leslie." Elly turned about, letting the door slam behind her. "Where have you been? I was summoning you with the bellpull."

Leslie slapped his forehead with the palm of one hand. "So *that's* what that infernal ringing was that I heard in the kitchen. And it's also why I don't remember why I wanted to see you. I never did want to see you. *You* wanted to see *me*. Don't do that, dearest Elly, please; you frightened me for a minute. I thought I was being more scatterbrained than usual. What did you want?"

Elly shook her head in defeat. "Nothing, now. Leslie, I must go out for a while. Oh, Hugo," she said as the giant came into the foyer, a half-eaten apple in one large paw. "What are you doing here? Never mind, I'm happy to see you. Tell me, please, is your master at home?"

Hugo nodded, taking another bite of apple as Leslie commented, "John? What do you care where he is, Elly? Just the other day you told me you were tired of him forever kicking his heels upon our doorstep. Said you wouldn't trust him across the street, too, if I remember it correctly—that and wishing him in Jericho a time or two. What do you want to see him about, Elly? Surely you aren't going to throw him out of the cottage? I shouldn't like that above half, Elly, truly I shouldn't."

"The selectivity of your memory, my dearest brother," Elly returned in resignation, "never ceases to astound me. No, I am not about to evict John from the cottage. I merely have some small matters to discuss with him," she told them, picking up her bonnet from a table near the door. "Leslie, you and Hugo stay here in case the Biggses need you for anything."

Leslie immediately looked crestfallen. "They don't want me, Elly," he told her sadly. "I took Mrs. Biggs some of my prunes and prisms gruel and she threw it out the window—bowl and all. Sick people aren't always nice, you know."

"Yes, dearest," Elly answered vaguely, her mind concentrating on how she was going to tell John Bates that she had announced their "engagement" to Lieutenant Fishbourne. Even worse, she was going to have to confront him with her latest conclusion—the one that, if correct, would most probably put a period to their entire association. She opened the door and stepped out into the bright sunshine, feeling like a prisoner walking to the gibbet. "I shan't be long."

THE MANTEL CLOCK chimed out the hour of two, and still Harry hadn't come to tell him that Elly was up to seeing visitors. Alastair continued to pace the carpet in the overcrowded main room of the comfortable, quaint cottage, trying to wish the hours away until he could stand before her at Seashadow and tell her the truth.

A knock at the front door interrupted his thoughts and he nearly ran in his haste to open it, only to find the object of his thoughts standing on the smooth stone doorstep.

He looked around quickly, just to see if she was alone, then pulled her unceremoniously inside the cottage, slamming the door behind them. "What in blue blazes is the matter with Harry? How could he have let you out by yourself at a time like this? And here I always thought he was the smart one."

Disengaging her elbow from his grip, Elly walked toward the oak settle, stripping off her bonnet as she sat down. "Harry?" she asked, fiddling with the strings of her bonnet.

"What has Harry to say to anything? And why are you acting as if I shouldn't be seen coming into your cottage? Not that I should be, but as no one was about to chaperone me, and this cottage is quite isolated, I didn't think it would matter. We've been alone before, John, if you'll recall."

She was as nervous as a Christmas goose around a chopping block, Alastair decided as he walked across the room to sit on the oak settle that faced hers. Had she heard something? Had she sensed some change in the atmosphere? Had there been another attempt on Leslie's life? "What are you doing here, Elly? I was planning to visit you at Seashadow once you were feeling better. You are feeling better, aren't you?" he asked, eyeing her pale face intently.

"Doing here?" she answered before biting her lip as she looked around the room that was crowded with so much furniture that Alastair had been forced to banish Hugo from its confines for fear he would forget himself, turn around too quickly, and demolish something. "And I'm just fine, thank you, although most of the Biggses are now suffering from the same complaint. My, what a lovely corner cupboard that is, John. I do believe it is mahogany. There is quite a wealth of furniture in here, isn't there? You are comfortable here, I trust? I imagine I should have stopped by sooner, to be sure you were. How many rooms are there in the cottage, all together, that is?"

Something was wrong. Elly was babbling, and she wasn't the sort of women who babbled. "Four, and yes, I am very comfortable, although the ceiling could be a foot higher for Hugo. Would you now like to discuss the weather—which continues to be very fine—or would you like to tell me what really brought you here before you wad that poor ribbon up past all saving?"

He watched as she looked down to see the havoc her

nervously twitching hands had wrought on her bonnet strings, smiling as she deliberately smoothed the ribbons and laid the bonnet to one side. "John, can we talk with the buttons off?" she asked, staring straight up at him, her eyes wide with apprehension.

Finally! He was beginning to think he was going to have to shake Elly's news out of her. Alastair crossed his legs, leaning back against the settle. "I certainly don't see why we shouldn't, my dear. We certainly haven't skirted around each other's sensibilities up to now, have we? What do you want to talk about?"

She took a deep breath, then said, "Lieutenant Jason Fishbourne!"

Alastair sat forward, his attention caught. He could have thought of a half dozen subjects she might wish to discuss—perhaps an even dozen. But Lieutenant Jason Fishbourne? *"Who?"*

"Lieutenant Fishbourne is investigating smuggling and spying that may be taking place right here at Seashadow. Then you don't know him," Elly said, as if convincing herself. "Well, he knows you. He knows all about you—or as much as anyone knows about you. He's very suspicious of you, John. Very suspicious."

"He thinks I'm a spy—or a smuggler? No, don't tell me. I'm *both!*" Alastair guessed, barely able to keep a straight face. So much for the investigative arm of His Majesty's Preventive Service! He was pleased he had told Wiggins to keep the good Lieutenant in the dark as to his true identity. The man was obviously incompetent.

Elly leaned forward, as if to comfort him. "Don't fly into the boughs, John. He just mentioned to me that he has investigated your background to find that you were never in the army. He finds that—and Hugo's presence—very dis turbing. But he didn't actually make any accusations. He just kept referring to his infernal copybook.''

From the look on her face as she mentioned the copybook, Alastair deduced that Lieutenant Jason Fishbourne was not Elly's favorite Preventive Service officer. "So he came to you with his doubts and suspicions? I have been out of touch. Is it customary to involve private citizens—especially female private citizens—in hunts for spies and smugglers?''

"You're upset, aren't you?''

Alastair decided that his beloved Elly was a master of understatement. Was he upset? Of course he was upset! How dare this Lieutenant involve her in this whole affair? "I object to his tactics. He was using you, Elly, wasn't he?''

The bonnet strings were once more within her grasp and she began shredding one of them with her fingers. "Not really, John. He visited Seashadow earlier to ask if I would report any strangers or unusual activities on the beaches. It was all quite congenial, really.'' Her head and her voice both lowered as she ended, "Until today.''

"And what was different about today?''

She rose to examine the mantel clock, which kept her features away from his sight. "He all but accused you of being a spy—or a smuggler. I think he was leaning toward your being a spy. And—and he wanted to know why I hadn't reported your presence at Seashadow. He, or his men, have been watching our every movement—and he has recorded it all in his little copybook, just like a schoolboy at his sums.''

Alastair rose to stand beside her, his hand lightly caressing her shoulder. "I see. I believe I should like to meet this Lieutenant Fishbourne, just so that I might give him a good pop in his nose. And what did you tell him, Elly? What reason did you give for not reporting me like any loyal citizen should?''

''I told him we were—'' the rest was unintelligible.

''You told him what?'' Alastair pressed, leaning closer, the better to hear her.

''Betrothed!'' she all but shouted, turning about to face him. ''I told him we were betrothed. And then I invited him to join us all for dinner tomorrow night at Seashadow because you were away somewhere today visiting your doctor for that nonexistent wound to your leg. But I didn't do it so that you could give him a good pop on the nose. I figured I could give you some time to get away before he could arrest you. There! Are you happy now?''

Happy? Alastair was ecstatic. She had lied for him. She had covered up for him, even while believing that there could be some truth to the Lieutenant's wild accusations. She loved him. Oh, yes she did, whether she admitted it or not. Alastair's smile was so wide, it threatened to crack his face in two.

''Will you help me pack my bags, dearest Elly? I should leave before the tide turns, don't you think, if I want to rendezvous with my froggie friends in Calais. You are free to accompany me if you wish, but I will understand if you refuse and want to cry off from our engagement.''

Her complexion deepened to a becoming dusky pink for a moment before she drew herself up straight and declared with some heat, ''Stop it! Don't you try to bamboozle me with your nonsense, John.''

He grabbed at his chest, as if her words had stung him to the quick. ''Me? I wouldn't be so brave. How am I trying to bamboozle you?''

She shook her head in exasperation. "You're no more a spy than Leslie is."

"Then I'm to be a smuggler?" he asked, not quite liking the look in her eyes. She wasn't just watching him; she was examining him from head to foot, as if measuring him for a suit of clothes.

"No," she answered, shaking her head, "you're not a smuggler either. I don't know why I didn't see it sooner, but I know now *exactly* what—or should I say *who*—you are."

"Then what am I, Elly? And why are you protecting me from the good Lieutenant?"

"You're Alastair Lowell, Fourteenth Earl of Hythe— *that's* who you are, John—and I think I hate you very, very much!"

Her words had Alastair hunting blindly for the hard wooden settle before his knees gave out from beneath him. So much for struggling with himself all during a long, sleepless night, trying to decide how to break the news to her in the kindest way possible.

"I'm right, aren't I? Oh, of course I am—it's written all over your face. I can see your guilty expression straight through that horrid beard. Oh, John, how could you?"

How could he? How could she have guessed? "Wh-what gave me away?"

"Then it is true," she said fatally, looking down at him. "I had so hoped I was wrong." He watched as Elly sat down on the facing settle with a thump, her body folding in on itself like a bladder that has lost all its air. "I was packing away the Earl's clothing the other day. You're ex- actly the same size. You knew precisely where we keep the brandy. Mrs. Biggs wanted Big George to serve your fa- vorite dish, and lied badly when I asked her to explain how she knew what it was. You were too arrogant to be a lowly soldier, as you claimed, and you have no calluses. So many little things," she told him quietly. "Oh, my poor, poor Leslie. Misfortune seems to dog his every footstep. Whatever will he do now?"

"He'll have to find himself a new studio, for one thing," Alastair was stung into saying, for he found he disliked intensely the fact that Elly had stolen his thunder—and all because of stuffed capon and calluses— "while I try to find another billiards table as good as the one he ruined."

Elly now glared up at him, her slanted brown eyes swimming with tears. "Your billiards table. Is that all you can think of, John—my lord?"

He was instantly contrite, for it was obvious that her whole world had just been shattered. Quickly sliding down from the settle to rest on his knees before her, Alastair reached out to take hold of Elly's elbows. "Not 'my lord,' dearest Elly, never 'my lord.' My name is Alastair."

He felt himself begin pushed backward as she hopped to her feet, putting as much space between the two of them as the small room allowed. "Alastair? Hardly, my lord— and I am not your *dearest* anything!" she exclaimed, flinging her hands wide. "Call yourself Judas, or Benedict, for you are the most two-faced, self-serving monster in all England! How dare you give Leslie false hope? How dare you come sneaking around here, checking up on your successor and telling all sorts of lies for your own amusement—in aid or your own twisted little game?"

Alastair's shoulders sagged for a moment as he considered her charges, then he straightened as he heard her call his actions a game. "Games, is it, Miss Dalrymple? And what sort of game is it to conk someone over the head and then dump him overboard to drown? Perhaps you can give me the name of this game, as I don't recognize it."

His words seemed to stop her from barreling out of the cottage, probably following hard on the heels of some dire warning concerning her wish never to see him again. "You—you didn't *fall* overboard?"

Alastair smiled. Yes, she was an intelligent puss. "No, Elly. I didn't fall overboard. Nor was I drunk—well, no more than two parts drunk anyway. I was pushed. If it hadn't been for Hugo, I would have drowned. As it was, it was two weeks until I came around, and nearly another two until I was fit to travel here."

"To find Leslie installed as the Earl," Elly finished for him, coming back to sit down once more. "But why didn't you announce yourself alive and reclaim your title immediately?"

"Would you?" Alastair asked, sitting down beside her and taking one of her cold hands in his. "Someone had just tried to kill me, Elly. I decided to hide away here, at Seashadow, until I could figure out who wanted me dead."

She pulled her hand away. "And so you settled on Leslie?"

Elly might have stumbled onto his true identity through the backdoor, but she was certainly heading in the right direction now, for a moment later she turned to him to screech: "No! Anyone could see that Leslie wouldn't hurt a fly. You thought *I* was the one who wanted you dead! Don't try to deny it. That's why you were so nice to me—you were trying to worm your way into Seashadow while you decided how to unmask me for the criminal you think I am. Oh, John, how could you?"

There was, Alastair had learned over the course of the years, a time for truth and a time for lies. This was a time for lies. "How could you ever think such a thing, Elly—after all we have been to each other?" he exclaimed with as much umbrage as he could muster. "I came here to discover who wanted me dead, yes, but not because I thought you or Leslie was the culprit. Far from it. I hadn't even known of your existence. I came here looking for the spies or smugglers who wanted me out of the way so that they could use my beaches undisturbed. I'm hurt, Elly, hurt to the quick, that you could think such a thing of me."

He turned away from her, silently praying that his half-truth would be acceptable. Besides, his mention of spies and smugglers hopefully might have jogged her memory about her own barely masked suspicions of him—not to mention her several disparaging statements about the late Earl made in his presence.

"You're working for the government?" she asked weakly after a few moments.

He turned back to face her, his smile deliberately guileless. "In a manner of speaking. I am working with Captain Geoffrey Wiggins, who is connected to the War Office."

"I'm terribly confused."

That makes two of us, Alastair thought silently, but he knew better than to share his confusion with Elly. Instead, he slid an arm around her shoulders, pulling her against him. "It's very simple, my dear. I am here incognito, working to unmask the spy who has been using Seashadow's beaches as his stopping-off point on his way back and forth from London to France. Once everyone in the chain has been captured—including the bounder who tried to do me in—I shall announce my lucky escape from a watery grave and resume my customary hey-go-mad place in Society, with no one being the wiser that I have, in reality, been a contributing member to the war effort."

"Leaving Leslie to crawl back to obscurity and his two hundred pounds a year," Elly ended in a very small voice, leaning her head against his shoulder. "How I shall detest eating turnips again."

"Not necessarily, my pet," Alastair told her, knowing he was dragging the thing out but feeling he was getting a little of his own back for having to listen to her tear his reputation to shreds more than once. "There is still the small matter of our betrothal. I had, of course, entertained hopes—but as I had yet to speak to your brother, I am all ears to hear the details of this recent engagement between us."

"Oh, aren't you just," Elly snapped, pulling her head away. "I certainly wasn't serious about the thing, you know. You had pretended an interest in me in order to get into Seashadow, and I had simply taken a page from your book in using the supposed betrothal to put Lieutenant Fishbourne off the scent. We are not truly engaged."

He pulled her head back against his shoulder once more. "And you are that set against it, then, dearest Elly? Think about it. Leslie would have his studio—a separate studio on each of my holdings—and you would never have to stare down another horrid turnip. I should think you'd jump at the chance."

Elly pushed his arm away and stood, glaring down at him. "You're laughing at me. I suppose I deserve it, for saying all those nasty things about you—and for thinking you might be a spy, for I did think that for a while, and if you think I believe for one moment that you hadn't harbored the thought that I was the one who tried to drown you, you're sadly mistaken—but I don't think I should have to stay here and be insulted. Good day to you, my lord Hythe! Leslie and I will be gone in the morning."

"And where will you go?" Alastair asked, also rising.

That question stopped her, as he had been sure it would. "Oh, do be quiet!" she ordered, bending to pick up her bonnet. "I have to think. I can't have an answer for everything, you know."

"Seashadow is a great barn of a place—although it is the smallest of my estates. You could stay there for a while without too much danger of the two of us stumbling over each other. I am going to take up residence now, you understand—out of consideration for Hugo's poor head, that keeps making its acquaintance with the lintels of this charming cottage, and in order to be closer to Big George's kitchen. Then there is the matter of the person who is trying to kill Leslie."

He watched, entranced, as Elly's eyes got very wide. "Someone—someone is trying to kill Leslie? I don't believe it!"

He shrugged. "Why not? Someone tried to kill me when I was the Earl of Hythe, in order to have access to Seashadow's beaches. Why wouldn't he try to kill the new Earl of Hythe, who cropped up unexpectedly when no heir was expected to surface? Leslie has been shot at, you know, and more than once. I was witness to the latest attempt yesterday afternoon just minutes after you left us—although Leslie will be angry that I've told you about it, fearing that you won't allow him outside any more. That's why Hugo is at Seashadow, to guard Leslie. We may be dealing with an inept murderer, but his luck is bound to change sooner or later."

Elly spread her hands. "But now that *you're* the Earl again, no one will be after Leslie," she deduced, to Alastair's mind, entirely too clearly. "My brother will be safe the moment you make your announcement."

"And in danger the moment I'm really dead," Alastair pointed out, trying his best not to succumb to the urge to strangle her for so blithely whistling *his* safety down the wind. "Besides, what makes you think I'm going to make any announcements? I'm still working with Wiggins. My identity has to remain a secret until all the spies are captured. I will merely be residing at Seashadow, as Leslie's guest."

"You-you'd deliberately put Leslie in danger?" Elly questioned, clearly incensed. "How could you be so cruel?"

"Leslie is in no danger, now that Hugo is taking care of him. As a matter of fact, I do believe Hugo has already saved your brother once—that day on the cliff—although I'm convinced we'll never understand exactly what happened. But since late yesterday, when I was witness to an attempt on Leslie's life, Seashadow has been patrolled by my mea, with Harry leading them, and Leslie hasn't been out of Hugo's sight. The only thing I don't understand is how Harry let you slip past him to come to the cottage."

CHAPTER SEVEN

"I ALREADY TOLD YOU, John," Elly answered absently, for her head was still reeling from all that had happened to her today. "The Biggses are all sick in their beds—all except Rosie, who has gotten better and Lily, who is less than useless, sick or well. Are you really going to move in at Seashadow and hide behind Leslie while attempting to uncover the person or persons who tried to kill you?"

She watched as John—Alastair—winced. "When you say it like that, it doesn't sound very noble, does it, Elly? But, yes, that is exactly what I propose to do. Our murderer will think twice about striking again if he learns that his first attempt on me failed. He'd go straight to ground, not to resurface for months to make another attempt. I want this over and done with as quickly as possible, for I want to get back to London and my life there."

"Your life in London! Is that all it means to you—that you have to be away from the gaming tables and your...your painted ladies? It's almost as if you're doing all of this as a sort of lark. I take back every kind word I ever said about you!" Elly pronounced feelingly.

Alastair only shrugged at this insult, making her more angry than before. "No matter. There can't have been more than two or three of them at best anyway—kind words, that is. If you only knew how trying it was for me to sit back and do nothing while, time after time, you threw my past in my teeth. As a matter of fact, you just did it again, didn't you? Now, Elly, if you are through surprising me with your brilliant deductive powers, and done accusing me of hiding behind your brother's skinny legs, perhaps we can have a serious discussion.''

Now, why did she know they weren't going to talk about their supposed engagement, the one he persisted in pretending to be real? Was it because he had just told her he wanted to get back to his life in London? Of course it was. She didn't have to be hit over the head with a red brick to know that he had all but forgotten her already. ''What do you wish to discuss, John?'' she asked, settling herself once more on one of the wooden settles.

''Good. That's very good, Elly. Continue to address me as John. It would be too easy to trip up with Fishbourne or anyone else who may be about if you tried to call me Alastair in private and John when we are in public.''

Elly nodded and nervously bit her lower lip. She hadn't realized that she had called him John. But there was no John, was there? The John who had walked the beach with her was gone, to be replaced by a monied, titled peer who wanted nothing to do with a silly, suspicious spinster who thought that taking down her hair could change her into a lovable, desirable woman. She was being silly—feeling as if she would like to have a quiet period of mourning to mark his passing before having to deal with the overpowering Alastair Lowell, Earl of Hythe.

Good lord! Alastair was the Earl of Hythe! How long would it take before she could say those words, even think those words, without a stab of real physical pain cutting into her heart?

Oh, her poor, poor Leslie! It wasn't just his life that was in danger. She raised a hand to her head, Alastair's mention of her brother bringing back her other worries. How was she ever going to tell Leslie he was no longer the Earl?

And wherever would they go? They had given up their small leased cottage in Linton, and they had precious little funds left to secure another one. How difficult it would be to leave Seashadow and the beach they had both grown to love. How difficult it would be to leave John—Alastair—a man she really didn't know, yet a man who already meant more to her than the very air she breathed.

"Elly?"

She shook her head, purposely banishing all depressing thoughts of a future without Alastair from her mind. "When do you wish to take up your chambers at Seashadow?" she asked, praying her voice was steady. "I just aired them the other day—as Leslie didn't wish to occupy them—and your clothes have all been packed away in the attics. I suppose I could have them ready for you by this evening, if I can get Lily to help."

She looked up at him as another thought struck her. "Lily! She knew, didn't she? No, don't answer. Of course she knew—and she used the opportunity to flirt outrageously with you that night you first came to dinner. The little minx!"

Alastair smiled, and she suddenly longed to rip out his beard, one blonde hair at a time. "So that still rankles, does it? Yes, I had forgotten that Lily and I will now be under the same roof. You know, she has *blossomed* quite nicely since my last visit to Seashadow," he commented, stroking that same beard.

"You wouldn't!"

"I wouldn't what, dearest Elly?" he responded, continuing to smile a moment more before sobering. "Of course I wouldn't. Is your opinion of Alastair Lowell still that low?

I am an engaged man, remember? You told me so yourself. You told Lieutenant Fishbourne. Have you sent notices to the papers as yet, or are you going to leave at least that much up to me?''

It had been a very trying twenty-four hours for Elly. She had been dreadfully ill for a large part of it, for one thing. Then there had been that distressing interview with the so pompous, so suspicious Lieutenant Fishbourne. And, as if that were not enough, she had learned that her worst imaginings about John Bates were founded in fact—and that she and Leslie were about to be dispossessed.

Having Alastair joke about her lies to Lieutenant Fishbourne, having him tease her with wild hopes that could never be fulfilled, was simply more than she could endure. Elly jumped up from the settle, brought back her right hand, and swung from her heels, landing a loud, stinging open-handed slap directly to Alastair's left cheek.

A moment later Elly was wrapped in Alastair's arms and his mouth was against hers, his kiss warm and deep and seemingly full of passion. She should struggle, she knew she should, but all the fight had suddenly gone out of her, to be replaced with her overriding need of this infuriating man.

She allowed her hands to creep up Alastair's broad chest, to entwine themselves behind his neck, just as his hands moved upward to the pins in her hair, removing them one by one so that her curls tumbled down past her shoulders.

She felt free, she felt reborn, she felt as if she were the most beautiful, desirable woman in all England. Opening her eyes to peek at him, she could see that Alastair's eyes were squeezed shut, as if he was intent on what he was doing, intent on kissing her until she either fainted or went mad.

Her toes were curling inside her jean half boots before he finally broke the kiss, but it was only to push her head against his chest, his fingers still deeply tangled in her hair, his arms still holding her a willing captive.

She touched her fingertips to her bruised mouth. "I detest that beard," she mumbled against his waistcoat, saying the first thing that came into her mind. "It scratches."

She sensed more than heard the rumble of his laughter. "It itches, too—and it will be the first thing to go once I am free to announce that I am still alive. As a matter of fact, my pet, if you wish to make a list—I understand from Leslie that you are partial to them—I shall be doing three things once the people who want me dead are safely locked up. One, I shall remove to London to reclaim my estates—for they do not run themselves, you know. Two, I shall shave. And three, I shall announce our engagement in all the papers, so that I don't have to be slapped anymore. You are quite strong for a little thing, you know, my pet. In fact, now that I think of it, perhaps numbers two and three should be reversed—just for the sake of my personal safety."

Elly pulled slightly away from him—his arms were not about to let her move much farther—and asked, "You are serious, Alastair? You really do want to marry me? I mean, this isn't another rig you are running? Another game you are playing? You really, *really* want to marry me? Why?"

She watched as his brow furrowed. "Dear Elly, always so full of doubts. Do you know what, Elly? I really don't know why. I've never wanted to shackle myself to anyone before. I only know that you are the most inquisitive—I'm sure I should dare to say nosy—female I have ever met; a woman who is as beautiful as she is intelligent, and as loyal and courageous as she is foolhardy."

"I am not foolhardy," Elly replied, stung by his last

word even as she gloried in most of what had come before it.

He leaned down to place a kiss on the tip of her nose.
"You flirted with me in the most outrageous way, all to
keep my interest while you delved into my life to see if I
was a smuggler, or a Bonapartist spy. If that isn't foolhardy
enough for you, my dear, allow me to point out that you
are now standing alone with me in this cottage—our bodies
pressed tightly together, knee to neck—with no chaperone
about and your beloved thinking delightful thoughts that
have no business being in his head until after our marriage."

"Wretch," Elly grumbled, removing herself from his
embrace, her head bowed so that he could not see the hot
color that had invaded her cheeks. She reached behind her
for her bonnet. "You are lucky that I am so very old, or
you wouldn't have me swooning, you know. I had better
leave now, I imagine?"

"That would be best, I suppose, although I don't like
it—and you are not old. You are just right." Alastair took
the bonnet from her hand and placed it on her head, arranging her long blonde hair around her shoulders before
neatly tying the ribbons beneath her chin. "I'll walk with
you to Seashadow and send Hugo back for our things and
to close up the cottage. You'll see, Elly. We'll all be as
merry as grigs."

BIG GEORGE HAD recovered sufficiently to prepare a simple
meal that evening, after which Leslie, Hugo, Alastair, and
Elly repaired to the drawing room, where they now sat,
Leslie and Hugo at the far side of the room playing spilli-
kins, Alastair and Elly sitting side by side on the settee,
holding hands.

"Tell me all about Hugo, dearest," Elly asked, smiling as the giant let out a roar at winning yet another game.

"'Dearest,'" Alastair repeated, squeezing her hand. "I think I like that."

Elly blushed. It occurred to her that she had blushed more since meeting Alastair than she had ever done before in her life. "It seemed a good compromise," she told him. "This way I cannot possibly call you Alastair when I should be addressing you as John. You don't mind, do you?"

She watched as he lifted her hand to his mouth and placed a gentle kiss in her palm. "I like it excessively, to tell you the truth. But, as it can lead nowhere for some time, I will do my best to take it in my stride and not allow my emotions to overwhelm me. Now, tell me, what else do you want to learn about my good friend Hugo? I've already told you that he rescued me from a watery grave."

Elly closed her fingers around the palm that still burned from the imprint of Alastair's kiss. "What?" she asked, her train of thought hopelessly jumbled by his romantic action. "Oh, yes, Hugo. I was just wondering how he came to have his tongue cut out. You had told me it was cut out, hadn't you?"

Alastair reached into his pocket and withdrew the letter Hugo had placed in his keeping. "This is all I know," he said, handing her the paper. "I recopied the note he carried—his mother had dictated it to explain his condition—as this one has seen better days. I'd like to keep it with Seashadow's other important documents as it is very valuable to Hugo."

When she had finished reading the letter, there were tears in Elly's eyes. She carefully folded the paper and handed it back to Alastair before searching in the pocket of her gown for her handkerchief. "That's terribly sad, isn't it? And yet Hugo is so gentle, so loving."

Alastair nodded. "And he's not a jaw-me-dead either. All I have to do is close my eyes, and I can't hear him."

"For shame! I would be angry with you if I could believe you aren't merely saying that to upset me. You and Hugo are good friends. However, Leslie is absolutely dotty about him."

"Leslie, my love, is dotty about everything. Which is why I am happy you've agreed with me that we should keep my identity a secret from him for a while longer. It will be enough for him to handle the fact that he is no longer the Earl. But you have to own it, knowing that someone is trying to erase him from the face of the earth may be too much for him to take in."

"Well, that's that," Leslie said loudly, rising from his chair to come across the room to where Elly and Alastair sat, so that Elly could not remind Alastair that she had never really agreed with his plan to keep her brother in the dark as to the facts. "He won every game. Devilish acute, Hugo is, John, as I just taught him the game. I say, Elly, you're looking pinched. Stomach still upset?"

"Leslie," she said tightly, as Alastair was squeezing her hand in warning, "you will remember to take Hugo with you everywhere you go, won't you?"

Her brother smiled down at her, shaking his head. "Of course I shall, Elly. Haven't you told me a dozen times tonight that Hugo is feeling lost in this big house and I should be responsible for him?"

"Maybe she'd like to embroider it on a pair of garters for you," Alastair teased, earning himself a searching look from his beloved.

"No," Leslie replied, obviously believing Alastair to be

serious. "Can't knit—stands to reason she can't embroider either. I say, John, would it be all right if Hugo and I went to my studio? I promised him I would show him my collection of grasshoppers."

Alastair agreed immediately, causing Elly to wonder if perhaps, at last, she could feel free to ask him some questions that had been burning in her head the whole time she had been dressing for dinner.

"I'd like to hear more about Captain Wiggins, if you please," she informed him once Leslie and Hugo were gone. "I don't quite understand his part in any of this."

For the next quarter hour Elly listened as Alastair brought her up-to-date on everything that had happened from the first time Captain Wiggins had been ushered into the drawing room of Alastair's London town house to the moment the spy and smugglers had landed on the beach at Seashadow.

"You saw the smugglers—and the spy?" she broke in as he seemed to digress from his story for a moment, to concentrate on the perils of half burying one's body in insect-infested sand, a tale that, to her mind, had precious little to do with capturing spies and smugglers. "And you did nothing? They're still out there, running about somewhere?"

"I wouldn't say that we did nothing, pet," Alastair answered with maddening calm. "We counted them. Geoffrey is very big on counting—but that really doesn't matter anymore. According to my latest communication from the good Captain, who has been so kind as to keep me fully informed, the spy's connection in London has been neutralized—I believe that is the word Geoffrey used—so all that remains is to pretend to capture the spy himself when he attempts a return to France. According to the phases of the moon, that should be any time now.''

"*Pretend* to capture the spy. *Count* the smugglers." Elly thought she was going to scream. "Is this the way we are winning the war, Alastair? You're not making any sense! If you don't want to tell me the truth—if you think my female brain is not capable of absorbing the ins and outs of such intrigues—please have the goodness not to lie so outrageously. Pretend to capture the spy, indeed. You're trying to gull me."

"Please, pet, don't descend to cant, especially just as I am determined to mature myself. Besides, I am not *gulling* you. The spy has been given a fistful of erroneous information bound to have a good portion of Napoleon's forces chasing their own tails while Wellington advances toward France unscathed. It is a good plan, bordering on brilliant, actually, which is why I am so surprised Wiggins thought of it."

Elly was quiet for a while, trying to absorb all the information she had received, mentally separating the wheat from the chaff. After a lifetime of dealing with Leslie, sorting out the pertinent information contained within Alastair's tale was not that difficult.

"There's going to be some action on the beach at Seashadow very shortly, isn't there, John?"

"Dearest. You were going to call me dearest," Alastair reminded her, giving her a kiss on the cheek. "I don't know why women have such a reputation for being devious, when you cannot even seem to keep my name straight, my love."

She pushed him away. "Don't distract me," she ordered, refusing to melt beneath his careless charm. "You said Captain Wiggins is going to pretend to capture the spy. Why would he want to do that, if you want the spy to take incorrect information to France? And I thought you wanted to capture the spy—who is most probably behind the attempts on your life, and Leslie's. Maybe you're right, and this is all beyond a mere female's mind.''

Alastair raised her hand to his lips once more. ''Don't frown, pet, and don't think unkindly of yourself. It really is quite convoluted. Now look—the traitor in the War Office has been captured, but that doesn't mean our spy knows this. So he will also not think his identity or whereabouts is known to us—allowing him to feel free to leave England the way he came to it, via the beach at Seashadow. That's why they chose my section of the coastline, you know. It is a natural harbor, and away from any real population.''

Elly nodded. ''All right. I understand you so far. Go on.''

''As we know who the spy is, we can follow his every movement, and be on hand as he waits on the beach for the smugglers he has hired to transport him to row in to the shore.''

''So that you can pretend to capture him? No, it still doesn't make sense.''

''It does once you know that the spy that will be waiting for the smugglers on the beach will not be the real spy,'' Alastair said, his expression smug as he gave her this last piece of information.

Elly sat back and gnawed on the right side of her thumb as she considered everything Alastair had said. ''If Wiggins captures the *real* spy at the last minute, and replaces him with his *own* spy—making sure the man has to run full tilt to the boat to evade certain capture, so that the smugglers are too fully occupied outrunning the soldiers to check his identity too closely—he can be safely out at sea under cover of darkness and delivered to France without anyone on the boat being the wiser! It's brilliant!''

Alastair slipped an arm across her shoulders. "Yes, I thought so myself."

Suddenly Elly sat front, Alastair's arm falling away from her shoulders. "No—it's not brilliant. How will our spy know what to do when he gets to France? He'll be exposed and captured—and *executed!*"

"No, he won't. Wiggins has been a very busy little bee and learned exactly what the spy will have to do once the boat docks. All he has to do is enter a certain small tavern on the waterfront—The Cold Heart is, I believe, the English translation—sit at the second table from the door, the hood of his black cloak pulled down low over his eyes, and wait for a barmaid named Yvette.

"She will place a tray on the table, he will place the information on the tray, and that will be that. Oh, yes, I believe our spy will also pick up some information from Yvette—which can only be considered a lovely bonus, Wiggins says.

"The spy will then be free to return to England immediately, his smuggler cohorts having waited for him. Within twenty-four hours—once the smugglers are once more nearing our shores, a Preventive cutter will pick them up, rescuing our spy before the light of day can give him away."

She leaned back again, snuggling into his embrace. "You were right. It is brilliant. How I envy the man who is going to be able to engage in such an invigorating scheme."

"Yes," Alastair said, pulling her close. "I imagine it will be something a man would wish to tell his children about someday. We are going to have children, aren't we? I mean, I think Leslie is a wonderful fellow, but I couldn't rest easy in my grave, knowing he was systematically destroying every last one of my estates with his paint pots and projects."

Elly pulled slightly away from him, to stare up into his face. "You're not—I mean, you wouldn't consider—you couldn't possibly be—" she began nervously.

"I couldn't possibly be what, my darling Elly?" Alastair asked, playing with a lock of blonde hair that had fallen forward onto her forehead. "Have I told you yet that I love you, pet? I do, you know, most desperately."

He looked so young, so wonderfully attractive, so gently loving. He wouldn't get himself involved with such a dangerous mission. She was being silly, overreacting because she had already lost Robert to this miserable war that seemed to be dragging on forever. Besides, this Wiggins fellow sounded capable. He wouldn't leave such an important mission in the hands of an amateur.

Yet it wouldn't hurt to ask him, would it? After all, they were betrothed. He wouldn't lie to her now—maybe once, but not now.

"Dearest," she began, careful to use the term of endearment they had agreed upon, "you would never do anything dangerous, would you? I mean, Captain Wiggins seems to have it all planned out so nicely and all. Once the spy and the smugglers are captured, you and Leslie will be safe and we can get on with our lives. You don't feel any need to be *personally* involved beyond what you have done, do you?"

"Me?" she heard him answer, his tone comfortingly incredulous. "Don't be ridiculous, my pet. My mission is to keep my identity hidden and Leslie out of the line of fire until Geoffrey is done playing at his little games. After all you have learned about me and my self-serving, devil-may-care, ramshackle existence—which ended the moment I met you, my darling—can you really believe I would ever consider endangering myself on purpose?"

''No, I suppose not,'' Elly agreed softly, feeling his fingers reaching beneath her chin to raise her face for his kiss.

''Whoops! I seem to have come in at an inopportune moment, haven't I, John, old man. Sorry about that. I didn't know the two of you were so chummy. I'll knock next time.''

Elly looked across the room to see her brother about to leave. ''What did you want, Leslie?'' she asked, amused by her brother's total lack of outrage at seeing his sister being ruthlessly kissed by a man who was a guest in their house.

Leslie turned back to face them. ''It's really not all that important, I guess, Elly—and I am in a bit of a rush. Just carry on,'' he suggested with a wave of his hand.

''Your sister and I are to be married, my lord, if it suits you,'' Alastair announced, rising. ''I know this is a terrible breach of good form, and that I should have asked your permission first, but as Elly is of age and all—''

Leslie flapped his arms wildly, as if impatient with Alastair's explanation and in a hurry to be gone. ''Yes, yes, whatever you want. I have more pressing matters myself. Wait a minute. Elly—since you're not busy now—I have to ask. You did say I was to take Hugo with me everywhere, didn't you?''

''Yes, my dearest,'' Elly agreed, marveling at the ease with which Leslie took the news of her betrothal. ''I did say that.''

The arms flapped again, as Leslie began to do a little dance. ''Well, Elly, the thing of it is—I have to visit the— that is—do I have to take him *everywhere* with me?''

Alastair fell back onto the settee, roaring with laughter, earning himself a poke in the ribs from his beloved.

''No, Leslie,'' Elly choked out, trying not to succumb to

a similar fit of hysterics, "you do not have to take Hugo with you when you go *there*."

Elly and Alastair hung together, laughing until there sides ached, long after Leslie had sprinted out of the drawing room, all thoughts of spies and smugglers forgotten.

ALASTAIR STOOD contemplating his reflection in the large mirror in his chamber, wondering if it would be possible for him to remove his beard without the help of his valet, Albert, who was still in London. "Probably eating his head off in my town house, when he isn't cavorting on my bed with the upstairs maid, that is," he told himself, his eyes narrowing at the thought.

Having spent a restful night in the familiarity of his own bed at Seashadow—probably the most restful night he'd had since his dunk in the Channel—Alastair was more anxious than ever to have the business of his attempted murder behind him so that he could get on with his life.

Marriage. Who would believe it? It was amazing. A few months ago, prior to his dunking, the mere mention of the word would have put him in full flight—to Scotland or some other remote, primitive place where men hunted and fished and did other manly things that did not require the company of women. As a matter of fact, the only thing they did require was the total *absence* of the fairer sex.

And she was fair, his Elly. *His Elly.* Even spoken silently, within the confines of his own mind, the words sounded incredibly sweet. What had he ever done to deserve her? After hearing Elly tell him about Robert Talmadge, her one-time fiancé who had given up his life for his country, he was even more sure of the course he was about to take, more certain that he should have to *earn* her love, and no be satisfied to have simply stumbled onto it, the same way one would stumble onto a four-leaf clover.

Picking up his tan hacking jacket—the one he'd had made for him last year at Weston's—Alastair sauntered out of his bedchamber in search of his betrothed, hopeful of spending a restful interlude with her on the beach while he waited for his summons from Wiggins.

"Hallo, *John*," Lily Biggs cooed, coming out of one of the bedchambers to step directly in front of him as he neared the staircase. "Ain't yer a treat, all dressed up in the old Earl's duds?"

"Thank you, Lily," Alastair said, moving to his right, to pass by her. He wasn't in the mood for one of Lily's childish attempts at seduction.

She stepped in front of him again. "I wonder what that handsome Lieutenant would think ter learn wot yer about, *Johnny?* Mighty interested in yer, the Lieutenant is or so I heard him say ter that Dalrymple woman yesterday."

"Is that right? That Dalrymple woman is your mistress, if you'll remember." Alastair stood quietly as Lily reached out to take hold of his lapels, using them to pull herself closer, so that their bodies were pressed together. "You're not too old to spank, Lily," he warned quietly.

"Oooh—a spankin'," she trilled, grinding her hips against him. "I think I might jist like that, *Johnny*."

Alastair reached up to disengage Lily's hands from his hacking jacket. "You have quite a future on your back, Lily, if Billie or Big George don't kill you first. Now, let me get this straight, just so that we don't misunderstand each other. You're threatening me, aren't you, little one? What exactly do you want?"

Lily smiled, her pointed pink tongue coming out to moisten her upper lip. "Wot does I wants, Johnny? I should think yer'd know. I heared about yer when yer were younger, when yer used to come here with all yer fine friends. I jist wants a little fun—a little tickle.''

Alastair smiled as he looked down at the girls full half-exposed bosom, disbelieving that the gods would do this to him now, just when he had decided to become a sober, responsible citizen. If Lily were not a Biggs, if he had never heard of a small firebrand named Elinor Dalrymple, he would most probably already be pulling the girl back into his bedchamber.

''You don't have the term quite right, Lily,'' he heard himself say. ''It's not just tickle. It's 'slap and tickle,' if memory serves.''

The tongue appeared once more, as well as a provocative dimple in her left cheek. ''I guess yer'll just have ter show me, Johnny,'' she purred, her hands dropping to his waist.

''I guess I just will,'' Alastair answered shortly, grabbing her by both hands and all but dragging her down the hall to his bedchamber. Once inside the room, he closed and locked the door before sitting down on the side of the wide bed. ''Come here to me, Lily,'' he commanded softly.

Smiling, her hips exaggeratedly swinging from side to side, Lily approached the bed and sat down on Alastair's lap. ''Ooooh, this is nice, ain't it?'' she remarked, collapsing against him.

A moment later Lily was lying facedown across Alastair's lap and he was delivering the first of a half dozen stinging slaps to her rounded bottom.

When he was done, he allowed her to slide to the floor, where she sat looking up at him, her eyes filled with tears—and all the hate a sixteen-year-old girl could muster. ''Wot did yer go and do that fer?'' she screamed at him.

''I decided it was time to teach you a lesson, Lily,'' he

said as kindly as he could. "Never threaten a man, my dear little girl. We're bigger than you are. Now, we'll keep this between us, as I wouldn't want your mother and father upset."

Not waiting to hear whether or not she agreed with him, Alastair left the room once again, more eager than before to find Elly. Thank God he had her love, for if he had survived his spill into the ocean only to return to a life filled with Lilys—a life he had formerly exulted in—he would rather have drowned!

He passed Billie Biggs—who was standing at the open front doors directing Iris as the child diligently scrubbed the steps with a brown brush—and walked out into the sunlight to see Leslie Dalrymple skipping across the gravel drive.

Alastair frowned. Where was Hugo? He shook his head and started forward. Obviously Leslie had slipped his leash, and now it was up to him to fetch the runaway home again. "Leslie!" he called out loudly, and the young man whirled about—a wide, childish smile on his vacantly handsome face—just as a shot rang out. A moment later, clutching his left shoulder, Leslie crumpled to the ground.

CHAPTER EIGHT

"Ah, there you are, my dear. I thought I might find you in here. I suppose you want to tear out my guts and feed them to the crows—and as it would be mean of me to hide and rob you of your pleasure, I came seeking you. Unless, that is, you've forgiven me, and you didn't mean what you said earlier when we met outside. I didn't know you knew such terrible words, truly I didn't. I was quite shocked, I tell you."

Elly's hands stopped in the midst of rearranging the bed pillows. "*You!* What do you want in here? Get out! Haven't you already done enough damage? Or are you lurking around here to inspect the results of your indefensible tactics?" She turned back to the bed after dismissing Alastair, intent on arranging Leslie's pillows behind his head.

How dare he come in here so blithely—and how dare he mention her temporary loss of control as Hugo had gently lifted a moaning Leslie to carry him inside? Blinking back traitorous tears she didn't want Alastair to see, Elly could still feel his presence in the chamber as she fluffed the feather pillows to within an inch of their lives, earning herself a whining rebuke from her brother.

"I say, Elly, leave off, do," Leslie told her. "I want to lie back now. You picked a plaguey queer time to be arguing, Elly. I'm not well, you know. And why are you angry with John anyway? He didn't shoot me, did he? No, of course he didn't. He wouldn't.''

"No, Leslie, I didn't. I wouldn't. It must have been those pesky poachers again. Poachers can be the very devil, can't they, as they have such poor aim. And yes, Elly, leave off, do," Alastair repeated from the foot of the bed. "Perhaps I was wrong and you don't have designs on my internal organs, dear heart. I can live with that. But if you are upset over Leslie's accident and want to punch something, I'll volunteer myself for the job."

Elly could hear the amusement in his voice—and the implied warning. He still didn't want her to say anything to Leslie. Although she felt he had been wrong to hide the danger from her brother, she agreed that it would serve no purpose to enlighten him now, after the fact.

But that didn't mean she had to be nice to Alastair. How dare he volunteer himself as a target for her anger, just as if she had gone stark, staring mad and he was the voice of reason? Of course she was angry with him—and he deserved every bit of it!

"And so you should, *John!*" she exclaimed hotly, helping her brother to lie back, as his bandaged shoulder was making it difficult for him to manage the maneuver on his own. "And stop acting the willing martyr, for I am unimpressed. How can you joke at a time like this, with Leslie lying here, at death's door."

"Well, in matter of fact, Elly, I'm not exactly at death's door," Leslie corrected, looking up at his sister, who found herself momentarily wishing the bandage had been around his mouth.

"That's it, Leslie," Alastair exclaimed. "Pluck to the backbone. It would take more than one bullet to dampen your spirits!"

"Doctor Wallingsworth said it couldn't have been a nicer wound, what with the ball passing straight on through my arm the way it did without hitting anything even remotely important. There must actually be unimportant parts inside us, I suppose, although I can't imagine what they could be, for why else would we have them—if they weren't important for something? I would think the Almighty planned it better than that. Anyway, I should be up and about in a day or two, Doctor Wallingsworth said, and with this lovely sling and everything."

"Yes, Elly, he even has a lovely sling," Alastair agreed as she glared at him, not knowing whether it was anger or fear that had kept her temper simmering just below the boiling point ever since she had been summoned outside to see Leslie lying propped against Hugo's massive arms, a slowly spreading red stain on his shirt sleeve.

Simmering, except for that single, lamentable lapse during which she had employed a few words learned at her father's knee when that man had been fairly deep in his cups; she looked toward the object of her anger. "Oh, shut up," she said succinctly.

He seemed to be oblivious to her mood. "And it's his *left* arm into the bargain, so that his painting and whatever else it is that he does—and you do it all *very* well, dear Leslie—can go on uninterrupted. Wasn't that lucky?"

"Eh?" Leslie looked down at the sling, then at his right arm, and smiled. "By Jove, so it is, Elly. How about that! You are quite right, John. Thank you for pointing that out. I'm so very glad you have moved in with us until your roof can be patched. I may not have noticed my good fortune so quickly, if left to my own devices. I was indeed very lucky."

"You're very welcome."

Elly knew what Alastair was about, knew that he was trying to keep the situation light so as not to worry Leslie, but she just couldn't take it anymore. Her brother was much too gullible for words, and Alastair had no more sense than a newborn babe.

"Lucky?" she exploded. "*Lucky!* I don't know if the two of you are crazy and I'm sane—or if I am the one who should be carted away in her own straight-waistcoat. How can you call being shot lucky? Oh, I can see that I have to get away form the both of you for a while! Leslie, lie still."

She brushed past Alastair and out of the room, only to turn on him as he followed her into the hall. "Alastair, you *promised* me!" she hissed, looking up at him, daring him to contradict her.

"Quietly, pet, so Leslie doesn't hear. There's no need to set him off again, is there? Elly, I know you're probably feeling mad as a baited bear, but—" Alastair began.

She cut him off, not interested in what he might have to say in his own defense. She had things to do, and he was dreadfully in the way. "You promised me Leslie would be all right. Hugo would take care of him, you said. It would all be over very soon, you said. There was no real danger, you said, as long as we did what *you said.* Well, you were *wrong,* Alastair—terribly wrong—and I don't think I shall ever be able to forgive you!"

"Well, I certainly hope someone forgives me," Alastair remarked, taking Elly's elbow against her will and leading her off down the hallway. "Am I heading you in the right direction, my dear? good!—for I am terribly depressed. I am also a victim, if you'll remember, and yet now I find myself cast in the role of villain. Hugo is completely out of charity with me—and if you have never been screamed at for a quarter hour by a very large someone who knows what *he* is saying, while *you* are totally in the dark, let me advise you not to actively encourage such an encounter— and Billie Biggs has gone so far as to threaten to have Big George take a birch rod to me. I think perhaps she has been in charge here too long, and considers me to be no better than the worst of her children.''

Elly did not pull her arm away, as Alastair's touch was comforting after her hours of fear for Leslie, and because she still loved this infuriating man very much—but that did not mean she was going to forgive him too easily.

''The fact that Leslie was shot at all *is* your responsibility, Alastair, as you were the one who insisted he not be told he was in danger. I knew I should have told him— which is probably why I am so angry. However did I let you talk me into not telling him? Leslie would never have slipped away from Hugo to walk outside looking for a thistle if you had told him not to do so. Leslie is very obedient—when he remembers what he is to be obedient about. But that is nothing to the point. He was never even warned.''

''Leslie was looking for a thistle?''

''He thought it would be above everything wonderful if he could use one as a sort of paint brush—but that's not important.''

''Why do I know that you are now going to tell me precisely what *is* important?''

''You're absolutely right—for once. What's important is that you told me you had everything under control when in fact you didn't—you don't. Hugo couldn't have been more than three paces behind Leslie, and he couldn't save him. You've been treating this entire thing as some sort of entertaining intrigue, when in fact it is deadly serious. You may not have any great sense of self-preservation, but it wasn't enough that someone tried to kill you, was it? Oh, no. You couldn't rest until you had placed Leslie in danger as well. I cannot wait any longer to do what I have to do. I'm going to send a note round to Lieutenant Fishbourne immediately.''

"Lieutenant Fishbourne? Tonight's dinner guest? How curious. This is, I suppose, the same pompous, full-of-himself fellow—and you told me this just last night, as I recall—who could bore paint into flaking off a wall?''

Prudently holding up her skirts as the two of them descended the staircase into the foyer, Elly nodded, noting that Alastair's memory was much like Leslie's—a steel trap when it came to remembering every verbal misstep *she* ever made.

"I did,'' she admitted crossly. "I never said I particularly *liked* the gentleman, Alastair. I just think it is time we called him in on this. You've already told me that your Captain Geoffrey Wiggins had been wanting to inform the Lieutenant all along, only you have refused to allow him to do so.''

Alastair guided her into the drawing room, where Mrs. Biggs had already placed the tea tray and a silver plate piled high with pastries. She knew she wouldn't be able to eat a single bite.

"And for good reason,'' he told her. "Your so estimable Lieutenant has had ample time to capture the spy and has not done so. Why do you think Geoffrey came to me in the first place—because he was impressed with my winning smile?''

Elly bit her lip as she looked at Alastair. He was a wonderful man, really he was. He was loving, caring, full of good humor, and handsome into the bargain—and she still found it hard to believe that he really loved her. But he was also a Lowell. Her mother had been a Lowell. Leslie was also a Lowell. And Lowells were not known for their over-whelming sense of responsibility—or their keen under-standing of basic common sense. Mostly they were just lov-able.

She herself, Elly had long ago decided, must be a throw-back to some commonsense paternal relative or, if not that, an exception to the Lowell rule. Each generation seemed to produce at least one responsible Lowell—or in this case, Dalrymple—whose sole purpose on this earth was to ride herd on the rest of the Lowells, protecting them from their own follies. She had fallen in love with Alastair, yes, but in doing so she had also placed herself in the role of care-taker of his bound-to-be irresponsible ways.

Elly sighed, her sympathies with Alastair since she could see the hurt in his eyes. "Look, dearest," she began gently, taking hold of his arm with both hands, "I can only try to understand how upset you must be by what you can only see as my *deplorable* lack of confidence in you, but—"

"I want the two of you moved to my estate in Surrey as soon as Leslie is able to travel," Alastair cut in abruptly, rising to pace back and forth in front of her as he spoke, his gaze directed at the carpet.

"What?" The question was all she could muster, for his commanding words had rendered her nearly bereft of speech.

"Please don't interrupt, pet. My mind is quite made up. I've already set things in motion. You should be able to leave before the week is out, according to Doctor Walling-sworth, if you take the trip in stages. I should have sent you two days ago, when I first learned Leslie was in danger, but you were ill. Then yesterday, when we seemed to come to an understanding, I couldn't bear to let you leave me. I was a selfish fool, but that is all over now. Your safety is my primary objective—everything else is secondary.''

She stared up at him in amazement. ''You—you want us to leave?''

He turned to face her. ''I don't *want* you to leave. I'm telling you that you are leaving. It's the only way. Surely you can see that, darling?''

Elly shook her head. ''No. No, I don't see that. Not unless you are prepared to leave as well. If we were all to go away, there would no longer be any reason for the spy to try to eliminate us, Captain Wiggins could set the trap you told me about, and everything would be over. But you're not planning to leave with us, are you, Alastair?''

He walked around the table to take hold of her upper arms. ''Of course I'm not! What sort of coward do you think I am? Is your estimation of me still so low? A spy is operating from *my* beaches, Elly. Not content with that, he is also doing his damnedest to rid the world of every last Earl of Hythe. I'm not about to leave his capture up to the Lieutenant Fishbournes of this world. This is a personal fight. He's *mine,* Elly—and I'm going to be a part of his downfall!''

Elly had never seen him so serious, never seen him without a twinkle in his eyes or a smile on his lips. This was a new Alastair Lowell, and one who frightened her even as he thrilled her. She put her hands on his chest. ''What are you planning, Alastair? Surely you're not going to—''

''Lieutenant Fishbourne ter see you, ma'am,'' Iris interrupted quietly from the doorway. ''He said ter tell yer he used the knocker this time. Should I tell him yer busy? Yer sure as check look busy ter me. Good mornin', m'lor—sir.''

Alastair's grip on her upper arms tightened for a moment.

"Alastair?" she asked, searching his face for some hint of how she should proceed. "What shall I do?"

His smile flashed white between the golden whiskers of his beard. The Alastair Lowell she had fallen in love with was back. Yet, she saw, his eyes weren't shining with humor. They were glinting silver-grey with determination.

"Do, my pet?" he answered softly, rubbing her cheek with the back of his fingers. "I should think you would follow your heart. I'll be outside on the porch, as I would rather not face the good Lieutenant at the moment."

Elly's hands fell to her sides as Alastair took two steps back, turned smartly on his heels, and walked quickly through the open doorway to the porch.

"Ma'am?"

She closed her eyes in confusion. What was she to do? How had she been put in this untenable position? It would be so easy to turn to Lieutenant Fishbourne, confess exactly what had been going on at Seashadow—tell him of Alastair's existence and the attempts on Leslie's life—and deliver responsibility for the capture of the spy-cum-murderer into the lap of the Preventive Officer.

But what would that do to Alastair—to them both? How could she profess to love him if she didn't trust him to protect his own? How could he love her if she showed so little faith in him?

"Ma'am, I'm needed in the kitchens. I'll jist tell the Lieutenant I couldn't find yer."

"No!" Elly ordered, whirling to face the young girl. "That won't be necessary. Please, Iris, show the Lieutenant in at once."

She sat down behind the tea tray and willed her hands not to shake as she poured herself a cup of tea, only spilling a few grains of sugar as she added a full two teaspoonsful to the dark, steaming liquid.

"Lieutenant Fishbourne, ma'am," Iris announced from the doorway, and the soldier strode into the drawing room, his hat tucked beneath his arm.

"Good day to you, Miss Dalrymple," he said, not bothering to sit down. "Thank you for seeing me. I can only stop for a moment, as I have pressing matters to attend to in Hythe."

"Good day to you, Lieutenant," Elly returned, happy to hear that her voice was not shaking as she looked up at the tall blonde man. His skin was slightly flushed, and he looked almost human. "You appear to be excited. Would these pressing matters possibly have something to do with the spy who has been operating in the area?"

She watched as his expression became grim, inwardly moaning as she feared he was going to launch into another of his overly patriotic, dry-as-dust dissertations. "That they do, ma'am, but I am afraid I am not at liberty to discuss them with civilians. You understand, don't you, Miss Dalrymple?"

Elly smiled, taking a sip of tea. "Indeed yes, Lieutenant," she assured him brightly. "We females have no head for intrigue anyway. Oh! I just thought of something. You aren't here to cry off from my dinner invitation, are you? That would be too bad, for Mr. Bates is *so* eager to meet you."

She thought she heard something—some slight choking noise coming from the porch—but the Lieutenant didn't react. Elly took a deep breath and pinned her smile more firmly on her face.

He sat down gingerly, on the very end of the chair across from her. "As I am eager to meet him, ma'am," he vowed in earnest tones. "But, alas, duty prevents me from participating in what I am sure would have been a very entertaining evening. I would have sent round my apologies, but I wished to explain my reasons to you in person. Is your brother the Earl about?"

"Leslie?" The question surprised her, as he had never before asked to be introduced to her brother. Surely word of his injury could not have traveled so quickly. "Why do you ask?"

He hopped to his feet, pulling on his gloves. "No reason, really," he answered lightly. "I had just wished to warn him that we've had word of poachers operating in the area, and I shouldn't like to think either you or the Earl could accidently stumble across a pack of the scoundrels in the woods. It is enough that my men are out there. But you can warn him for me, I imagine. You won't forget, will you, ma'am?"

"As I *forgot* to tell you about Mr. Bates, Lieutenant?"

"Exactly," he agreed with a smile, making Elly long to box his ears. Obviously his opinion of women was not high. How he must have regretted his initial impulse to enlist her in his cause. "Well, I must be going. There is no limit to my work this day, but tonight should prove to be the end of it. Please, Miss Dalrymple, keep away from the beach for one more day, no matter if you hear shouts, or shots, or whatever."

Elly carefully placed the teacup on the platter and rose to walk over to where Fishbourne stood. "There is something very important going on, isn't there, Lieutenant? Are you expecting that terrible spy—or some smugglers—to come ashore at Seashadow tonight? How terribly—" she searched for an adequately "female" word "—terribly *exciting!* I should like above all things to see this fearsome group in shackles. You are so *brave*, Lieutenant! How I envy you men your perilous exploits, not that I should ever wish such a dangerous experience for myself.''

There was another sound from the porch—and this was definitely a low rumble of male laughter—so that she quickly coughed delicately, to cover the sound.

She watched as the Lieutenant pulled himself up very straight, the sun streaming through the open doorway glinting off the shiny metal buttons of his uniform jacket. ''It is all in the course of my work, Miss Dalrymple,'' he said with, she supposed, his impression of manly modesty. ''You and the Earl—and Mr. Bates, of course—will stay clear of the beach until you hear from me again, won't you?''

Elly pressed her clasped hands to her breast. ''I should think so! And then, perhaps, when this horrid business is over, you shall consent to be guest of honor at a celebratory dinner here at Seashadow?''

''I should be honored, ma'am,'' Fishbourne told her, bowing. ''Good day, ma'am.''

He had just regained the foyer when a slight sound—the one she had previously recognized as suppressed laughter—reached her clearly from the porch, and she turned to see Alastair walking into the room, his hands applauding softly.

''I hear Mrs. Siddons is about to retire, pet,'' he told her, coming over to plant a kiss on her cheek. ''If we were to quarrel and you should cry off from our engagement, I do believe you have quite a future treading the boards. 'You are so *brave*, Lieutenant!' That was the absurd, posturing idiot you wished to entrust with our safety? I wouldn't be surprised if half the village shows up on the beach tonight, if that was an example of how well the man keeps a secret.

I can only thank my own good sense for keeping the fact of my existence safely from him.''

Elly sat down, putting one hand to her forehead, for she had developed quite a headache. "Don't tease me, Alastair," she warned tersely. "I did what you wanted, didn't I? Now, tell me what you are going to do. It is definitely tonight, isn't it? This isn't just an ordinary smuggling run. The spy is going to try to leave England tonight. That is why the Lieutenant had to cry off his invitation to dinner."

"The good Lieutenant has other duties tonight, yes," Alastair answered, sitting down beside her. "I received a little missive from Geoffrey confirming the event only an hour ago."

"He warned you to stay away from the beach tonight?" Elly asked hopefully, knowing she wasn't going to like his answer.

"Yes, pet," she heard Alastair say, and her heart plummeted to her toes. "That is exactly right. It would seem that the good Captain is very concerned for my welfare. Poor Geoffrey."

"RICE. RICE! Where the devil is the fellow? This is no time to be answering a call to nature! O'Brien—find Rice, now!"

"Softly, my friend, softly," Alastair warned congenially, sliding into the shallow, hollowed-out ditch the Captain had made in the sand some thirty yards to the left of the spot the smugglers had last used to land their boat. "Rice won't be coming, Geoffrey. He is, um, all tied up right now. But not to worry. He kindly loaned me his cloak before he left, so I can just take his place."

"Lord Hythe!" the Captain rasped, recognizing the voice

of the Earl even if he couldn't see the man's face in the darkness. "You didn't!"

"Ah, Geoff, but I did. You knew I would, deep in your heart of hearts. Admit it, man, and let us move on to more important matters. Where is our genuine spy? Safely tucked away in some guardhouse hours ago, I suppose, before I could safely slip away from Seashadow. Good work. I like your hat, by the by, even if it is a bit large. I suppose it keeps you from having to rub lampblack on your head to keep down the shine? It's called a sailor's toque, isn't it— the headgear, that is. Yes, it's very attractive, Geoff."

"Yes, it is, and thank you," the Captain muttered, shaking his head so that the large, drooping knitted cap slipped down over one eye. "What on earth am I thanking you for!" he exploded, which was difficult to do, as he knew he had to keep his voice low. "My lord, you would try a saint, and that is someone I most definitely am not! But you wanted to know about the spy, didn't you? We intercepted him three hours ago, on the road. Impertinent young fellow by the name of Bunk. Now what, sir?"

"You know what I want, don't you, Geoffrey? I fully intend to sail away on that boat—that is the smuggler's boat signaling to us, isn't it? Don't you think they're expecting some sort of answer from their passenger? You only gave me a broad outline of your plan, remember."

Captain Wiggins rolled his rotund body onto his back— reminding Alastair of a turtle tipped onto its shell—angling his head for a better view of the dark waters of the Channel.

There was no moon and it was as dark as the inside of a pig's bladder, so that it was nearly impossible to miss the flashes of light emanating from the lantern that one of the smugglers was alternately covering and uncovering, obviously in hopes of receiving an answering signal from the beach.

"O'Brien, flash the bloody lantern!" Captain Wiggins whispered the harsh command as Alastair—who had already recognized the rather anonymous-looking shadows to be no less than ten soldiers, who were scattered about the beach and dug into shallow ditches just like their Captain—concentrated on the movements of the smuggler's craft.

"Probably busy scratching at a flea," Alastair observed charitably, as at the moment he was engaged in a similar pursuit. "Ah, there it is. Good show, O'Brien," he called quietly across the sand.

"This is not a game, sir," Wiggins pointed out through clenched teeth.

"Indeed, no, Geoffrey," Alastair agreed quickly. "I should say it isn't. I trust that tomorrow you will allow me a few minutes alone with our spy before you ship him to London? I want to be sure he is the man I'm after—just so that all the ends are neatly tied, if you know what I mean. Now, if you'll be so kind as to give me the papers, I shall be on my way to The Cold Heart and the lovely Yvette. It may not be good form to keep a fellow spy waiting."

Wiggins looked toward the Channel, to see that a small rowboat was heading toward the beach, with two strapping men at the oars. It was either move now or lose the entire project. But how would he explain this change of plans in London—especially if the Earl bollixed the mission and ended up at the bottom of the sea with his throat cut? Yet, the Captain considered further, as the Earl was already supposed to be dead—what difference would it make anyway?

"Geoff," Alastair prodded, "the papers, if you please. My excuse to Miss Dalrymple for coming out tonight was unbelievably lame, and she's as suspicious as a wife whose husband has suddenly started walking around the house smiling and whistling. You wouldn't want her showing up here, now would you?''

The Captain reached inside his jacket and pulled out a fat packet in oilskin. ''You'll be careful, won't you, sir?''

''Why, Geoff, I didn't know you cared so much.'' Alastair reached across the sand to pull off the Captain's toque and plant a smacking kiss on the man's bald pate. ''You will tell the men to shoot over my head, won't you? Thank you so much. See you at dawn, my friend. I would appreciate it greatly if you were not late.''

''Lieutenant Fishbourne and his men are most probably already at sea, ready to follow at a safe distance, and we'll be doing likewise the moment you are safely gone,'' Wiggins assured him as Alastair rose, pulling the hood of the black cloak down over his face. ''You'll never be completely alone.''

''How that comforts me, Geoffrey,'' Alastair told him, only slightly mollified, as he was not unaware that he was embarking on a very dangerous mission. The two pistols he had tucked into his waistband, and the very long knife that was concealed in his boot, added only marginally to his assurance. ''I've had one nocturnal encounter with the cold waters of the Channel and do not relish a second.''

''They've took the bait and landed, Captain,'' came a whisper from the darkness. ''Is Rice movin' his arse this night or not, d'ya know?''

''He's moving,'' Alastair whispered back, drawing one of the pistols from his waistband and brandishing it in the air. He began to run down to the shoreline at full tilt, spouting unintelligible French while being careful to keep his face averted as he pointed the pistol behind him and fired.

The bark of ten firearms going off nearly at once was all

but deafening, the flash of the guns splitting the dark night with red fire and smoke.

A heartbeat later the fire was being returned from the rowboat as Alastair ran, his cloak flying out behind him, his boots kicking up loose stones and sand. He could feel bullets whizzing past him—at least one of them coming close enough to give credence to his haste in flinging himself face-first into the rowboat and yelling, *"Se presser, vous! Se presser!"* which was rather inelegant French for "Get a move on!"

Clambering to the front of the boat, Alastair missed the thin wooden bench and inadvertently sat himself down in the very bottom of the boat, wetting himself thoroughly in the fetid seawater that sloshed inside as the bow cut into the waves, the oarsmen straining to reach the speedy Dutch dogger that was already weighing anchor.

"Shut yer froggie mouth an' git yer bleedin' carcass outta m'way so's Oi kin git ter this oar better," one of the smugglers ordered, kicking at Alastair's feet. "Else they'll be off an' leavin' us behind fer gallows bait."

Wiggins and his men were standing at the water's edge now, still firing, but already their shots were falling short. Alastair looked forward to see hands reaching for him, to rudely hoist him onto the deck of the Dutch dogger, a ship that was probably swifter than whatever slug of a boat Lieutenant Fishbourne would be using to follow them.

He was leaving England, leaving his beloved Elly, with only a slight hope of ever seeing either one of them again. It really was quite oppressive, being a man of honor.

"Wot in bloody blue blazes happened?" a very large, bearded man demanded, grabbing Alastair roughly by the shoulder and whipping him around so that he had to lower his head to keep his face hidden. The hand remained on his shoulder, the strong fingers squeezing viselike until Alastair's arm went numb. "Oi don't like this. There weren't apposed ter be no troubles. This'll cost yer, froggie!"

Alastair was a born gambler, and he gambled now, with his life as the stakes. He savagely hit the large man's hand away and growled, "Unhand me, Englisher, and go about your business. You weel be paid. Feel-thy *cochon*. Do you wish for to talk, or do you wish for to have ze gold in ze pockets?"

The man grunted, raising a closed fist, then seemed to think better of it and moved away, turning back to warn gruffly, "But I'm tellin' yer now, froggie, this here is the last trip yer'll be makin' with Blackie Baxter. Yer musta bin gettin' careless, that's wot. Oi'd druther end m'days in a bleedin' jail."

"I only hope I can accommodate you, Blackie," Alastair murmured under his breath, finding himself a dry, out-of-the-way corner where he would sit, rub his sore shoulder, and ride out the hours until they landed in France.

CHAPTER NINE

ELLY WATCHED, one hand pressed to her mouth so that she wouldn't cry out, as Alastair ran across the width of the beach to the sea, bullets flying over his head. She continued to crouch at the crest of the hill, her dark brown merino cape concealing her trembling figure, as the rowboat made its rendezvous with the larger smuggler craft.

Only when the dogger had begun to move out to sea and the soldiers on the beach turned to climb back up the hill did she speak. "Captain Wiggins? Yoo-hoo!" she began tentatively. "Don't shoot me, please. This is Elinor Dalrymple speaking. Which one of you is Captain Geoffrey Wiggins?"

"Criminy! Who's that?" O'Brien asked his commanding officer. "It sounds like a woman. And what would a woman be doin' here, Captain, d'ye think? Do ye knows her?"

"And that's just what I needed—the suspicious fiancée," Wiggins muttered under his breath, allowing O'Brien to help him up the steep incline until he was standing face-to-face with Elly. "His lordship didn't think he had fooled you, ma'am," he said without preamble, puffing slightly from his recent exertion. "Luckily, I think he did succeed in pulling the wool over the smugglers' eyes."

Elly squinted through the darkness to get a better look at the Captain, whose short, rotund frame would have inspired her confidence had he been her vicar, or even the village baker. He did not, she decided, cut half so imposing a figure as Lieutenant Fishbourne. Yet she immediately felt she could trust him with her life—and Alastair's life—not that her fiancé's reckless heroics had given her much choice.

"Where is Lieutenant Fishbourne, Captain?" she asked, searching the faces of the other soldiers and not finding that of the Preventive Officer.

"Fishbourne? How did you—oh, never mind," Captain Wiggins said, shaking his toque-covered head. "I should be used to it by now. Tell me, ma'am, is there anything Lord Hythe neglected to tell you?"

Elly smiled. "You like him too, don't you, Captain?" she said, falling into step with the man as they walked toward the path that led to the small pier where she had earlier spotted a black-painted Coast Guard yawl.

"Yes, ma'am, that I do," Geoffrey Wiggins admitted, offering his elbow to Elly, as the path was strewn with small rocks. "I only hope he can carry this off." He called back over his shoulder, "O'Brien—have you found Rice yet? It would serve him right if we left him tied up in some dank cave the whole night long, but I need him to escort Miss Dalrymple back to Seashadow."

"On the contrary, Captain," Elly corrected quietly. "I shan't need Mister Rice's accompaniment at all—as I shall be sailing with you. That's very ingenious, you know, painting the yawl black. Are the sails black as well? You are sailing, aren't you?"

The Captain stopped abruptly in the middle of the path, so that one of the soldiers nearly cannoned into his back. "You want to go with us on the yawl? That is totally out of the question, ma'am! I cannot allow you to put yourself in danger."

Wiggins's small outburst wasn't lost on his men. "A

woman 'board ship, Captain?'' the man directly behind him questioned, obviously horrified. ''Say it ain't so, sir. We'll have bad luck fer sure.'' His mates, all breaking into agitated chatter, seemed to agree with him.

Elly, however, had figured on just such a reaction, and so was prepared for their protests. Reaching into the voluminous pocket of her cape, she withdrew an ugly-looking pistol she had coerced Mrs. Biggs into liberating from the locked gun cabinet at Seashadow.

Poking the business end of the thing into Captain Wiggins's soft belly, she said tersely, ''I think you should convince your men that they are mistaken, Captain. Deciding to leave a woman—this woman in particular—onshore holds twice the danger of taking her aboard ship.''

Wiggins looked down at the pistol—noting that it was, indeed, cocked—and raised his hands above his head. No wonder she and the Earl got on like a house on fire. They were both mad as hatters. ''Now, ma'am,'' he began nervously, ''don't you think this is going too far? I mean, the smugglers are getting farther and farther out to sea with each passing moment, with only Lieutenant Fishbourne and his men in pursuit. We don't have time for this foolishness.''

Elly was so nervous, she could feel the heavy pistol shaking in her two-handed grasp. ''As you already know Alastair's destination, Captain, and do not intend to stop the smugglers' ship until they are away from the French shore and once more safely in English waters, I fail to see the rush. But you are right—we are wasting time. I suggest you order your men to go ahead and raise the mainmast and jiggermast, so that we can be on our way. The breeze is fresh, but we cannot depend on it lasting.''

''Mizzenmast.''

Elly leaned slightly to her left to better hear the man who had spoken. "What?"

"It's not a jiggermast, ma'am," O'Brien told her, reaching swiftly across her to knock the pistol harmlessly to the ground. "A mizzenmast is what it is, don't you know. Captain? Are ye ready now, or are ye goin' ta stand here jawin' all the night long?"

How could she have been so stupid—so careless! Elly grabbed on to the Captain's arm, ready to beg him to allow her aboard ship. She knew she had been overreaching herself to threaten the man with a pistol, but she just had to be on that yawl when it set out to sea. Alastair might need her. Besides, she would go insane if she had to stay behind and wait for someone to come to Seashadow in the morning and tell her that he had been shot, or worse. "Captain Wiggins—" she began tearfully.

"Is it all right ye are, Captain?" O'Brien interrupted, bending to pick up the pistol. "Ye looked as nervous as a dog around an Irishman's boot for a minute there, if I do say so m'self." The soldier chuckled and shook his head. "Jiggermast. It's the same thing as a mizzenmast, ain't it?"

The Captain was looking at Elly assessingly. "Do you know what I mean, Miss Dalrymple, when I say the word 'abaft'?"

A glimmer of hope invading her chest, Elly nodded furiously and answered, "I've been reading about ships all my life, Captain Wiggins, as I have always known I would love the sea. That's why we came to Seashadow first, you know, so that I could be near the sea. But I'm babbling, aren't I? Abaft on a ship is aft—to the rear or stern. Is that where you'd like me to sit?" she ended hopefully.

Wiggins sighed. "I'd like you to sit in your parlor, ma'am, knitting socks. But if you were to sit very quietly—

allowing O'Brien here to guard your pistol—I think you
might come along with us. The way this night has been
going—and when my superiors hear of it, I wouldn't be
surprised to find myself guarding a lighthouse at John
O'Groat's—I may as well be hung for a sheep as a lamb.''

Wiggins found himself being kissed for the second time
in a half hour, a very disconcerting circumstance for the
crusty bachelor, and within a few minutes the yawl was
heading into the open water, Elly perched primly on a barrel
of gunpowder, her brown merino cape wrapped decorously
about her ankles.

A WOMAN NAMED Yvette should be blonde, Alastair
thought meanly, nursing his mug of inferior wine. Blonde
and petite—and with a dimple in her chin. Besides, she was
a spy, and a spy—or at least a female spy—should be glam-
orous.

His Yvette, however, was tall and dark and of an inde-
terminate age, and her chin sported not a dimple but a large
wart shaped much like the island of Sicily—with a single
black hair growing out of it. When she smiled, which the
unfortunate woman did often, it was to show a mouth sadly
lacking in teeth.

But he had not come to France for romance, Alastair
reminded himself, tipping back the last of his wine and
waving his hand for Yvette to approach with another mug.
As she plunked the thing down on the wooden tabletop,
sloshing some of it onto the scarred surface, he reached into
his pocket to extract the thick packet of papers Wiggins had
given him and pointedly placed it on the barmaid's tray.

''There had better be more in your pocket than that,''
Yvette gritted in gutter French, giving the packet a dis-

missing look. "But you are a pretty one, aren't you? Maybe you can pay me another way."

Alastair was nonplussed. He looked down at the packet, then toward the door, counting to be sure he had sat at the second table. Yes, he was in the right seat. Had he read the faded sign outside the tavern correctly? Christ on a crutch— was he in the wrong tavern…and with a pocketful of English gold but without a single French coin among them?

Smiling up at the barmaid as he replaced the packet in his jacket, he fought down his distaste and sudden apprehension to croon in what he hoped was equally fractured French, "*Ma petite chou!* I am so sorry, *mamselle*. I have come lately from Paris with this information for Yvette. I was told she was the prettiest barmaid at The Cold Heart— so when I saw you, *ma petit,* I naturally assumed—"

The barmaid turned her head to one side and spit at the floor. "Yvette!" she exclaimed. "Always it is Yvette! No one wants Berthe. Ah! *Quand on parle du loup, on en voit la queue!* Speak of the wolf and you see his tail! There is your Yvette, *m'sieur.* I wish you joy of her—and may you catch the pox!"

Berthe flounced away as Alastair leaned back in the chair, perspiration breaking out on his forehead as he watched the barmaid standing deep in conversation with another woman, the two of them looking over at him as they spoke.

The second woman, a small blonde whose major claim to beauty was nearly completely exposed by her low-cut peasant blouse, approached the table, her green eyes narrowed to slits. "I am Yvette. Who are you? And where is Emeri, *m'sieur?*" she asked quietly. "He promised me a pair of woolen drawers on his return. I want my drawers."

Woolen drawers? Alastair repeated mentally, racking his

brain in an effort to understand why the barmaid would want woolen underwear? Why not something pretty—like a shawl, or jewelry, or silken cloth? The answer hit him just as swiftly. England got those things from *this* side of the Channel. Woolen underwear, a mundane but useful product, was strictly an English invention.

Be that as it may, he did not have the dratted woman's drawers, damn the forgetful Emeri, who hadn't been carrying them—or else Wiggins most certainly would have given them to him.

"I know nothing of such things," he told her gruffly, reaching into his pocket once more for the packet. If he didn't get moving soon, the tide would turn, and he wouldn't put it past Blackie Baxter to leave him behind onshore. "Mine is an extra trip. Emeri had to stay over there a while longer—he should be back any time. Here."

Yvette gave an elegant French shrug—for the divisions of class faded into nothingness when it came to a Frenchman's use of his or her body to express emotion. "You do not lie very well, *m'sieur*. I'll take English gold instead. If I cannot be warm this winter, at least I will not starve. The Little Corporal is doomed, and Yvette must take care of herself."

She knew! The doxy knew! Alastair leaned forward. "What gave me away?" he whispered, for if he was about to be hauled outside and hanged from the nearest lamppost, he felt he deserved to know what he had done to betray himself.

Yvette picked up the packet, then withdrew a single folded sheet of paper from her bodice and laid it on the table. "The gold, Englisher," she prompted, holding out her hand until Alastair laid a small bag of coins in her palm.

"Emeri is my pig of a husband, *m'sieur*—over there,

behind the bar,'' she told him, quickly placing the bag where the paper had so recently resided and tucking the packet in her apron pocket. ''The man who was supposed to be here tonight is Leonard, my lover. You will hang him, no? No matter. He was cheating on me with Berthe anyway. But I did so want the woolen drawers. Go now, Englisher, before you catch a fly in that mouth of yours.''

ELLY WAS CHILLED through to the bone, her teeth chattering uncontrollably as she sat huddled on the keg of gunpowder, her eyes constantly searching the darkness for some sign of the Dutch dogger that was carrying Alastair.

The night had been interminable, both because of her fears for her beloved and due to the rapidly dawning realization that, although she might love the sea, her stomach obviously did not.

Captain Wiggins's yawl had made its rendezvous with Lieutenant Fishbourne's larger cutter several hours before, about five miles off the coast of Calais. The number of men and guns aboard the cutter did much to comfort Elly, although she sincerely hoped the smugglers would decide against making a fight of it.

The cutter had sent over a longboat for Captain Wiggins, who had spent at least an hour on the larger ship with Fishbourne, surely discussing strategy before returning to the yawl to tell Elly that so far everything was going according to their plans and it would all be over shortly.

She pulled her cape more firmly around her, her left hand clutching the belaying pin she had appropriated for use as a club when no one was looking. She didn't want a fight, but she knew she should be ready for one. And this time she wouldn't make the mistake of being distracted, so that she could be unarmed without a struggle.

Surely Geoffrey Wiggins's definition of ''shortly'' could not be the same as hers. What was taking so long? It would soon be light, and the smugglers would discover that Alastair wasn't their regular passenger. Were they in the right spot? The Channel was so very large—much larger than Elly had supposed. How could Captain Wiggins and Lieutenant Fishbourne be so sure that they would even be close enough to *see* the smugglers' boat as it went by on its way back to England, yet alone capture it?

So much seemed to depend on luck. This had to be the most ridiculous, farfetched, *impossible* plan in the history of man! Oh, why did the yawl have to pitch so—her stomach was so queasy!

''Would ye be wantin' a bit of good Irish whiskey, ma'am, jist ta take the chill outta yer bones?'' O'Brien asked, coming up to her, a small tin flask in his hand. ''Captain Wiggins wouldn't have ta know.''

The idea was very tempting. Elly eyed the flask, then looked down the deck to where the Captain was standing, his back to her. ''Thank you, Mister O'Brien,'' she said, reaching out her hand.

''It's jist O'Brien, ma'am,'' the soldier corrected her. ''I owes it to ye, after knockin' that barkin' iron outta ye hand. Ye sure are a spunky one. Me ma woulda loved ye. I didn't hurt ye any, did I? And don't ye be worritin' about his lordship. Old Bullie won't let nuthin' happen ta him.''

''Old Bullie?'' Elly questioned, coughing slightly as the heat of the whiskey burned the back of her throat. ''Oh, you mean Captain Wiggins, don't you?'' Her eyes were stinging from the potency of the drink, but already she could feel its warmth penetrating and easing her frozen limbs.

O'Brien took back the flask, turned to see if his superior

was watching, and quickly lifted it to his mouth to take a long pull of its contents. "And who else would I be meanin', ma'am, if not him? He's the best, ma'am. Glory be, and the stories I could tell ye—uh-oh!" The soldiers were beginning to bustle about the small craft, some manning the black sails, the rest holding their firearms at the ready. "If ye'll excuse me, ma'am, I think the dogger has come out to play."

Elly jumped up to grab O'Brien's arm. "What will happen now? How will Wiggins get the Earl off the smugglers' boat?"

O'Brien leaned back against the side of the yawl, his eyes scanning the horizon, and his rifle at the ready, but seemingly not disobliged to talk. "It's nearly daybreak, so we'll soon be in plain sight. We're two against one. Fishy will shoot a round across the dogger's bow. That oughta do it, and the dogger will heave to—unless the Gentlemen want ta try ta make a run for it."

What little Elly knew about the smugglers had led her to believe they were a desperate, coldhearted bunch, capable of anything. "But if they do decide to make a run for it, Mister O'Brien?" Elly asked, her heart pounding as she saw the speed with which the bow of the dogger was cutting through the water. "Lieutenant Fishbourne's vessel seems to fairly bristle with cannon, but surely he won't use them— not with the Earl aboard. It would be too dangerous."

The soldier lifted his cap to scratch his head. "Now ye got me, ma'am. I doesn't know wot we'll do iffen the dogger runs. I guess his lordship will jist hafta get himself wet, and swim for it."

The next ten minutes were the longest Elly had ever lived through as she watched the three boats maneuver in the choppy seas as the slowly rising sun lightened the sky. Finally the cutter was no more than a hundred yards from the dogger, and Elly strained her ears to listen for Lieutenant Fishbourne's order for the smugglers to strike their sails.

The order never came. As Elly watched, her heart in her throat, the dogger, definitely the faster of the two ships, began to move away.

Captain Wiggins began to jump up and down on the deck of the yawl, his toque in his hands, waving his short arms furiously and shouting to Fishbourne at the top of his lungs. "The bow, man!" he yelled frantically. "Shoot across their bow!"

A premature dawn exploded upon the water in the form of a full broadside from the cutter, an avalanche of shot crashing through the rigging of the dogger and ripping a gaping hole in the port side just at the water line.

"It's sinking!" Elly screamed while O'Brien, cursing under his breath, held her back, as it appeared she was about to leap over the side. She searched the debris-filled water frantically, praying for some sign of Alastair as the men aboard the dogger abandoned the rapidly sinking boat. "There—there he is!" she cried at last, pointing to a large black cloak that was floating atop the water. "Quickly, O'Brien! Quickly! Do something. We must save him!"

"I KNOW YOU MUST think me a sorry enough looking shrimp, Hugo," Alastair remarked, fighting back a groan as he waved his friend off and stepped, naked, onto the carpet, "but I promise you, I can still get myself out of a tub. Stop twittering over me like an old cockerel with a prize pullet."

"Aaarrgh, aaarrgh," the giant answered, gently wrapping a large white bath sheet around his master's bruised and battered form.

"Thank you, my friend," Alastair said, moving to sit

down on the edge of the bed, wondering how anyone could hurt so much and still be alive. "I am not sure what you said, but if I might recommend something to you—don't ever get blown up. It hurts like the very devil."

A half hour later, and against Hugo's unintelligible but vigorous protests, Alastair was on his way downstairs to face Elly—who he was sure was just waiting for him to show his face, biding her time to be sure that he would live, just so she could kill him.

What a night he'd had, he thought, leaning heavily on the cane he had once used in jest as he made his way haltingly to the drinks cabinet and poured himself a liberal three fingers of brandy. Between the explosions and Elly's coldly efficient care of his wounds once Wiggins had retrieved him from the sea—by the ignominious use of a grappling hook—he didn't know whether he would have preferred being a dead hero to his current condition.

Elly was livid, there was no denying it, but he wasn't so knocked about in his head that he was going to allow her more than five minutes of lecturing before he reminded her that she had been on the yawl—which wasn't exactly an innocent act.

He looked around the room, lighted by the late afternoon sun, wishing Elly would make her entrance, ring a peal over his head, and forgive him—for they still had a lot to talk about.

"There you are, Alastair. I may not yet be your wife and you may think I am overstepping myself to make demands on you, but you are to never, I say, never do anything like that again!"

He turned to face the doorway, a smile on his face. Bless her, she was right on time. "Good afternoon, my love. Don't you look all the crack. Parliament should pass a law stating that you must always wear your hair down. But you said something, didn't you? I was mentally counting my bruises, I'm afraid—as well as being hampered by this ringing in my ears that has not gone away since Lieutenant Fishbourne did his reenactment of Vesuvius erupting—and was not really attending. Was it anything important?''

''Oh, Alastair, I can't do it! I can't rage at you, even if I should!'' she cried, running across the room to launch herself into his arms—a move he would have enjoyed immensely if it weren't for the fact that his ribs ached abominably. ''You were so brave, and I was so afraid. Please, my darling, no more heroics. I don't believe I could endure it.''

He patted her on the back, happy she couldn't see his smile. ''Pish tosh, pet, don't turn into a watering pot on me now—not after you've been brave to the point of idiocy, following me to sea like that. Besides, how can you really see me if you have your face crushed against my chest? Don't tell me you didn't notice, my darling. I have a surprise for you.''

Pulling back fractionally in his arms, Elly looked up to see that Alastair was clean-shaven. ''Oh,'' she exclaimed, reaching up to stroke his cheek, ''you're even prettier than I'd imagined, although it will take some getting used to, I suppose. After all, I shan't be able to become angry with you and call you a great hairy brute anymore, shall I? I love you, Alastair.''

''As I love you, pet.'' He leaned down to kiss her lightly on the nose, neatly disengaging her arms from around his waist before he so unmanned himself as to wince with the pain she was unconsciously providing. ''I don't remember you ever calling me a great hairy brute,'' he commented a moment later, leading her to the settee so that he could sit down before he fell down.

"You probably never heard me," she told him, taking hold of both his hands as if she were afraid he would disappear if she let him go, "but I have called you several things, I'm afraid—many of which you were most unfortunately present to hear. I could have employed my time more wisely by thinking up horrible things to say about that terrible, bumbling Fishy."

"Fishy?"

Elly nodded vigorously. "Lieutenant Fishbourne. That's what Mister O'Brien calls him, so that I hardly think he's popular with the men. They call Captain Wiggins Old Bullie, but with him I'm sure it's a term of affection. Anyway, Mister O'Brien is one of the soldiers. He's the one who knocked the pistol from my hand when I was threatening Captain Wiggins with it so that he would take me aboard the yawl with him. And he gave me some whiskey when I was cold." She moved even closer to Alastair's side, squeezing his hands. "Darling, I've been thinking—"

"Yes, you've been—wait a minute!" Alastair sat up straight, looking down at Elly, his eyes wide. "You held a *pistol* on Geoffrey? Geoffrey *Wiggins?*" No wonder she had been so quick to forgive him for lying to her about his involvement with the capture of the spy and the smugglers. It would appear that the demure, ladylike love of his life had been up to her pretty little chin in some rather questionable activities of her own. "And just who was it who gave you whiskey—Wiggins or this O'Brien fellow?"

She let go of his hands and faced front on the settee. "It doesn't matter," she said dismissingly. "What matters is that Lieutenant Fishbourne disobeyed orders. I thought the Captain was going to have an apoplexy! Fishy was supposed to shoot a single cannonball across the bow of the smugglers' boat—not sink it with a full broadside.''

Alastair leaned back with a smile on his face as he replied idly, ''Geoffrey explained it to me. Fishbourne's men misunderstood his order and fired all the cannon instead of just the one. You held a pistol on Geoffrey—and *threatened* him?'' he ended, his head still reeling as he mentally pictured Elly pointing a pistol at Captain Wiggins.

Elly whirled about to face him. ''Would you stop babbling about Captain Wiggins? *Yes,* I threatened him. I had to do *something.* I couldn't just watch you sail away, not knowing what would happen to you. Now—will you please listen to me?''

Alastair sat at attention, waggling his eyebrows. ''Yes, ma'am,'' he said smartly, ''anything you say, ma'am. After all, I wouldn't want you to shoot me or anything. What did you want me to hear?''

''I think Lieutenant Fishbourne didn't want anyone to get off that dogger alive,'' she announced gravely, lifting her chin as if daring him to contradict her. ''And—to take my supposition a step farther—I think Captain Wiggins thinks so too. He expressly told me to tell you not to leave the house until he could finish with the smugglers who survived and come here—for a private conversation that had to do with your continued good health.''

Alastair's smile disappeared as he gave Elly his full attention. ''A guilty man would wish to eliminate any evidence pointing to him, wouldn't he? But do I believe Fishbourne was involved with spying and smuggling? He's so full of patriotic speeches—and he didn't try to kill the real spy, did he? No, I don't think it's possible. It doesn't make sense. Did Wiggins say anything else?''

Elly shook her head. ''Everything was very rushed on

the dock, what with you all but unconscious and many of the smugglers bleeding and shouting to wake the dead— but I did hear him say something strange. I didn't really understand what he meant."

"Which was," Alastair prompted, the short hairs on the back of his neck beginning to prickle with a growing suspicion that would go a long way toward explaining Fishbourne's attack on the dogger.

Elly sighed. "First you have to promise me you will stay inside until Captain Wiggins arrives. I don't think I could stand it if both you and Leslie were laid low by one of the 'poachers.'"

"I promise, Elly," Alastair said impatiently, wondering why women always felt they had to have their men promise them things, when everybody knew a man could not really promise something when he didn't know if he could live up to it. "Get on with it."

"He said that it was beginning to look as if you had been right all along. He said it was crazy—but it was possible. Now, what could he have meant by that? You came here thinking that either Leslie or I had tried to kill you in order to get the title—and don't shake your head, because you and I both know it's true. But Wiggins couldn't possibly mean that he now believes that one of us is guilty—could he?"

Alastair stood, reaching for his cane, and began to pace the carpet, absently rubbing at his cleanly shaven chin. "No, of course not, pet," he assured her, his mind racing as thought after thought hit him. "Although it must have something to do with that first attempt on my life, if Geoff doesn't even want me out-of-doors. It seems impossible, but—"

"*Nothing* is impossible, Lowell, except that you seem to have more lives than a cat."

Both Elly and Alastair turned at the sound of a male voice, directing their attention to the man who was standing just inside the open doors that led to the porch.

"Who in hell is—"

"Fishy!" Elly exclaimed, answering Alastair's unfinished question. "It can't be!"

The Lieutenant advanced into the room, a pistol in each hand. "Cousin Jason, actually," he said punctiliously, "although I had never heard of you or your brother until you showed up here at Seashadow, to ruin all my plans."

Eyeing the uncocked pistols, Alastair moved slowly to his left, to shield Elly from the line of fire. "Cousin Jason," he said affably, smiling wryly as he shook his head. "So you're the one I have to thank for my dunk in the Channel? For *both* my dunks in the Channel, as a matter of fact. I wonder how many other relatives I have rattling about that I have never met. I cannot believe my parents were so remiss as not to mention both you and the Dalrymples. But then, now that I think of it, it appears the Dalrymples were a surprise to you as well."

Fishbourne stopped walking, planting his feet a foot apart on the carpet, his hands steady as he visually inspected Alastair. "You cannot know what it was like," he said quietly, as if to himself. "I sat there in Hythe, day in, day out, waiting for word to come that I was the new Earl. I waited and waited. But nothing happened. Then one day I was ordered to come to Seashadow to tell the new Earl that his beaches were being used by smugglers."

"You must have been devastated," Alastair commiserated, motioning for Elly to stand up and move behind him.

Fishbourne used the barrel of one pistol to scratch his

temple. "And what an Earl!" he said in obvious distaste. "The man is a complete fool. He bought those toadstools from me without a blink. Yet he's such a lucky fool—all my attempts on his life came so close, only to fail."

"As you failed with your attempt on my life—although I must tell you that you do a commendable job when you try to blow up a boat," Alastair inserted, taking one small step forward, Elly nearly on his heels. "When did you find out that I was still alive, Cousin Jason? I had expressly told Wiggins not to mention it to anyone."

"When he came aboard the cutter last night," Fishbourne answered, his pale green eyes rather glazed, as if he still hadn't quite recovered from the shock of Wiggins's disclosure and was acting more from impulse than design. "He told me to be especially careful, as you were the rightful Earl of Hythe and he'd have my liver and lights if any harm befell you."

"At which point you immediately decided to do me as much harm as possible," Alastair slid in, taking yet another step, Elly once again moving right along with him.

Fishbourne smiled, as if in agreement. "It came to me instantly that I would have to blow the entire dogger out of the water. Wiggins could never let it be known you had died *twice*. It would be too embarrassing for the War Office. There would be no real investigation."

"And then you could get back to the business of killing my brother," Elly piped up, stepping out from behind Alastair. "You are totally despicable, Lieutenant Fishbourne— as well as a very bad shot!"

"Elly, for God's sake, don't get him angry," Alastair whispered out of the corner of his mouth. "He's wavering, don't you see that? Let me handle him."

"Hallo!"

"Leslie!" Elly hissed, grabbing Alastair's upper arm at the exact spot where a large piece of the Dutch dogger's splintered deck had struck, bruising the entire area, causing Alastair to wonder who was going to kill him first, Fishbourne or his betrothed.

"Isn't it grand—I'm back on my feet again, nearly as good as new," Leslie trilled from the doorway. "Oh, it was all right, being in bed, and I did get a lovely drawing of my big toe—although the angle wasn't quite right—but I'm up now, and happy to be downstairs. I told you—the bullet touched nothing at all of importance. Well, are you both just going to stand there? Isn't anyone going to congratulate me? Oh, I say—isn't that fellow holding a pair of pistols?"

"Leslie, be quiet," Elly ordered, grabbing her brother as he made to pass by her, most probably to walk straight up to Jason Fishbourne and introduce himself. "This is Lieutenant Fishbourne. He is the man who tried to kill you."

Leslie didn't hesitate—he immediately took two steps to the rear and fell to the carpet, to cower behind his sister's skirts. "John, Elly—what is he going to do?"

Alastair—or John, as Leslie still called him—turned slightly to look at Elly. "Yes, Elly, what is he going to do? Do you have any suggestions for him? Poor Cousin Jason here has only two pistols—two bullets—and now there are three of us. It presents quite a dilemma for the poor fellow, doesn't it? Not that he could have shot any of us and still hoped to cheat the hangman and take his place as Earl in any case. No, I think Cousin Jason's visit is more spur-of-the-moment than planned, don't you?"

There was a sound at the doorway from the foyer, and a moment later a loud, angry roar shook the chandelier. "Correction," Alastair amended wryly, looking toward the door

"There are *four* of us. Hugo—be a good fellow, please, and don't startle the Lieutenant with any sudden movements."

The giant—his great hands balled into fists—stopped in the act of plunging across the room, his mouth working furiously as he moaned his frustration and concern.

Alastair could sense Fishbourne's mounting terror. Nothing seemed to be going right for the man—what with not one but a pair of Earls who refused to cooperate and die, an inheritance that kept eluding him, an interfering lady who thwarted him at every turn, and a superior officer who was suspicious of his motives. A lesser man would have broken under the strain long ago.

For all the trouble the man had caused, Alastair found himself actually pitying the Lieutenant, who must have hatched his scheme within sight of Seashadow—within sight of what would have been his if not for an accident of birth.

Alastair took another step, holding out his hands. "Jason, it's over. Why don't you give me the pistols and we can all sit down and discuss our family tree? According to your cousin Elinor, we have more than our share of eccentrics hanging from the limbs. Was your father a gamester—or an artist? No? Perhaps a writer, then."

"He was an actor," Fishbourne spat, shakng his head. "A very bad actor. His father disowned him before I was born. But I am a Lowell—and I can prove it! If only those solicitors hadn't been so stupid! If only you had stayed dead! I'm a loyal English soldier. I have lived my whole life for my country. But what does my country do for me? It makes me stay in Hythe—where I can see all that I can't have. I deserve to succeed. I *deserve* Seashadow!"

Leslie peeked out from behind his sister's skirts. "I say,

John, what is he talking about? He can't have Seashadow. It's mine. Elly—tell him it's mine.''

"You don't deserve it!'' Fishbourne shouted, stepping forward, both arms extended. Just as he was about to shoot, Alastair brought up his cane, knocking both pistols harmlessly out of the way.

Unfortunately this action badly unbalanced Alastair, and he found himself crumbling clumsily to his knees as Fishbourne turned to flee the way he had come—across the porch—while Elly cried anxiously, "Stop him! We can't let him get away—he might do something rash!''

"I'll give him something rash!'' Alastair grumbled, picking up one of the pistols as he scrambled to his feet and broke into the best run his bruised body could muster. He got as far as the steps leading down to the lawns when he saw Jason Fishbourne, his back against a tree and Lily Biggs standing in front of him, her hands on his chest.

"Where was yer goin', Lieutenant?'' Alastair heard the girl purr as she moved her hips closer to the wild-eyed soldier. "Was yer lookin' fer me? I told yer yer could see me any time yer liked. I have some news fer yer—about that John Bates who's bin livin' at Seashadow. Would yer like to know what it is? *Umm,* you're breathin' kinda heavy, ain't yer, Lieutenant? Mayhap yer'd like it iffen Lily opened some of these buttons, hmm, so's yer could cool off?''

Alastair walked up to the pair, the pistol leveled at Fishbourne's chest, and said, "Lily, I always knew you would come in handy one day—no matter that you were trying to bring me down. You saved me quite a run, and I thank you. Now be a good girl and step back, if you please. The Lieutenant doesn't have time for you right now.''

"Yer—yer welcome, sir,'' Lily quavered, a new respect

ful tone in her voice. Then, her sky-blue eyes as wide as saucers as she continued to goggle at the pistol, she turned on her heels and ran for the safety of the kitchens as fast as she could, just as Hugo clapped a large paw on Fishbourne's shoulder and led the dazed man away.

"You were wonderful, darling," Elly said from somewhere behind him.

"Yes, stap me if he wasn't," Leslie agreed. "Absolutely wonderful. Tell me, Elly—what just happened?"

Dropping the pistol to the ground, Alastair opened his arms to Elly and they clung together, laughing until tears filled their eyes.

"And they say I'm strange," Leslie muttered to a butterfly that happened to be passing by. Then, since his sister and John Bates were kissing each other, he prudently took his leave.

EPILOGUE

"So, Geoffrey, I imagine you'll be off on some other adventure now that things are all settled here?" Alastair asked, standing with his arm around his bride of two weeks. "I should like to go with you if circumstances were different, but I'm a married man now, you know, and very busy. As a matter of fact I wouldn't be surprised if I spent the remainder of my life drooling over the girl."

"Alastair!" Elly scolded, blushing. "Don't listen to him, Geoffrey. He only says things like that to shock people."

"No, I don't, pet," Alastair corrected, giving her trim waist a loving squeeze. "I only say things like that because my beautiful wife blushes to such advantage."

"Wretch," Elly responded, blushing in spite of herself.

"Wretch," he repeated, grinning. "Marriage being what it is, I can't understand why I waited so long to experience its delights. See how much she loves me, Geoff? The dear child fairly worships the ground I walk on."

"She also has been known to carry a pistol," the Captain warned, winking at Elly. "Well, I must be off. I just wanted to stop by and tell you that you won't have to worry about Jason Fishbourne anymore."

As she and Alastair walked arm in arm along the drive, Elly asked, "He will be well treated in that asylum, won't he, Geoffrey? I feel rather sorry for him, actually, now that it's all behind us. Besides, if it hadn't been for Jason, Alastair and I would never have met.''

Captain Wiggins assured them that the Lieutenant was being well cared for and at last took his leave, glancing back as he was driven down the drive, waving to the newlywed couple.

''He's going, is he?'' Leslie said, coming up behind them, his clothing dusty and stuck with leaves, and a large cloth sack in his hands. ''That's too bad. I wanted to show him my latest discovery. John—would you like to see it?''

''Not John, Leslie,'' Elly corrected patiently. ''It's Alastair, remember? You're not the Earl anymore, but you are very happy about that because now you can spend all your time painting and creating and—Leslie, what do you have in that sack? It's moving!''

Leslie shifted the bag to one hand, striving to unlace the top. ''I'm not quite sure, Elly, actually. It looks rather like a cat, but its stripes are so odd. There are two large white ones—and they run down the entire length of its body. I say—where are you two off to now? Don't you want to see it either?''

Alastair, Elly's hand held tight in his as they scurried toward the house, called back over his shoulder, ''We just remembered we promised Hugo another lesson in printing his name. See you at dinner, Leslie, if you can make it— but please leave the 'cat' outside!''

Once they reached the safety of the foyer, Elly, whose sides ached from laughing, wrapped her arms around her waist and looked up at her husband. ''Why didn't you tell him, Alastair? We'll probably have to bury the poor boy up to his neck in the gardens to rid him of the stink.''

Alastair looked down at his wife and smiled. ''Not only that, pet, but I doubt he'll be fit company for a week. Now, seeing that we most probably won't be disturbed—would you care to adjourn to our chamber? Hugo's lesson can wait, but I can think of *several* things I should delight in teaching you.''

Smiling up into his eyes, Elly felt herself being lifted high in her husband's arms, and willingly accepted her fate.

''HAVE YOU HEARD the news?''

Lord Blakestone lowered his newspaper to glare overtop it at the young man who had dared to intrude on his peace. ''You again!'' he bellowed. ''It seems you're always running in here, hot to tell us all something we'd rather not hear. What is it now?''

Hopwood refused to be cast down, for his news was particularly wonderful. ''But—but I just heard. It's the most incredible thing! Lord Hythe is *alive!* And not only that, but he's a hero! He has captured a French spy, and an entire gang of smugglers, and—*and he's married!*''

Lord Blakestone stared at Hopwood until the young man was sure his lordship had succeeded in boring a hole clear through his brand-new canary waistcoat. ''Indeed,'' the older man said at last. Turning to see that Lord Godfrey had just entered the room, he called out, ''Freddie. I say, Freddie! This puppy says Wythe is alive. Didn't we just have a drink to mark his passing? Seems to me I paid for a wreath, too, come to think of it. And he's married to boot. How do you suppose he manages it?''

Hopwood, silently wondering what quirk in his makeup allowed him to continue to punish himself in this way, corrected wearily, ''No, no, Lord Blackstone. Not Wythe—*Hythe.*''

''Married, you say?'' Lord Godfrey questioned, seating himself heavily in the burgundy leather wing chair opposit

Lord Blakestone's. "How can that be right? How can he be married? That's impossible. Wythe's dead."

Hopwood spread his arms...opened his mouth to speak...thought better of it...shook his head in resignation...and walked slowly out of the club.

CHAPTER ONE

VALERIAN FITZHUGH stood before the narrow window he had pushed open in the vain hope that some of the stale, dank air trapped within the small room might be so accommodating as to exchange places with a refreshing modicum of the cooler, damp breeze coming in off the moonlit Arno.

Both the river that divided the city and the lofty dome of the Cattedrale di Santa Maria del Fiore were vaguely visible from Fitzhugh's vantage point, although that particular attribute could not be thought to serve as any real consolation for his reluctant presence in the tumbledown *pensione*.

Florence, birthplace of the Renaissance, had been one of Valerian's favorite cities when he had visited Italy during his abbreviated Grand Tour some sixteen years previously, although his youthful adventures had come to an abrupt halt when the brief Treaty of Amiens had been shattered. So it was with a willing heart that he had begun charting his current three-year-long return to the Continent in Brussels the very morning after Napoleon had been vanquished forever at Waterloo.

Touching a hand to his breast pocket, Valerian felt again the much-folded, much-traveled sheets of paper that had led him, two and one half years into his journey—and not without considerable trouble—to this small, dark, damp room on quite the most humble street in Florence.

It was damnably wearying, being an honorable man, but Valerian could not in good conscience turn his back on the plea from Lord Dugdale (his late father's oldest and dearest friend) that had finally caught up with him at his hotel in Venice—and the crafty Denny Dugdale, never shy when it came to asking for assistance, had known it.

So here Valerian stood, at five minutes past midnight on a wet, wintry night just six days after the ringing in of the year of 1818, waiting for the baron's difficult-to-run-to-ground granddaughter to return to her pitifully mean second-story room in a decrepit *pensione* so that he could take a reluctant turn at playing fairy godmother.

"…and chaperon…and traveling companion," Valerian said aloud, sighing.

He stole a moment from his surveillance of the entrance to the *pensione* beneath the window to look once more around the small room, his gaze taking in the sagging rope bed, the single, near-gutted candle stuck to a metal dish, the small, chipped dresser, and one worn leather satchel that looked as if it had first been used during the time of Columbus.

"One can only hope the chit knows the English word for soap." A second long-suffering sigh escaped him as he turned back to the window once more to continue his vigil.

"Chi é? Che cosa cera?"

Valerian hesitated momentarily as the low, faintly husky female voice asked him who he was and what he was looking for. He stiffened in self-reproach because he hadn't heard her enter the room, then a second later remembered that he had glanced away from the entrance for a minute probably just as she had come down the narrow alley to the *pensione.*

Slowly turning to face her through the dimness that the flickering candle did little to dissipate, a benign, non threatening smile deliberately pasted on his lean, handsome face, he bowed perfunctorily and replied, "*Il mio nome é* Valerian Fitzhugh, Signorina Crispino. *Parla inglese*, I sincerely pray?"

The girl took two more daring steps into the room, her arms akimbo, her hot gaze raking him up and down as if measuring his capacity for mayhem. "*Sì. Capisco.* That is to say, yes, Signor Fitzhugh, I speak English," she said at last, her accent faint but delightful, "which makes it that much easier for me to order you to vacate my room— *presto!*"

Instead of obeying her, Valerian leaned against the window frame and crossed his arms in front of his chest. His relaxed pose seemed to prompt her to take yet another two steps into the room, bringing her—considering the size of the chamber—within three feet of her uninvited guest.

"You speak, signore, but do you hear? I said you are to leave my room!"

"Do not be afraid. I am not here to harm you, signorina," he told her, believing her aggressive action resulted more from bravado than from fearlessness.

Her next words quickly disabused him of that notion. "Harm me? Ha! As if you could. These walls are like paper, signore. One scream from me and the whole household would be in here. Now, go away! Whatever position you are offering me, I must tell you I have no choice but to refuse it. I leave Firenze tonight."

"Position? I don't follow you, signorina. But, be that as it may, aren't you even the least bit interested in how I came to know your name?"

"Such a silly question." She threw back her head in an eloquent gesture of disdain at his blatant admission of ignorance. "Everyone knows me, signore. I am *famosa*—famous!"

Valerian's lips quivered in amusement. "Is that so? And modest too, into the bargain. However, if you don't mind, we'll pass over that for the moment and get on to the reason for my presence here."

She sighed, her impatience obvious as she rolled her eyes upward. "Very well, if you insist. But I have not the time for a long story."

Valerian spoke quickly, sensing that what he had to tell her was rough ground he would wisely get across as rapidly as possible. "I am not here to employ you. I have been sent here by your English grandfather, to fetch you home. How wonderful that your mother taught you her native tongue. It will simplify things once you are in Brighton. Excuse me, but what is that smell? There are so many vile odors in this room, but this one is new, and particularly unlovely."

"Smell? How dare you!" Her hands came up as if she were contemplating choking him, then dropped to her sides. "*Mia madre?* I don't understand. What do you know of my dearest *madre* signore? Or of my terrible *nonno,* who broke her poor heart?"

The hands came up again—for the urge to remove Valerian from the room had overcome her temporary curiosity. "*Magnifico,* signore! You almost deflected me, didn't you? But no, I shall not be distracted. I have no time, no interest. It's those terrible Timoteos. I must pack. I must leave here, at once. As soon as I eat!"

So saying, she reached into the low-cut bodice of the white peasant blouse Valerian had been eyeing with some interest—Miss Crispino might be a mere dab of a girl, the top of her head not quite reaching his shoulders, but her breasts were extremely ample—so that his disappointment could be easily assumed as he watched her retract her hand, holding up a foot-long string of small sausages.

His left eyebrow lifted a fraction, his disappointment tempered by the realization that the blouse remained remarkably well filled. "At least now I know the origin of that unpleasant odor I mentioned earlier. How devilish ingenious of you, Signorina Crispino. I should never have thought to keep sausages in my shirt."

She waited until she had filled her mouth with a lusty bite of the juicy meat before replying, waving the string of sausages in front of his face, "You never would have thought to steal them from the stall on the corner either, Signor Fitzhugh, from the look of you. But then you don't give the impression of someone who has ever known hunger."

"You filched the sausages?"

She took another bite, again thrusting the remainder of the string up near his face. "Ah! I congratulate you, signore. You have, as we say, discovered America—asked the obvious. Of course I filched them. I am a terrible person—a terrible, desperate person."

"Really." Valerian remained an unimpressed audience.

"This filching; it is a temporary necessity." She stepped closer, the nearly overpowering aroma of garlic stinging Valerian's eyes and aristocratic nostrils. "But I do not sell my favors on the street for food—or for anything! I make my own way, in my own way. You can tell *il nonno,* my grandfather, that when you see him—which will be in Hell, if my prayers to the Virgin should be answered. Now get out of my way. I must pack."

She turned to pick up the scuffed leather case but was halted by the simple application of Valerian's hand to her upper arm. "Oh, no, you don't," he commanded softly. "I have wasted nearly a month chasing you from one small *città* to another. I have stood here patiently and watched as you displayed a lack of good manners that would have dis-

tressed your dear mother to tears. Now you, signorina, are
going to hear me out.

"Duggy—your grandfather—is dying, and he wants to
ease his way through Heaven's gate by leaving his fortune
to his only grandchild. You, Signorina Crispino, more's the
pity, are that grandchild. I am here to offer my assistance
in returning you to Brighton, to"—he could not resist a
glance at the bodice of her blouse—"the bosom of your
family."

"*Basta!*" Miss Crispino turned her head to one side and
very deliberately spat on the scarred wooden floor.
"Enough! I spit on my grandfather! I spit on my mother's
family—seed, sprout, and flower!"

"How utterly charming," Valerian remarked, unmoved.
"Your aunt Agnes will positively adore you, I'm sure—
once she has recovered from her faint. Now, if you have
finally done with the overblown Italian theatrics, perhaps
you will take a moment to listen to what I have to say.
Duggy may have disowned your mother for marrying your
father, but he has lived to repent the action. He's dying,
signorina, and he wants to make amends for his sins.

"If you can't bring yourself to forgive him, perhaps you
can screw yourself up to the notion of inheriting every last
groat the man has collected over the years. It's not an inconsiderable sum, I assure you."

She pulled her arm free of his grasp and picked up the
satchel. "You begin to interest me, but *belle parole non
pascolano I gatti,* signore—fine words don't feed cats. How
do I know my fickle grandfather won't have had yet another
change of his dark heart by the time I reach this place, this
Brighton?"

Valerian answered truthfully, his job done—at least in
his mind—now that he had delivered Lord Dugdale's message. "You don't know that, I suppose. It is also true that

a woman—even one of your obvious, um, *talents*—would perhaps find it difficult to make her living in England alone. So, as you seem to be getting on so swimmingly here in Italy, I can see that you might be reluctant to trade all this luxury for the chance at a fortune.''

''You make fun of me, signore; you doubt me. But I do not care. My *talent* it is not inconsiderable.'' She busily pulled various bits of clothing from the dresser drawers and flung them into the open satchel. ''I inherited it from my magnificent *papà,* who was the master of his age! I am a most famous *cantante*—an opera singer—and I am in great demand!''

Valerian watched as she unearthed several rather intimate items of apparel and wadded them into a ball before stuffing them into the satchel, doing her best to keep her back between the undergarments and Valerian's eyes.

''Really? Then I stand corrected,'' he remarked coolly, peeking over her shoulder to see that her hands were shaking. ''But I have been in Italy for two months. Isn't it strange that I have not heard of you?''

''I have been resting, signore,'' she said, wincing, for the term was one that many singers used to explain why they were unemployed. She could find work every night of the week if she wanted to—if it weren't for those horrible Timoteos, curse them all to everlasting damnation!

''It's my throat,'' she lied quickly. ''It is strained. But I will be performing again soon—very soon—in Roma.''

''Which of course also explains your rush to quit this charming *pensione* in the middle of the night,'' Valerian said agreeably, wishing he was not interested in knowing why the girl was in such a hurry, or why her hands were trembling. ''I should have guessed it. Perhaps you will allow me to transport you safely to the nearest coaching inn?''

She pulled a length of rope from the drawer, using it to tie the satchel closed, as the clasp had come to grief months earlier, not by accident but merely by rotting away with age. She hefted the thing onto her shoulder. "You'd do that, signore? You aren't going to press me about accompanying you to England?"

Valerian shrugged indifferently. "If you're asking if I'm about to carry you off will-nilly against your wishes, I fear you have badly mistaken your man. I've been most happily traveling across Europe in a long-delayed Grand Tour of sorts, and interrupting it to play ape-leader to a reluctant heiress was not part of my agenda. No, Signorina Crispino, I have wasted enough time with this project. It is time I continue my journey."

She looked at him carefully, piercingly, for the first time, taking in his well-cut, modish clothes, his tall, leanly muscular frame, and the healthy shock of thick black hair accented by snow-white "angel wings" at the temples—although they didn't make him look the least angelic, but rather dashing in a disturbing sort of way.

"*Naturalmente*. If I had looked harder, I should have seen more. Like overcooked pasta, Signor Fitzhugh, you are appealing to the eye, but upon further investigation, can be quickly dismissed as unpalatable, being soft at the center and rather mushy. Now, if you will excuse me?"

Valerian merely bowed, her verbal barb seemingly having no effect on him.

Just as she turned for the door it crashed open, banging loudly against the inside wall and nearly ripping free of its rusted hinges. A heartbeat later a large masculine shape appeared in the doorway. "*Ha!*" the shape bellowed, his roar one of triumph as he caught sight of Signorina Crispino.

His elation quickly dissipated, however, when he espied

Valerian, who was once more standing near the window. The man turned to Signorina Crispino, asking, *"Chi?"* even as he extracted a small metal mallet from his breeches pocket, raised it above his head, and advanced in Valerian's direction.

"Bernardo, no! Un momento, per favore!" Allegra made to grab at the man's arm, but he flicked her away as if she were an annoying fly. "Signor Fitzhugh, be careful! He is crazy and won't listen to me! I can't stop him! You must run! *Bernardo farà polpette di tuo*—he will make meatballs out of you!"

"Sì, the little meatballs!" Bernardo concurred in heavily accented English, grinning his appreciation of that description of what he and his little mallet would soon be doing to Valerian, the weapon gleaming dully in the faint light.

Valerian was not by nature a timid man, far from it, nor was he incapable of protecting himself. He just, frankly, wasn't in the mood for a fist fight with a man no taller than he was but twice as muscular and at least five years younger. Was this Bernardo even real? No human should be so beautiful—at least not a man. Besides, the fellow was armed, and that didn't really seem fair.

He decided to even up the odds a bit. Reaching into his breast pocket, Valerian pulled out a small pistol and pointed it at Bernardo, halting him in mid-attack.

"Call off your dog, signorina," he ordered amicably enough, "before I am forced to place a small hole between the eyebrows on his pretty face. And I so abhor violence."

Signorina Crispino lifted her slim shoulders in an eloquent shrug before turning her back on the pair of them and heading for the door. "And why would I warn him, signore?" she called over her shoulder. "Shoot him, *per favore*. You will be doing me a great service. *Addio,* Bernardo."

The pistol wavered, only slightly and only for a moment, as Valerian watched the girl go, leaving him standing almost toe to toe with Bernardo, who was jabbering at him in something that sounded like Italian, but not like any Italian the Englishman was accustomed to hearing.

Now what was Valerian going to do? He certainly wasn't about to shoot the man—he had never really considered doing that—but with that option lost to him, the metal mallet did once more make the two of them an unmatched pair.

"Signorina Crispino—come back here!" he yelled as Bernardo growled low in his throat, raising the mallet another fraction as if unafraid of either Valerian or the weapon in his hand. "I warn you, I shan't hang alone. Come back here at once or I'll tell the authorities that you ordered the killing!"

Her head reappeared around the doorjamb. "You English," she said scathingly. "What a bloodless lot. You can't even put a hole through a man who is trying to bash in your skull. And as for honor—why, you have none!"

"It's not that, signorina," Valerian corrected her urbanely. "It's just that a prolonged sojourn in one of your quaint Italian prisons until explanations can be made ranks very low on my agenda. I've heard the plumbing in those places is not of the best. Now, are you going to call this incarnation of an ancient Roman god off or not? I'm afraid his notion of the Italian language and mine do not coincide, and I don't wish to insult him further with some verbal misstep."

Shrugging yet again, Signorina Crispino walked over to Bernardo and gave him a swift kick in the leg in order to gain his attention. *"Bernardo, tu hai il cervello di una gallina! Vai al diavolo!"*

"Oh, that's lovely, that is," Valerian interposed. "Although I hesitate to point this out, I could have told Bernardo here that he has the brain of a chicken. *I* also could have told him to go lose himself somewhere. Can't you just tell your lover that I'm harmless—that I'm a friend of your grandfather's?''

''My lover! You insult me!'' she exploded, throwing down the satchel. ''As if that were true—could ever be true!'' Her hands drawn into tight fists, she wildly looked about the small room in search of a weapon, seizing on the lighted candle that stood in a heavy pewter base, not knowing whom to hit with it first, Bernardo or Valerian.

Bernardo, who seemed to have tired of staring down the short barrel of the pistol, and who did not take kindly to the insults Signorina Crispino had thrown at him, took the decision out of her hands by the simple means of turning to her, his smile wide in his innocently handsome face. ''Allegra—*mi amore!*''

''Ah, how affecting. The Adonis loves you,'' Valerian said, earning himself a cutting glance from Allegra.

''*Fermata!* Stop it—both of you!'' she warned tightly just as Valerian's pistol came down heavily on the side of Bernardo's head and the man crumpled into a heap at her feet. She looked from Valerian to Bernardo's inert form and then back at Valerian once again. ''*Bene,* signore. *Molto bene.* I thought you said you abhorred violence.''

Valerian replaced the pistol in his pocket. ''I have learned a new saying since coming to Italy, Signorina Allegra: '*Quando sé in ballo, bisogna ballare.*' When at a dance, one must dance. Your Bernardo left me no choice. Thank you for coming back, by the way. It was cursed good of you.''

He looked down at the unconscious Bernardo. ''I didn't really wish to hit him. It was like taking a hatchet to a Michelangelo. I don't think I've ever seen such a pretty face.''

"Behind which resides the most bricklike brain in the good Lord's nature," Allegra retorted, giving Bernardo's inert figure a small kick. "He speaks some English, you know, but it goes straight out of his head—pouf!—when he has to do more than stand up straight and be handsome. *Sogni d'oro, Bernardo*—golden dreams to you. Now, Signor Fitzhugh, I suggest we take ourselves out of this place before he rouses, for Bernardo has a very hard head and won't sleep for long."

Valerian bent to retrieve her satchel. "A praise-worthy resolution, signorina. But I must ask again, in light of what has just happened—will you please reconsider accompanying me back to England? This Bernardo fellow doesn't seem like the sort to give up and go away. He has been chasing you, hasn't he? That's the reason you have been so difficult to locate—you've been on the run."

"I've been avoiding Bernardo, *sì*," Allegra bit her bottom lip, considering how much and what she wished to tell him. "Bernardo has convinced himself he wants to marry me, and won't take no for an answer. And he won't give up; I can see that now. Yes, I think I might go along with you, although it won't be a simple matter to cross over the border." She took the satchel from Valerian's unresisting fingers. "I have no passport, signore, so we will have to sneak out of the country. It may take some time."

"Valerian Fitzhugh forced to sneak out of Italy? What a lovely picture that conjures," Valerian remarked, closing the door behind them as they quit the room. "But I do have some friends located in Naples at the moment. We should find help there. It would mean a few nights on the road."

Allegra nodded once, accepting this. "Very well, signore. But I must warn you—I shan't sleep with you!"

Valerian looked her up and down, seeing her clearly for the first time in the brighter light of the hallway. She was wildly beautiful in her coarse peasant dress, this Allegra Crispino, her ebony hair a tousled profusion of midnight glory as it tumbled around her face and below her shoulders. Her eyes shone like quality sapphires against her fair skin, and her features were appealingly petite and well formed. Almost as well formed as her delightful body.

However, she was also none too clean, her feet were bare, and the smell of garlic hung around her like a shroud. "My hopes, signorina, are quite cut up, I assure you," he said at last, tongue-in-cheek, "but I would not think of despoiling Duggy's granddaughter. Your virtue is safe with me."

For now, he concluded silently, still holding out some faint hope for the restorative powers of soap and water.

THEY HAD QUIT the *pensione* and were nearing the corner of the small side street and Valerian's waiting carriage when two large men jumped out of the shadows of a nearby building to block their way.

His eyes on the men, Valerian asked softly, "Friends of yours? I sense a pattern forming, signorina."

"Alberto! Giorgio!" Allegra exploded in exasperation as Valerian's small pistol quickly came into view once more, the sight of the weapon stopping the men in their tracks before they could do any damage. "Am I never to be shed of these dreadful, thick-skulled Timoteos?"

Valerian eyed the two men warily as the coachman, who had seen his master's dilemma, hopped from the seat and came up behind them, an ugly but effective blunderbuss clutched in his hands. "Lord luv a duck, sir, but these sure are big 'uns. Oi told yer there'd be trouble in this part of town. Yer wants ter drop 'em? Oi gots the one on the right."

"Not yet, Tweed, but I thank you most sincerely for the offer," Valerian answered. "Signorina Crispino—tell your

hulking friends here to be on their way, *per favore,* or it
will be the worse for them.''

Allegra immediately launched into a stream of colloquial,
Italian like none Valerian had ever heard before, the whole
of her speech punctuated by exaggerated arm movements
and eloquent gestures that made him momentarily wonder,
were her hands ever to be tied behind her back, if she would
then be rendered speechless.

Giorgio and Alberto twisted their heads about to see
Tweed—the man extremely unprepossessing with his small
stature, skinny frame, and black patch that covered his right
eye. His blunderbuss, however—the barrel of which was
steadily pointing first toward one of them and then at the
other—was another matter, and the two Timoteos ex-
changed speculative glances before turning back to look at
Allegra.

''Bernardo?'' Giorgio questioned worryingly. *''Dove
posso trovare Bernardo? M-m-morto?''*

Allegra jabbed Valerian in the ribs with her elbow. ''Isn't
that wonderul? Giorgio thinks his brother is dead. Look at
him, Signor Fitzhugh—his knobby knees quiver like the
strings of a plucked violin. What shall I tell him? Shall I
tell him you killed his brother? That you made meatballs
of his pretty face? It would serve him right, *capisci,* for
what they have tried to do to me.''

''You're more than usually animated when you're bloodthirsty, signorina, but I don't think I can allow you to do
that,'' Valerian answered, watching as a single large tear
ran down Giorgio's cheek. The young man's features were
almost as perfect as his brother's, although the youth standing next to him, Alberto, must have been hiding behind the
porta when the family good looks had been handed out, for
he was as ugly as Bernardo and Giorgio were beautiful.

"Tell me, just for the sake of intellectual curiosity—are all three of them brothers?"

She shook her head. "Alberto is a *cugino,* a cousin. His mother must have been frightened by a *tarantola,* don't you think?"

"A tarantula? He is as darkly hairy as a spider, Signorina Crispino," Valerian agreed, looking at the unfortunate Alberto, "although I doubt he is as poisonous. But enough of this sport, diverting as it is. Tell them where they can discover their beloved Bernardo so that we may be on our way. I wish to leave the city at dawn, before these pesky Timoteos of yours can launch yet another sneak attack, as repetition has always held the power to bore me."

Allegra gave a mighty shrug, clearly not happy to end her sport so soon, and told the men that Bernardo was back at the *pensione*—"sleeping."

As the pair hastily disappeared down the narrow street, their heavy shoes clanging against the uneven cobblestones, Valerian thanked Tweed for coming to their rescue so promptly and helped Allegra into the closed coach.

"We will return to my hotel, rest for a few hours, *bathe,* and be on our way. Perhaps, signorina, you will amuse me as we travel to Naples by telling me why these Timoteos are after you—and most especially why Bernardo Timoeteo called you his 'love.'"

Allegra burrowed her small body into a dark corner of the coach, her full bottom lip jutting forward in a pout. "Sì, signore, if I must—but I warn you, it is not a pretty story!"

Valerian, his long legs stretched out on the opposite seat, his arms folded negligently across his chest, chuckled deep in his throat. "Somehow, signorina, I think I already suspected as much. Oh, and one more thing, if you please. When we reach my hotel you will enter it from the rear with Tweed—discreetly—then join me upstairs in my rooms."

Allegra sprang forward, her eyes flashing hot sparks in the dark. "*Impossible!* You would treat me like a *prostituta*—a harlot? To sneak into your rooms like some filthy *puttana?* Never! I shall not do it! I should die first!"

Valerian did not move except to slide his gaze to the left to see Allegra throw back her head in an already familiar gesture of defiance. "You're a tiresome enough brat, aren't you?" he offered calmly. "I am not treating you like a prostitute, signorina, even if your manner at the moment would insult one of that ancient profession. If you must know the truth, I do not wish to be seen strolling through a lobby with a barefoot young woman who smells like a sausage. If that is poor-spirited of me, so be it, but I do have some reputation for fastidiousness to uphold. *Comprende?*"

She shrugged expressively yet again, suddenly calm once more. "It is understood. You are *meticoloso*—a conceited prig."

Allegra subsided into the corner, her hand going to her bodice, where the remainder of the sausages still resided. "But I will hate you forever for your terrible insult, signore. Forever!"

CHAPTER TWO

"IT ALL BEGAN about six months ago, signore, shortly after my *papà* died."

Valerian sat at his ease on the facing seat of the coach as Allegra began her story. They had spent an uneventful evening at his hotel on the Via del Prato, with Allegra retiring to her rooms without a fuss, her bare feet all but dragging with fatigue.

That was not to say that the morning had been without incident, for she had refused to budge an inch from the hotel without bathing from head to toe in a hip bath she charged Tweed to procure—a sentiment Valerian sincerely seconded—and until she had been served a herculean breakfast of cappuccino, *bisteca alla fiorentina,* and *tortino di carciofi.*

Valerian, accustomed to a lighter breakfast since coming to the Continent, denied himself the opportunity to likewise partake of the thick sliced steak but did sample the eggs with artichokes, a dish whose aroma could not be ignored.

Besides her hygienic and epicurean commands, Allegra harbored only one other demand she wished imparted to Valerian. She had thought long and hard about it during the night, she had told him, and she was not about to travel along the road with him for the days and nights it would take the coach to reach Naples, no matter that no Englishman feels he has seen Italy unless he can claim to have bravely run down the inner slope of the long-dead Mount Vesuvius.

It was out of the question, this constant, unchaperoned togetherness, and so she told him—just as if she hadn't been running about Florence without so much as a *cameriera* in attendance! They were instead to make straight for the coast and the town of Livorno, whence they could hire a small boat to take them to Napoli.

She had even presented Valerian with a crudely drawn map listing a suitable stop along the way where they could sleep (in separate rooms, of course; this part was heavily underlined), change horses, and be assured of a decent meal of Chianti, minestrone, and *funghi alla fiorentina al fuoco di legna.* Allegra's appetite, it was becoming more and more obvious to Valerian, knew no bounds.

Once he had acquiesced to this plan (for any idea that would serve to lessen the amount of time he must spend inside a closed coach with only Allegra for company could only be looked upon as a blessing), they were on their way. Now, an hour later, the coach moving forward at a brisk pace once they had left the city behind them, Allegra finally seemed ready to tell Valerian about the Timoteos.

"Yes," he said, watching as her lower lip began to quiver at the mention of her father. "I learned of his death shortly after I began my quest to locate you. An inflammation of the lungs, I believe?"

Allegra nodded, averting her eyes, then lifted her chin. "It was that terrible Venezia. So beautiful, you know, but so damp. He died in my arms, just as my dearest *madre* breathed her last in his three summers earlier in Modena."

Smiling again, she raised her hands, palms up. "But enough of that! I am the *orfana*—the orphan—but I make my own way. My fame had already begun to spread and my voice was in demand everywhere. I could have been a prima donna—I could still be a prima donna—the best! If only it weren't for that stupid Erberto. Erberto was my manager, you understand.'' She spread her hands wide, comically rolling her eyes. "Erberto's mouth, signore—*tanto grossa!*"

Valerian chuckled in spite of himself. Allegra was so alive, so mercurial, that he felt constantly on the alert—and continually entertained—by her antics. "And what did Erberto's big mouth do?" he asked as she collapsed against the seat.

She sat forward once more, balancing her elbows on her knees as she spoke so that the lowcut peasant blouse gave him a most pleasant view of her cleavage. Oh, yes, Agnes Kittredge was going to take to her bed for a week once she clapped eyes on her grandniece. "We were in Milano, where I had just had a magnificent triumph at the Teatro alla Scala—"

"You sang at La Scala?" Valerian's tone was openly skeptical.

Allegra tossed back her head, impaling him with her sapphire glare. "No, signore," she shot back. "I swept the stage after the horses were taken off! Of course I sang! Now, if you are done with stupid questions, shall I get on with it?"

Valerian shook his head. "Forgive me, signorina. You must possess a great talent."

She shrugged, then grinned, her natural honesty overcoming her pride. "*Dire una piccola bugia*—it was just a small fib. In truth, I was only one of the chorus—although I did get to die during the finale. It was a very good death—very dramatic, very heart-wrenching. They had no *buffo* that night—no comedy—so I did not get a chance to really show my talent. But, be that as it may, Erberto and I retired to a nearby *caffè* after the performance—for singing always makes me *very* hungry—and that is when it happened.''

''Let me hazard a guess. Erberto opened his big mouth.''

''*Sì!* It is like this. Erberto is a *fiorentino,* a Florentine, and naturally thinks himself a wag and a wit. But mostly he is a *grullo,* a fool. He is always building himself up by poking fun at someone else. This night his wicked tongue lands on Bernardo Timoteo—something to do with seeing cabbage leaves sticking out of his ears, I think. It is a simple enough jest, hardly what you'd call a triumph of the language, and I am positive it does not linger in stupid Erberto's memory beyond his next bottle of Ruffina.''

''But Bernardo takes—I mean, *took* umbrage, and has been chasing the two of you ever since. Now I understand why you were running. But where is this Erberto fellow?''

Allegra leaned forward another six inches, her hands on her hips. ''Who is telling this story, signore, you or I? Take umbrage? No, Bernardo does no such thing, for he is not very smart. Beautiful, yes, but very, very stupid. For myself, I believe it is only sometime later, when one of Milano's good citizens takes the time to explain the insult to Bernardo, that the trouble starts.

''You see, the man probably didn't much like it that an outsider had infringed on what the people of Milano consider theirs—the God-given right to tickle themselves by poking fun at all Timoteos. Oh, yes, signore. I was in the *caffè* long enough that night to hear almost everyone there take a turn at poking fun at *il bello calzolaio*—the beautiful shoemaker.''

''Ah,'' Valerian said ruminatingly, interrupting her yet again. ''That would explain the metal mallet, wouldn't it?

Oh, I'm sorry, Signorina—please, go on. I'm hanging on your every word, really I am.''

Allegra leaned back, making a great business out of crossing her arms beneath her breasts. ''No. I don't think so. My English is rusty since my *madre*'s death. You are making fun of me.''

Valerian inclined his head slightly, acknowledging her refusal. ''Very well, signorina, if that's what you have decided. I shan't beg, you know.'' So saying, he pushed his curly brimmed beaver down low over his eyes, showing all intentions of taking a nap as Tweed tooled the coach along the narrow, rutted roads.

He had only counted to twenty-seven when Allegra blurted, ''Three nights after the incident in the *caffè*—with the help of his brother, Giorgio and his hairy spider cousin Alberto—Bernardo waits in the shadows for Erberto to emerge from the opera house after the performance.''

Her voice lowered dramatically. ''They have, in their ridiculousness, begun the *vendetta*—a hunt for revenge— against my manager! Bernardo taps—boom!—on Erberto's poor skull with that terrible mallet of his even as I watch, helpless.'' She spread her hands, palms upward. ''There is blood everywhere!''

''Erberto is dead? I had no idea, signorina,'' he said, pushing up the brim of his hat, the better to see Allegra. Valerian had been reasonably impressed when Bernardo's size (as well as the potential for mayhem provided by the metal mallet the man had carried), but he had not really believed the gorgeous young man capable of murder.

''You poor creature, to have been witness to a murder. And they are after you now, to kill you as well in order to cover their tracks. Please, tell me the whole of it.''

She quickly turned her head away, but not before Valerian had seen her smile. "No, no, signore, I won't go on boring you with my tale of woe. Continue your nap, *per favore*."

"Little Italian witch," Valerian breathed quietly, knowing he had been bested by a mere child, and a female child at that. He sat up straight and offered his apology for teasing her, then begged her to continue with the story of the Timoteos.

"Erberto is not dead—more's the pity. For even Dante's terrible inferno is too good for him," she went on, happy to speak now that she was sure she had Fitzhugh's undivided attention. "Once he regained his senses the coward beat a hasty retreat—probably all the way to his uncle's in Sicilia—leaving me alone to starve, for the night of the attack was also the final night of our engagement in Milano. He ran like a rabbit—and took every last bit of my wages with him! I spit on Erberto!"

"Not in *my* coach, you don't!" Valerian cut in firmly, lifting one expressive eyebrow.

She shot him a withering glance. "Of course I won't. Last night I only wished to shock you. You wanted me to be terrible, and I did not wish to be so unkind as to disappoint you. But you would spit on Erberto too, signore, if you knew the whole of it! Bernardo had seen me as I sat in the alley, you understand, holding that thankless Erberto's broken head in my lap—and the fool fell fatally in love with me at that instant!"

"Then Bernardo really is in love with you?"

"Will you never stop asking silly questions and listen? Consider, signore. There I was, still in my stage costume— and a lovely costume it was, all red and glittering gold— sitting in the moonlight...my sapphire eyes awash with tears for the worthless Erberto...my glorious ebony tresses loosed about my shoulders…Erberto's broken head cradled in my lap. I am very beautiful, you know, and I believe Bernardo saw me as a *caritatevole Madonna*."

"A beneficent madonna? Really?" The child was a complete minx, and Valerian was having a very difficult time keeping his face expressionless as Allegra lifted a hand to push at her hair, striking a dramatic pose. "Don't you think you might be overreacting—not to mention overacting?"

Her right hand sliced the air in a gesture that dismissed Valerian for a fool. "He follows me, does he not—dogging my every footstep these past six months so that I cannot find work, so that I cannot live without looking over my shoulder? He tells Giorgio and Alberto that, with Erberto gone, the *vendetta* is now directed at me, so that all three of them have abandoned the shoemaker shop to make my life a misery. They would not follow him else, you understand.

"But Bernardo has told me—once, when he almost caught me—that he wants only to marry me, to make up for the trouble he caused me by chasing Erberto away. *Stupido!* As if I should spend my life with that empty-headed creature and his beautiful, empty-headed children! No—I choose to run—to spend my life running, a wild pack of Timoteos forever barking at my heels!"

Valerian reached up a hand to straighten his cravat. "I see now that Duggy's change of heart and imminent demise have come just in time for you, signorina. Considering all that you have told me, I'm surprised it took you so long to accept his offer, for I must admit I too can't believe you have the makings of a dutiful shoemaker's wife."

Rather than become angry, Allegra appeared amused by Valerian's opinion of her worth as a wife for Bernardo. "I should probably take his little metal mallet to his thick skull within a fortnight, signore,'' she admitted with a grin. "But what is this—we are slowing down!''

She scooted over to the window to see that they were coming into the outskirts of a small town. "Ah, Empoli, and just in time! The inn I directed Tweed to take us to has the most delicious *bruschetta* in the region!''

"Bruschetta?" Valerian repeated, scowling. "That's bread drenched in garlic, isn't it?''

"It is nothing so simple. The bread is sliced thick and toasted ever so lightly, then rubbed most generously all over with none but the freshest garlic, olive oil, and salt. I adore it!''

"You will adore it from a distance today, signorina, or else ride up top with Tweed to the next posting inn,'' Valerian warned her, his expression as stern as his voice. "I am entranced by Italy in general, but I have never learned to share your national love of garlic.''

Allegra's chin jutted out as her breast heaved a time or two while she considered this ultimatum. It was raining, and had been raining ever since they had left the hotel. She had been an outside passenger in the wintertime enough to know that she did not wish to be one again. "I will have the minestrone, signore,'' she said, giving in even though it pained her. "But you will not know what you have missed!''

"Oh, but I already know what I will miss, signorina,'' he corrected her, reaching for the door as Tweed pulled the coach to a halt. "I will miss an afternoon in peace and quiet while you bear Tweed company—probably the last peace and quiet I shall have until we reach Brighton.''

As Valerian pushed down the coach steps, his back to Allegra, she almost gave in to the urge to lift her foot and push him headfirst through the door and out into the muddy inn yard.

"Ah, signore," was all she said a moment later, comically rolling her big blue eyes as Valerian handed her down from the coach, "you must have a saint on your shoulder. You don't know how lucky, how very lucky, you are!"

Valerian stared after her as she made her way confidently to the inn's entrance, her dark head held high, her step fluidly graceful. The feeling that he was in some sort of unrecognizable danger from this small spitfire of a child was growing ever larger in his chest.

THEY REACHED NAPLES two days later, docking at the bottom of the Via Roma just at sundown, and proceeded directly to the rented villa of Mark Antony Betancourt, Marquess of Coniston, and his wife, Candice. The two were good friends of Valerian's who, upon leaving Rome in October, had instructed him to visit them in their uncle's villa in Naples after the New Year.

His fingers figuratively crossed that the couple would be in residence and not entertaining this evening, Valerian descended from the hastily rented carriage, bidding Allegra to remain behind while he assured himself that the Marquess was at home.

"Will your Marchesa of Coniston bid me to enter through the servants' door as well?" Allegra asked, reluctant to move. Her stomach and legs had yet to acknowledge that she was back on dry land, because, as she had told Valerian, she didn't have "sailor's feet."

She waited until he had walked away before adding peevishly, "Or do Englishwomen have better manners than Englishmen?"

Valerian, who had already mounted the three shallow

stone steps to the front door, turned to smile back at her. "Candie stand on ceremony? I should think not, signorina. I'm sure she'll make us both feel most welcome."

Allegra sniffed and withdrew her head back into the carriage to await developments, as her pride still smarted from having to climb the back stairs at Valerian's hotel in Florence. Her stomach grumbled as she waited for Valerian to summon her and she smiled, knowing that her appetite was returning to normal. With any luck there would be a good Neapolitan cook installed in the villa's kitchen.

Five minutes passed before Valerian opened the door to the carriage and held out his hand for her to descend to the narrow flagway.

"I'm to go to the servants' entrance?" she asked warily.

"The servants' entrance?" exclaimed a female voice from the doorway. "Valerian, what have you been up to with this poor child? I've never before known you to be mean. Cuttingly sarcastic, yes, but never purposely mean. Oh, Tony, Uncle Max—just look at her! She's beautiful! Have you ever seen anything so small as her waist?"

"And I don't think it's her waist we men are looking at, *aingeal cailin,* don't you know," replied a short, rather pudgy man in a curiously lilting baritone. "Reminds me a bit of your sister, Patsy. Isn't that right, m'boyo?"

"I wouldn't know, Max," a third voice supplied, chuckling. "I'm a married man now, you know, and beyond such things."

"Exactly like your sister, Patsy, my love," the Marchioness answered, not sounding in the least upset. "I've always said I would gladly trade her this tiresome hair for her lovely, full bosom."

Allegra, whose gaze had been concentrated on Valerian's face as she tried to take some silent signal from him as to how to go on (a signal which, no matter how hard she looked, never came), lifted her head to confront the three people who had spoken of her as if she weren't really there to listen. Almost instantly her mouth dropped open as she looked at the Marchioness of Coniston, a woman whose ethereal loveliness literally took her breath away.

The Marchioness was tall, and reed-slim, and her beautiful, pale-complexioned, heart-shaped face was animated by a lovely pair of slanted, lively sherry eyes. But it was her hair, a thick mane more white than blonde which fell nearly to her waist, that totally entranced Allegra. Until the Marchioness smiled, that is. Then Allegra was captured and won by the open friendliness in the young woman's expression.

"Come inside, Signorina Crispino, do," the Marchioness commanded, taking Allegra's hand in hers. "Tony, Uncle Max, come along. Valerian looks as if he could use a tall glass of Chianti."

"What a wonderful idea, Candie. And it's a great thirst I've worked up this day myself, being good," Maximilien P. Murphy answered brightly as the five of them headed inside, passing by a small group of interested servants.

Valerian slipped his arm around the older man's shoulders as they walked across the marble foyer and into the main *salotto*. "It's strange that you should mention being good, Max," he said companionably, "for I've been wondering—how would you like to be *bad* for a while? Nothing terrible, you understand, just perhaps a momentary resurrection of the Conte di Casals, the Italian Count Tony told me you played to perfection in London. Would you impersonate him again—just long enough for the Conte to procure a passport for Signorina Crispino here?"

"That's it? One tiny passport?" Maximilien answered,

frowning. "That's no harder than tripping off a log. Done and done, my boyo!"

"Valerian! Shame on you. And shame on you, Tony, my love, for telling tales out of school!" the Marchioness, over-hearing, accused. "Uncle Max doesn't do that sort of thing anymore, Valerian. You know that. After all, now that Tony and I have our sweet little Murphy, we want our son to get to know his uncle as a free man—and not just as a poor wretch we take oranges to at the local *prigione*."

Allegra, who had been led to a chair by the Marquess, looked up at Lady Coniston in confusion. "Prison! Your uncle is a criminal?" she asked, biting her lip at the insult. "*Scusi!* I mean to say—" She turned to Valerian, who was now holding a wineglass and looking very much at home and at his ease. "Well, don't just stand there! Help me, Fitzhugh, *per favore!* What did I mean to say?"

Lady Coniston promptly sat down beside Allegra and patted her hand. "Don't apologize, my dear, for it was an honest mistake. You see, dearest Uncle Max and I traveled about the world for many years before Tony and I married, and we—well, you might say we indulged in a wee bit of stage-playing from time to time when the need arose."

"Is that right? And 'tis that what you call it now, me fine *Marchioness?* We lived higher than O'Hara's hog on that 'stage-playing,' if memory serves," Maximilien re-torted, his round face turning a violent red, although Alle-gra, watching him, was very sure he was not really angry, but was only indulging in a little more stage-acting of his own. They were an unusual group, she acknowledged si-lently, but there was a lot of love in this villa, and she felt a momentary pang at the remembered loss of her own fam-ily.

"High as O'Hara's hog, is it? And twice as much time

was spent lower than O'Malley's well, *Uncail.* I remember that as well,'' Lady Coniston shot back, not without humor. ''Now, do we waste time splitting hairs, or do we help Valerian and Signorina Crispino with their little problem? Uncle Max, your Conte di Casals may get the passport, but I don't wish to hear how. I'm a mother now—and, like my husband, 'past such things.'''

''It's turning into an Irish shrew ye are, darlin','' Max groused before downing a glass of wine.

''Valerian,'' she went on, unheeding, still holding Allegra's hand as she turned to her other guest, ''all we heard when Tony and I last saw you in Rome was that you were off to find Lord Dugdale's long-lost granddaughter and transport her to Brighton. I see the granddaughter before me, and I congratulate you on your success, but I sense that more is involved in this story. Please, if I promise to have the servants lay out some refreshments in the *sala da pranzo,* you must tell us everything, from the very beginning!''

Allegra's ears pricked up at the mention of food, her recent seasickness forgotten, and she squeezed Lady Coniston's hands appreciatively. ''I will tell you everything, dear Marchesa, I promise, all about my singing, my life, and even the terrible Timoteos—directly *after* we have eaten!''

A FULL TWO WEEKS passed in relative bliss for Allegra, for in the Marchioness of Coniston she had found her first true female friend since childhood. Lady Coniston, or Candie, as she had begged Allegra to address her, was more than gracious, more than interested—she was a true sister of the heart.

For Candie had not always led a life of comfort; she had

known poverty, she had known fear, and she had learned to make her own way, by whatever means she could. But, like Allegra, she had never sacrificed her honor in order to fill her belly.

Candie had been rewarded for her purity with the love of Tony Betancourt, a man Allegra found to be immensely wonderful, and with the birth of their son, Murphy, an adorable blond cherub of two years who held his uncle Max's heart in his chubby little hands.

Could there be such a similarly rosy future in Brighton for someone like Allegra? Somehow, she doubted it, no matter how enthusiastic Candie was about her prospects.

To that end, and over Allegra's protests, Candie had set out to provide her young guest with a complete new wardrobe the very morning after Valerian and Allegra's arrival in Naples. Although Italian styles were still woefully behind those of Paris, there existed enough modistes sufficiently schooled in the art of copying for Allegra to acquire a fairly extensive wardrobe that would be considered not only acceptable but wonderfully stylish by the ladies of Brighton.

But the Marchioness was not content to merely dress her young guest in fine feathers. Oh, no. She spent long hours schooling Allegra in proper deportment (including at least one stern lecture concerning Allegra's tendency to gesture with her hands as she spoke, an entirely too Italian habit), and had helped her to weed most Italian words and phrasing from her vocabulary, permitting her to use only those considered suitably Continental and sure to impress her English relatives.

"I was the Conte di Casals's niece Gina more than once in the past, you understand," the Marchioness had informed her as the two sat alone late one night over Allegra's lessons, "so I have a fairly good notion as to how you should go on. Have I told you about the time—I was just a young girl, I believe—that Uncle Max wrangled us an audience with the Pope?''

''His Holiness!'' Allegra had exclaimed, much impressed. ''I once sang a solo for the Bishop of Bologna, but it is not the same, is it?''

Yes, there were many lessons, but there were just as many stories, and just as many shared reminiscences between the new friends, quite a few of them having to do with the at-times-almost-bizarre courtship of Candice Murphy by Mark Antony Betancourt, Seventh Marquess of Coniston. The Marquess, it seemed, had until his marriage been known all over London as Mister Overnite: a carefree, heartbreakingly handsome man who supposedly had held the modern-day British record for dallying the whole night long in more society matrons' beds than half the husbands in the Upper Ten Thousand.

It hadn't been easy for Tony to understand that his bachelor days were effectively over from the first moment he'd clapped eyes on the mischievous Miss Murphy, but—as Candie, blushing, told Allegra—he had lived to give proof to the adage that reformed rakes make the *very* best of husbands.

As for Allegra's singing career, it had been left to Valerian to explain to her that this, alas, was over, finally and completely. It was not to be mentioned in company, it was not to be considered as a viable part of her future—it simply was not to be thought of, ever again!

Only the quick-witted Tony had been able to save Valerian from Allegra's employment of a particularly vile Italan curse, which he did by quickly pointing out that there was nothing wrong with Allegra considering herself a talented amateur.

"Why, as a matter of fact," he had interjected cleverly, winking at his appreciative wife, "Prinny himself is quite a devotee of Italian opera. You're bound to be the sensation of the age, Allegra, once you sing for him, for many of his guests perform at the Marine Pavilion after one of his Highness's hours-long dinner parties."

"Yes, the dinner parties," Valerian had added, knowing by now where to aim his darts where Allegra was concerned. "I heard it said that there are often two dozen main dishes served in one evening," he slid in, watching as Allegra's sapphire eyes opened wide. "That's not to mention the many side dishes, cakes, puddings, pastries, and the rest. Although I have not yet had the pleasure, Duggy is one of Old Swellfoot's cronies, signorina, so you are sure to be invited, if you can just learn to behave yourself."

All in all, Allegra had become not only resigned to leaving Italy but anxious to reach England and her mother's birthplace, although it was with tears in her eyes that she waved good-bye to the Betancourts as the ship pulled away from the pier, her newly obtained passport safely in Valerian's possession.

Then, suddenly, all her new finery to one side and her more refined English forgotten, she pointed to the dock, hopping on one slippered foot as she exclaimed, "*Impossible!* It is that terrible Bernardo—here, in Napoli! How has he found me? Again he shows up unwanted, *come un cane nella chiesa*— like a dog in a church!"

As Bernardo ran to the very edge of the pier, tears streaming down his handsome face and looking for all the world as if he was about to throw himself into the water in order to swim out to the ship, Allegra struck her right arm straight out in front of her, tucked her middle two fingers beneath her thumb, and shouted dramatically, *"Si rompe il corno!"*

Immediately Bernardo stepped back as if stunned, clutching his chest.

"You're going to break his horns?" Valerian asked from beside her, watching bemusedly as her small but voluptuous figure was shown to advantage by her antics. "Why don't I believe that is some sort of quaint Italian farewell?"

Allegra threw back her head, her long black hair blowing in the wind, since she had shunned Candie's suggestion that she wear one of the new bonnets Valerian's money had bought her. "I wished evil on him, signore. Great evil such as only another Italian can imagine!"

"Oh, you did, did you? And now you will kindly take it off again," Valerian commanded, shaking his head. "Otherwise the lovesick fool will be on my conscience forevermore. You're leaving Italy, signorina, so you can afford to be magnanimous. Bernardo Timoteo and his cohorts can no longer harm you."

Allegra turned to Valerian, her face alight with glee. *"Magnifico,* signore! You are right! I, Allegra Crispino, will be magnanimous!" She leaned over the railing, waving a white handkerchief at the openly sobbing Bernardo. *"Addio, caro Bernardo addio!"* she called brightly, until the handsome young man on the pier heard her and began waving in return.

Valerian, well pleased with himself, smiled and waved to Bernardo as well, hardly believing he was actually on his way to Brighton at last, to achieve the long-awaited removal of the mercurial Allegra Crispino from his guardianship.

An odd, unrecognizable sensation in his stomach at the thought of depositing Allegra with Lord Dugdale and then walking away prompted him to turn his head and look down at the strange young girl.

"Allegra!" he was startled into saying, for she was gripping the rail with both hands, huge, crystalline tears running down her wind-reddened cheeks. "Why are you crying? Surely you're not going to miss having the Timoteo dogs barking at your heels?"

"I shall never see my beloved Italia again, Valerian," she answered in a small voice, her gaze still intent on the rapidly disappearing shoreline as she gave out with a shuddering sigh. "My *madre,* my *papà* they live in that earth. They are lost to me forever; all of what is home to me is now gone, while I sail away to an uncertain future with a grandfather I don't know. I didn't know how much it would hurt, Valerian, or how very much frightened I would feel."

Before he could think, before he could weigh the right or the wrong of it, Valerian gathered Allegra's small frame close against his chest, where she remained, her arms wrapped tightly around his waist, as, together, they watched the only homeland she had ever known fade from sight.

CHAPTER THREE

AGNES KITTREDGE sat in the outdated drawing room she would most happily have given her best Kashmir shawl to redecorate, awaiting the arrival of her children, seventeen-year-old Isobel and her older brother, Gideon, who had reached the age of three and twenty, Agnes was sure, thanks only to his fond mama's most assiduous nursing of his delicate constitution.

Mrs. Kittredge's brother, Baron Dennis Dugdale, was upstairs in his rooms, his gouty right foot swathed in bandages Agnes would much rather see bound tightly about his clearly disordered head.

She was furious, Agnes Kittredge was, pushed nearly to the brink of distraction by the disquieting thought that her beloved brother, Dennis, could have the nerve to recover his health after he had most solemnly promised that his demise was imminent. Was there no one, who could be trusted to keep his word anymore, not even a brother?

Not only had her aging sibling once more become the possessor of depressingly good health, but his general demeanor had reverted to one of such high good humor that Agnes, who had never been a tremendous advocate of levity, was lately finding herself hard-pressed to keep a civil tongue in her head whenever the jolly Baron was about.

Lord Dugdale's near-constant, jocular remarks alluding to a "change in the wind," and his oblique hints at a coming "surprise to knock your nose more sideways than it already is, Aggie," were not only most depressingly annoying, they were beginning to worry her very much.

Everything had always been so settled, so regulated, in the life they all lived at Number 23 in the Royal Crescent Terrace. Agnes ruled, Isobel preened, Gideon gambled, and dearest Denny paid the bills. It was all so simple, so orderly. Now Lord Dugdale was making noises as if this arrangement no longer could be regarded as the ordinary, and that soon there would come a major readjustment in all their lives.

Agnes had agreed with this notion in part at first, when the Baron had spoken so earnestly of his imminent demise. There most assuredly would be changes at Number 23 when that unhappy day finally dawned.

Agnes would still rule, Isobel would still preen, Gideon would still gamble. But forever gone from the scene would be Lord Dugdale and his annoying habit of closely questioning the amount of the bills his family presented to him with every expectation that they be paid at once, and without his first issuing a sermon about the evils of incautious spending.

Once her brother, rest his soul, was safely underground, Agnes would be free to run the household exactly as she wished, without the wearying necessity to beg for every groat. This sort of "change" Agnes had looked forward to with great expectation, nearly unmixed with sorrow for the soon-to-be-departed brother, who, after all, had led a good long life and deserved his rest.

It was all that new doctor's fault, Agnes had decided when her brother, far from sliding conveniently into his grave, began to make a near-miraculous recovery from a violent uproar of the bowels. Who ever heard of such a thing? No bleeding. No leeches. No thin gruel. Just plenty of fresh air, exercise, and good, hearty food. The treatment should have killed the Baron, but it hadn't.

Agnes hadn't allowed the doctor back in the house since the first day Lord Dugdale had sat up and loudly called for his pipe and a full bottle of his favorite cherry ripe.

"Not that it did me a penny worth of good," she groused, arranging her shawl more firmly about her bony shoulders as she thought of her brother's refusal to suffer an immediate relapse. "The man's body has been restored at the cost of his wits. It had been nearly three months, and still we must hear daily about this surprise of his. It is time and more I consider placing the poor, sainted man in an institution where there are those trained in dealing with delusional lunatics such as Denny."

"Talking to yourself, Mama? I must admit I do know of some who do so from time to time, but then I believe those people are usually rather deep in their cups. Have you been nipping while my back was turned, Mama? It isn't like you; but then this entire household has been rather irregular for weeks on end now, hasn't it?"

Agnes Kittredge looked up at the sound of her beloved Gideon's voice. "Darling!" she exclaimed, patting the space beside her on the settee. "Come sit down and tell me how you feel this morning. You were abroad quite late last night, I believe. The damp night air isn't good for you, you know. Have you breakfasted? I expressly ordered the eggs be poached this morning, as they are much more suited to your delicate constitution in that form than the hard-cooked variety you persist in eating whenever my back is turned."

He sat down dutifully, spreading his coattails neatly as he did so. "I shunned eggs entirely this morning, Mama, in favor of dry toast dipped in watered wine, for I woke with the most shocking headache. Do you think it's coming on to rain? It couldn't have been the canary I partook of last night, for you know I never drink to excess.''

"Indeed no, Gideon. You would never do that, not with your fragile system.'' Agnes turned to look adoringly upon her son. Gideon Kittredge was as handsome as his mother and sister were plain—although how this quirk of nature came about no one save Lord Dugdale, who once mentioned the idea of his sister having played her husband false at least the once, had ever been able to understand the phenomenon.

Gideon had been born scarcely five months after his parents' marriage, a sickly babe whose small size and poor chances for survival lent at least partial credence to the outrageous fib that he had been born much too soon due to an unfortunate fright his mother had taken at the sight of a tumbling dwarf in the small traveling circus she and her husband had chanced upon the same day Agnes was delivered of her first-born child.

When Gideon didn't expire as expected, Agnes, through guilt over her lie or natural motherly devotion only she knew, threw her entire energies into coddling and protecting the child well past the point of necessity or even common sense.

Gideon's sniffles were a sure sign of a lung inflammation, his cough no less than threatening consumption, his sighs a dire portent of some crippling, disabling condition that must be averted at all costs. Isobel was conceived and born almost without Agnes's notice and shuffled off to a separate nursery so that she could not contaminate her brother's air.

When Mister Kittredge had the misfortune to break his neck in a hunting accident, Agnes had little time for grieving, for she was too busy thanking her lucky stars that the man hadn't instead decided to succumb to some lingering illness that might either be passed on to Gideon or take her away overlong from her main project in life, that of taking care of her son.

That Gideon had grown from a whining, totally unlovable child into a self-indulgent adult concerned only with his own wants and desires could not be surprising. Even less of a revelation was that he thoroughly disliked his mother, the woman having earned his disgust because of his easy ability to manipulate her.

Moving closer to her now, Gideon laid his dark head on Agnes's shoulder and gazed up into her watery blue eyes. "You appear distressed, dearest Mama. Is there anything I can do to help? I promise I shall not let this crushing headache stay me from performing whatever deed you should ask of me. After all, I owe my life to you, as well I know."

Agnes blinked twice, masterfully holding back loving tears. "I shouldn't think to bother your aching head, my darling," she declared passionately, daring to touch a hand to his smooth cheek. "It's just your uncle Denny again. I fear he is becoming worse with each passing day."

Gideon turned his head slightly and stifled a yawn. "Really? In what way?"

"Why, this morning he is insisting on coming downstairs, even though his foot is still wrapped up like some heathen mummy, and his valet has told me your uncle actually intends to see his tailor this afternoon to order an entire new suit of clothes. Now why would he need new clothes? It isn't as if he doesn't have a closet full of them."

"All displaying his love of food, for the dear man seems to find it necessary to wear what he eats," Gideon supplied helpfully.

"Precisely so, my dear," Agnes concurred feelingly. "I

should think he'd be more concerned with the fact that you have been seen in the same evening dress at least three times this year. If anyone is in dire need of a new wardrobe, dearest, it is you, who shows his tailor to such advantage.''

There was a slight movement at the doorway, followed by a decidedly unladylike snort from Miss Isobel Kittredge, who had just entered the room.

''Toadeating Mama again, Gideon?'' the young lady asked, taking up a seat across from the settee. ''I'm surprised you haven't hopped into her lap to ask her to tell you a story. Or would you rather tell her a story, possibly the one about your latest venture into the land of the sharpers?''

Agnes wrinkled her forehead, at least as much as the tightly done-up bun perched atop her head allowed her to do. ''Sharpers? What are sharpers, Gideon? I don't believe I've ever heard the term.''

Gideon, sitting up smartly once more, shot his sister a fulminating look. ''Pernicious little brat,'' he gritted from between his even white teeth as Isobel, obviously well pleased with herself, made a great business out of straightening a lace doily on the table beside her.

''Pernicious, am I?'' she countered, lifting hazel eyes as depressingly watery as her mother's to her brother's face. ''Since you have roused the energy necessary to be insulting, I can only imagine that I am right and you are scorched again.''

''Gideon?'' Agnes prompted, fighting the feeling that yet another score of gray hairs were about to sprout overnight on her already nearly white head. ''Is your sister correct? Have you been gambling again?''

Sparing a moment to send his sister another fulminating, I'll-see-to-you-later look, Gideon picked up his mother's left hand and held it firmly between both of his. "I must admit to a shocking run of bad luck, Mama, but it is nothing to fret about, I promise. The devil was in it last night, that's all, but I'll come about as soon as you can get Uncle Denny to advance you a small pittance on the household allowance."

Agnes's thin face took on a pinched expression. "How much, Gideon? I cannot fob your uncle off with another story about the price of candles. He has his wits about him again, you know, at least in the area of his finances. Tell me quickly, before I conjure up some horrendous sum."

"A mere monkey, Mama," Gideon mumbled into his cravat. "Five hundred pounds. Four hundred, actually, but I also placed a small wager with a certain party about the outcome of a race. Dratted horse stumbled going round the turn."

"Five hundred pounds! I will never be able to extract so much from your uncle as that!"

"Of course you will, Mama—for me." He brought his mother's hand to his mouth, firmly pressing his lips against the papery skin. "And I promise, Mama, I shall eschew racing from this moment on. I don't know how I got involved in such a harebrained thing, for you know I can't abide horses. It was all George Watson's idea—he goaded me into the wager when my spirits were at a low ebb!"

"Of course he did," Agnes agreed immediately, pressing her cheek against her son's hands. "I never did like that George—and his grandfather smells entirely too much of the shop to suit me, as I recall. You would be wise to eschew George in the future as well, my darling."

"George tied him up and forced him to make a wager against his will," Isobel spat mockingly, shaking her head. "Honestly, Mama, he takes you in like a green goose, over and over again. Gideon is a dedicated gamester. When are you going to get that fact into your head? Why, he probably has a wager with George right now on how long it will take you to come up with the blunt to settle his latest debt.''

"Isobel!" Agnes exclaimed, stung. "You will apologize at once! I vow, your overweening jealousy of your brother makes me wonder if I have nurtured a viper at my bosom."

Gideon took that moment to cough delicately into his fist.

"Now look what you've done!" Agnes exclaimed, immediately pressing a hand to her son's forehead to check for fever. "You've brought on one of Gideon's spasms. Such an unnatural child!"

"It wasn't—*a-ahumph, a-ahumph*—my dearest sister's viperish tongue—*a-aumph*—that upset me, Mama," Gideon corrected quickly, his strong voice giving the lie to his continuing bout of coughing. "It is the money that worries me. George can be so demanding—and it is, after all, a debt of honor. If only I should be assured that Uncle Denny won't cut up stiff—''

"No, no, of course he won't. I shan't even mention your name," Agnes assured her son even as she shot her smirking daughter a quelling look. "I shall approach your uncle this afternoon."

"Without fail?" Gideon asked, somehow managing to produce a slight sheen of feverish perspiration on his smooth upper lip.

"Without fail, my darling," Agnes vowed, then gave a quick silencing wave of her hand as she heard her brother's limping gait approaching outside in the hallway.

"La, yes," she exclaimed quickly in an overly hearty voice that was sure to carry as far as the foyer. "I have just come from prayers in my room, yet again thanking the good Lord on my knees for your uncle's miraculous recovery. I should think the fine air of Brighton has had much to do with his renewed good health, but the good Lord must be thanked for that good air as well, mustn't He, children?''

''Spouting gibberish again, Aggie?'' Lord Dugdale asked from the doorway, where he stood leaning heavily on the bulbous head of his cane. ''If you wish to thank anyone, thank Valerian Fitzhugh—for it's he who saved me, sure as check. Great faith I have in that boy, and it's sure to be rewarded any day now with the most wonderful surprise a man could push himself up from the brink of the grave to accept.''

He took two more steps into the room before Isobel rose to take his arm, helping him to the chair she had just vacated. ''You mustn't push yourself, Uncle, not on your first day downstairs. There you go,'' she complimented as the Baron lowered himself heavily into the chair. ''Now if you'll just let me place this footstool here for you to rest that leg on—there! Mama, Gideon—doesn't Uncle Denny look much more the thing?''

Lord Dugdale looked from sister to niece to nephew, his squat, heavy body all but wedged into the chair as he presented himself for their scrutiny. What his relatives saw, other than the truly magnificent cocoon of snowy white bandages stuck to the lower half of his right leg and foot, was a no-longer-young man with a sparse, partial circlet of gray hair banding his head directly above his ears, leaving his shiny bald pate to cast a glare in the afternoon sunlight coming through a nearby window.

His eyes, the same watery blue of his sister's but with a multitude of cunning if not intelligence lurking in their depths, returned their piercing looks, yet his round-as-a-pie plate face was carefully expressionless. Yes, it was the same old Baron Dugdale they had known forever—complete to the food stains on his loosely tied cravat and too-tight waistcoat.

"Well, this is something new, Uncle Denny," Isobel piped up at last, perching her thin frame on a corner of the footstool as she looked up at the Baron. "You've been hinting about this surprise for weeks, but I've never heard Mister Fitzhugh's name mentioned before this moment. Why, it must be three years or more since he's been home to Brighton. Ever since Waterloo, I imagine. Is that the surprise? That Valerian—I mean, Mister Fitzhugh—is returning home?"

Gideon rose to stand behind the settee. "Don't drool, Isobel; it doesn't become you. Why, you were scarcely out of swaddling clothes when Valerian Fitzhugh took off for the Continent. Don't tell me you still fancy yourself in love with the man. Lord, that's pathetic!"

Isobel's normally sallow complexion visibly paled and a small white line tightened about her thin lips. "Gideon Kittredge—you take that back!" she gritted, pointing a shaking finger in his direction. "Mama! Make him take that back!"

"I won't take it back," Gideon declared, moving to stand more directly behind his mother. "You've been embroidering slippers with his name on them every Christmas in the hope he'll come back from the Continent and sweep you off your feet and into his waiting arms. Well, let me tell you, sister mine, those slippers will grow whiskers before Valerian Fitzhugh tosses more than a crust of bread in your direction!"

"Children—children! Stop this at once!" Agnes pleaded, sure that Gideon would soon overheat himself with his exertion. "Isobel, remember your brother's frail constitution."

"Odds bobs, woman," Lord Dugdale chortled. "The little bugger has the constitution of a horse, if only you'd scrape the scales of mother love from your eyes long enough to see it. Now, does anyone wish to hear about my surprise or not? With Valerian's letter reaching me the very day I turned my head away from death's dark door, I figure the time is about right for my little announcement. Any later and it will most probably be too late.''

"I fear, dear Baron, you have already left it too late, if I have guessed correctly and you have failed to acquaint your family with the purpose of my mission," pronounced a smoothly articulate voice from the doorway to the hall. "Pardon me for having bypassed your butler and choosing to announce myself, but after all this time I could barely contain my anxiety to present you with my traveling companion."

"Valerian!" Isobel all but screamed, hopping up from the footstool to raise a trembling hand to her nonexistent breast. "Mama, Gideon—look! It is Valerian!"

Fitzhugh walked fully into the room to make his bows to the company. "Such a rousing welcome, Miss Kittredge," he said, inclining his head over her outstretched paw. "I vow I would have returned to Brighton much earlier had I known I would be accorded such a heartwarming greeting. I left you a child, but I have returned to see the woman."

He turned to the Baron. "Having seen no crepe hatchment on the knocker, I had already assumed you still lingered, awaiting my return, but now I see that you have made a full recovery. This knowledge makes my time spent fulfilling your request even more personally rewarding, as I have a sentimental heart and shall greatly enjoy this coming family reunion."

Baron Dugdale snorted once, pushing himself about in

the chair so as to get a look at the now vacant doorway. "Never mind all that sweet talk, man—where is she? You wrote from Florence, promising to have her here within three months. What did you do—leave her at the dock to guard the luggage? Must I fetch her the rest of the way myself?"

"Her?" Agnes directed a long, dispassionate stare at her brother until at last, her eyes narrowing even as twin flags of color began waving brightly in her thin cheeks, she declared tightly, "Dennis Dugdale—you *didn't!* You *couldn't!* You *wouldn't!* How dare you? I won't have that foreign baggage in my house!"

With Agnes's words the drawing room was immediately transformed into a hotbed of mingled questions and accusations, all delivered in full voice and with the sharp rapidity of gunshots.

"Your house? *Your house!* I could be three days dead and it would still be my house, woman. It will always be my house!"

"Who did Valerian bring from Florence, Mama? Do you know her? Is it some relative of Aunt Mary's husband? But I thought Uncle Denny disowned Aunt Mary years ago, and Aunt Mary's dead, isn't she?"

"A foreign woman? I knew you were off to France and such. So you've been in Italy as well, have you, you lucky dog? Tell me, are Italian women as hot-blooded as I've heard, old man? Does she sing? I hear they all warble like little songbirds. What's Uncle going to do with her—give her to Prinny?"

"My hartshorn! Where is my hartshorn? Quickly, Gideon—my hartshorn. I shall perish in a fit, I just know it!"

"I'll give you a fit, you daft female! Odds bobs, but I don't know why I've put up with you all these long years!"

"Rompere le uova nel paniere di qualcuno."

Immediately there came a crashing silence throughout the drawing room as all the voices cut off abruptly and all heads turned to locate the person who had uttered the foreign gibberish.

Valerian turned as well, to see that Allegra had entered the room, still clad in her traveling cloak, to stand slightly behind him, her hand barely touching his arm. "Yes, indeed, Signorina Crispino," he agreed quietly, "it certainly would appear as if we have well and truly broken the eggs in someone's basket. In *all* their baskets, as a matter of fact, save your grandfather's. He is that gentleman seated over there—the gentleman wearing that extremely wide smile."

Valerian turned back to the occupants of the room, bowing once more. "Mrs. Agnes Kittredge, Miss Isobel Kittredge—Gideon. Allow me to present to you Signorina Allegra Crispino, daughter of the late Mary Dugdale Crispino and only granddaughter of Baron Dennis Dugdale. Signorina Crispino—your loving, devoted family."

"Come state?" Allegra asked, her chin high as she dared anyone to say a single word more. *"Grazie per la cordiale accoglienza!"*

Valerian looked down at Allegra curiously, wondering why the young woman had chosen to speak in Italian after all of his and Candie's warnings to the contrary, but he decided to go along with her for the moment, for he was sure she was justifiably nervous at this first meeting.

"Signorina Crispino asks how you all are and thanks you for your most *cordial* welcome. Italians, you may infer from her words, are not unconversant with sarcasm," he added quietly as her fingertips dug into his forearm.

"We've had a most arduous journey here from Naples, what with storms at sea and Signorina Crispino's lack of what she delightfully terms 'sailor's feet,' but we are here now, having dispensed with the signorina's temporary chaperon at the dock a scant hour ago. Her baggage will be delivered directly, at which time I am sure she will wish to retire to her rooms for a rest. In the meantime, I am assured you, Mrs. Kittredge, will endeavor to make your niece as comfortable as possible.''

''But of course!'' Agnes exclaimed quickly, seeing the warning in her brother's eyes and not daring any further revolt—at least not at this moment. ''We must make dear Mary's child welcome! Unfortunately, we have no room ready—thanks to my dear brother's misguided love of surprises—but we shall just have to make do, won't we, Isobel? How long will the dear child be staying in our country? This is just a visit—isn't it?''

Allegra's slightly husky voice was low and laden with disdain. *''Tu hai il cuore di un coniglio.''*

Valerian's lips quivered appreciatively as Allegra's quick remark threatened to unleash a bark of laughter that could only serve to shatter the already tense atmosphere in the room into a million jagged pieces.

But Allegra had taken one look and seen straight through the woman to her self-serving core. Indeed, as Allegra had said, Agnes Kittredge possessed the heart of a rabbit. The woman might detest the thought of being kind to Allegra with every fiber of her being, but she wasn't about to jeopardize her own position in the household by standing on her principles in front of her clearly determined brother.

''Signorina Crispino says for me to tell you that you are very kind, Mrs. Kittredge,'' Valerian said at last, when the prolonged silence had become almost unbearable, Allegra's ever-tightening grip on his forearm threatening to shut off his blood supply to that necessary limb.

"Yes, yes, enough of that, boy," the Baron interrupted testily. "This is demmed awkward, but I can't get up just anytime I want. This miserable foot, you understand. Bring the gel round here so I can get a good look at her. I never thought I'd live to see the day my Mary's child would be here with me. I did her mother a terrible wrong, you know, cutting her off without a farthing when she ran off with that Italian bastard—but it's time and more I made amends.

"Ah, there she is," he said, sighing, as Valerian all but pushed Allegra forward so that she stood in front of the footstool. "Take off her cloak, for pity's sake, so I can really see her. Little thing, ain't she—all eyes and hair."

Allegra's small hands balled into fists at her sides and she glared up at Valerian accusingly. Leaning down close to her ear as he helped her off with her cloak, he whispered in Italian, "It isn't my fault the old boy's still alive. Besides, I think you'll fare better this way than if you had to deal directly with your aunt. She'd make the Timoteos look like a stroll in the park, to my way of thinking."

A moment later Allegra was divested of her cloak, to stand before her grandfather in the modishly styled morning gown of green-and-white sprigged muslin Candie had deemed demure enough, yet sufficiently sophisticated, to give a good first impression.

Lord Dugdale rubbed his hands together in glee as his watery blue eyes made a careful assessment of his granddaughter. "Oh, this is more than I could have hoped for, Valerian, truly it is. Why, she'll have half the bucks in Brighton drooling all over her slippers! She doesn't much favor my Mary, except perhaps a little around the chin—it's Mary's stubborn chin to the life—but I don't see any of the father in her either, thank God. Yes, with her looks

and figure—and the plum I plan to give her—she'll do jus
fine!''

"A plum! Never say you're going to give her a plum!'

This outburst came from Gideon, who had been remark
ably quiet up to this point as he had been very preoccupie
in cudgeling his brain to find some way of bringing th
conversation around to his crushing need for five hundre
pounds before nightfall. However, the mention of a dowr
of one hundred thousand pounds had served to bring him
unhesitatingly to attention. "Why don't you give her th
house and all the rest while you're at it?" he asked face
tiously.

"I plan to, nephew," Lord Dugdale responded swiftly
still looking at Allegra. "But not quite yet. I've more tha
made up my mind to stay above-ground a while longer, jus
so that I can see my granddaughter comfortably settled."

"The—the house? *This* house? And all your fortune
Denny—what about me? What about Gideon—my chil
dren?''

Lord Dugdale reached out to take hold of Allegra'
hands, smiling up into his granddaughter's stony face
"What about 'em, Agnes? You'll all have your allowance
as usual and a roof over your heads. But that's all I ca
give you. I had a vision, you see, whilst I lay dying. A
angel came to me and asked how I thought I could fac
Saint Peter at the Golden Gates, knowing what terrible si
I had committed against my only child."

He sat forward, not without great effort, and looke
around Allegra to his sister. "I'll feed you and yours, Ag
nes, and I'll house and clothe you, but you must understand
I'll be damned for a bloody fool if I'll burn in Hell fo
you!''

Allegra tugged at Valerian's sleeve so that he bent dow

to hear her whisper in Italian, "I've heard enough for now. I think it would be a very good time for me to drop into a most graceful, affecting swoon, don't you? Please catch me, *per favore,* for I shouldn't wish to fall on *Nonno*'s poor foot."

Before Valerian could protest, Allegra raised a hand to her temple, moaned once—a truly wonderful, anguished, theatrical moan—as her huge sapphire eyes fluttered closed behind a thick veil of long, sweeping black lashes.

A moment later, and much against his inclination, Valerian found himself cradling her small, limp body against his chest.

CHAPTER FOUR

VALERIAN STOOD outside the small bedchamber into which he had ten minutes previously deposited the limp yet curiously clinging body of Allegra Crispino, still wondering how he, a normally well-regulated, rational man of no mean intelligence, had come to be in his current insane position.

Much as he had been simultaneously attracted to and repelled by Allegra during the time they had spent together in Italy, he had more than once rejoined in her inability to leave her cabin after their ship had put to sea. This lengthy respite from her volatile presence, which had lasted for the entirety of their journey to Brighton, had almost totally cured him of his curious attraction for the imp—or so he'd thought, until the moment she had "fainted" into his arms.

He'd had every intention—every serious, well-thought-out intention—of depositing Allegra with her English relatives within an hour of docking and then retiring to the comfort (and personal safety) of his own estate just outside the seaside town for a well-deserved rest.

He knew now, however—intentions being what they were, and Allegra being who she was—that the "thought" never really had much chance of being transformed into "deed." Besides, if nothing else, he could console himself with the notion that he was just too curious to leave.

He should have realized Allegra was up to something the moment the little minx had opened her mouth downstair and spoken in Italian, rather than the English he and Candie had warned her would be a major asset in having her accepted by her mother's family.

But why should he have been taken off guard? Allegra's actions since entering the Baron's residence, Valerian thought now—considering the day he'd already had—should not have surprised him in the least. They should only have made him wonder if there existed any limit to Allegra's capacity for outrageous unpredictability.

He once more considered the fact that she'd had the audacity to emerge from her stateroom this morning looking as fresh and as lovely as only a naturally beautiful woman could appear. If she really had been ill for the length of the journey, as her hastily employed English chaperon had most earnestly informed him she was, the ravages of mal de mer certainly hadn't shown either in her face or on her still petitely voluptuous figure.

Her adorably vibrant face; her soft, yielding figure. Valerian shook his head, banishing such dangerous thoughts, and brought himself back to the matter at hand.

She had cried illness, yet she appeared even more healthy now than she had after a week of rest and indulgence in Naples. He had very much wanted to question her about this seeming inconsistency, but Allegra had kept him so busy answering her rapid-fire questions about Brighton as the carriage had rumbled through the streets that there hadn't been time.

No. He had to be honest with himself. He hadn't wanted to ask her how she'd managed to banish her supposed seasickness so quickly. What he had really wanted to know, still longed to know, was why she had felt the need to take such pains to elude his company while they had been aboard ship. Was he truly that repulsive to her?

If only they'd had more time to talk. If only her arrival hadn't thrown the entire household into such turmoil, thanks mostly, Valerian had decided, to both Baron Dugdale's refusal to expire as promised and his decision to keep his granddaughter's advent into the Dugdale household a secret.

He had been embarrassed for the lot of them, Valerian had, but he could not in all honesty say that he had expected less from the Kittredges or the Baron, none of whom were known for either their tact or their reticence.

Valerian pulled out his pocket watch and marked the time, suddenly once more anxious to be on his way. He should have quit the house the moment he had safely deposited Allegra on the bed. That's what any sane man— even a very curious sane man—would have done. Perhaps he could convince himself it had only been Allegra's swift delivery of a discreet yet painful warning pinch to his ribs when he had voiced to Agnes Kittredge his intention to depart that had kept him here so long.

Valerian took a deep breath and let it out in an aggrieved sigh.

No matter what the reason, no matter which excuse he chose to employ, here in the hallway he would remain, like some caged, pacing tiger, his mind a muddled mess, waiting for the performance to begin in the center ring of the circus—or Allegra's newly designated bedchamber, which, to Valerian's mind, was much the same thing.

The door behind him opened, putting an end to his agitated travels up and down the hall carpet.

"She's calling for you, Valerian," Agnes Kittredge said her tone grudging as she exited the bedchamber to stand in front of him in the hallway. Her displeasure at having to deliver such a message was clearly evident on her thin, pinched face.

"I somehow sensed that she would," Valerian returned, sighing.

"This Allegro person," Agnes persisted, "does she speak any English at all? How can she claim to be English and not know her mother tongue? Foreigners are such a contrary lot, refusing to learn our language. Mary has a lot to answer for, bless her departed soul, if this person truly is who you claim her to be."

Valerian, who felt he had already borne more than he should, and knew he was most probably going to have to bear a great deal more when he presently confronted Allegra, looked down at Agnes with minutely narrowed eyes.

"Are you suggesting I have foisted an impostor on your brother? I hesitate to point this out, but if you were a man, madam, I should be obliged to meet you on a field of honor for such an insult."

Agnes was quick to deny what she had so clearly implied, adding, "All the girl spouts is popish gibberish, save for your name, and might I say that I consider it very strange indeed that you have gifted her with the casual use of your Christian title. And, oh yes—did you know the chit wears no stays? To my way of thinking, that's just another indication of her sadly uncivilized nature."

Valerian passed over this outburst, not feeling quite up to a discussion of women's undergarments at the moment, and inclined his head toward the door. "I believe you said Signorina Crispino was asking for me? I presume there is a maidservant inside, to act as chaperon?"

Agnes rolled her watery eyes, giving up the fight, if only for the moment. "Betty is with her, yes. I will await you downstairs in the drawing room. Please tell me if the girl wishes us to send for a doctor.'' She brightened momentarily. ''Perhaps she needs to be bled. She does have a very high color, doesn't she?''

His hand already raised to knock on the door, Valerian shot Agnes an amused look that implied that he, a functioning member of the male species, found Allegra's ''high color'' to be more in the way of an attraction than a telltale sign of ill health. ''I'll be sure to ask your niece if she wishes her dearest aunt to call for the leeches, madam. Now,'' he added as the maid opened the door, ''if you'll excuse me, I believe I have kept the signorina waiting long enough.''

Entering the bedchamber, Valerian motioned for the maid to return to her seat in the far corner of the darkened room and approached the side of the high tester bed. ''You rang, signorina? I am entirely at your command, not that you would have it any other way. Perhaps you would like me to plump your pillows? Or maybe I might toddle down to the kitchens and get you a bite to eat, for you must be famished after your performance.''

Allegra peered across the room to see Betty's head already nodding as if the maid was almost asleep; then she smiled brightly up at Fitzhugh. ''I *was* wonderful, wasn't I, Valerian? I have always been very good at stage-acting, although I much prefer to be singing. My goodness—are they always like that? My new family, you understand. They buzz so angrily, like bees all after the same flower.''

''So the 'flower' in question decided a timely 'wilt' was in order, is that it? I'll say one thing for you, Allegra. You do know how to break up a conversation.''

Allegra dismissed his words with a small wave of her hand. ''Someone had to do something before they all came to blows—and it certainly didn't appear as if *you* were going to take control any time soon. Did you hear my *nonno,* Valerian? He still intends to make me his heir, even though he has not yet died as promised. Tell me, is a hundred thousand pounds a great deal of money? It is not so much in lire, although it is very generous, but my cousin Gideon seemed quite impressed with the figure.''

"Let me put it this way, my dear. For a hundred thousand pounds *I* might even be induced to offer for your hand—if I didn't already know you better, that is,'' Valerian told her, pulling up a chair so that he could rest his weary body. "But that's enough idle chatter. I would like an explanation of your almost totally unaccented speech, young lady. Your English seems to have improved a hundredfold since our journey began in Naples.''

Allegra pushed herself up against the backboard of the bed, her smile wide and unaffected. "Then you have noticed! How wonderful, for I have been working ever so hard to rid myself of any lingering accent. *Madre* had taught me very well, and it is only since her death that my English became lazy.''

That said, she changed the subject. "Did you know, Valerian, that dearest Signorina Shackleford was returning home to London after fifteen years as governess to the children of one of Napoleon's many cousins? No, of course you didn't. Men never ask important questions like that, do they? All they want in a chaperon is a respectable-looking female who eats little and keeps her mouth shut.''

"I would dearly love to learn just where and how you formed that opinion, Allegra,'' Valerian remarked, "but I will forgo the urge for the moment in order to learn more of your arrangement with Miss Shackleford. Max found her for us, as I recall, the same day he procured your passport.

I should have known she wasn't just someone he chanced
upon in the street. Please, go on.''

Allegra pulled a face at him, but answered anyway. ''Signorina Shackleford is a particular friend of *Uncail* Max's.
She had been trapped in Napoli thanks to the war, you
understand, and then could not bring herself to leave until
the last little Bonaparte was raised. She is a very strict task-
master, Signorina Shackleford is, but as I was very determined, and *Madre*'s lessons came back to me once I applied
my mind to the exercise, she was kind enough in the end
to kiss me good-bye and tell me I had developed into one
of her most apt pupils. Isn't that nice? Valerian—do you
think you could send down to the kitchens for some food?
Fainting seems to make me extremely hungry.''

''*Breathing* seems to make you extremely hungry,'' Valerian complained absently, his mind still struggling with
the information Allegra had already supplied. ''Tell me,
how did you apply yourself so assiduously to your studies
while suffering from such extreme seasickness? Miss
Shackleford told me you could barely lift your head from
your pillow and were not up to entertaining visitors in your
stateroom.''

Allegra's expressive hands came into play once more as
she pushed his words aside. ''Oh, that. It was only a tiny
fib, actually, for I really do not much like to sail, but I could
think of no reason to stay out of your way for the length
of the trip. You sometimes get a very strange look in your
eyes, Valerian, as if you would find the world a much more
pleasant place without me. I decided I would not much care
for being tossed overboard if I inadvertently did something
to upset you.

''But in the evenings, after the sun was well down, Signorina Shackleford and I took the air outside our cabin

for I should never have been able to spend the entire trip locked within four walls, even if the food was plentiful, though not especially tasty. Besides, I wished to surprise you with my progress, as a gift for being so nice as to rescue me from those terrible Timoteos, and for introducing me to dearest Tony and Candie and Murphy and *Uncail* Max—and most especially for holding me so close while I had my dearest Italy good-bye.

"Oh, dear. You've got that strange look in your eyes again, Valerian. Are you angry with me yet again? I should think you'd be pleased. I've improved my English, I've become a much better sailor, and I did not pester you with my presence aboard ship. Honestly, I begin to believe I shall never understand you. But that is of no matter now. Tell me—what do you think of my *madre*'s relatives. I really do value your opinion—above everything!"

"Oh, you do, do you? I see Miss Shackleford has also taught you it is always good to flatter a man if you wish him to be cooperative." Valerian leaned back in the chair, crossing one long leg over the other before giving her his answer. "Very well, I shall tell you what I think of the inhabitants of this little nest of toothless vipers."

He took a deep breath and began. "Gideon is a dedicated but woefully inept gamester who alternately loathes his mother and sponges from her. He would also sell her to any passing tinker if he could get a good price. To put it bluntly—if I were ever to be involved in a fight, I should not long for Gideon Kittredge to guard my back.

"Your aunt Agnes is an overweening, meddlesome blockhead who will fawn over you if necessary to keep her position in this household, but who privately curses your mother for not strangling you at birth. She is totally obsessed with her son, so that I should expect she'll be throwing him at your head before the day is out in order to gain back her longed-for inheritance through your marriage.

"Isobel is a painfully plain, spiteful child—not entirely without cause—who believes herself a great beauty. Whatever you do, Allegra, don't let her have the dressing of you.

"Lastly," he said, marveling at the way Allegra's eyes seemed to grow wider with his every word, "we come to your grandfather. Now here is an old man trying to use his granddaughter—please don't think he loves you, pet, for he loves only his cherry ripe, and perhaps the Prince Regent—to buy his way into Heaven. Of the lot of them, I think I like Duggy the least, for the rest of them are fairly up front with their vices. Now, tell me your impressions."

Allegra's lower lip jutted out as she prepared her answer. "I think," she said at last, sighing, "that *Cugino* Gideon is a very pretty boy, much like Bernardo, but with all the vices the silly shoemaker lacks. *Zia* Agnes I do not like at all, and not just because she calls me Allegro, as if I were a musical direction and not a person. *Cugina* Isobel is a sad little underfed creature, looking much like a bad morning while her brother resembles a good night. Did you take notice, Valerian—*Cugina* Isobel's teeth are so jumbled that it makes me think she did not grow them, but must have stood across the room and had someone toss them at her, so that she had to quickly catch them with her mouth as best she could."

Valerian suppressed a chuckle as Allegra opened her mouth and moved her head from side to side, as imitating Isobel's teeth-catching technique. "And your grandfather?"

Allegra's antics came to an abrupt stop. "He is my *madre*'s father, and he broke her heart. He did not even have the courtesy to write back to my *papà* when he sent him word that she had died. I should hate him—I always *have* hated him.'' She gave a wholly Italian shrug, shaking her head. ''But now—''

''But now?''

''I think he is sincere in wishing to make amends for his shabby treatment of my *madre*. He plans to use me to make his sister and her children uncomfortable, I am not so silly as to not understand that, but I saw something else in his eyes—just for a moment, you understand—when I performed my little faint. He was very worried. Yes, even if you cannot like him, Valerian, I think I should like to watch my *nonno* for a while longer before I pass the judgment.''

Valerian stared at her for a long moment, his estimation of her intelligence rising another notch. ''And is that why you played the uncomprehending ignoramus downstairs earlier? So that you could learn your relatives' true opinions and motives?''

''*Chi non fa, non falla,* Valerian,'' she answered, smiling. ''He who does nothing makes no mistakes. *Uncail* Max told me to first see what he called the lay of the land before I showed myself to them.''

''*Uncail* Max?'' Valerian remarked, realizing that he was feeling slightly abused by the thought that Allegra, whom he, at least intellectually, wished to move out of his life, had sought advice from someone other than himself. ''My, that little Irishman does get around, doesn't he? What else did he tell you?''

''He also reminded me of another Italian warning. *Non Cercate i peli nell'uovo.* I should not go looking for hairs inside an egg. In other words—''

''In other words,'' Valerian interrupted, rising, ''you should not go looking for trouble. Hence the propitious swoon. All right, Allegra, I believe I understand everything now, an admittance that frightens me more than you know.

I think enough time has passed for you to have recovered your senses. Would you like to rejoin the family? It is, after all, nearing the dinner hour.''

At his last words Allegra sat forward quickly and swung her feet over the side of the bed, holding out a hand so that Valerian could help her descend from the high mattress to the floor. "I can only hope we will be having some of this famous roast beef Signorina Shackleford has told me about. It sounds delicious, although she says garlic is not a part of the dish. I can't imagine such uninspired cooking, but Signorina Shackleford says your English puddings are very nice. My *madre* never learned how to cook as a girl, so I have never eaten this bland-English before. You will stay to dinner, won't you, Valerian? I am ashamed to admit it, but my relatives frighten me, and I should be glad of your company for a while longer.''

At the touch of her small hand, Valerian's best intentions took to their heels yet again and he found himself agreeing to her proposal. "But do not expect me to become your permanent champion, Allegra,'' he warned in self-defense. "I have been away from my estate for over two years, and must get on about my business as soon as possible.''

Allegra gave a dismissive toss of her head. "If you have left it this long, Valerian, I should think one of two things has happened. Either your estate has been raped by your manager and fallen into rack and ruin, or it has prospered in your absence, which would mean you are not needed there at all. No matter which it is, I don't see that one little dinner can make much difference.''

Opening the door to the hallway, Valerian acknowledged her maddeningly logical comment with a slight nod of his head, adding, "Polite Englishwomen—polite women everywhere—do not employ the use of the word 'rape.' Although

I know what you meant, some words, Allegra, do suffer in translation. Kindly remember that in future, please.''

"I will remember, Valerian," she said meekly, although her sapphire eyes twinkled.

He pulled her unresisting arm through his and they began the descent to the first floor of the town house. "Now quickly, Allegra, before we rejoin the family—to what great miracle do we credit our sudden discovery of your mastery of the English language?''

"AND SO, DEAREST *NONNO,* you see it was all very silly of me," Allegra said from her perch on the footstool at Baron Dugdale's feet, "but my extreme excitement at finally meeting my beloved mother's family caused all of my carefully learned English to totally desert me. *Pouf!* Why, if I hadn't fainted, I don't know what would have happened.''

"I can only suppose, cousin, that you would have heard my dear, distraught mother call you vile names a dozen times rather than the mere half dozen you did hear," Gideon put in smoothly from his position across the room, leaning negligently against the marble mantelpiece.

"Gideon, you're such a cold, heartless wretch," Isobel inserted from her seat on the settee. "Really, Mama, I don't know why you can't see straight through him.''

"All I see," Agnes returned forcefully, staring directly at the back of Allegra's head, "is that this young woman, this Allegro, has descended on our peaceful home, and within the space of a single afternoon all the rest of its inhabitants are at each other's throats, saying vile, hurtful things to each other, even threatening each other with the loss of all the things in life that mean the most to them.''

"Allegra—with an A at each end," Allegra correctly sweetly, turning to face her aunt. "Forgive me for bringing it to your attention, *Zia* Agnes, but I know you shouldn't like to address me incorrectly.''

"'*Zia* Agnes' don't want to address you at all,'' Gideon put in from his new position behind the settee. He had the most unnerving habit of moving about without making a sound, almost, Allegra thought, like a snake sliding through deep grass. "You've given her—indeed, all of us—quite a turn, you know. We always thought we was Uncle's heirs.''

"There must be half a score of sharpers holding your vowels that will be likewise displeased to hear of Allegra's existence, once the word gets out,'' Lord Dugdale put in, chuckling into his cravat. "For your sake, nevvie, and the sake of your still intact knees, I hope you haven't been playing too deep on your expectations.''

"Denny, please!'' Agnes pleaded, her hands flying to her scrawny breast.

Lord Dugdale leaned down to address his granddaughter. "The boy was counting heavily on me sticking my spoon in the wall, you know, and then gleefully gambling away my life's savings within a fortnight. Queered him good, I did, by living, and I shouldn't be surprised to wake up dead one morning just so's he can make good on his markers.''

He looked up at Valerian. "You'll be my witness, boy. If I come to an untimely end before I can have my will changed over to benefit this sweet girl here, can I count on you to take Gideon's name to the nearest magistrate?''

Agnes gasped and quickly began fanning herself with a small lace handkerchief. "I don't think I can bear much more of this. Truly I don't.''

Allegra reached out to place a hand on the Baron's knee. "There is no need to trouble Valerian, *Nonno,*'' she said, her voice deceptively gentle. "If you should die before your time, I would make the *vendetta* and go directly to *Cugino*

Gideon myself and slice out his ungrateful heart with a kitchen knife. We Italians are a bloodthirsty lot when it comes to family, you know.''

Agnes gave a single, ladylike shriek. "Did you hear that! We shan't any of us be safe in our beds! Denny, you must do something at once—or else I shall be forced to quit this roof before nightfall.''

The Baron looked askance at his sister, who was clinging to her rigidly resisting daughter as if to protect her from the heathen in the midst. "If only I could believe that, Agnes, I should rise from this chair this very moment and do a lively jig. But you are as firmly entrenched here as this damnable gout is in my big toe. Now if the lot of you would please be quiet, I wish to speak further with my granddaughter.''

"Speak with your granddaughter, then, you heartless creature," Agnes retorted, struggling to rise, "but don't expect me to sit here and listen!''

"Mama, reconsider, please," Isobel begged, tugging at her mother's shawl as the older woman made to rise. "You cannot be so rude to our new-found cousin"—she looked up at Valerian, her heart in her eyes—"or to our guest.''

"Oh, Mama, do sit down," Gideon ordered in disgusted tones. "You know you wouldn't miss a word of what Uncle Denny has to say—no matter how much he insults you.''

"*Basta!*" Allegra interrupted just as Valerian was beginning to feel that Waterloo, when compared with the scene in the Dugdale drawing room, could only be described as a slight skirmish. "Enough! I wish for *everyone* to sit down—now—for *I* have something to say!''

Valerian's lips twitched appreciatively as all three Kittredges subsided into chairs, their attention directed to Allegra as she fussed momentarily with her skirts, prolonging the newly fallen silence until she felt her audience was ready to hear her speak. She was a minx all right, he knew, but he couldn't help but feel proud of her at this moment.

"Now, *Nonno, Zia* Agnes, Isobel—and you too, Gideon," she began at last, looking piercingly from one to the other as she spoke, "I would have to be blind and deaf not to feel the strain my appearance has caused to come to this family, and I have decided it is time we cleaned the air."

"Cleared the air, imp," Valerian corrected, his eyes flashing her a warning as he deliberately tried to keep her from saying anything in haste that she might repent later.

"Cleared the air, yes. Thank you, Valerian," she said tightly before turning back to her relatives. "Now, where was I? First of all, I think you should know more about me, as I am a stranger to you. For one, my disposition is not always so calm—"

"I can vouch for that," Valerian slid in neatly, propping himself against the side of Lord Dugdale's high wing chair, his arms crossed against his chest.

Allegra shot him a look guaranteed to freeze lava if it should ever again dare to descend from Vesuvius. "I am also, when sufficiently pushed, malicious enough to strike back twofold for any injury I sustain."

"I can vouch for that as well," Valerian agreed happily as Allegra continued to glare at him. "But if it's any consolation to you, Agnes, she doesn't spit anymore."

"Don't pay him any attention, *Nonno,*" Allegra cautioned her grandfather. And then she smiled as inspiration struck. "You see, Valerian is just angry because I refuse to love him."

"I'm what?" Valerian, who had thought he was at last prepared for anything Allegra might say or do—and who had actually believed himself to be in charity with her only

a second earlier—belatedly closed his mouth and fought the urge to strangle the little vixen on the spot.

"Don't bother to deny it, Valerian." Allegra's lips twitched at his outburst and she lowered her gaze—not seeing the strange, cold look that had crept into Isobel's watery hazel eyes.

Gideon, however, noticed his sister's involuntary flinch, and he did not bother to hide his glee. "How titillating, dear Cousin Allegra," he crooned, his mouth just beside Isobel's ear as he leaned over the settee. "Do go on."

Allegra shot Gideon a withering look, then turned back to her grandfather. "It is true. Valerian is deeply in love with me—as are so many men; a circumstance I find very troubling to my tender heart. But, alas, I cannot love Valerian, or any man. I am, you see, completely dedicated to my art."

"You draw pictures?" Lord Dugdale questioned blankly as Isobel—unnoticed again by any save her brother, who made a habit of storing up miscellaneous information he could possibly put to some malicious use at a later date—raised a hand to her mouth and bit down hard on her knuckle. "What do you draw, child? Pictures of castles and the like? I guess that's all right. Prinny favors faces, though, and horses. Can you draw horses?"

"I do not draw, *Nonno*," Allegra answered patiently, still purposely avoiding Valerian's sure-to-be-condemning eyes. He might have warned her against it, but she had to tell the truth. "I sing. Like my *papà* before me, I am a great singer. People pay money to hear me sing. I tell you this, not because I am proud, but because I wish you to know that I do not need your conscience money. If you were to disown me today as you disowned my *madre* twenty years ago, I should not starve. Orphan that I am, I can make my own way."

Gideon came around the settee to sit down beside his mother. "Well, good. She's a resourceful puss, unlike my dear sister, who can only embroider slippers—and only ones with the same name on them at that. It's settled, then. Cousin Allegra is to set herself up as the town warbler. But don't think we're completely without compassion, dearest cousin. You may still stay for dinner."

"Gideon," Isobel said quietly.

"Yes, sister mine? Is there something you require?" the young man responded, grinning widely in appreciation of his own humor.

"Yes, there is. I'd like your silence, Gideon," Isobel suggested succinctly, her thin, sallow face so pinched it reminded Allegra mightily of a Tuscany olive left too long in the sun.

At this point, and high time it was for the man to make a move, Baron Dugdale took the conversational bit firmly beneath his teeth. "Odds fish, but she's got all her mother's fire! Mary was my daughter to the bone—and a rare handful, which should have told me that once she'd made up her mind to marry that *I*-talian bloke, I shouldn't have tried to stop her. Well, the apples don't fall that far from the tree, like they say, and what you get with the mother you're just as likely to see in the daughter. I'm going to enjoy you, Allegra, even though we probably will fight like cats in a sack most of the time."

"Thank you, *Nonno*," Allegra said, feeling the threat of tears behind her eyes for the first time since she had left Naples. "But please don't think I wish more than a roof over my head. I can make my own way without having you push *Zia* Agnes and her children out into the gutter."

"If that's where they belong, then that's where they'll land," the Baron answered shortly, glaring at his sister. "But if they behave themselves—" He allowed this last sentence to dangle, waiting for Agnes to pick up his hint.

He didn't have long to wait. "I have never been known to be less than civil, Denny," she said, lifting her pointy chin. "If you wish me to take Mary's child under my wing, I shall be happy to do so. What is it you want me to do? Educate her in the ways of polite society? Teach her the intricacies of acceptable behaviour and prudent speech? Introduce her to the finer points of modest dress—to *stays?*"

"Stays?" Lord Dugdale ejaculated, his gaze resting on Allegra's remarkably fine figure. "What would she be wanting to truss herself up like a Christmas goose for, I ask you? If it's her chest that's bothering you, Aggie, I think you're fair and far out there. She has a lovely chest—probably comes from all those deep breaths singers take, don't you think, Valerian? Valerian? Now where the devil did the fellow go?"

They all looked to where Valerian had been standing just a few moments earlier, but he wasn't there. Without his dinner, without bidding any of them farewell, he had gone.

"How rude!" Agnes exclaimed, aghast.

"Oh, dear. Do you think Cousin Allegra's silly remarks upset him?" Isobel questioned, her voice hopeful.

"He was aboard ship a long time. Probably decided he needs a woman," Gideon offered helpfully, if only to watch his sister's thin cheeks go pale.

"A woman, is it, nevvie?" the Baron snorted. "And what would you be knowing of women—you who never got close to any save the Queen of Hearts?"

As the Kittredges and her grandfather launched themselves into yet another argument, Allegra sat on the footstool, staring into the middle distance, a decidedly pleased smile on her face.

For Allegra knew where Valerian had gone. He had gone to ground, in order to get away from her. But he would be back. Oh, yes. One way or the other, he would be back.

CHAPTER FIVE

It took slightly less than three days for Allegra, always a highly emotional girl, to fall totally in love with Brighton. The bracing sea air that made her feel so alive, the crash of the surf, the winding streets and lovely narrow houses— all this and more Allegra enjoyed during her lengthy daily walks along the Steine with a grumbling Betty in tow, complaining that she would doubtless have to spend the remainder of her wretched life brushing crusted sea salt out of her new mistress's hair.

But more than anything else, Allegra had fallen under the enchantment of the Prince Regent's Marine Pavilion. It reminded her of a snow-white castle out of some marvelous fairy tale, a glorious confection of swirling onion-shaped domes, pinnacles, minarets, and intricate lacelike embattlements that seemed too delicate, too ethereally beautiful to be real.

But even more than the sea air or the neat houses or even the fantasylike Pavilion, Allegra fell in love with the Prince Regent. She had not seen him, of course, for he was in seclusion, only a few months having passed since the tragic childbed deaths of his daughter, the Princess Charlotte of Wales, and his grandson, and no one really saw him.

Allegra loved him because he was suffering, and her emotional Italian heart felt a high degree of *simpatia* for a man in mourning. But she felt even more in charity with him because Prinny, no matter what his faults, loved music. He loved music so much that, even in his grief, he allowed his most excellent German musicians to play outside on the Pavilion grounds in order to entertain the citizens. Allegra had been immediately enthralled to hear the great works of composers such as Bach, Haydn, and Beethoven wafting through the windblown trees, and when the band broke into a familiar Italian *sinfonia,* she ached with the desire to hum along.

But if she had learned nothing else in her first days in Brighton, Allegra had learned it was not wise to call too much attention to herself. Brighton might be lovely, but the people she met along the Steine were very strange indeed. They were displaced Londoners all, Betty had told her, hangers-on of the Prince Regent who would follow the great man to the ends of the earth, simply for an invitation to the Pavilion.

Mostly older, the women were a sad, over-stuffed collection of molting peahens, while the gentlemen seemed to vary in age but no inclination, eyeing Allegra as a hungry wolf would eye a spring lamb. The younger women who passed by, some of them with faces painted as if for the stage, were, according to Betty, "milliners." Allegra, although not familiar with English customs, had no difficulty in understanding that these ladies' closest proximity to bonnets came about only when they were wearing them.

Betty, who had lived in Brighton all her life, became a veritable fountain of information for Allegra, who could not seem to locate the bottom of her deep barrel of questions about the town in which her mother had grown up.

"She must have loved my *papà* very much, to leave such a wonderful place," Allegra said to Betty as they stood outside the Pavilion, watching as a weak sun glinted off the main onion dome and danced against the stained-glass windows.

Betty was quick to correct her. In 1796, the year Mary Catherine Dugdale had slipped down a rope made of knotted bed sheets and into the arms of her Italian lover, the Marine Pavilion had been little more than a discreetly amended farmhouse, a modest residence the Prince shared with Mrs. Maria Fitzherbert, "the lady he should have stuck with, rather than that terrible Lady Jersey or the naughty Princess Caroline, and most especially not any of those fat old hens that roost with him now."

Yes, according to Betty things were a lot different in 1796, even if the Prince's rowdy bachelor friends sometimes pulled silly pranks on the townspeople and kept everyone up half the night with their drinking and rowdy ways.

"It was that bad when that Lady Jersey got her hooks into him, missy," Betty told Allegra as they sat together in the latter's bedchamber near midnight of her fourth evening in England, the two of them rapidly having gone past the usual mistress-maid association. "It was Lady Jersey what stole the Prince from Mrs. Fitzherbert and then talked him into marrying that German person, who was mother to Princess Charlotte, Lord rest her dear soul. And where was her mother when poor Princess Charlotte breathed her last? Nowhere to be found, that's where!"

"Yes, Betty," Allegra responded, handing the maid a sugarplum. "I have already heard your opinion of Princess Caroline and her travels with her Italian Chamberlain. What I want to hear about is Brighton itself."

"We had some hard times after your mother left. I blame it all on that terrible Lady Jersey, who started the fuss in the first place. You know, the people of Brighton so loved

Mrs. Fitzherbert, and so disliked Lady Jersey, that when Lady Jersey's coach passed through the streets the citizens hissed at her and called her names. The Prince didn't much care for that, and the year your mother left he didn't even come to Brighton, but went to Bognor with his terrible lady. It was as if the whole world had forgotten us. Shops closed. People moved away. Your grandfather, the Baron, was so beside himself he nearly sold this house and moved to London. We all suffered mightily in the next four years, until he made it up with Mrs. Fitzherbert and came back to Brighton.''

"And is Signora Fitzherbert still here with the Prince?" Allegra asked, her mouth full of sugarplums as she sat cross-legged on the bed. "And if she is, who are all the fat ladies you mentioned?"

Betty screwed up her plain-as-pudding, face. "Mrs. Fitzherbert is still here, but she finally had enough of the Prince's goings-on and refuses to see him." Betty leaned forward in her chair to impart quietly, "I hear he still wears a likeness of her in a locket around his neck, the silly old fool." She sat back once more, folding her arms. "But no, the Prince spends his time now with fat old women like that Lady Hertford and that other one before her, Lady Conyngham. He does not want a wife now, missy; he longs for a mother who will tell him that he is a good boy."

Allegra sniffed a time or two and wiped at a tear with the back of one hand. "He sounds so sad, Betty, and so alone. It must be terrible to be a prince forever when you long to be King. Oh, I know he must be a terrible man, but he loves beauty so much, in both form and music, that I cannot believe you English understand him. In Italy we have many great men—lovers of art and music and literature—who are not always very nice people. Why, just think of the Medici! That may be the price of genius, don't you think?''

Betty sniffed as well, but not to stifle the threat of tears. ''My sister Clara once worked as housemaid at the Pavilion, missy. Clara told me she spent the whole of the time with her back to the wall so as not to be pinched by this genius of yours. No, missy,'' she ended firmly, ''he should have stayed with Mrs. Fitzherbert. She knew how to keep him in line. But you'll see it all for yourself soon enough, I wager. The Baron is one of the Prince's closest chums here in Brighton, and the whole lot of you will probably be going over there for dinner any time now.''

This brought Allegra's attention away from the Prince and onto one of her favorite subjects: food. Valerian had already told her a little about the enormous feasts that lasted for hour upon hour, and she looked forward to an evening in the great Pavilion's Banqueting Room.

''One hundred and sixteen separate dishes for a single banquet, Betty!'' she exclaimed, rubbing her flat belly. ''All eaten beneath a huge chandelier suspended from the claws of a ferocious dragon clinging to a plantain tree on the ceiling! Oh, yes, *Nonno* has already told me a great deal about this magnificent Banqueting Room. It all sounds so grand that I cannot believe the Prince Regent is English. There must be a secret Florentine lurking about somewhere in his family tree, to have him love beauty and food so much.''

''If there is, I wouldn't mention it to your grandfather,'' the maid advised, reaching for one last sugarplum. ''From what I've heard below-stairs, even though he's that tickled to have you here with him, he still isn't so happy with anything *I*-talian.''

Allegra popped the last sugarplum into her mouth, then

leaned forward, squinting at the maid. "What have you heard, Betty? The terrible Kittredges don't worry me, but I should not like to think my *nonno* is still harboring a grudge against my poor *papà*."

Betty's dark eyes slid away from Allegra's searching gaze. "Nothing, missy, I heard nothing. At least nothing important. Just something about how he missed you and your mother all those years you were traipsing all over that heathen country like a band of gypsies, following your da from one place to next just so's he could sing. That's all. Yes, I'm sure now that was the whole of it. My, it's late, missy. Would you like for me to turn down your bed?"

"Betty?" Allegra felt ill suddenly, which might have been due to the niggling feeling that something she wasn't going to like was about to happen. It also could have been due to the fact that, between them, they had succeeded in eating an entire candy dish full of sugarplums, but Allegra didn't think so.

"Yes, missy?" Betty was looking decidedly pale as she fidgeted in her chair.

"My *nonno* sent a note to me this evening, saying he wishes for me to meet with him in his study after luncheon tomorrow. I thought we were going to talk about *Madre* again, as we have done every day since I arrived. We aren't going to be talking about her tomorrow, are we?"

Betty rose and made a great business out of whisking bits of sugar from the satin bedspread. "Please, missy, don't ask me to say more, because I really don't know. The Baron had his solicitor here this afternoon and Bates, one of the footmen, heard the master cursing and yelling about *I*-talians. So I don't really know why he wants to see you or what the two of you will be talking about." She straightened up and looked her new mistress, her new friend straight in the eye. "I only feel sure you probably aren't going to like it. I'm that sorry, missy. Truly I am."

THE NEXT MORNING dawned gray and misty, with a fog rolling in from the ocean. The weather matched Allegra's mood, for she had spent a restless night wondering about her grandfather's summons, only to fall into a fitful sleep near dawn that included a strange dream in which Valerian Fitzhugh figured prominently.

They had been running through the streets of Brighton, she and Valerian, with some unknown assailant hard on their heels. It was very dark, so that no matter how often Allegra looked behind her, it was impossible to learn the identity of their pursuer. Her hand clasped tightly in Valerian's, all she could do was run, and keep on running, even though she was singing an aria at the top of her lungs at the same time.

Then the scene had changed, and Allegra had seen herself standing at the end of a long aisle, her arm through that of her smiling grandfather as he led her toward a candlelit altar. How lovely! She was to be a bride! As she walked along she strained to make out the identity of her groom, but just as she thought she was close enough to discern his features, a great wind roared through the church, blowing out all the candles and plunging the interior into complete darkness.

"Sing, Allegra!" a voice cried to her from the altar. "Sing, and I shall find you."

Allegra, her grandfather mysteriously gone from her side, opened her mouth to sing, but nothing happened. She had no voice, no way to signal to her groom.

"Throw coins, Allegra!" a second voice commanded

from the altar. "Throw coins, and by their lovely jingle I shall find you."

Allegra reached into her pockets to find some coins, but all she found there were sugarplums. Dozens and dozens of sugarplums. Desperate, she flung them in the general direction of the altar.

"I'll tap, Allegra!" called a third voice, this time in Italian. "I'll tap my little hammer so that you can find me. First I'll tap on the head of your *maestro,* and then I shall tap on the head of this silly gamester. Tap, tap, tap, until I find you, *mi amore.*"

"Bernardo!" Allegra had awakened then, drenched in perspiration, the shoemaker's name bursting from her lips before she could clap a hand over her mouth. She rested her throbbing head in her hands. "What a terrible nightmare," she said, moaning as she slid from the bed to get a drink of water from the pitcher that stood on a table at the far side of the bedchamber.

After a leisurely breakfast in bed, as Betty helped her to bathe and dress, Allegra was still troubled by the dream. The first part of it was easily explained, probably nothing more than a delayed reaction to her months of flight round Italy to avoid Bernardo and her rescue by Valerian.

Also easily explained was the groom who wished her to throw money. He could be none other than Gideon. As she had already recognized Bernardo by both his voice and the words "little hammer," she was puzzled only about the identity of the groom who commanded her to sing.

She would have very much liked to believe that it had been Valerian, but he had time and again warned her against singing—he, who had never so much as heard her hum. "Which probably explains why I couldn't sing for him—if it was him," she said aloud as Betty stood behind her, buttoning the last of the buttons on the buttercup-yellow muslin morning gown.

"Pardon, missy?" Betty asked, turning Allegra about to inspect the evenness of the hem. "Who would you be singing to at this hour of the morning?"

"Who indeed?" Allegra answered without answering, moving past Betty to check her appearance in the mirror above the japanned dresser. The reflection that met her eyes pleased her. Betty, bless her, had a wonderful way with long hair, so that Allegra's ebony tresses had been tamed without losing their vibrant life. The yellow muslin was demurely cut, with two-inch-wide white lace ruching about the neckline that set off her pale skin to advantage.

She looked, even to her own eyes, extremely English—except perhaps for the dancing life in her lively sapphire eyes.

"Do I look presentable, Betty? Do I look like the good granddaughter?" she asked, twirling about, holding her skirt away from her ankles.

"You look beautiful, missy," Betty replied, although she bit at her lower lip as if there was something about Allegra's appearance that bothered her. "You forgot all about what I told you last night, didn't you, missy?"

Allegra blinked three times, then smiled. "Forgot about what, Betty? Did you tell me something upsetting last night?"

Betty exhaled on a deep sigh. "Thank you, missy. For a minute there you had a look in your eyes that—well, never mind me. I'm just getting old, I suppose. I like my place in this household, even if Mrs. Kittredge can be as cheap as meat on a chicken neck. That is—I mean, I wouldn't want to leave you, missy. Not for worlds."

"It's all right, Betty. There is nothing my *nonno* can do

to upset me. I was alone and lost in Italy until he sent for me, and I am not so stupid as to refuse to be grateful. Besides, I am too happy in this beautiful place not to be in charity with the world. I promise I shall be on my very best behavior.''

Allegra skipped across the room to pat the maid's round cheek, then dashed out the door, eager for luncheon to be over and her meeting with the Baron to begin. She deliberately pushed any lingering thoughts of the past night's strange dream from her mind.

For three days her grandfather had pretty much left her to her own devices. For three days the Kittredges had been icily polite to her. But it would appear her lovely, carefree time of adjustment was about to come to an end.

Allegra passed another mirror in the upstairs hallway and glanced into it, wondering if Valerian Fitzhugh would approve of her ''English'' appearance. Then she shook her head back and squared her shoulders, deliberately pushing thoughts of Valerian—who still insisted upon hiding himself on his estate somewhere just outside a village called Pyecombe—to the back of her mind.

She had made a promise to Betty, a solemn promise between friends she sincerely believed she could keep, but she could not entirely fight off the feeling that she was going to need all of her wits about her for the next few hours.

''YOU ARE IMPERTINENT!''

''*No!*'' Allegra rounded on her grandfather—her black-as-night curls swinging about her shoulders, her eyes flashing blue fire, her cheeks flushed with fury—looking every inch the hot-blooded, emotional Italian. ''You are wrong! I am Allegra Crispino. *You, Nonno,* are impertinent!'' She then launched herself into a stream of Italian that, had he been able to understand it, would have had her grandfather's sparse halo of hair standing on end.

"Knock, knock. A thousand apologies for what I can only see as my untimely interruption. I have arrived at a bad time, haven't I? Haven't you fed her yet? She growls more on an empty stomach, you know. My goodness, but I think my ears are burning. Duggy—I'm surprised all the paint hasn't blistered right off these walls. What's going on in here that our little Italian fishwife has come to the conclusion that your parents neglected to exchange marriage vows?"

Allegra and the Baron turned as one to see Valerian Fitzhugh lounging against the doorjamb, one leg crossed over the other at the ankle.

"Valerian!" Allegra exclaimed, running to his side to drag him willy-nilly into the room. "It has been so long. I thought we might only see you every death of a pope."

"Fitzhugh, thank God!" Baron Dugdale bellowed from his seat, his bandaged foot propped on a footstool in front of him. "Odds fish, but I'm glad you're here. You speak her lingo. Maybe you can talk some sense into the gel."

Valerian disengaged himself from Allegra's grasp, not without some difficulty, and sat himself down in the leather chair facing the Baron's. "Do I have to, Duggy? I have been enjoying my homecoming, believing you and Allegra to be agreeably settled. It would pain me unbearably if you were to undeceive me now by telling me that something is amiss."

Allegra dropped to her knees in front of him, her yellow muslin skirt billowing out to make her look as if she were sitting in a soft puddle of spring sunshine, and put her hands on his knees. "Valerian, you are this moment to stop amus-

ing yourself at my expense!'' she commanded tightly, her
grammar slipping a notch in her agitation. "This is a very
serious thing we have to discuss."

Valerian very deliberately wiped the smile from his face.
"Oh, we are to be serious, Allegra? What terrible thing has
your grandfather done—cut back on your rations?"

"Food! Always it is food with you. Can't you think of
anything else? And don't be stupid, Valerian. *Nonno* would
never starve me. He would only *kill* me! He would only
tear my heart into little pieces!" She turned her head to
shoot a quick, angry look at her grandfather, then continued.
"He has ordered me to call myself Crispin. Allegra *Crispin!*
He wishes for me to forget I am Italian, to forget my
papà!"

Valerian looked down at Allegra, saw the tears standing
brightly in her deep blue, soul-wrenching eyes, and then
raised his head to confront the Baron. "Is this true,
Duggy?"

"Odds bobs, of course it's true!" the man exclaimed
hotly. "Had my solicitor in here yesterday, you know, to
change my will, but I couldn't do it. It stuck in my craw
to put the name Crispino in it. What kind of a name is
that—Crispino? Damned *I*-talian nonsense, throwing vowels around like pebbles in a brook. My granddaughter is
English. Now, *Crispin*—that's a good English name. Nothing to be ashamed of in a Crispin, eh?"

Valerian felt the muscles in his shoulders tightening as
he longed to jump up and push his fist squarely into Dennis
Dugdale's ignorant face. Instead, he pinned a small smile
on his features. "Being just a bit of a prig, aren't you,
Duggy? I mean, it is only one letter."

"Only one letter? Only one letter! *Stupido!*" Allegra
hopped to her feet, her bosom heaving in her agitation as

she began to pace. "It is not only a letter! I am my *papà*'s daughter as well as my *madre*'s. He would ask me to give up my *papà*, Valerian, as if that sainted man never existed. No! I will not have it. *Viaggio come un baule*. I have traveled like a trunk, taken a trip from Italy to England, and gained nothing from the experience! I do not call having my heart stepped upon a gain. No! I have made up my mind, and you cannot change it. I am very sorry for it, for I have come to like this place, and I will miss Betty, to whom I have broken my solemn promise, but I must return to Italy."

"Tell her she can't do that, Valerian," the Baron piped up, trying to move his unwieldly bulk about in the chair so that he could see Allegra, who had moved to the window. "Tell her she has to stay with me. A plum, Valerian—I'm giving her a plum. Doesn't the child understand that?"

"*Basta!*" Valerian watched as Allegra reversed her direction, to run back to her grandfather. Leaning down so that her hands rested on the armrests on either side of him, she spoke directly into his face. "A plum is money, *Nonno*. Only money. And you are giving it to me only in order to spite your sister and her children. I had thought it might be different—hoped it might be different—but it is not. You are a horrible, hateful old man, just like Valerian said, and I hope that when you do meet Saint Peter, he orders you thrown into the deepest, darkest pit in all of Hades."

The Baron cringed, as if trying to burrow into the back of the chair, and swallowed hard. "Now, Allegra," he began in a small voice, "you must remember. I am not a well man. I could die at any time. Did—did Fitzhugh really say that?"

"Never mind what he said!" Still hovering over him, her eyes shooting sparks of blue fire, she said, slowly and distinctly, "In Italy we have a saying. *Quando nascono sono tutti belli, quando si maritano, tutti buoni e quando muoiono, tutti santi*. What I have said, *Nonno*, is that people, when they are born, all are beautiful; when they marry, they are all good; and when they die, they are all saints."

"That—that's a very nice saying, Allegra," the Baron squeaked, still trying to burrow into the back of the chair. "Fitzhugh? You still there?" he called softly, as if for help.

"No, *Nonno*, it is not *nice*. Not all babies are beautiful, nor are all brides good. Most especially, death does not turn a sinner into a saint. We would all like to believe it to be so, but it is not true. You, *Nonno*, have made yourself a bid for sainthood, but you have failed. You are a terrible, nasty, self-serving old sinner. Dying won't change that, or make the world remember you differently.

"Now I know why my *madre* could leave this beautiful Brighton. And now I know why she sometimes cried at night. Not for you, *Nonno*—it could never have been for you. She cried for Brighton. For her beloved England. I have enough English blood in my veins to love this place myself. But you ask too much, *Nonno*, and you do not ask it for the right reasons. *Now* do you understand?"

Valerian, who had just moments earlier believed Allegra might completely lose control of her emotions and begin throwing things, settled back in his own chair and clapped his hands together softly. "I may live to be proud of you yet, imp," he said as Allegra whirled about to face him.

She was suddenly all smiles as she turned her head in Valerian's direction. "Then you agree with me, Valerian?"

He rose to stand looking down at her. "Do I agree that you should be allowed to return to Italy? No, I cannot agree with that, for it is a very long swim and I doubt you can afford to pay for your passage. Do I agree that you should be allowed to keep the surname given to you by your father? Yes, I most certainly do. Lastly, do I agree that your grandfather, your *nonno,* is a sure candidate for an eternity of hellfire and brimstone? Oh, yes, imp, I most assuredly do agree. I might even go so far as to say I endorse it.''

"You too, Fitzhugh?" The Baron's bottom lip jutted out and he allowed his chin—both his chins—to fall onto his egg-stained cravat. "Odds fish, I never thought one little letter could cause such a fuss. I am a fool, Allegra. A stupid, stubborn old fool. Very well, then. You may keep your name—and my fortune. Only please, granddaughter—don't leave me. You're the only member of my Mary that I have left.''

The old man's self-pitying tone was Allegra's undoing. Abandoning her threatening stance, she threw herself at the Baron's neck, giving him a resounding kiss on the cheek. "Ah, *Nonno,* I am such a terrible person myself. Truly, I did not mean it when I said you had the scruples of a hungry shark. Nor do I really wish for your big toe to blow up like a pig bladder and burst, or for a wart the size of a melon to grow on the very tip of your nose, or for—''

"I think the Baron accepts your apology, imp,'' Valerian interrupted. "You don't have to give him a recital of all the nastiness you were wishing on him when I arrived.''

Allegra stepped back from the chair, smoothed her hair, and folded her hands together in front of her, somehow managing to look as innocent as a novitiate about to take the veil. "You're right, of course, Valerian, although I know my behavior was most shameful.'' She looked up, her sapphire eyes twinkling so that he could see a flash of her usual fire peeping out at him. "But I was much provoked, wasn't I, Valerian?''

"Yes, imp. You were much provoked,'' Valerian agreed

as Allegra once more took up what seemed to be her usual position, perched on the edge of the Baron's footstool. He looked piercingly at the older man. "Now tell us, Duggy, do you have any more little surprises in store for your granddaughter, or can I leave now, secure in the knowledge that Allegra won't be wishing for a very large, very heavy brick house to fall on your head any time soon? Italian curses can be the very devil, you know."

The Baron made a great business out of picking a stray piece of breakfast ham from the folds of his cravat. "Well, boy, now that you mention it—there is one other thing. That's why I sent for you in the first place. You will help me, just to show that the gel here was wrong and you don't really think I'm a bad man?"

Allegra smiled in delight, for anything that would keep Valerian—who had championed her plea to retain her identity—nearby could not possibly serve to upset her.

The Baron coughed once, and continued. "It's Aggie, Valerian. She's cutting up stiff about taking Allegra here to her dressmaker and all those other places women go to spend my money. Seems to think the girl's figure is an embarrassment, or some such drivel. Isobel offered to escort her cousin, but I'm not so daft as to let that one have the dressing of her."

Valerian conjured up a mind picture of the underfed, overdressed Isobel of the crooked teeth. "Really," he said, desperately trying not to pay attention to the comical face Allegra was making at that moment.

"Think about it, Valerian. M'niece considers herself a beauty, you know, when even an old man like me can see she's as scrawny as a wind-burned dead tree, so it's sure as check she thinks Allegra here is some freak of nature. Why, I heard her just yesterday, telling Aggie that what this girl here needs is to have her hair all cut off and gowns that button to her chin."

Valerian looked down at Allegra, seeing the creamy expanse of skin that peeped out above the neckline of her gown and feeling a sharp shaft of envy at the familiarity with which her heavy black curls caressed her gently sloping shoulders. "Madness," he said softly.

"Madness, indeed! And I won't have it, you understand!" he ended, slapping his knee for emphasis, which set up a terrible throbbing in his badly swollen toe. "Damme, but that hurts like the very devil! Valerian—you have to do something. We're to go to the Pavilion Thursday night!"

Valerian reluctantly tore his attention away from Allegra's bodice, which rose and fell ever so slightly with her every breath. "I'm afraid I don't have a cure for gout stuffed in my pocket, Duggy. Sorry." Valerian refused to even seriously consider the Baron's outrageous request concerning Allegra. It was too dangerous, for both of them.

Allegra, for her part, had become awash with several different emotions as her grandfather spoke. She knew herself to be tinglingly aware of Valerian's presence, standing as he was, so close behind her that if she were only to lean back the slightest bit, her spine would make contact with his knee.

She had been thrilled to think that a reason had been found to keep Valerian by her side, then immediately confused to think that she wanted him by her side for any other reason than to torment him for bringing her to England and then abandoning her.

She had been hurt, but only mildly, as she listened to her female relatives' opinions of her. She had been also hurt, most severely, by Valerian's obtuse and most obvious skirt-

ing of the Baron's request for assistance. And lastly, she
had been struck by her grandfather's obvious pain.

Putting all else aside, she asked, "Are you eating the
ciliegie, Nonno—that is, lots and lots of cherries? Deep red
cherries are the best kind. There was a music master we
met once in Gargano who swore by them to relieve the
swelling of gout. *Zia* Agnes surely has you eating cherries.
And no pepper, *Nonno*. Pepper is very bad for your toe, I
think."

Dugdale looked at his granddaughter, tears forming in
his eyes. "Did you hear that, Valerian? She's an angel, an
angel sent to me in my affliction. Cherries, eh? I like cherries. Now why didn't Aggie know that? Do you think we
can get any cherries here in Brighton this time of year?"

Allegra knew opportunity when it struck and, to her
mind, it was banging most mightily on the door at precisely
that moment. She sprang to her feet, grabbing onto Fitzhugh's forearm. "Valerian will know just where to go,
won't you, Valerian? Why, we shall leave this very moment, just as soon as I fetch my wrap, and scour Brighton
from one end to the other until we find cherries. And if we
should find a dress shop or two along the way so that I
might discover some gown suitable for wearing when dining beneath a chandelier held by a dragon, well, wouldn't
that be above everything wonderful?"

Before Valerian knew what had hit him—actually, he
knew what had hit him but found himself unable to resist
either Allegra's enthusiasm or the chance to be with her for
just a little while—the two of them were going out the door.

CHAPTER SIX

ALLEGRA CLUNG closely—dared he stay *too* closely?—to Valerian's arm as they walked along the windblown Steine, the first part of their mission accomplished. It had taken inquiries at six different shops, and her refusal of one basket of hothouse-grown cherries as being entirely too hard for her liking, but at last Allegra had pronounced herself satisfied.

Valerian had paid for a clerk to deliver the fruit to Number 23—and paid for the cherries as well, as Dugdale did not keep an account at that particular shop—and now they were merely walking and talking, enjoying the day.

If anyone had told Valerian that he could take pleasure in window shopping with a young miss not yet out of her teens, listening to her chatter about ribbons and flounces and the merits of silk linings, he would most probably have laughed out loud. Yet he knew himself to be happy in Allegra's company.

Now that he thought of it, he was almost always happy in Allegra's company. Or angry. Or amused. Or confused. Well, at least he was never bored. She was an intelligent little minx, well traveled—if only in Italy—and not in the least bit missish or shy. She seemed to be endlessly delighted with everything and everybody, and Valerian found himself thinking how wonderful it would be to repeat his tour of Europe with her by his side.

"Cold, imp?" he asked as Allegra gave a delicate shiver. "Ladies usually shun walking for carriages in February, you know."

She looked up at him, the brim of her green velvet bonnet grazing his shoulder, and he could see that the wind had brought a flattering bloom to her cheeks. "Do they really, Valerian? I have always liked to ride on San Francesco's horse—which you know means to go on foot, as did the good Saint Francis. What a shame your English ladies do not like walking, when it is so very invigorating to face down the elements."

"Always looking for another challenge, aren't you, Allegra? I imagine you'll be trying the bathing machines one of these days."

"Oh, yes, indeed. Betty has told me all about them, and this woman, this very strong Martha Gunn, who dips ladies into the water. I love the seaside, don't you? But I think I most love to look out over the ocean and think of the places that lie beyond the water, the people who live there, the wonderful sights I could see. Valerian—have you ever traveled to America? We discovered it, you know. We Italians, that is. Our Christoforo Colombo, in 1492, I believe—although the silly Spanish like to take credit for it, of course. Isn't that always the way of it?"

Valerian's lips twitched in amusement. "The silly Spanish might have thought that, as they had put down the money for the project, they deserved some recognition. And no, I haven't yet traveled to what we still would like to call our colonies. Would you like to go to America, Allegra?"

"Oh, my, yes!" she exclaimed, skipping a bit as they passed over an uneven patch of flagway. "I have wanted with all my heart to tour in America—singing, you know— and in Paris, and in Vienna, and in Moscow, and maybe even in faraway Japan, where women do not sing.'' Her face fell and she added, ''But I never shall, I suppose, or at least not for many years to come. For now I must be a supporting prop to *Nonno,* and then later, well—how could I enjoy myself on my poor dead *nonno's* money?''

''You couldn't, could you?'' Valerian directed their steps to a wooden bench along the side of the flagway. Once they were seated and he could see into her eyes, he asked, ''What do you intend to do with your inheritance then, imp? Stuff it into boxes and bury it all in the back garden?''

She lifted her chin in what, to him, was now her easily recognizable expression of defiance. ''And what good would that do? You are making sport of me, Valerian, and I don't think that is very nice. No, I have already decided what I shall do once dear *Nonno* is gone—which I can only hope will not be for a very, very long time. I shall take just enough money to keep myself until I can find employment as a singer, and give the rest to my *zia* Agnes.''

''You're going to do *what!*'' It was a good thing Valerian was sitting down, for he otherwise probably would have fallen, giving himself a nasty bump on his head while he was about it.

He longed to throttle her. How could he feel so in charity with this infuriating child one minute and long to strangle her the next? ''Are you telling me that I gave up my trip and dragged you all the way to England just so you could turn up your nose at a fortune—and then give it to those ignorant, bloodsucking Kittredges into the bargain? Of all the stupid, harebrained—''

''Valerian!'' Allegra interrupted, putting her gloved fingers against his lips to stifle his protests. ''You have not brought me to England in vain. You saved me from Bernardo, for one thing. And you have given me back my

family, after I thought myself to be all alone in the world.
If I live to be one hundred I cannot thank you enough for
what you have done.''

"If you mean to put me to the blush, imp, you are fair
and far out,'' Valerian told her, speaking around her fingers.
''From what I've heard, I've done nothing more than land
you in a nest of vultures who wish to strip you of your
name while dressing you up like a dowager in mourning.''

Allegra laughed. ''*Nonno* is not the soft, cozy grandfather
I could have wished for, I will admit that easily, but he is
at heart a fine, if shallow, man. The Kittredges, for good or
ill, are the only other family I have—and the most *sorry*—
looking trio I have ever seen. But they are also totally useless to themselves, I think, and it is not their fault that I
was born. How can you believe I should sleep nights if I
allowed *Nonno*'s plan to make friends with the good Saint
Peter end with my *zia* and *Cugina* Isobel sleeping in the
damp gutters of Brighton? *Cugino* Gideon, I must tell you,''
she added with a smile, ''I do not find it so terribly easy
to worry about.''

Valerian hated to admit it, but the child made sense, bless
her generous heart. He could feel all his anger fading away
and raised a hand to hold her fingertips against his lips a
moment longer. ''It might help them build character,'' he
then suggested with a wry smile, trying to picture Gideon
Kittredge camping in a gutter.

Allegra drew back her hand, doing her best not to pay
attention to the way her fingertips now tingled in such a
delicious manner. ''You won't tell my *nonno*, will you,
Valerian? It makes him so happy to think he is making his
sister's life a misery.''

Valerian's left eyebrow rose a fraction. ''And that
doesn't bother you?''

"No. Should it? *Zia* Agnes is not a nice woman. It does not hurt me to see her suffer for a while when I know she will come out right at the end. Besides, as long as she believes she will lose all *Nonno*'s money when he dies, she will take very good care to keep him most happily alive. And, before you ask me, I do not feel the least bit naughty spending *Nonno*'s money for him now—money that should have been my *madre*'s—great heaps of money—while he is able to see where it goes. *Capisci?* Understand? I still think I must get my sometimes terrible temper from my dear *papà*, but if I am mean, it only proves my Dugdale blood."

Valerian helped her to her feet. "And whom do we blame, imp, for your twisted logic? No, don't bother to answer, for I think I know. You are a woman. That is answer enough. Now, even if you are not cold, I am—as well as dizzy from listening to the way your mind works. I suggest we return to your grandfather's house before you tell me anything else and I slide into a sad decline."

She slipped her hand once more around his forearm and allowed herself to be led back the way they had come. "*Uncail* Max warned me that you were a difficult man," she said, sighing. "Do you think, Valerian, that I am a difficult woman?"

"I think, imp, that you are a very generous child—although perhaps you are also still a little confused by all that has happened to you in the past weeks. I can only suggest that you give yourself some time before you make any binding decisions."

"Of course, of course," Allegra answered absently, pulling him toward a shop window. "Oh, Valerian, it is beautiful, is it not?" she asked, pointing to a gown hanging just behind the display in the bow window. "It's like *un ro-*

manzo rosa—a pink novel. A perfect love story of a gown.''

Valerian sighed and closed his eyes. Allegra might be different in many ways, but she was proving very much like all other women when it came to her wardrobe. He knew what would happen if he stepped inside this shop with her. He would be trapped for hours.

He felt her tug at his arm once more and sighed, knowing what he had to do. Reluctantly, he led Allegra into the shop.

Once inside, Valerian was in for a surprise as Allegra, upon being greeted by a thin, sallow-faced Frenchwoman, immediately launched herself into a torrent of faultlessly accented French that left him standing with his mouth open. Within a matter of minutes Allegra had disappeared into a dressing room, the shopkeeper trotting behind holding gown, shoes, hose, cape, and elbow-length kid gloves.

It had taken Allegra only that long to make her selections, eyeing the contents of the shop from one end to the other with the sharp eye of one who knows exactly what she wants.

How different this was from Valerian's previous experiences in such places, when he had accompanied his mistress of the moment to Bond Street in the years before he'd learned that a simple gift of money was just as appreciated, if not more so. He had hated the experience then and he had believed he should hate the experience now, but so far Allegra was proving him wrong. Finding himself a seat in a corner, he sat down beside a vase filled with large feather plumes that insisted upon drooping onto his left shoulder, to await further developments.

He didn't have long to wait. After making him promise to "squeeze your eyes closed, ever so tightly, Valerian, and do not open them until I tell you," Allegra stepped out of the dressing room, the Frenchwoman walking behind her, wringing her hands and weeping at the beauty of the sight in front of her.

"All right, Valerian." Allegra spoke from somewhere in front of him. "I will allow you to open your eyes now."

He obeyed, not realizing that his world was about to change forever.

Valerian, at the age of two and twenty, had taken a fall from his favorite horse, landing flat on his back so that all of his wind had been knocked out of him. He hadn't been able to curse, or to yell, or even to breathe. He had only been able to lie there, not really hurt, but just looking up at his mount, disbelieving that the animal could have surprised him so.

He felt the same way now. Unable to talk. Unable to think. Unable to breathe. Able only to look.

The gown Allegra wore had been fashioned of the richest taffeta and was white without really being white, but more like a deep, rich cream. The body of the gown was magnificently simple, hugging her tightly just beneath the breasts, then sweeping downward to a simple hem adorned only by a modest edging of taffeta flower petals sewn with tiny seed pearls.

The entire bodice, what there was of it, and to Valerian's mind there was precious little, was similarly decorated, each of them at least one hundred separate, pearled petals so cunningly placed on both the bodice and the short, off-the-shoulder puffed sleeves that Allegra's shoulders and head seemed to rise from the gown like a perfect summer rose in full bloom.

Her breasts were not overly exposed, but only gently hinted at, the slight cleavage revealed by the cut of the bodice rendering the illusion of enticing innocence rather than deliberate enticement. With every breath she took, the pearled petals trembled delicately, subtly, causing Valerian's blood to pound heavily against the base of his throat.

Allegra's naturally pink lips and cheeks, sparkling sapphire eyes, and deep-as-midnight curls gave the only real color to what, to his bemused mind, could only seem to be a painting of some glorious angel come to Earth.

Was this the same dusty termagant he had discovered in Florence—the barefoot urchin with a string of garlic sausages stuffed in her bodice? Could this glorious creature possibly be the same child he had teased about her voracious appetite, or been ashamed to be seen with in public, or even the one he had dismissed as a child who—although intriguing—was not really a woman, and most definitely not the woman for him?

Valerian fought the sudden urge to flee for his life.

"Well—are you going to say something or are you just going to stand there? What do you think? I am a thing of beauty, yes?" Allegra took hold of the skirt on either side and made a half-turn, looking back over her shoulder at him. "Madame Mathieu says she has poured her life into this gown but there has never been anyone she wished to sell it to—until now. I do so love to be in costume, and this is just like a costume, isn't it? Oh, that I might ever appear on stage in such a magnificent creation! I should then be the real prima donna!"

Allegra turned back to her still mute audience of one, frowning. "Valerian, you are once more looking at me in that strange way. Say something quickly, please, for you are beginning to make me nervous, and I do not like it."

Valerian rose, not without effort, unable to stop staring

at Allegra's animated face. "She—" He had to stop and clear his throat. "She'll take it. What else do you have, madame?"

AGNES KITTREDGE, of course, had been appalled. First of all, no real lady frequented a dress shop with a man. What were people to think? Only kept women did such things. Thankfully it had only been that strange little "Madame Matthew's" shop, where no one of any importance would even think of making a purchase, yet alone browse, so perhaps they could scrape by without a major scandal.

Next there was the price! Ships had been launched for less. Armies had been fed for less. For Allegra had not stopped at that single gown, or the accessories so necessary to set it off. Oh, no. With that bewitched Valerian Fitzhugh's help, she had all but bought out the shop, blithely sending the bill to her grandfather.

Her grandfather—ha! To Agnes, this perhaps was the unkindest cut of all. The insolent chit didn't even know how to spell the man's name. Agnes knew, for Agnes had peeked at the bill when the mountain of striped boxes had been delivered—with even more to be delivered in the next few weeks.

"To be paid for by the Baron Dennis Dugdale*o*," Allegra had scribbled across the bottom of the bill in a bold, almost masculine script. The chit had put an O on the end of the reverend Dugdale name, just as if Denny were Italian! Why, it was almost enough to make a grown woman—a grown woman who had not herself seen a new gown in nearly three months—weep.

It *was* enough to make a young woman weep, which was precisely what Isobel did when she, while Allegra and Betty were out on yet another of their lengthy walks, sneaked into her cousin's bedchamber and took a peek into the armoire.

Pinks, yellows, greens, whites, lavenders, and robin's egg blues. Silks, velvets, taffetas, bastistes, percales, and muslins. Morning gowns, redingotes, tunics, spencers, and shawls. Even a cashmere *canezou,* or hussar vest, edged with bands of sable. There was so much it threatened to spill from the armoire in a pastel rainbow of colors.

But that was not all. To supplement the fine but fairly meager wardrobe she had brought with her from Italy, Allegra now also had drawer after drawer filled with the finest linen handkerchiefs, kid gloves, silk stockings, lace-trimmed petticoats, chemises—and not a single corset.

There were three embroidered silk purses, five pairs of silk slippers, a pair of overshoes, a multitude of combs and artificial flowers to be worn in the hair, two ivory fans, and three bonnets—any one of which Isobel would have gladly died for, not that she would ever tell her cousin that.

The worst, the very worst of it all, was that there existed nothing in the armoire or the drawers that even vaguely suited Allegra. Didn't Valerian know that, even if her silly half-foreign cousin was too blinded to see it?

Allegra should never have been encouraged to buy such pale, flowery shades or such close-fitting styles. Her disturbing physical "faults" needed to be subdued, not accented. Egyptian earth. Pea green. Tobacco brown. And whiter-than-white whites. Those were the colors Isobel would have chosen for Allegra. And high necks. And lots and lots of lace. Yes, definitely a multitude of lace, to hide the girl's "embarrassing" figure.

She told her mother as much, unfortunately while Gideon was in the room, so that the startled young man found himself forced to submit to a half-dozen sharp slaps between his shoulder blades from his frantic mama in order to relieve himself of the bite of muffin that had, thanks to his nearly hysterical laughter, become wedged in his throat.

This did not make for a reconciliation of brother and sister after a lifetime of spats, which otherwise might have transpired, considering the fact that they both had so much to lose if Allegra were truly to be named the Baron's heir. It also did not endear Isobel to her mother, who had, just for a few single heart-stopping moments, believed she was about to see her beloved Gideon turn purple and expire, right in her lap.

"Mama, Uncle Denny doesn't seem to care a whit that Allegra is spending his money as if he is already below-ground," Isobel added once her brother had finished wiping his streaming eyes and again taken up his familiar stance in front of the mantelpiece, totally neglecting to mention that the crime with which she had just accused Allegra could also most easily be laid at the collective Kittredge feet. "We have to do something quickly, Mama, before she spends his last groat!"

"Or marries Valerian Fitzhugh," Gideon slid in neatly, so that Agnes was forced to cough discreetly into her hand-kerchief at her adored son's great wit.

"Mama!" Isobel cried, pushing at her mother's shoulder. "Make him stop!" She turned to her brother. "You're horrid, Gideon. Perfectly horrid." Her eyes narrowing, she attacked in her turn. "How long are you going to hide out behind Mama's skirts like some cringing coward, avoiding your creditors? That's why you're haunting the house, isn't it, instead of running the streets with your ramshackle gambling friends? Because you don't dare stick your nose outside for fear someone will break it for you?"

"That will be enough, Isobel!" Agnes unceremoniously pushed her daughter back against the settee cushions, putting an end to this distasteful exchange. "I should have known better than to think that Isobel could put aside her petty jealousies to help us, Gideon," she said, rising to go to her son. "But you, my darling, are not so foolish, are you?"

Gideon, who was indeed that foolish and did not have the faintest idea what the woman was talking about, placed a kiss on his mother's cheek and murmured, "Ah, Mama, you know me so well."

Isobel sighed, giving up the fight as she always did, for she was intelligent enough to know that after a lifetime of losing every battle to her brother, she was not about to win this one. "You don't seem to be completely cast down by Allegra's latest mischief, Mama. Do you, perhaps, have some sort of plan to rid us of her?"

Agnes walked to the doorway, looked both ways into the hall, then shut the door and locked it. "I do have a plan, my children," she all but whispered, "and it will benefit both of you—all of us—although it will take some personal sacrifice on Gideon's part."

Gideon stood up very straight, "*Me,* Mama?" he said, incredulous. Why, he had never been asked to do anything personally sacrificing in his life—except maybe that time, at the age of twelve, when he had been forced by his mama to write a thank-you message to his paternal grandmother for giving him, upon that man's death, his late grandfather's pearl stickpin. He stuck out his bottom lip, instantly turning mulish. "What must I do *now?*"

Agnes Kittredge threw back her thin shoulders and lifted her head, the movement remotely possible of convincing any onlooker that she did indeed possess a chin. "It is quite simple, actually. Isobel will have a free run at Fitzhugh—although why she should think he wants her remains a mystery to me—we shall have our fortune back, and Gideon, you shall have all the blunt you need at your fingertips. All you have to do, distasteful as this may be to you personally, is to *wed* Allegra Crispino!''

Isobel gave a small shriek, pressing her hands to her mouth. ''It is a glorious idea, Mama! But wait—that would mean that Allegra would still live under this roof. I do not think I should like that, for she is not the most temperate person, and seems to actually enjoy flying into rages.''

But Agnes wasn't listening. She was concentrating on the expression that had stolen, unbidden, onto her beloved son's face, a look that could only be termed ''lascivious.'' It was so difficult to believe, so crushing to learn that her son, her adorable little boy, could possibly be susceptible to carnal urges.

''Gideon!'' she exclaimed, tottering to a nearby chair, as she was feeling decidedly faint. ''Show some respect! You are in the presence of your mother!''

IT WAS THURSDAY AT LAST, and Allegra was rapidly becoming a bundle of nerves, just as she did before every important performance.

She had spent an hour that morning simply standing outside the Marine Pavilion, imagining herself as she would look sitting beneath the great chandelier in the Banqueting Room, or walking, arm in arm with the Regent himself, through the Long Corridor, and then—would her heart never stop its fearful pounding that made it feel as if it would burst?—standing directly beneath the vast dome of the Music Room as she gifted her host with an aria from the great Alessandro Scarlatti, father of the modern opera.

''Or perhaps I should do something lighter, something from Rossini's *Il Barbiere di Siviglia*,'' Allegra mused aloud as Betty tucked a single soft ivory silk rose into the mass of curls that had been combed through so carefully and then heaped atop Allegra's head. She looked up at the maid. "I do that very well, you know."

Betty turned her mistress's face back toward the mirror. "I'm sure you do, missy, iffen it's anything like what you was singing earlier in your tub. That was proper wonderful. I had to shoo two of those nosy footmen from your door, they were listening so hard. Was that song from this *Sivi— Sigl*—oh, you know what I mean."

Allegra smiled at her reflection, liking the dramatic touch the rose, set just behind her ear, had given her. So she'd had an audience, had she? It was good to know that her voice had not become too rusty. "It is called, in English, *The Barber of Seville*. The work is a comedy, you see, and very new, first performed less than two years ago in Roma. My *papà* always said comedy is my *trionfo*—my triumph. And yes, the song I sang in my tub was from that opera."

Happy to have an audience, and hoping to rid herself of some of her nervousness, Allegra proceeded to hum some of the first aria, only to be interrupted by a loud knocking on the door to her bedchamber.

"There you are, gel!" Baron Dugdale bellowed, barging into the room without waiting for an answer to his knock. He walked slowly—as his immense bulk would have had him do even if it were not for his bandaged foot and un- wieldly, gold-topped cane—carrying a large flat velvet box in his right hand.

"Here," he said, pushing the box at Allegra, who had stood up, smoothing the front of her ivory gown. "These belonged to your grandmother. It's only fitting, I guess, that you should have them. And there's plenty more where these came from, only pearls is for purity, you know. Yes, your grandmother always told me Mary should wear the pearls first."

Allegra looked at the jewelry box, knowing whatever lay inside it should have graced her *madre*'s neck, and hesitated.

"What? Are you waiting for me to tell you how beautiful you look, eh? Well, you do, you know. Pretty as a picture. I shall have to use my cane here to beat the men away from you. Now, put these on. I don't want to be late."

"Yes, *Nonno*," she responded quickly, shaking off her momentary melancholy. She took the box and gingerly opened it, as if a snake might have taken up residence atop the satin bed within. Then, all restraint flown, she gasped, "Oh, *Nonno*, they're beautiful!"

Betty helped Allegra put the heavy old-fashioned gold-and-pearl earrings in her ears, then lifted the waist-length double strands of lightest pink pearls over her head.

Allegra turned back to the mirror, her hands going to the pearl ropes as they skimmed over her bare skin and lay lightly against the ivory flower petals. Then she touched the tips of the earrings that cascaded from her ears like miniature waterfalls.

Tears stung at her eyes as she saw her grandfather's reflection in the mirror, his face nearly puce with what had to be pride. She whirled about and stood up on tiptoe, giving him a resounding kiss on each cheek.

"Yes, well—" he blustered, pushing her away. "Are we ready to go now, or are you going to stand there preening all the night long?"

Taking his arm, Allegra asked, "Is *Zia* Agnes ready, *Nonno*? I have not seen her all of the afternoon, or Isobel."

"Aggie?" The Baron threw back his head and laughed. "She's not invited. Nor that die-away daughter of hers either. Whatever could you be thinking, gel? Prinny don't like prickly weeds cluttering up his beautiful Pavilion."

They made their way slowly down the stairs, a footman at the Baron's left side to add his support as they went. "Took Aggie the once you understand, but it didn't work out. She complained the whole night long." He pulled a face and mimicked his sister in a high, singsong voice. "'It's too hot. There is too much food, too many dishes. The singing is too loud, the ladies' dresses too low. The music is too hearty.' Odds fish! I'd rather ride bareback on a greased pig than live through another night like that! The woman has no appreciation!"

Betty, who had run on ahead, met Allegra at the bottom of the stairs with the pink-lined ivory cape that matched Allegra's gown, its neck a wide ruff of pearl-studded flower petals.

"Oh, dear, I didn't know," Allegra responded, trying to appear downcast after her grandfather had given her what, to her, was the most exciting news of the evening: she would not have to feel *Zia* Agnes's frowns following her everywhere she went. "Well, I promise not to complain about the amount of food the Regent serves. I can hardly wait, and have purposely starved myself all day in anticipation."

"Meaning, I should imagine, that you carefully limited yourself to no more than two desserts at luncheon. How very brave of you, imp."

"Valerian!" Allegra whirled about to see Fitzhugh standing at the entrance to the small drawing room, her heart pounding even more furiously than it had when she thought of performing for the next King of England. "You didn't tell me you too have been invited to the Marine Pavilion.

You are going, aren't you? You look entirely too magnificent for just an ordinary evening.''

It was true. Valerian had dressed himself very carefully, daring to wear formal evening clothes made expressly for him during his time in Paris. His black velvet breeches fit him like a second skin. The matching single-breasted, split-tailed coat, piped and lined in the finest white satin, was left open over a form-fitting black waistcoat, the white silk being repeated inside the tails of the coat, at his lace-ledged cuffs, and in the formally tied neckcloth and frills that peeped above the shawl collar of yet a second, white satin waistcoat.

White silk stockings and black leather pumps completed the outfit, as he could not bring himself to wear the remainder of the French Restoration *ensemble,* which consisted of a sword hung from a special belt, limiting himself to his usual restrained jewelry. He did, however, carry a black ostrich-fringed felt bicorne under his arm, knowing the hat to be *de rigueur.*

He had left his estate an hour previously, confident he looked his best, but now, with Allegra walking fully around him, her eyes wide in awe, he silently wished he had remembered the name of his French tailor so that he might send the man a gift.

He had given a brief consideration to turning down the Prince Regent's invitation to what was known far and wide to be an interminable evening at the Pavilion—but it had been only a very brief consideration. Allegra was to be present. Allegra, dressed in that beautiful gown, smiling that heartbreaking smile. Allegra, so alive, so vital, and doubtless to be the cynosure of all male eyes. Allegra, who would be the recipient of a dozen compliments—and two dozen invitations to go riding, driving, or otherwise engage in some other pursuit meant to allow a man some time alone with a comely young woman. Would he go to the Pavilion? A herd of Hannibal's war elephants couldn't keep him away!

"Do I pass inspection, imp?" Valerian asked once she had rejoined her grandfather.

"Oh, Valerian—you, you—" Allegra threw up her arms, unable to find words to explain just how wonderful he looked. "Do you know how nice your angel wings look when you wear black?"

"Angel wings? I have been likened to many things, imp, but never anything remotely heavenly."

"No, no. I mean only the bits of white hair among the black above your ears. I think of them as angel wings."

Valerian's spirits plummeted, for Allegra had just unwittingly reminded him of the more-than-fifteen-year difference in their ages. It was strange, but when he was with Allegra he did not usually feel the least bit old.

"We all are as imposing as the richest box holders at the *Teatro alla Scala*," she went on, heedless of Valerian's pain. "*Nonno*, don't you think Valerian is magnificent? You should wear two waistcoats, *Nonno*—if only to make it easier to catch more of the little drips when you eat."

The Baron, who had been noticeably quiet throughout this exchange, stepped forward, his eyes narrowed. "I didn't know you was invited, Fitzhugh. You ain't exactly one of our set, you know. Prinny don't usually invite young pups."

Valerian smiled, his good spirits restored. "That's true enough, Duggy. I may not be as young as Allegra, but I don't as yet have one foot in the grave either, do I? But no matter. It seems our dear Regent has heard of my extensive travels and wishes for me to regale him with stories of my adventures. I understand, in fact, that I am to sit at his right hand tonight, beside Lady Hertford, of course.''

"Eh? Is that so? Well, I suppose that's all right, then,'' the Baron said as a footman jumped about, struggling to throw a cape over the man's bulk. "Shall we be off, then? I assume we will be taking your carriage, Fitzhugh?''

"Would you have it any other way, Duggy?'' Valerian answered, holding out his arm to Allegra. "My dear? Shall we go?''

CHAPTER SEVEN

THE MARINE PAVILION was everything Allegra had hoped it would be, and more. Much more. Perhaps, as the hours spent at the heavily laden dining table ground on and the gas chandeliers above their heads hissed out light and enthusiasm-wilting heat, *too* much more, even for her.

Seated as she was, between her constantly chattering grandfather, who seemed to be in his element here, and an aging peer whose only claim to celebrity had been the dizzying speed with which he had run through a fortune it had taken his family six generations to amass, Allegra could not even see Valerian, much less hear a word of the lively conversation going on between him and the Regent.

Perhaps that was why she had unconsciously eaten so heartily of *les filets de volaille à la marcchale,* forgetting to heed Valerian's hastily whispered warning as he left her to go to his assigned seat that she should be careful not to partake overmuch from any one course, as another dozen equally appealing courses were sure to follow.

What seemed to be—and in reality was—several hours later, after having to wave away the tempting *les gâteaux glacés au abricots,* a truly heartbreaking denial, she forced herself to sample *les truffes à l'italienne,* if only to judge for herself the authenticy of the chef's claim. Truffles, she soon found to her delight, did survive translation.

When it came time to leave the Banqueting Room—a

departure was announced none too soon, Allegra mused, deciding that the temperature in the room now missed exceeding that of Hades by no more than a single degree— she was quick to seek out Valerian and ask his opinion of the meal.

"There was a meal?" he quipped, discreetly wiping his forehead with an handkerchief pulled from his pants pocket. Obviously, in this heat, the black velvet, no matter how flattering, had been a mistake.

"Prinny kept me talking for so long that I must have missed it. The man is insatiable, Allegra. If it weren't for his duties and the war, I should imagine he would have spent his entire life tramping from country to country just to see the sights. You know, Allegra, it had never before occurred to me that a man such as our Prince Regent, a man who has so much, could in some ways be so deprived."

Allegra smiled sympathetically as they followed the rest of the company of nearly a hundred overdressed guests down the hallway and toward the Music Room. "I had sensed that the Prince is not very popular in England, Valerian, but you sound as if you almost like him."

"I do, imp, don't I? But mostly I feel sorry for him. He lives in a dream world now, all alone, and I doubt that even he can sometimes distinguish between what is real and what is not. Do you know, he as much as told me tonight that he had been at Waterloo with Wellington, distinguishing himself in battle against Napoleon."

Allegra frowned, failing to understand the significance of what Valerian had just said. "And he was not? I thought all princes and kings were great soldiers. They are in operas."

Valerian directed Allegra to the sight of the bulky Prince

Regent, who had chosen to leave off his stays after his daughter's death, as two footmen helped lower the man into a chair.

"Not our Prince, Allegra. Until a few years ago, Prinny needed a winch to hoist him onto a horse. Now, well, now he doesn't even try. A great soldier? I think he will most probably go down in history more as a great spender of his subjects' money. I earlier heard someone say that the main chandelier alone in the Banqueting Room cost over five thousand pounds. If I sound bitter, Allegra, it is only because the real veterans of Waterloo, like Tweed, my coachman, have not fared half so well."

Allegra recalled Tweed, and the black patch the man wore over the place where, before he had gone to war, his right eye had allowed him to look at the world through two eyes. "I suppose that is true, Valerian. War is a terrible thing. But the chandelier is a pretty thing, Valerian, and I think the world sometimes needs pretty things as well, even more than it can know."

"There are moments, imp," Valerian said softly, squeezing her gloved hand, "when you make me feel a complete fool."

Allegra felt much depressed as Valerian withdrew his hand, and she began looking about the enormous room in hopes of finding something that would lighten her spirits, something of which her companion did not know the price. It didn't take her long to discover that there existed not a single thing within the Music Room that failed to please her.

Her spirits soared, so that she felt more as she had done when first they had arrived at the Pavilion—before *les filets de volaille à la marcchale* and Valerian's sad stories about the Regent.

She truly did not know where to look first—at the strange pillars with bronze serpents coiling down them headfirst, at the exotic red Chinese laquered panels, or at the ribbon-wound bamboo side ceilings that were topped by an immense central dome made up of first blue, then gold scales, as if it mimicked the protective skin of some elegantly painted reptile.

There were chandeliers everywhere, lighting the room as if it were still daylight and showing off the strange gilt furniture that seemed to encourage people to lie half reclined rather than sit. But of premier importance to Allegra was the orchestra of at least seventy musicians who sat on one side of the room, their instruments at the ready.

"*Magnifico. Molto magnifico!* It is just like a great cathedral, Valerian, only pretty—and maybe just a tiny bit naughty," she declared fervently, which encouraged Valerian to laugh out loud.

Yes, everything in the Music Room pleased her, except perhaps a few of its occupants who seemed to be a little the worse for drink and prone to make disparaging remarks about their host, who had yet to join them. She couldn't help noticing the looks she was receiving from many of the gentlemen present—looks not difficult to interpret—nor did she really like the way the ladies seemed to ignore her in droves. Only one, a rather faded redheaded lady dressed in purple, had actually spoken to her at dinner, and then only to demand imperiously that she reveal the name of her dressmaker.

As he caught sight of a twice-widowed Marquis making his way in their direction, all but smacking his lips as he eyed Allegra's bodice, Valerian led the girl, who was still gazing upward in rapture at the immense dome, to a pair of blue brocade satin chairs at one side of the room. They sat down, only to rise again as the Regent entered, a heavily painted and ostrich-plume-topped Lady Hertford on his arm.

For the next two hours the Regent performed for his guests, playing the cello and then singing "Mighty Conqueror" and "Glorious Apollo" for them in a surprisingly pleasing baritone before commanding the assembled musicians to play—as he beat a hearty accompaniment on his knee—a nearly endless selection of his favorite musical works with, to Allegra's mingled delight and dismay, a most telling emphasis on Italian rococo.

It had passed eleven before Allegra, who had found herself growing weary in the overheated room, noticed that many of the guests were taking their leave, and made to follow them.

Valerian held her back. "No, imp, you aren't rescued yet. Duggy told me we are to be a part of the select few who have been honored with an invitation to retire with the Regent to a nearby drawing room for a cold supper."

"Supper?" Allegra clapped a hand to her mouth as her exclamation seemed to echo in the rapidly emptying room. "Valerian, you can't be serious! I couldn't possibly eat a thing!"

"There you are, gel!" Baron Dugdale approached slowly, favoring his bandaged foot. "Good news, m'dear. I told Prinny all about your singing and he has agreed to hear you after supper. You singing, Lady Brownley playing at the harp—Lord help us—and the Earl of Somewhere-or-another is going to scrape away at a violin or some such nonsense."

He leaned forward, peering intently into her eyes. "You weren't funning me, gel, were you? Poor fellow seemed so pleased to hear he had a real *I*-talian here to sing for him, though for the life of me I don't know why. He just had some other foreign warbler here last month. They sing in their own lingo, you know, so that you can't understand a word of it even if you was to try, which I surely don't. Seems a waste of time to even listen to 'em, don't it? Well, never mind that. You'd best be good. It isn't smart to get on the wrong side of the next King of England.''

Allegra had relaxed, having given up all hope of performing that night, but now her nervousness was back in double force, not that she would allow her grandfather to see it. ''*Nonno*, I once sang for the Bishop of Bologna,'' she announced, her head thrown back challengingly. ''I do not believe I should be an embarrassment to you—that is, *if* I should choose to sing tonight.''

Valerian thought for a moment that Lord Dugdale was going to reach out and slap his granddaughter. ''*If* you should choose to sing tonight? *If!*'' He turned to Valerian. ''Fitzhugh, what is the gel talking about? What does she mean—*if* she should choose to sing tonight?''

''*Hai messo il carro davanti ai buoi, Nonno.* You have put the cart before the oxen,'' Allegra retorted hotly, stepping directly in front of her grandfather so that he would stop looking to Valerian for answers that should be coming from *her* mouth.

Lord Dugdale employed the bottom third of his cane to push his granddaughter to one side, then all but bellowed at Valerian, ''What's she talking about, I asked you? Didn't she talk about singing here? Isn't that all she talked about in the carriage on our way? Besides, I ain't asking her to sing! Odds fish—I'm *telling* her!''

Allegra stepped in front of Dugdale yet again. It was true. She was dying to sing for the Regent, and had been longing even more to perform for him ever since hearing the most wonderful acoustics of the domed Music Room. But some things were more important than her deathly desires.

"Ah, *Nonno,* now you have hit the nail with the mallet! I am a great artist. It is just like I told my manager, that thickheaded Erberto. It is *I,* and I alone, who must be allowed to choose the time and place of my performances. And I do not think I choose to perform alongside what are sure to be hapless harp ladies and violin-destroying Earls."

Valerian stuck his head past Allegra's shoulder and addressed the Baron. "Perhaps, Duggy, if Allegra and I might have a few moments alone?" he asked, hoping that for once in his life the older man would show some intelligence.

"Alone?" the Baron repeated, frowning. "I don't know, Fitzhugh." Then he brightened. "Odds fish, I guess it ain't like the two of you haven't been alone plenty before this, eh? In many ways you're almost sort of her guardian."

"Thank you so much, Duggy," Valerian responded, the other man oblivious to the fact that he most sincerely wanted to throttle him.

The Baron looked about to see that nearly everyone else had either departed for the evening or proceeded to the supper room. "Now I'm in for it! Prinny's already at table. Look, Fitzhugh—Valerian—be a good lad and talk some sense into this gel here, won't you? I suggest the small salon down the hall. Everyone uses it when they want to— well, never mind about that. You just make sure this gel sings!"

"POOR *NONNO.*" Allegra collapsed, giggling deliciously, onto a striped satin settee in the discreetly placed salon. "I most probably should not have done that, but he must learn that I am not someone to be ordered about. I am a singer!"

"You sang mostly in the chorus, if memory serves,"

Valerian reminded her, sitting beside her after closing the door to the salon. "Now tell me, what are you going to perform for the Prince?"

Allegra sat forward, frowning. "He has dismissed the orchestra, you know. Oh, yes, I saw that most distinctly. They will not be back." She then rattled off a long stream of possible selections, holding each out verbally for inspection before, one by one, eliminating them all. She leaned against the back of the settee, which somehow was now draped most comfortably with Valerian's black velvet sleeve. "Oh, I do not know what I shall do."

Valerian looked down at her, seeing the adorable pout that had appeared on her enticingly pink lips, and swallowed hard.

He had to retain the knowledge that she was little more than a child.

He had to remind himself that he was a man of the world, an honorable man, and knew better than to steal a kiss from an innocent girl.

He had to remember that he, although so much older than she, and the possessor of angel wings, was still a reasonably young man of five and thirty, and not nearly ready to settle down and start his nursery.

He had to keep it clear in his mind that—"Oh, the hell with it!"

Valerian quickly shifted himself on the settee so that he sat slightly forward, turned in Allegra's direction, and took her chin between his fingers, "Imp," he said, his voice husky, "if you think I'm going to ask your permission for this first, you're fair and far out!" So saying, he lowered his head to hers and allowed himself to succumb to the sanity-destroying attraction of her moist, pouting mouth.

Allegra did not resist him, but rather welcomed him to

her, winding her arms around his neck as he dared to deepen the kiss. He sensed rather than knew that this was her first kiss, for her reactions, although enthusiastic and wonderfully cooperative, were not at all practiced.

He could feel her body trembling under his hands and imagined that the hundreds of pearled petals were all rustling in a sweet summer breeze off the ocean. He could feel his own body begin to tremble as the passion Allegra's innocent seduction wove around him penetrated to the very heart of his being.

If he didn't stop soon, if he didn't remember who he was and where he was and what he was about to do, he would be hopelessly lost, caught forever in Allegra's magical spell. He should draw back. He should break off the kiss, apologize for his boorish behavior, get them both out of this exotic, tempting salon made for dalliance, and return Allegra to her grandfather.

He should. But he wouldn't. Not when he lifted his head a fraction, opened his eyes, and saw the blissful, rapturous expression on Allegra's beautiful face. He couldn't. If all of Prinny's dragons chose that moment to come to life and breathe their hottest fires or if all the bronze snakes began to hiss his name, Valerian could not have broken away from her.

Taking hold of her bare shoulders, he crushed her to him once more.

"Now, and isn't this a most lovely picture, don't you know? The toadeating old man is in the supper room, none the wiser, chatting up Old Swellfoot. And while the cat's away, I always say, the mice will dance. Is that how it goes, my boyo?"

Valerian broke from Allegra so quickly that he nearly toppled backward onto the floor. "Max!" He couldn't believe it. Maximilien Murphy in Brighton? In the Marine Pavilion? Why? How? He turned to see a short, pudgy man dressed in the formal wear and powdered wig of Prinny's Banqueting Room servants. "What are you doing here?"

"Yes, it is I, Maximilien P. Murphy, at your service." Max made his stunned audience a most magnificent leg (considering the tightness of his breeches), closed the door, and walked across the room to kiss Allegra on both cheeks. "What am I doing here? Up to a few minutes ago I was helpin' to clear up the mess you people made over dinner, if you must hear it. Coulda fed all Dublin and half of County Clare on the scraps, don't you know? Isn't this the place, though? I don't think I've ever seen such a mess of grandeur."

"*Uncail* Max," Allegra said, hopping to her feet to throw her arms about his neck, "it is so wonderful to see you again. Candie, and Tony, and the so-adorable Murphy—they are all fine?"

"Fine as shamrocks on a sunny day, child, though I'm wagering Candie wouldn't be so happy to see what's been going on in here. Then again, knowing my Candie, I must reconsider. She probably would be cock-a-hoop! Why, I remember her telling me how Tony, that rascal, climbed in through her bedroom window and—"

"Never mind that," Valerian broke in hurriedly. "Max, I repeat—what are you doing here? Here in Brighton, and most especially here in the Pavilion? I thought you were living in Italy because you're a wanted man in England."

"Well, and of course I am, my boyo. And why d'you think I'm wearing this blasted, itchy wig?" He turned to Allegra. "You shouldn't be letting him kiss you, don't you know. Lovemaking always did have the power to rattle a man's brains."

Allegra blushed very prettily, and she did so now, murmuring, "Yes, *Uncail* Max. I'm very sorry."

"No, you're not," Murphy shot back at her, winking. "Fib, m'darlin', for a good fib may take you anywhere, but never lie."

Valerian crossed to the door, opened it, and looked out, to be sure the hallway was clear. "Never mind that now, Max," he commanded, all his passion now fled, and his thoughts again directed to the happenings of the moment. "What's wrong? It has to be something very important for you to take the chance of coming to the Pavilion."

"It could be and it couldn't be." Max sat himself down beside Allegra on the settee and reached a hand into a nearby candy dish, popping a comfit into his mouth. "But it can wait, boyo. Could you and the beautiful little colleen here meet me tomorrow on the Steine, say at two in the afternoon? You won't know me, so I'll find you. We'll make our plans then."

As Max started for the door, Valerian grabbed his arm, pulling him back. "This could have waited for tomorrow, couldn't it, Max? You only sneaked in here, right under Prinny's nose, for nothing more than the thrill of the thing, didn't you?"

The Irishman grinned from ear to ear. "Ah, boyo, you're an apt student of human nature. I like that in a man." He looked past Valerian to wag a finger in Allegra's direction. "And it's a good thing I came here tonight, I'm thinking. If it's designs on turning into a hoyden you have, m'girlie, you'd best think again. First the ring and the promise—then the kiss. Remember that, darlin'."

"Yes, *Uncail* Max," Allegra replied, her sapphire eyes dancing. "I'll be very sure to remember that." She looked toward Valerian, who was in his turn glaring at Max. "I always remember *everything.*"

"IN BOCCA AL LUPO," Valerian whispered as Allegra rose from her chair, using an Italian saying meant to wish her good luck, but that sounded much better in Italian, as it translated to English only as "in the wolf's mouth."

He watched as she stepped to the exact center of the Music Room, curtsied deeply in the Regent's direction, and rose to stand facing the future King, her hands decorously folded at her waist.

Allegra was the last to perform, a condition she had laid down to her grandfather, saying that it wouldn't be fair to the other two performers to have to follow her lead. The occupants of the room, some of them more than half drunk and all of them yawning into their hands, could be heard squirming in their seats, eager for the interminable evening to come to an end.

Allegra waited until all sound had stopped, her chin high. The chandeliers threw a bright but flattering light, calling attention to her small, beautifully clad, regally erect frame.

Valerian thought he would burst with pride. He tore his gaze from her and sneaked a quick look around the room, smiling, he was sure, like a preening old hen with one chick. She held every occupant in the palm of her little hand, and she had yet to sing a note.

He could not know that, inside, Allegra was trembling so violently she thought she might become ill. He could not know that she would sing that night, not for the Regent, not for all the titled ladies and gentlemen, not even for her own enjoyment. Tonight she would sing for Valerian. Tonight she would give the performance of her life!

Just as Valerian was beginning to worry that Allegra

might be hesitating too long, that she had become a victim of her own bravado and in truth could sing nary a note, she opened her mouth and, with the first pure, sweet sound that issued forth, dispelled his every fear.

She sang an aria from some Italian opera or other—Valerian did not readily recognize it or even care—her voice even more beautiful than she, if that were possible. The aria asked a lot from her—laughter, deep sorrow, amusement, elation, despair—and she gave herself over to the music most generously, her hand movements eloquent, her face animated, her eyes twin sapphire mirrors of deeply felt emotion.

Somehow—he would never afterward remember precisely when or how it had happened—he found himself standing, unable to remain seated in the presence of such beauty. He had always enjoyed attending the opera, in a social sort of way, but never had he been struck by anything as he was now by Allegra's effortlessly soaring voice. He knew, just as well as he knew his name, that the memory of this night would comfort him every time he looked into her eyes and, if she were ever to leave his side, haunt him unceasingly into his grave.

When it was over, the room remained silent, echoing only the last, long note of Allegra's musical story. She turned toward him, her expression questioning, just as Prinny leapt from his chair, clapping loudly and calling, *"Bravo! Bravo!"*

A heartbeat later the Music Room exploded into pandemonium. The previously sleepy, jaded audience came to life, rushing to follow its host's lead, each person trying to outdo the other with either praise or applause.

Valerian did not join them. He did not clap. He did not shout. He simply stood there, he and Allegra looking at each other as if no one else were in the room, until the crush of people eager to congratulate her took her from his sight.

"You've gone beyond hope, you know," Max Murphy said from somewhere behind him. "I've seen it all before, with Tony and my Candie, and I know all the signs."

Valerian didn't even bother to turn around. "I don't know what you're talking about, Max," he said, knowing that no one, least of all someone as astute as Maximilien P. Murphy, would ever believe him. "And shouldn't you be going before you're found out? Not to be nasty, Max, but you're not half so young or sleek as the rest of Prinny's servants, and you're beginning to stick out like a sore thumb."

"It's goin' I'll be doing now, boyo, until tomorrow at two," Max said, chuckling, clearly not taking offense at anything a silly, lovestruck soul should say to him. "But it's too late for you to be goin' anywhere, no matter what the time. Your heart, don't you know, has already flown."

ALLEGRA DANCED about her bedchamber, her arms held wide, unable to contain her ecstasy. She felt like a child who has just been granted its most favorite wish, unable to sit still, but forced by her own inner excitement to constantly remain on the move.

"Oh, Betty!" she exclaimed, grabbing onto one of the bedposts and leaning back, swinging herself lightly from side to side, dressed only in her chemise. "You cannot know, you cannot imagine it! I am the *sensazione!* The pudgy Prince, he adores me, he *weeps* in adoration! And, ah, Betty—my *nonno!* My *nonno* puffs and preens and so forgets himself as to rush into the multitude of supplicants crowding about me and allows some stupid person to step on his poor toe! And still he doesn't care. No! He tells everyone, 'This is *my* granddaughter, to whom I am giving a plum!' Betty, I cannot tell you how I enjoyed myself!''

The maid, who had spent the last hour chasing Allegra around the room in order to divest her of her gown, and who had been trying without success since then to get her mistress to bed, at last collapsed onto the mattress herself, saying, ''Yes, missy, you *can* tell me. You have *been* telling me, over and over again. And if you don't stop gallopin' about the place singing little bits of that foreign stuff, you'll be telling the whole household!''

Allegra abandoned the bedpost to dance across the room and snatch a flower from a nearby arrangement. She sniffed of its delicate fragrance, then tucked its dripping stem into the top of her chemise as she looked at the drowsy maid. Betty, it would appear, was becoming bored. Well, Allegra would soon put an end to that! ''Ah, you terrible grouchy person, I refuse to listen to you. But did I tell you of my assignation—I think that is the correct word—with Mister Valerian Fitzhugh in one of the small salons?''

''Your *what?*''

Allera hopped up onto the mattress, sitting on her knees. ''Ah, I had thought not,'' she teased, grinning mischievously. ''He kissed me, Betty,'' she whispered confidentially, leaning toward the bug-eyed maid. ''He kissed me twice. He dragged me off to a private salon and we were all alone, just the two of us, in the beautiful Pavilion. It was most delightful! And I had not yet even sung for him!''

Betty rolled her eyes, sighing deeply. ''Oh, laws, now what? Does your grandfather know?''

Allegra collapsed onto her back on the bed, her ebony tresses splayed out fanlike on the pillow, her fingers lightly stroking the deep pink flower petals lying against her breasts. "*Nonno?* No, he does not know. It is our secret, Betty. I wish to hug it to myself for a while longer. You do understand, don't you?"

Betty sniffed derisively, her common-sense mind far from clouded with rosy romantic images. "I understands it all right, missy. You've gone and compromised yourself good. And to think I always thought that Mister Fitzhugh fella to be a fine gentleman. He should be ashamed of himself!"

Allegra turned her head on the pillow, her eyes shining with mischief. "Oh, I think Valerian is very much ashamed with himself, Betty. I turned to him when my aria was done and caught him looking at me in that strange way I told you about, the one that makes my toes curl up in my slippers. That look used to worry me, but now I like it very much, as my toes curled up the same way tonight, when he kissed me."

Betty clapped her hands over her ears. "Please, missy, I don't think I want to hear any more about this kiss."

"Two kisses, Betty. Betty? Valerian barely had a word for me all the way home, except to tell me he will be coming by tomorrow to take me walking on the Steine. He will propose marriage to me then, yes?"

Betty made a great business of pulling the bed-clothes up over Allegra's slim body. "He'll be proposing somethin', missy. I've lived long enough to be sure of that! Now you'd best get to sleep or it will soon be time to get up." She walked to the door, blowing out candles as she went, only to turn back and say, "You know, missy, you shouldn't be in such a big hurry to wed. You'll have plenty of gentlemen to choose from before you're done. Why, I heard it below-stairs when I went down for tea that Master Gideon is planning to ask for your hand."

"Gideon!" Allegra sat up, her smile wide. "Oh, yes, Betty, I can see Gideon now, down on one knee in front of me in the drawing room, begging to be allowed to make passionate love to my inheritance." She collapsed once more onto the pillows and gave way to another attack of the giggles. "Gideon for my *nonno*'s fine fortune and, I am thinking, sad, silly Isobel for poor Valerian, whom she is so sure she loves. Oh, My. *Prendi due piccioni con una fava,* Betty. *Zia* Agnes, I think, wishes to catch two pigeons with one bean! Now I am even more impatient for tomorrow to arrive so that I can tell the other pigeon!"

VALERIAN'S DISPOSITION, as he continued pacing the length of his study two hours after arriving back at his estate just outside Pyecombe, was not quite so carefree as Allegra's.

His mind insisted upon spinning backward in time, trying in vain to discover just where it was that he had made a small turning in the road, leading himself unwittingly, unknowingly, into quite the most confusing, confounding, intriguing chapter of his life.

Had he sealed his fate the day he had opened the missive from Baron Dugdale enlisting his aid in locating his lordship's long-lost granddaughter? Or had he set the stage for his downfall only after agreeing to act as Good Samaritan for the Baron?

He swallowed the last of his fireside-warmed brandy and ran a hand distractedly through his hair. Perhaps it had been the moment Allegra, barefoot, smelling of sausages, and clad in her soiled, peasantlike dress, had turned to him and announced quite clearly that she would not sleep with him.

He poured another snifter and rubbed the glass between his palms, warming it.

Failing that memorable moment in Florence, he knew he

would always remember their departure from Naples and the way Allegra had cried so brokenheartedly against the front of his greatcoat, her slim arms wrapped tightly about his waist as if he were the only remaining solid thing in life that she had to cling to.

Or could he have taken the fatal step that first day in Brighton when, against his better judgment, he had remained at the Dugdale residence, impatiently awaiting Allegra's summons to her bedchamber, rather than following his inborn self-protective masculine instincts and taking to his heels just as fast as he could?

He took a deep sip of the brandy, grimacing as it burned the back of his throat. No, it had been none of those times. Yes, they all had something to do with his current pitiful condition, that he acknowledged, but none of them were the single, telling blow, the final determination that, for good or ill, he would never be the same man he had been before Allegra Crispino had come literally crashing into his heretofore neat, orderly life.

It was arriving home at his estate after first delivering Allegra to her grandfather that had done it for him, finally made him realize he had crossed the river to real love for the first time in his life and then, without ever once considering the danger, had proceeded to burn all his bridges behind him.

Everywhere he looked, in each room of his house, in his gardens, while riding across his budding fields, he had seen Allegra, envisioned how she would look if she were there, sharing each moment with him. Without her, without Valerian being able to see his surroundings the way she would see them, through eyes shining with innocent wonder, his whole world had turned to a lifeless gray, and he would not have been able to stay away from Brighton another moment, with or without the Baron's request that he attend him.

He sank into his favorite chair, smiling ruefully at the memory of that day.

The time spent with Allegra, hunting down elusive hot-house cherries for the Baron, walking and talking as they wove their way together through the streets of Brighton, had only served to prove once and for all that he, Valerian Fitzhugh, was a doomed man.

But he had still secretly held out hope that he could be wrong, that he was only suffering from a temporary delusion that had him dreaming wistfully of carefree days listening to Allegra's chatter while he feasted on her beauty, and of quiet nights spent in front of the fire, Allegra's dark head trustingly pressed against his shoulder.

And then there would be the travel, the places he would take her to just so that he could see them again through her eyes, and the children they would have, sapphire-eyed, dark-haired girls and little boys who had their father's features and their mother's unquenchable spirit...

"Damn it!" Valerian's fist came down on the arm of the chair, making a loud, smacking sound in the quiet room. He shouldn't have kissed her! No matter what his excuse, no matter how terrible the temptation, he should never have kissed her!

He threw back his head and laughed out loud at his own foolishness. He shouldn't have kissed her? No! He shouldn't have *stopped* kissing her! He should have kissed her, and held her, and loved her, until he was so lost, so completely at her mercy, that he would have dared there and then to ask this most delightful, beautiful creature to do him the supreme honor of becoming his wife.

But Max, blast his interfering Irish soul to Perdition, had put an end to all that.

Now it was too late. Now she had become the newest sensation in a society that lived for the next sensation. From this night on she would be fêted and pursued and fawned upon from the mighty on down. Now he would have to bide his time, allow her to bask in the full glow of her triumph at the Pavilion, and hope that she would deign to allow him some few small crumbs of her attention.

Only when she had been allowed to indulge herself in her newly found popularity, only after she had had her well-deserved Season as a Diamond of the First Water at the Assembly Rooms in Brighton and the ballrooms of London, only then could he in clear conscience dare ask her to become his wife.

He sat slumped in his favorite leather chair and stared into the dying fire. Yes, that was what he would have to do now. He would have to play a waiting game. Unless, of course, he thought—rallying slightly as he remembered Max's appearance at the Pavilion—some other, less painful way was to present itself!

CHAPTER EIGHT

VALERIAN WAS going quietly out of his mind. It seemed as if he and Allegra could advance no more than three feet in any one direction before they were stopped by someone who wished to issue an invitation to her, speak to her, praise her, be seen with her.

As he smiled, and bowed, and tipped his hat, his eyes kept darting in every direction, endlessly searching for some sign of Maximilien Murphy, who was, by Valerian's pocket watch, a full twenty minutes late for their appointment.

Not that he seriously expected the wily Irishman to show his face in the midst of this crush. Was there no one left in London? Had every fool and his wife come to Brighton to be with the Prince? Valerian looked about him for a convenient side street down which, hopefully with Max watching, from some not-too-distant vantage point, he and Allegra might somehow escape this ridiculous crush of humanity.

Finally, just as Allegra was floundering badly in a rather one-sided conversation with Lady Bingham, who was imploring Allegra to attend a "small party in your honor on any evening of your choosing," Valerian mumbled some vague excuse, bowed to her ladyship, and all but pushed his companion around the corner and onto St. James's Street.

"You were rather rude, weren't you, Valerian?" Allegra

questioned, tugging her arm free of his hold as they began walking down the nearly deserted street. "I have always much preferred someone to ask my permission before pulling me along as if I were no more than a sack of tomatoes on the way to market."

Valerian smiled down at her. "I stand corrected, imp. From now on I shall be sure to gain your agreement *before* I pull you along like a sack of tomatoes. Now, if you have done with accepting applause for your performance last night, perhaps I might drag your thoughts back to the project at hand?"

Allegra's full bottom lip jutted out as she made a great show of pouting before once more taking Valerian's arm and giving it a friendly squeeze. "I am very bad, am I not, Valerian? But I did so enjoy myself, with everyone complimenting me on my singing." She shook her head. "There were even flowers delivered from the Regent himself this morning. Did I tell you that? Yes, I suppose I did."

"Counting now, Allegra, you have told me four times," Valerian answered tightly, wishing he had had the presence of mind to send a bouquet himself.

"And to think I had worried that I should not be liked. I am very popular, yes?"

"I refuse to answer that, imp, or else your head might succeed in outgrowing that fetching bonnet. Now, did you see Max anywhere?"

Allegra instantly sobered, shaking her head. "I looked for him, but I could not find him anywhere, and then there were all those people around us, so that I could not see anything. Oh, dear!" she exclaimed, suddenly understanding. "He could not dare to approach us while we were surrounded by all my new friends, could he? Valerian, do you think he has taken fright and gone away?"

"Max, frightened? Allegra, he dared to come inside the Pavilion last night, no doubt serving up vegetables to three dozen lords and ladies he had talked into parting with a good deal of their money at one time or another. My only concern right now is finding him so that we may discover what brought him to Brighton when he promised Candie he would stay in Italy."

"He's got something boiling in the pot," Allegra declared, nodding. "I think perhaps Max has heard of some trouble concerning me. Or else Erberto has returned, to give me back my wages, and Max has brought my money to me. Pooh! That cannot be it. Erberto would never do such a thing. Ah, but only to say his name is to see him!" She began, alternately clapping her hands and pointing down the street. "*L'uomo del giorno!* It is the man of the day! Isn't he wonderful?"

Valerian looked in the direction Allegra was pointing, frowned, then looked again. "Max?" he asked as a short, stout woman approached them, leaning heavily on a battered cane, her other arm encumbered by a wicker basket filled with small bouquets of rapidly wilting flowers. "Good Lord, man, is it really you?"

"Violets! Violets! Who'll buy my sweet violets?" Max called loudly, drowning out both Allegra's delight and Valerian's question. He sidled up to them and lowered his voice to a harsh whisper. "Of course it is Max. Who was it you was expecting, boyo, the Queen of the May? And, Allegra, much as you are delighted by my presence, m'darlin', I would ask you to stop kicking up such a devil of a wind about it, please. I'd like to be seeing this day."

Valerian covered his mouth to stifle his laughter. He could barely believe Max's peasant-woman appearance, and the gray wig that covered the man's head could only be termed a master stroke. "Max," he said, grinning, "my compliments. You, as you Irish say, make a fine doorful of a woman."

Max ignored this insult, turning to concentrate his full attention on Allegra. "Quite the rising comet you are, m'darlin'. Yes, it's watching you I've been, lugging these posies about—made m'self a few pennies doing it, by the by—and I'm here to warn you not to take all this boot-licking to heart. The sheep only go where Prinny leads 'em, and he'll be leading 'em somewhere else before the cat can lick her ear, so you keep that in mind and make the most of it for yourself while you can."

"Ah, sage words of wisdom from the Bog Lander in the petticoats. Allegra, mayhap you should embroider them on a pillow for your bed." Valerian turned to Max, frowning. "What would you have the imp do, Max, charge a fee for gracing their parlors and end up in disgrace? Is that why you've come here, to set yourself up as her new manager? Allegra's singing career is over. She's an heiress now, and has no need of your help in that direction."

Max lifted a bunch of violets and pressed them into Allegra's hands. "That'll be twopence, sir, and the lady thanks you very much," he said, holding out his upturned palm to Valerian for payment. "Didn't sleep well last night, did you, boyo? You're showing a mean streak I never saw before, don't you know?"

Valerian had the good grace to feel ashamed of himself and said as much to Max, adding, "It's just that I've been waiting all day for this meeting. What has happened that you felt the need to come to Brighton? Is Allegra in any danger?"

Max pocketed the coins, sneaking a look out of the corners of his eyes as if to make sure no one was close enough

to overhear his next words. "It was bored I was, watchin'
as Tony and my Candie billed and cooed, so I amused myself a bit by keepin' an eye on that Bernardo fellow. Besides, after sendin' m'dear Louisa—that's Miss Shackleford
to you, Fitzhugh—along to chaperon Allegra, I thought I
might just as well drop myself over here for a space and
see how she's doin'."

"*Uncail* Max? You and Miss Shackleford are in love? I
didn't know. Valerian, isn't that wonderful? Will there be
a wedding?"

"Don't be daft, girlie. Max Murphy will never wed. My
wife's intended mother died an old maid. No, it's a warning
I've come to deliver to the both of you. The handsome
shoemaker is on his way. Thanks to my generous Candie,
I was able to take a faster ship, but he'll be here any time
now, to claim his bride."

"His bride? How could he continue to believe that I
would ever—oh, no!" Allegra rounded on Valerian, shaking the bouquet of violets in his face. "This is all your
fault! You were the one who said I should wave to the fool
as the ship left the dock. He probably thought I was sorry
to leave him behind and wished for him to follow me. Oh!
We are in a lovely pie now!"

"It would seem so. Persistent fellow, isn't he?" Valerian
mused, shaking his head, oblivious to Allegra's anger. He
had wondered if Bernardo's impending arrival could be the
problem Max had alluded to last night, but he hadn't been
quite able to bring himself to believe the Italian's devotion
would cause him to do anything so desperate. But then, he
mused further, Allegra was a difficult woman to forget.

"Don't be beating on Valerian, m'darlin', for it's need-
ing him again you'll be, I'll be thinking," Max interrupted
just as Allegra looked about to deliver a punch to Fitz-

hugh's middle. "Bernardo comes alone, which evens up the odds a bit, but unless you wish to have the man serenading you outside your window at midnight, you'll have to find some way to convince the shoemaker you will never be his."

Allegra, who had been feeling much abused, rallied. "You're right, *Uncail* Max. Valerian is a true ark of science—very smart. He will figure out just what we are to do. Something must be done. I cannot live my life with that foolish Timoteo forever chasing behind me like some hungry dog after a bone."

Something was bothering Valerian. "Max, exactly how did Bernardo learn that Allegra was bound for Brighton?"

Murphy made himself very busy rearranging his remaining bouquets. "And what am I to be now, boyo, a mind reader? Unless I had a little slip of the tongue when I sat sipping wine with the lad in a local *caffè*, trying to discover what he planned."

He turned to Allegra. "It's on the water wagon I've been since the morning after you left, m'darlin', but I confess I took a most terrible tumble from it the day you and sweet Louisa sailed away—and you as well, Valerian. I'm that sorry, that I am, and not just because Candie read me one of her memorable scolds just while my head was pounding like to make me believe someone was doin' a jig behind my eyes."

"Oh, *Uncail* Max," Allegra all but groaned, shaking her head. "But I forgive you, for you must have been sorely tried to lose your Louisa. You forgive him as well, don't you, Valerian? Valerian?"

"Hmm?" Inspiration had struck Valerian with a force so hard he almost reeled under its onslaught, so that he hadn't really been listening. Could he do it? Would he be able to pull it off? And if he did do it, would it last? He looked at Max, his expression purposely blank. "I suppose—and this may be just what you were thinking yourself, Max—we could defuse Bernardo's ardor by telling him that Allegra and I are betrothed."

"Betrothed! What can you be thinking?" Allegra exploded, causing two female passersby to peer at her intently and then move on, their heads pressed together as they giggled and whispered to each other.

Valerian looked down at her, seeing her flushed cheeks and overbright eyes. "Is it so inconceivable?" he asked as Max continued to busy himself with the basket of violets. "Am I so old and undesirable that Bernardo wouldn't believe you could ever marry me?"

"Don't be so silly, for you are not old at all, even with your angel wings." Allegra sighed, reluctant to explain the obvious, for she had just told Max that Valerian was brilliant. "But only think, Valerian, if an ocean couldn't stop Bernardo, how do you suppose a betrothal could do what the ocean could not? No, he will only bring out his silver mallet and tap-tap on your head as he did on Erberto's, and then the chase will be on once more. No, I think, Valerian, that you shall just have to kill Bernardo for me. There simply is no other way."

Max threw back his head and laughed aloud, nearly dislodging his wig. "Kill him! Oh, boyo, she's a colleen after me own heart! You talk of marriage and she talks of murder. Either way, as I see it, my friend, *you're* a dead man."

"Max—" Valerian began warningly.

"Well, I must be going," the wily Irishman broke in quickly, for a lifetime of living by his wits had given him a fine sense of timing when it came to calling it a day. "I'll be around, checking the dock and the stagecoaches just so

I can let you know when our love-bedazzled, shoemaker reaches Brighton—if he doesn't get lost and end by landing in Cornwall.''

''Where are you staying?'' Valerian called after him, reluctant to see Max leave, though why he should feel that way he was at a loss to explain, even to himself. ''I might want to reach you.''

But Max just kept on moving, disappearing into a nearby alleyway so quickly that Valerian realized it would be impossible to give chase to the man without deserting Allegra in the middle of the flagway.

''Damn the man!'' he swore under his breath, then turned to his companion, thoroughly out of charity with her. ''Kill him, Allegra? How do you propose for me to go about it, hmm? A knife? A pistol? Or perhaps a heavy brick applied to the back of his head in a darkened alleyway might do the trick. And will you come watch me hang, or would that prove too upsetting, even for your bloodthirsty Italian sensibilities?''

Allegra saw the pain in Valerian's eyes and longed to throw her arms around him, begging his forgiveness. She wanted nothing more from life than to hear his proposal, but not this way, and not for the reason he had given. But he was not to know that. She would die a thousand terrible deaths before she would let him know that!

''Oh, Valerian,'' she said, turning to retrace their steps to her grandfather's house, her hand tucked tightly around his arm. ''Why are you Englishmen so carelessly brave? Bernardo would not think twice before tapping on your head.''

Valerian sought to find solace where he could. ''So you have turned down my suggestion of a betrothal purely to protect me? It had nothing to do with whether or not you could *ever* consider a betrothal between the two of us?''

She looked up at him, wishing with all her might that she could believe he truly cared how she answered his last question. ''If—if you were to really mean it, Valerian, I suppose I should not be offended by your proposal,'' she answered at last, trying to be very English about the thing while her Italian blood urged her to tell him exactly what was on her mind. ''Would—would you consider asking me for my hand if it weren't for Bernardo?''

Valerian didn't know how to answer. To tell the truth would end his misery once and for all, for he was not so blind as to be unaware that Allegra looked upon him favorably. And there were their shared kisses at the Pavilion to give him hope as well. But he had already decided that she should experience more of life in England before tying herself to a promise she might live to regret.

''Ah, imp,'' he said, seeing Lord Halsey—and temporary rescue—approaching from the opposite direction. ''There are some questions well-behaved young misses just do not ask. Now smile, Allegra, for unless I miss my guess, his lordship is about to compliment you on your performance last night, and as you and Duggy are promised to him for this evening, I suggest you be polite.''

ALLEGRA SAT ALONE in the Dugdale drawing room, nursing her dark mood. Who did Valerian Fitzhugh think he was, to lecture her on proper deportment as if she were some simple-witted dolt? Who did he think he was talking to, a silly schoolroom chit who had never sung for the Bishop of Bologna? And how dared he tease her about quite the most serious question she had ever asked in her life?

She had all but bared her soul to him, right there on the

street, and he had laughed at her, then quickly changed the subject, just as if her question had been of no importance. She had been nonplussed by his action, completely at a loss as to how to go on, and could not remember a word Lord Halsey had said to her. Only now, once Valerian had deposited her back at Number 23 Royal Crescent Terrace and run off like the hounds of Hell were after him, could she think of what she should have done.

She should have turned to him, right there on the street, and asked in a very loud, very carrying voice, "But, Valerian, why then did you take me to a private parlor in the Pavilion—with the Regent in residence and my grandfather in the building as well—and kiss me on the mouth, not once, but twice? I do not know all your English rules of propriety, but in Italy you could not do such a thing without either proposing marriage or being prepared to face my grandfather's vengeance. Isn't that right, Lord Halsey?"

Allegra took a large bite of the pastry Betty had filched from the kitchens for her and nodded emphatically. Yes, that's precisely what she should have said. After all, Valerian had compromised her last night. Even *Uncail* Max had said as much. But all Valerian had done today was to parade her about the town like some prize pullet and then weakly offer his proposal only as a way to thwart Bernardo.

Hadn't the man even considered punching the persistent shoemaker on his perfectly sculpted nose and sending the man back to Napoli on the next ship to leave port? Hadn't he given so much as a moment's thought to protecting her in some other way than by offering her a pretend engagement? And if he had really meant his words, why hadn't he repeated them, telling her the truth?

Her head ached with all this civilization. It was so much easier in Italy. People told you what was on their minds—

screamed it at you, actually—so that there could be no doubt as to how they felt. Here, in Brighton, everyone merely danced about, saying things that only implied what they meant, only hinted at the thoughts behind the words. Well, she decided, taking another savage bite of the tart, she could be devious too—even more devious than any Englishman—for she had Italian blood in her veins!

"Ah, there you are, cousin," Gideon said, breaking into her thoughts as he entered the drawing room, closing the doors on the empty hallway behind him. "I was just in the morning room with my dearest mama, lamenting to her how I have not seen you above a few precious moments since your great triumph last night at the Pavilion. We are all very proud of our little Italian cousin, you know."

Allegra glared at him. Gideon was a prime example of what she had been thinking. He never said what he meant, and his mocking tone proved it. He didn't care two sticks about her "great triumph" at the Pavilion. And he wasn't proud of her—none of the Kittredges were proud of her. They merely wanted her inheritance. That's why Gideon had sought her out, and that's why he had closed the doors to the hallway as he entered, so that they would not be interrupted. As a matter of fact, if Betty had been correct, the man was probably about to propose to her.

She felt her temper rising. Two insincere proposals in one short day were just too much. Valerian Fitzhugh might not be here for her to vent her spleen on but Gideon was. She sat back, prepared to make him pay for what he was about to do. It was time she showed these English amateurs what the word *devious* really meant!

"Good afternoon, Gideon," Allegra began, smiling brightly even as her stomach did a small sick flip, for it was not really in her nature to be cruel. She laid the half-eaten strawberry tart back on the plate, her appetite gone, and went on the attack. "Are you here to propose to me, *cugino?*"

"What?" Gideon threw back his handsome head and laughed aloud. "Whatever gave you that idea, cousin?" he asked, slipping his body close beside hers on the settee. "Oh, dear. Has my dearest sister been tattling? I suppose I have been caught out. She heard me baring my soul to Mama yesterday, I suppose, telling her of my deep affection for you, and my hopes for the future. How terrible of Isobel to betray me, not that I should be surprised. She lives to make me suffer for her own well-deserved unhappiness."

He had recovered from his shock so swiftly, lied so smoothly, that Allegra was forced to admire him. "And are you suffering very badly with this great love you bear me, Gideon?" she asked, picking at the tart once more, for her appetite had reappeared as quickly as it had gone into hiding. "Please, you must tell me everything."

Gideon needed no encouragement, his arm snaking out to rest lightly against her spine. This was going to be even easier than he could have hoped. It was his handsome face, he was sure. His handsome face, and his brilliant tailor.

"I was struck by your great beauty the day Fitzhugh and Uncle Denny dropped you into our laps, my fiery darling, but I knew I had to wait before I could dare to speak of my love."

"And I was much struck by you, Gideon," Allegra answered truthfully, gazing down at her hands, which she had demurely folded in her lap. She had been struck—by his arrogance and total lack of human feeling, not that she was about to tell him that.

Gideon took courage from Allegra's admission and pressed on. "Mama, bless her generous heart, has already given us her blessing, saying that nothing could be more fitting than to have her only niece's child and her own child united in marriage. Tell me, Allegra—dare I hope?''

Allegra knew she was being naughty, but she was also thoroughly out of charity with all men at the moment, and banished any lingering doubt as to what she would do. ''Hope, Gideon? You are daring to hope?'' She studiously removed his hand from her waist. ''I think, *cugino,* you are daring *many* things. Have you approached my *nonno* and asked his blessing?''

''Uncle Denny?'' Gideon leaned back, crossing one well-tailored leg over the other. ''Actually, my sweet, I had hoped you might do that for me. You know how Uncle Denny feels about me. He might just cut up stiff if I were to ask him. But he likes you, don't he? He'd accept our engagement, coming from you.''

Now she had him. Gideon had swallowed the bait and all that was left was to reel him in. Allegra hid a smile by taking another bite of her snack. ''But, *dearest,*'' she said, blinking rapidly, ''I could not do that. *Nonno* must hear the question from your mouth.'' She pressed her fingertips against his lips as he tried to protest. ''No, no, do not say anything else. Not another word. I cannot promise my hand, I cannot even promise to listen to your proposal—which you have not yet presented—until you have gained permission from *Nonno* to court me.''

Gideon leapt to his feet, his eyes haunted. ''But he'll skin me alive! He'll throw me out of the house! Think, Allegra! Could you bear for that to happen to the man you love?''

Her furious blinks had done their job, and she produced a single sparkling tear. ''Ah, Gideon, you break my heart!'' she exclaimed in her best tragic voice. ''If you cannot fight for me—'' Her voice broke and she buried her face in her handkerchief.

Gideon stood very still, considering his options. He wouldn't fight for Allegra—or anyone, for that matter—if it were his only means to Heaven. However, for a plum, and for the rest of the Dugdale fortune (which would be his the moment he deposited his mother and sister in some far-off cottage in the north of England), he would consider walking through fire in his stockinged feet. Of course— being Gideon—more than anything else, he would consider lying to get what he wanted!

Dropping to one knee in front of her, he vowed fervently, ''I will do as you say. I'll promise him that I will never set foot in a gaming house again. I'll give up my friends, the ones he says are leading me to rack and ruin. I'll never lay another wager on a horse race, no matter what the odds. Anything! I'll promise him anything. Only please, Allegra, promise *me* that your answer will be yes!''

''Really, Gideon? You would do this? You would do this for me?''

Gideon swallowed hard. ''I will do this!''

Her grandfather was going to enjoy the coming conversation, Allegra consoled herself, picturing Gideon on his knees in front of his uncle, promising to mend his wicked ways.

She turned her head to one side, the handkerchief now clutched dramatically against her breast as she struck a theatrical pose. ''No! I cannot! This is wonderful, but I cannot say another word of what lies in my heart, *dear* Gideon, until you have *returned* from *Nonno* with his blessing. Please—I beg you—do not ask me again!''

She held out her hand for his kiss, and continued to hold it out until he belatedly grasped it and pressed his lips to her palm, an action that set her teeth on edge. "I will do as you ask, Allegra, but you must give me time. A few days? A week?"

"I shall not smile again, nor even breathe, until it is done," she vowed earnestly, stealing a line from a very bad play she had once seen in Rome. "Now go," she added, remembering another line from the play, "before my tortured emotions betray me."

Gideon rose, unable to resist the need to brush off the knee of his new fawn breeches. "Thank you, Allegra. Thank you for making me the happiest of men," he declared, turning on his heel and heading, shoulders back, head erect, for the door.

Once she was alone again, Allegra gave way to a fit of the giggles. "I so love Italian opera, even as it is done by silly Englishmen," she said aloud, taking another bite of her strawberry tart just as Isobel—who had seen her brother in the hall and said something nasty to him, only to have him ignore her—entered the room, looking perplexed.

"Was my brother just in here, Allegra?" she asked, taking up a chair on the other side of the small table that sat in front of the settee.

"Yes, indeed, my cousin was here," Allegra answered, still trying to control her happiness, for she was feeling quite pleased with herself, and rather vindicated. "And now you are here. It is so nice to have so many visitors. Will my *zia* Agnes be joining us, do you think? No? Ah, well. Would you like one of these strawberry tarts, *cugina?* Betty got them for me from the kitchens when the cook turned her back. They are very good."

Isobel primly denied the offer. "Perhaps if you did not love food so much, cousin, you would not have so many unseemly bulges in your gowns," she suggested, eyeing

Allegra's ample breasts while ignoring the evidence of the other girl's slim waist. "But I am not here to remind you of your faults, dear girl. I am here to congratulate you on your triumph at the Pavilion. Uncle Denny has told us all about it, and I have seen myself the multitude of invitations that have already been stacked high on the mantel. You must be feeling rather smug."

Allegra, who was in fact feeling very smug indeed, only smiled, waving her hands as if dismissing the fuss that her singing had caused. "You are too kind, Isobel. But it is true enough, I suppose. Everyone wants me to sing for them now." Isobel's insults she would ignore, for she could not bring herself to care what the other girl thought.

Isobel, her eyes narrowing, leaned forward, saying, "Yes, they do, don't they? I think it is so unfair of them, to ask you to sing for your supper—to give your talents away for nothing—when you were so celebrated in Italy. That is why," she continued, sneaking a quick look toward the hallway, "I have come to you—to suggest a way you can make them all pay for such shabby treatment."

Allegra frowned, taken off her guard. Isobel acted as if the fashionable people of Brighton had insulted her and she—her loving English cousin—resented it. "But, Isobel, *Nonno* didn't seem to think anything was wrong. Nor did Valerian. Besides, I have no need of money anymore."

Isobel shook her head. "I know that. They are only men, and see no more than the obvious. But just think, Allegra. There are still so many poor soldiers, back from the war all these years, and still without the payment promised them by that fat old man in the Pavilion. Wouldn't it be wonderful if you could do something to ease their pain? Valerian would be greatly pleased, for I have heard him speak so eloquently about the horrors suffered by those wretched men. Valerian has many of them in his employ, you know—men without eyes, men who have lost limbs.''

Allegra, remembering Tweed, Valerian's one-eyed coachman, was hard-pressed not to be carried along on the flood tide of her emotions. She would give anything to help other people. She would give anything to please Valerian. But she was not so simpleminded that she did not recognize that Isobel was purposely directing her along a path she, Isobel, had chosen.

''Please, *cugina,* go on,'' she begged, for she did long to hear exactly what was on the other girl's mind. It appeared that Gideon was not the only devious Kittredge in the household.

Isobel smiled in unholy glee, which was truly a painful thing to watch. ''Then you are interested in my idea! How wonderful! What I have in mind is for you to give a performance—just a single performance—at the Theatre Royal in the New Road.''

It was becoming clear now, Isobel's plan. ''But *cugina,* if I were to charge money I would be singing professionally again. Valerian has most expressly requested that I do not do that.''

Isobel hastened to reassure her. ''No, no, Allegra. Listen to me! It would not be that way. You would not be keeping the money. It would go for the poor soldiers, the widows, the orphans. You would be a saint!''

She would be ruined for life! She would be thrown out of Society, her grandfather would cut her off without a penny, and a life spent with Bernardo behind his little shoemaker shop would begin to seem a blessing. Allegra leaned forward, smiling. ''A saint, Isobel? I would so like to be a saint.''

''Then you'll do it?''

Isobel, Allegra thought, would starve if she ever chose to go on the stage, for the girl had no talent for playing a part. Her greed and her envy and her longing to destroy her cousin were all quiet clearly stamped on her thin face.

Allegra rose, turning toward the door. "I will think about it most carefully, Isobel," she promised, then turned back to her cousin as inspiration, suddenly her friend, struck yet again. If it had worked once, she reasoned quickly, would it not work twice? "Yes, dear cousin, I *will* think about it— but only if you go to my *nonno* and ask him for me if the performance would be all right with him."

"Me?" Isobel's smile disappeared in a heartbeat. "You want me to ask him? But, Allegra, Uncle Denny barely even *speaks* to me!"

Allegra set her chin defiantly. "As I told your dear brother just a few minutes ago, I do nothing without my *nonno*'s blessing, no matter how much I may wish it." She unbent a little and leaned down to look Isobel squarely in the eye. "You will do this for me, *cugina?* Besides," she added just for good measure, "I do *so* wish to please Valerian."

Hearing Allegra speak Fitzhugh's name lent new starch to Isobel's spine. That, and the mention of her hated brother's name in almost the same breath.

"Gideon is going to approach Uncle Denny—for your hand?" she guessed, knowing that if the Baron agreed to the match, she would no longer need to destroy Allegra's chances with Valerian by making her a laughingstock in front of all of Brighton. Not that she had much faith in her mama's estimation of Gideon's ability to talk Allegra around to marrying him—which was why she had felt it imperative that she come up with a plan of her own. "And then you will accept him? If he gets Uncle Denny's permission?"

Allegra's sapphire eyes all but danced in her head as she leaned even closer and asked, "You can keep a secret, dearest Isobel?"

"Yes, yes! Anything!" Isobel answered, her heart pounding with excitement.

"You will swear it on your eyes?" Allegra persisted. "Think, *cugina,* for this is a very dangerous curse to wish on yourself. Italian curses often are, you know."

Isobel shivered, crossing her fingers behind her back. "I swear. On my eyes," she whispered hoarsely.

"Then I will tell you," Allegra answered brightly. "Yes, Gideon is going to ask *Nonno* for his permission to woo me. And no, I shall not marry him. I could not do this, you see, because I have already decided to marry Valerian."

Isobel's eyes all but popped out of her head at exactly the same time that her stomach plummeted to her toes. "Valerian! Do not tell me Valerian has asked you to be his wife?"

Allegra dismissed this question with a wave of her hand. "No. But he will. He loves me, *sotto sotto*—deep down. He just does not know it yet, I think, poor man."

This was all very confusing to Isobel, whose full concentration had been on her own plan, so that she could not see that Allegra was playing out a small stratagem of her own. "Then I truly don't understand. Why did you allow Gideon to hope in the first place? It seems very cruel."

"I did it because Gideon does not love me, but only the plum I will receive when I marry. I did it, dearest Isobel, because I wish to watch as your silly brother puffs himself up to a great height, only to collapse into a great airless heap. I think *Nonno* will not be so nice to him either, and that also pleases me. Does it please you?''

''Oh, yes,'' Isobel responded earnestly, rubbing her hands together. If Allegra didn't stand in the way of her happiness with Valerian, Isobel might even think she was beginning to like her Italian cousin. ''And it serves him right too, trying to use you to pay off his horrible gambling debts.''

Then she sobered, realizing that Allegra's admission took them both back to the question of Valerian. She would have no choice but to continue with her plan to disgrace Allegra if Gideon's suit was destined to be denied. But even Isobel was not so thick as to overlook the obvious. ''And why are you sending *me* to Uncle Denny, Allegra? Are you hoping he will not be nice to me either?''

Allegra did her best to appear puzzled by the question. ''And why would that be, Isobel? You said yourself that I would be doing a great thing, singing for all those widows and the tiny *bambinos*. Surely *Nonno* will not object to your most wonderful idea. But you see, because *Nonno* loves me and wishes to make up for leaving me abandoned all these years, he may give his agreement just to please me, which is something I could not let him do. So you must ask him for me, just as if *I* knew nothing about the plan.

''Besides,'' she added, in case her reason hadn't completely convinced Isobel, ''your English, um, *she* is so much better than mine. *Comprende?* And *Nonno* does admire you so much for your great intelligence—as well as your beauty. I have seen it in his eyes when you talk to him.''

''Yes,'' Isobel answered hesitantly, preening a bit at the inferred compliment, ''I suppose you're right about all that, but—''

"Then it is settled!" Allegra bent to kiss Isobel on both cheeks. "I shall be so eager to hear that you have done me this small favor so that I might give my concert. We must devise a special invitation for the Regent, don't you think?"

"Missy?"

Leaving Isobel to muddle through everything that had gone on, Allegra turned to see Betty standing by the open doors, looking decidedly nervous. "You said for me to tell you when your new bonnet got here."

Her new bonnet? Allegra didn't have the faintest notion of what Betty was telling her. She looked at the maid and asked carefully, "And which bonnet would that be, Betty?"

Betty spoke through clenched teeth, surreptitiously motioning with her right hand—the one that held a folded sheet of paper. "The *Irish* green bonnet, missy, if you take my meaning. It's at the servants' door right now, waiting on you."

Allegra shot a quick look at Isobel, who seemed lost in a brown study. She would have loved to stay a while and watch her cousin attempt to puzzle out what had happened in the past ten minutes, but she had more important things to do now than to amuse herself by turning the tables on Isobel and Gideon Kittredge's plans for her future.

"If you'll excuse me, Isobel?" she asked, already heading for the hallway.

"Yes, yes, you go on now," Isobel answered vaguely, her mind concentrating on precisely how she was going to present her plan for the Baron's permission and at the same time make him think the whole thing had been her mother's idea.

CHAPTER NINE

BETTY WAS still occupied in helping Allegra don her cherry-red cloak as the younger woman entered the kitchens.

"I cannot believe it. He is arrived so soon?" Allegra questioned, seeing Max seated at his ease at the table, a fresh strawberry tart in his hand, the bottom half of his face hidden behind a truly glorious red beard.

"Love sails on wings, I suppose, m'darlin'," Max answered, holding out his arm as he rose and began walking toward the servants' entrance.

"Missy!" Betty cried, wringing her hands as she watched her mistress leaving on the Irishman's arm. "Whatever am I to say to the Baron iffen he should ask for you?"

"Lock my door and tell everyone who asks that I am lying down with the headache," Allegra offered quickly, turning to face down a lingering scullery maid and the Dugdale cook. "And if *anyone* is heard to say differently, Betty, give me their names and I will call down a most terrible curse upon their heads, so that their betraying tongues fall out and all their fingers tie themselves into knots. I am *Italiana,* and I can do these things!"

The Dugdale servants, one of them visibly quaking while the other quickly made the sign against the evil eye, both promised not to breathe a word of what they had seen, and as Max chuckled his delight at her ingenuity, Allegra quit the house for the alleyway.

"Where is Bernardo now? Have you sent a messenger to Valerian? He has gone back to his estate, yes? I am sure he has, as we did not expect the shoemaker so soon as this. Have you put Bernardo where no one can see him? Do you think anyone will recognize me with my hood pulled down this way? Yesterday I should not have worried, but today I am famous, you know. Oh, everything is happening so quickly!"

Max was huffing and puffing, having some difficulty keeping up with both the pace Allegra was setting and her rapid-fire questions. "Bernardo is safely tucked up in my room at a small inn near Chapel Street, though it wasn't an easy thing, don't you know, to talk him out of running up and down every street in Brighton, calling your name. It's a determined fellow he is, your shoemaker."

"He is not *my* shoemaker, *Uncail* Max," Allegra corrected, ducking her head as a familiar face passed by. "But you have not told me about Valerian. Will he be meeting us at this inn?"

Max would have laughed, but he was rapidly getting out of breath. "And thereby hangs a tale! Valerian was the one what brought Bernardo to me. It's underestimating the boy I've been doin', I think. Not only did he ferret out the place where I'm staying, but he beat me to Bernardo as well. And, bless him, the fellow already has cooked up a plan to explain the shoemaker's presence until we might straighten this thing out once and for all. It's a very good plan it is, too, if only we can pull it off, which I've no doubt we can. Do you think, mayhap, there might be a drop of the Irish in Valerian? Yes, a fine broth of a boy!"

They were nearing the waterfront and Max prudently

took a quick peep behind them before pulling Allegra into a narrow alleyway and entering the third door on the left.

Together they tiptoed down the hall past the inn's common room and climbed the staircase to the top of the high narrow house, to come to Max's room. The Irishman knocked twice, waited, then knocked twice more before Valerian opened the door to allow Max and Allegra to step inside.

Instantly all was chaos.

Bernardo, who had been slumped dejectedly beside a sloping wooden table, his elbows on his knees, spotted the love of his life and leapt to his feet, his smile so wide and blightingly white that Valerian felt obliged to turn away.

Allegra, in her turn, espied the shoemaker and instantly burst into a scathing stream of Italian that had a lot to do with the great disrespect with which she regarded Bernardo's brainpower and little to do with greeting a fellow countryman who had come to the English shore.

As Bernardo stood there, a glorious, sad-eyed angel whose wrists stuck out a full two inches from the bottom of his coat sleeves, Allegra continued her assault, her musical voice rising and falling as she berated the shoemaker with a barrage of insults, her entire body taking part in the tongue-lashing as she gave emphasis to her words with expressive hand gestures and eloquent shrugs.

She finally ran down, ending her scolding with a stern warning to Bernardo that if he so much as tried to utter a single word in his own defense she would personally see to it that her good friend, the Prince Regent, had him hauled to the very top of the Marine Pavilion and then deposited, rump down, on the extreme tip of the largest, most pointed onion dome on the entire building.

Max collapsed onto the side of the narrow bed, wiping

his brow. "Ah, and it's grand to listen to her when she's in a rage, isn't it? Takes the cockles off m'heart, don't you know."

Exhausted by her own vehemence, Allegra subsided into the chair Bernardo had vacated and began fanning herself with a handkerchief she had pulled from the pocket of her gown.

"*Brava! Brava!*" Valerian applauded from the vantage point he had taken up in front of the single window in the small, meanly furnished room. "I begin to think, imp, that you give your most impassioned performances in ramshackle inns, although I see your months in civilization have robbed you of the ability to spit in order to lend credence to your threats. I hesitated to point that out, but I find that, since meeting you, I must take my pleasures where I might find them."

"Valerian!" Allegra ran to him, throwing herself against his broad chest, and tightly wrapped her arms about his waist. She had temporarily forgotten Fitzhugh in her sudden, overwhelming anger upon seeing Bernardo standing in the room big as life, grinning as if she would actually be pleased to see him.

From his position in the middle of the room, Bernardo began to growl low in his throat, one hand going beneath his shirt in search of his metal mallet—the same metal mallet Valerian had prudently demanded the man put into his keeping earlier, before he would agree to allow Max to fetch Allegra.

"*Arrah* now, do sit down, you beautiful dolt," Max ordered from the bed. "You're becoming a bloody nuisance one way or the other, don't you know? And what are you glowering at in the first place? Can't you see you've lost her? All that remains now is to ship you straight home again before anybody here becomes the wiser, for it's a fine mess you could make for this sweet colleen, and no mistake, even if Fitzhugh here has a plan, which I'm thinkin' now might not be so good as it first seemed.''

As if the words had conjured up the deed, the door to the room burst open and Gideon Kittredge stepped inside to look about, his avid gaze taking in all of the occupants. ''My, my, and what do we have here, hmm? I thought I saw you pass by the coffeehouse, and I was right. That's ten pounds Georgie Watson owes me.'' He put a hand to his ear. ''Listen? Do you hear that, cousin? Ah, what a pity. It's the sound of my dear uncle's bellow, calling for his solicitor so that he can change his will yet again.''

It was Max who spoke first, shaking his head sadly. ''Candie is right, boyo, and it's getting past it I must be. I had no idea we were being followed. It's that sorry I am, don't you know.''

''Valerian?'' Allegra questioned quietly, her eyes wide with apprehension as she looked up at him. Everything was becoming so confused.

''Just be very quiet, imp, and we may wriggle out of this yet. It's time to put my plan, such as it is, into action,'' he answered softly as he gently disengaged her death grip around his waist and stepped forward, his hand outstretched, to welcome Gideon to their little gathering.

Gideon's hand came out automatically, although his eyes remained puzzled as he stared at Bernardo, who, unbelievably, appeared to be even prettier than he, as if that were possible. ''Fitzhugh,'' he said blankly. ''What are you doing here? Who are these people? Isn't m'cousin here for an assignation with that bearded fellow over there? I don't understand.''

''You *don't* understand, do you?'' Max sniffed indelicately, although it had to have pleased him that Gideon believed that he, who would never again see the sunny side of fifty, might be having an "assignation" with a young, beautiful colleen like Allegra. "And there's nothing so surprising in that, I'll be thinking, you miserable buckeen, for you have the look of one what has a great deal of knowledge outside his head."

"Quiet, Max," Valerian warned softly, motioning Gideon to a chair. A lot depended on these next minutes and he disliked having his concentration broken by the Irishman's wit. "Now, Gideon, I suppose you'd like to know what's going on here. Of course you would, as would I if our positions were reversed."

"Yes, well, I suppose so!" Gideon sat briefly, made to rise, then sat down once more, all the time staring at Bernardo. "Is that fellow *real,* Valerian? He looks like a painting."

The shoemaker, who had been blessedly silent for so long, took it into his head at this moment to add his mite to the conversation. *"Il mio nome é,"* he announced proudly, rising to his full, impressive height and jabbing one long forefinger into his chest as he introduced himself, "Bernardo Sansone Guglielmo Alonso Timoteo—"

"Conte Timoteo to you, Gideon," Valerian broke in quickly, unceremoniously pushing Bernardo back down into his chair and stepping in front of the shoemaker before the fool totally destroyed Allegra by adding "premier shoemaker of Milano!"

Gideon peered past Valerian to take in Bernardo's humble garb. "Conte Timoteo? Shouldn't he dress better than that? Not that my tailor would have him, of course. He has far too many muscles to allow a jacket to lie smoothly. And look at his thighs. They're positively obscene. As a matter of fact, Valerian, I think the only thing good about him is those boots. Magnificent work, don't you think?''

Bernardo, whose command of the English language thankfully remained somewhat limited, stuck out one boot and beamed a smile at Gideon. ''My *stivali? Sì*. He is *magnifico!*''

A sharp explosion of rapid-fire Italian from Allegra silenced the shoemaker and he lowered his head, giving in once more to the overwhelming sorrow of at last acknowledging that the single great love of his life refused to love him back. He was lost, at sea—adrift without a hint as to what would become of him now. His hope gone, his brother and cousin calling him mad and deserting him to return to the shoemaker shop, Bernardo had nowhere to go, nothing to live for, and nothing—considering the sad, empty state of his pockets—to live on even if he should wish to go on living, which, of course, he did not.

He would have to fling himself into the cold, dark sea. He would have to end it all, a broken-hearted shell of a man who could not find anything left in all the world to give him hope. He would—*"Che cosa?"* Bernardo's head snapped up. What was it the tall man with the silver wings in his hair had said? *Conte Timoteo?* Who was *Conte* Timoteo?

Bernardo straightened in the chair and began to listen very carefully to what Valerian was telling the skinny, flour-white-skinned man who had admired his boots.

''...and so you see, Gideon, Allegra's cousin, the Conte, had no choice but to apply to his only remaining relative for assistance. His house and grounds lost to him in a debt of honor—surely you of all people can understand the Conte's need to satisfy his gaming debts—he spent his last penny, even sold his wardrobe, to procure passage for his loyal servant, Max, and himself to come to Brighton.''

Max growled low in his throat, but Valerian silenced him with a look.

"To continue," Valerian said firmly, redirecting his attention to Gideon, a young man in whom the light of knowledge did not, thankfully, burn brightly. "Not wishing to embarrass his cousin by showing up at the Baron's door in his shabby clothes, he sent Max to bring Allegra to him. It is all quite simple, really, when you think about it. Oh, yes, the only thing the Conte could not bear to part with was his magnificent boots," he added as an afterthought. "It seems we men, too, can be vain."

Kittredge scratched at the side of his head, looking toward Allegra, who was at that moment whispering into Bernardo's ear—a far happier Bernardo than the shoemaker had been a few moments earlier.

Clearly Gideon had misunderstood the situation. Everything was still all right. He could still approach his uncle Denny for Allegra's money—no! He gave a slight shake to his head, making a mental erasure. He could approach him for Allegra's *hand*—he must remember to ask for her *hand!* It would appear he had some more work to do on the speech he had been preparing with Georgie Watson at the coffee-house.

"Yes, yes, I think I understand now," Gideon mumbled at last, just as Max, who had been growing impatient with Kittredge's excruciatingly slow mental processes, had been about to explode in frustration. "But I still don't understand what *you're* doing here, Valerian."

As Valerian hesitated—for he had not taken his plan far enough to consider what he would say if they were caught out here at the inn—Allegra, whose father had often praised her for her ability to cover beautifully for another singer who suffered a mental lapse on stage, stepped forward to effect a rescue.

"Max—*Cugino* Bernardo's valet—summoned Valerian before he came for me. My *cugino* and Valerian had met in Milano, you see, at the Palazzo dell'Ambrosiana, and it was he, my *cugino,* who helped him to locate me in Firenze in the first place. *Capisce?* Do you understand now, Gideon?"

This overabundance of Italian proved to be too much for Gideon, who only nodded, saying, "Yes, I see. I see—I think."

Allegra, flushed with her success, continued. "And that is why I was hugging dear Valerian when you came in, Gideon. Valerian, being such a dear, dear friend, had just offered to house Bernardo and clothe him until such time as his so-very-sickly uncle passes away—an uncle on his mother's side, so that I, unfortunately, cannot share in the bounty—and Bernardo inherits the man's fortune and can return to his own estates. It is all quite simple, yes?"

Valerian, who had, halfway through Allegra's speech, turned to her in mingled astonishment and dismay, belatedly found his voice. Speaking through clenched teeth, he said, "So if you don't mind keeping our secret until the Conte is better outfitted to meet the Baron, perhaps we can get on with it. I would like to quit this room as soon as possible. Can I trust you to escort your cousin home, Gideon?"

By now Bernardo understood as much as he, with his already remarked-upon limited brain-power, would probably ever understand. He had lost his beloved Allegra. But he had gained a title, and new clothes, and something to eat besides the moldy bit of cheese that was all he had left in his pocket, and could even look forward to having a roof to cover his head that night. Wasn't he a lucky shoemaker? Wasn't this England wonderful?

His smile bright, Bernardo exuberantly dashed about hugging everyone and soundly kissing them on both cheeks—including a thoroughly disgusted Gideon, who made short work of extricating both Allegra and himself from the room.

As Valerian stood looking at the door that had just closed behind Allegra's back, Max walked up to him, rested a hand on his shoulder, and said, "That little girl can spout lies that would shame a tinker, Lord love her. Now, boyo, my *master* has need of at least three suits of clothes, excluding his evening dress, and all of the other bits and pieces that go with them. I'll have the shops send the bills round to you, but I shall be needin' a bit of the ready to tide me over, don't you know."

Valerian looked down at the pudgy Irishman and the hand the man was holding out to him and saw the gleam in the man's eyes. "We'll do this shopping together. Much as you might think my brains have been addled by all that has gone on here, Max, I'm not so confused as to give you carte blanche with my money.

"But first," he said, picking up his cloak and motioning for the still grinning Bernardo to follow him, "I think we might stop downstairs and split a few bottles. Perhaps I am just getting old, but I am suddenly very much in need of a drink."

"A cup of the creature wouldn't do any of us harm, I'm thinkin'," Max agreed readily, turning to Bernardo. "*Vino*, you paper-skulled Adonis?"

Bernardo nodded emphatically, tossing his tattered cloak and small worn satchel into Max's arms just as if he had lived his entire life surrounded by servants. He lifted his head imperiously and brushed past Valerian, to be the first through the doorway. "*Vino, sì! Vino* for Bernardo—*Conte Timoteo!*"

Valerian laughed out loud. "Taking his heart-break rather well, isn't he, Max?" he suggested, following the shoemaker.

Bringing up the rear, loaded down with Bernardo's belongings, Maximilien Murphy launched himself into a string of Irish curses that could have blasted a hole in an iron pot.

"*ODDS FISH! Say that again, boy! I don't believe I'm hearing this!*"

Baron Dugdale's incredulous roar could be heard throughout the house, and everyone within earshot raced to discover what had happened, each harboring her own fears—and even hopes—as to precisely what had launched the Baron into the boughs.

Isobel had been sitting alone in the drawing room, still carefully composing the impassioned plea she would employ to convince her uncle that Allegra should perform for money, while still letting him know that the inspiration behind this glorious idea came from something her mother had said—just in case Uncle Denny should cut up stiff at the idea.

Her arguments, already three days in the making, were starting to sound feasible even to her, so that Isobel was beginning to harbor serious doubts that a charity performance by Allegra would have the expected result—that of forever disgracing her cousin in Valerian's eyes.

But what other choice did she have open to her? Allegra had already told her that she would never accept a proposal from Gideon—who was even now closeted with her uncle—because she expected to receive an offer from Valerian. And Isobel would die, simply die, if that were ever to happen.

But if Isobel were to approach her uncle with the idea of a charity performance, and if that stupid Prince Regent should give it his blessing, the whole thing could end with Valerian being even more in charity with Allegra than he was at this moment. In which case—and this was the point that bothered Isobel most of all—why should her mother get the credit for thinking of such a wonderful idea in the first place while she, Isobel, the true genius, received no recognition at all?

The Baron's bellow had interrupted these tortured thoughts and Isobel had run into the hallway, only to cannon into her mother, who had just dashed from the morning room, twin dots of color giving life to her otherwise sallow face.

"Look out, you little idiot!" Agnes screeched, hastily pushing her daughter to one side, so that Isobel was forced to pick up her skirts and run behind her mother, each of them fighting to be in the lead.

Agnes, who had been mentally redecorating the morning room with some of the plum that would come to her the day Gideon and Allegra were wed, and who knew that her beloved son was with her brother at that moment, immediately thought the *worst*—which, she supposed, grinning, might just as easily turn out to be the *best!*

Obviously, Agnes told herself as she and Isobel (now side by side, as youth and speed had little difficulty overcoming age and greed) ran toward the study door, Denny had exploded in wrath at the mere idea of Gideon marrying his granddaughter. That was most probably to be expected, she knew, although still depressingly ignorant of the man. Why couldn't her brother bring himself to see the obvious—that her son was the most wonderful, lovable creature on earth, and his precious Allegra should thank her lucky stars that he should deign to toss his cap her way.

But if the worst were to happen and the Baron denied the suit, the strain of screaming at her son caused by her brother's inevitable anger might prove to be too much for the man's heart. Why, even now her dearest Denny could be prostrate on the floor, breathing his last. A plum was lovely, but to gain the entire inheritance in one blow was even lovelier!

Unless, of course, as Gideon had supposed, the dratted man had summoned his solicitor again and already changed his will! That chilling thought lent wings to Agnes's steps, and it was only with some difficulty that Allegra, who had been descending the staircase at the moment her grandfather had called out—Betty having told her that Gideon was meeting with the man, and eager to listen at the door while her *nonno* tore a verbal strip off the younger man's hide— was able to be the one to throw open the door to the study.

The trio of women took two steps inside and skidded to a halt to survey the damage.

The Baron was not either clutching his chest in pain or collapsed in his chair, which greatly depressed Agnes's hopes for recovering the morning room chairs in the lovely gold brocade material she had seen in that little shop on Dean Street.

Gideon, it would seem, however, hadn't fared nearly so well as his still upright uncle, for he was on his knees in front of the fireplace, his forearms pressed protectively against the top of his head.

Isobel, who had come to a halt just behind Allegra,

twisted up her mouth in disgust, not as disappointed by her brother's failure to gain permission to woo Allegra as she was by her own momentary hope that the simpleton might have somehow pulled it off and Allegra, who seemed to place so much faith in her grandfather's judgment, would then agree to go along with the engagement.

Lastly, there was Allegra, the architect of the scene that was even now playing itself out in the Dugdale study. She, if anyone were to apply to her at the moment for her thoughts, would have announced herself greatly pleased with the sight of Gideon groveling on the hearth.

Even if she hadn't already wished her arrogant cousin at the opposite end of the earth, his actions of the past three days—days that had dragged along interminably, as neither Valerian nor Bernardo had yet to present themselves at Number 23—had proved to her that no punishment that befell Gideon could be too terrible.

For Gideon had been making her life a misery ever since discovering her at the inn with Bernardo, plaguing her with questions about "her cousin the Conte" for which she had no answers. How rich would the Conte be when his sick uncle died? And if the Conte were to die—perish at sea or some such thing on his way back to Italy—would his money then go to her, Gideon's wife? And then there was this palace of the Conte's to consider. Were there many servants? How many bedrooms did it have? It was the out-side of enough! Gideon, she was sure, was so greedy he must have heard the coins jingling in his mother's pockets before he was born!

The Baron belatedly became aware of his feminine au-dience, bowed, and pointed to his kneeling nephew with the tip of his cane. "Come to see the show, have you, eh? It seems everybody but me was privy to what this ignorant puppy was about, yipping around my heels with his blasted proposals. Here, now, boy," he said, prodding at Gideon's shoulder with the cane, "let's hear that last part again, so that everyone can see how low you can sink."

Gideon turned his head to see his mother, sister, and cousin standing just behind him. He looked up at his uncle, his eyes silently pleading with the man not to put him through this torture. He had tried and failed. He had lost a fortune, and most probably his mother's good graces. Wasn't that enough? Did he have to be made a figure of fun in front of his sister, who looked to be enjoying every second of his disgrace?

Taking refuge in the tried-and-true, Gideon put a hand to his mouth and coughed.

"Oh, never mind!" the Baron growled in disgust, lifting the cane so that Gideon could rise. "Tell a lie once and it lives forever, I say. There's no need to hear all that drivel again. You, Aggie—you're the one who's behind this anyway, unless I miss my guess. *He* don't have the wit to think up such nonsense by himself. Did you really think I'd believe this worthless scamp could ever stop his gaming and be a good husband to my granddaughter here? I'd as soon believe Prinny will send word to Calais tomorrow to fetch Brummell back for another go at being his bosom beau! Now get out of here—the lot of you. Except you, Allegra. I want to talk to you."

"Perhaps you'd best consider a repairing lease at Papa's cousin Bertrand's in Wolverhampton, Gideon, until your creditors forget you," Isobel suggested happily as her brother brushed past her, coughing into his hand. Agnes quickly followed him out of the room, mumbling something about having Betty fetch the lad's restorative tonic.

"You're a cruel, unnatural child, Isobel," her mother

took the time to declare feeling, which only served to make Isobel laugh out loud as she closed the door.

Once everyone was gone Allegra turned to her grandfather, smiling. "Does your toe pain you, *Nonno?*" she asked, waiting until he sat down before settling herself on the footstool at his feet.

"My toe?" the Baron questioned blankly, looking down at his bandaged foot. "Why, bless me, I do believe it's healed. And to think I didn't even notice, being so busy yelling at that idiot. Imagine him thinking I'd give you over into his keeping! Daft fool! That boy isn't fit to mind mice at a crossroad. Haven't enjoyed anything half so much as seeing him on his knees, though, telling me how he loved you and how he would never go gaming again." He peered intently at his granddaughter. "How did you know the gout was gone?"

Allegra shrugged, smiling in real pleasure. "The cherries helped, I suppose, but I also remembered something my father once told me, *Nonno.* He said that a happy man, a laughing man, has no room inside him for pain. You see, the proposal was not all *Zia* Agnes's idea, for I allowed Gideon to hope I would agree to a match between us if he came first to you."

"Eh? And why would you do a thing like that, child? You couldn't want him."

"Never! I only thought having Gideon ask for my hand might amuse you—although I must not lie. I am also a little naughty, *Nonno,* and wished for you to bellow at Gideon, for I do not much care for him, even if he is your nephew. I did tell you that I am not always nice. You are pleased?"

The Baron, who was not so old that he could not recognize the fine hand of a woman's revenge, threw back his head and laughed aloud. "Odds fish, but that's good! I always thought you *I*-talians were downy ones. Tell me, child, do you have any plans for that scheming Aggie—or that die-away daughter of hers? You never know when the gout might be back, eh?''

Allegra, who had begun to feel some small remorse for her meanness now that the deed was done, was saved from answering as the butler entered the room, cleared his throat audibly, and announced: ''The Conte Timoteo and Mister Fitzhugh to see you, my lord.''

THE FOLLOWING TWO HOURS remained mostly a blur in Allegra's memory.

Valerian had handled the introductions brilliantly, beginning with his greeting, which had included the words ''Look, dear Allegra, at the *surprise* I have brought you.'' Taking her cue from him, she had pretended to be astonished by Bernardo's arrival in Brighton, although her astonishment at Bernardo's appearance as he stood in her grandfather's study was not feigned, for Valerian had surely wrought a miracle.

The shoemaker, always handsome, had been transformed into a heavenly vision whose brilliance almost hurt her eyes. His unruly blond locks had been tamed and styled so that they surrounded his face like a gilt picture frame, with a few of the golden ringlets dropping carelessly onto his smooth forehead.

Bernardo's fine body—long, powerful legs and muscular upper torso—had been poured into a modish suit of clothes that, if it were possible for mere fabric to speak, would doubtless thank all the angels and the saints for the opportunity to serve such a glorious purpose.

Perhaps his memory of polite behavior had been prodded by recollecting his years spent as a ''companion'' to a lonely English lady in Italy, or perhaps it was just that all Italians seem to have a flair for performing—but Bernardo himself had been wonderful.

Saying little, and employing much of his mother tongue, the shoemaker had dazzled the Baron and the Kittredges as well—except, perhaps, for Gideon, who had crept back into the room to stand at a distance and eye Bernardo's expensive tailoring with open envy.

Valerian's explanation for Bernardo's appearance had satisfied the Baron as easily as it had Gideon—for none of the purely English inhabitants of Number 23 was especially acute. Even Agnes fluttered and giggled, and Isobel, who had thought herself hopelessly in love with Valerian, transferred her loyalties to Bernardo within five minutes of his arrival on the scene.

All in all, Bernardo's entry could only be termed a brilliant success. It was only later, while the ''Conte Timoteo'' and Isobel took a stroll about the garden and Allegra and Valerian stole some time to themselves in the morning room, that Allegra could voice her fears.

''*Nonno* wishes to take Bernardo with us tomorrow to the Pavilion,'' she told Valerian, her sapphire eyes clouded with apprehension.

''And you are wondering how you will explain the dear Conte's propensity for eating with his fingers?'' Valerian offered, seating himself beside her on the striped satin settee. ''I admit it might prove difficult. Shall I have him develop the plague, or will a simple inflammation of the lungs be sufficient to have him cry off for the evening?''

Allegra's bottom lip came out in a pout. ''Do not make sport of me, Valerian,'' she commanded testily. ''I have not had a very nice day—a very nice several days. Why did you stay away so long?''

"Did you miss me, imp?"

Allegra shot Valerian a look that delighted him no end. Until she spoke. "I need to make a small confession, I suppose. I have been very naughty, Valerian—though it is all your fault."

He raised one eyebrow, looking down at her expectantly. "Of course it is, imp. Heaven forbid you should do anything that is *your* fault."

She sprang up from the settee to begin pacing the carpet and Valerian leaned back, content to admire the sight of his dearest Allegra in a dither. "You were mean to me, Valerian, saying that polite young ladies do not speak of proposals and the like. You remember this, yes? I was very hurt—*very* hurt. And when I am hurt I do not always do nice things, although I am always sorry for them later."

Valerian looked about the room, noticing that all the vases and mirrors were still in one piece. "Is the damage confined to your room, then? I see nothing amiss here."

She rounded on him, her small hands drawn up into fists, her ample breasts heaving in agitation. "*Stupido!* Why must you persist in thinking I know no other way to show anger than to scream or break things? I can be devious, you know. I *was* devious! And I am now so ashamed of myself!" With that, and totally without warning, she burst into tears, launching herself on Valerian's chest.

It took some time, but at last Valerian succeeded in getting the entire story out of her—all about her plans to pay Gideon out for his lies and greed while punishing Isobel for her scheme to lure Allegra into social disgrace.

He could not, he found, discover in his heart any sympathy for either Kittredge. Gideon had deserved his punishment, and as for Isobel—well, wasn't it true that all was fair in love and war? He did, however—since Allegra had told him *everything*—feel impelled to ask her how she had come to the conclusion that he was going to propose to her.

"You already did!" she exclaimed, now sitting beside him once more and dabbing delicately at her still moist eyes. "Oh, I know it was only to protect me that you thought of it, but you *did* think of it, when there were so many other things you could have done. You did not like me over-much when we were in Italy, as I did not very much like you—but that has changed. You love me now, Valerian."

Valerian rose, finding that it was now his turn to pace the carpet. It was true. He loved Allegra. He loved her with all his heart, Heaven help him. But he also loved his well-ordered life, the life he had lost the moment he had first learned of her existence. Suddenly, without warning, he felt trapped, backed into a corner.

The devil with his earlier notions that she was too young to make up her mind about marriage when she had yet to see London, let alone experience a Season. That had only been an excuse he'd used to delay the inevitable. If there was one thing he had learned about Allegra, it was that the child had very definite opinions.

And how could he forget his dreams of traveling the world with her at his side, or his visions of their sons and daughters playing on the lawns of his estate? *He* was the one he had believed to be too young to be tied to a spouse and children.

Yes, she was lovely. Yes, life since meeting her had been exciting. Yes, he dreamed about her at night and looked for her all the day long. Yes, he was fast on his way to becoming obsessed by his longing for this small, exciting, exotic scrap of explosive femininity.

His sigh was so deep and heartfelt that he saw Allegra's

hand go out to him, as if he might be ill. There was nothing else for it. He loved her. She had accepted it. Now it was his turn to face it.

Valerian's head came up and his shoulders straightened. His decision had been made, and it was final!

But *he* would do the asking, dammit, when *he* considered the time to be right! That's what was wrong. That was why he felt so trapped. It wasn't that he didn't love her. It was only that she wasn't playing by the rules. If, as the saying went, it was best for one to begin in the way one planned to go on, it was time he took charge of the situation!

"While it is true enough that there were other avenues open to me—killing Bernardo was your suggestion, as I recall—a pretended betrothal merely seemed to be the thing to offer at the time," he said at last, deliberately avoiding her eyes. "But as for loving you, imp—as for wishing to marry you—I'm afraid that *I* must be the one to tell you that—"

He never got to finish his poorly conceived confession, for Allegra was on her feet and running for the doorway, her hands tightly clapped to her ears. She had almost escaped him before he caught up with her, whirling her about to face him.

"Listen to me, imp," he begged, seeing tears standing in her eyes once more. "You think I am rejecting you, when I am only trying to explain how I feel about—"

"No!" she exclaimed, pushing herself out of his embrace. "I have made the *idiota* of myself. You were kind to me, and in my foolish vanity I believed that this kindness came from love. Forgive me, Valerian, if I have abused that kindness. *Addio!*"

"Allegra, wait!"

But it was too late. Bernardo, with Isobel hanging from

his arm like a limpet attached to a strong outcrop of solid rock, had appeared in the doorway, and all Valerian could do was watch helplessly as Allegra brushed by them and ran upstairs.

CHAPTER TEN

GIDEON HAD, in desperation, retreated to his bed, which was as far from his increasingly demanding creditors as he could conceivably hope to travel without applying to his uncle for funds—a consideration which by itself was enough to make the young man believe that, for once, he was really ill.

Adding to Gideon's melancholy was the all-but-constant presence in the house of Conte Timoteo—and the Conte's wardrobe Gideon found out very rapidly that it is extremely difficult to spend the entirety of one's life believing that one is the most handsome, well-turned-out gentleman in the vicinity, only to have one's own mother and sister fawn over some rosy-cheeked, vacant-eyed Italian who probably didn't understand every third word spoken to him!

If watching his scrawny sister make a cake out of herself hadn't been debilitating enough, his own mother—a woman who had clothed herself in half-mourning for the past sixteen years—had thoroughly sickened him by parading around the house waving an ivory-sticked fan boasting a hand-painted silk rendition of no less than the Coliseum itself!

Yet taking to his bed had not helped. Gideon coughed, and his mama sent Betty with the restorative tonic. Gideon moaned, and his mama told him to be a good little soldier and stuff a handkerchief in his mouth. Gideon asked if he could be set up on the settee in the drawing room, a blanket over his knees, and his mama refused, saying he might then give his latest illness to "our dear Conte, who had just endured an arduous sea voyage."

Why, it was enough to make a grown man healthy.

So it seemed to Gideon that insult was about to be heaped upon injury when there came a knock on his bedchamber door and Allegra peeped her head in to ask if she could speak with him.

"*You!* I know now what you were about. I saw your face when Uncle Denny turned me down. You tricked me. You were never going to marry me. And now you've come to crow over me!" he accused, turning his head toward the windows. "Well, I won't have it, so you can just go away again. Go on—go away!"

Allegra closed the door behind her and walked across the room to the bed. "Poor *bambino*," she sympathized, knowing that he had been at least partially correct. She *had* wanted Gideon to feel the rough side of her grandfather's tongue. She *had* enjoyed it. But that was not why she had come to her cousin's room.

She pulled up a straight-backed chair, taking from it the worn, velvet, floppy-eared rabbit that had been Gideon's since childhood, and sat down, the rabbit in her lap. "Are you feeling very ill, *cugino?*"

Gideon rolled onto his back, his bottom lip jutting out in defiance. "Yes, I am—and a lot anyone around here cares, if I live or die! It's all 'the dear Conte this' and 'the dear Conte that.' I'd like to take that stupid Italian and ship him straight back where he came from!"

"You do not like Bernardo, do you?" Allegra asked, knowing that it was not a brilliant question. "I fear I do not much like him either. He is too puffed up, too full of himself since he came to Brighton. He is a very different

Bernardo from the one I knew in Milano. Perhaps you are right, Gideon. Perhaps if we two can between us discover some way to get him to go back to Milano, he will become the same old Bernardo again, and not *un cane grosso*—this big dog!''

She had, needless to say, succeeded in garnering Gideon's undivided attention. He sat up, running a hand through his hair. "Get him to go back to Italy? We could do that? But—but the Conte doesn't have any money!"

"*I* have money, *cugino. Nonno* has given me an allowance. I have one thousand pounds. We could give this to Bernardo. It is enough money, yes?"

Gideon's eyes all but burst out of their sockets. "Uncle Denny gave you *what?* Then it's true—he is dicked in the nob! His only nephew deep in dun territory, and he's giving *you* a thousand pounds to buy hair ribbons!" His eyes retreated back into his skull as his eyelids narrowed speculatively. "You wouldn't wish to make your dearest cousin a small loan, would you, Allegra? Say, ah, *half* your thousand?"

Allegra shook her head. "I am so sorry, Gideon. I know I should loan it to you, if just to make up for teasing you so with *Nonno,* but I cannot. I shall need it all for our passages, and until I am once more up on my toes in Italy."

If Valerian had been privy to this conversation, he could have corrected Allegra by saying, "You mean back on your feet, imp." Valerian might have said it, but it is doubtful that he would have done so. Instead, just as Gideon did now, he most probably would have exploded, "*You're* going back to Italy!"

However, unlike Valerian's explosion into speech, which would have doubtless carried more than a hint of incredulity, Gideon's voice eloquently conveyed his elation—and his sudden and complete recovery from his latest "illness."

Allegra shrugged, her fingers idly stroking one of the rabbit's worn velvet ears. "I have no choice, *cugino*. Italy is my real home. Much as I am grateful to *Nonno* for asking for me, I now know I can never be really happy here. But I will need help, Gideon, to sneak away."

Gideon passed over Allegra's unhappiness without regret, concentrating on how this latest development would affect him. "All right," he said, swinging his legs over the edge of the mattress—which was not all that shocking, since he had been lying fully clothed beneath the satin coverlet.

"Give me a minute to think this thing out. You wish to return to Italy. Where you go, the Conte goes. If you go, Uncle Denny's money reverts to Mama. If the Conte goes, Mama reverts to me. Isobel? Who cares where she goes?"

He snatched up the rabbit and began pacing the floor, rubbing the velvet animal's hide against his cheek. "I know. Isobel will sink into a sad decline. Yes, and Uncle Denny will go tripping back to the Pavilion to act the toad-eater. Mama will once more get to handle the family purse strings, and I—ah! I get to live again! I can pay my debts and maybe even buy a half share of that racehorse Georgie told me about! A real goer, Georgie said."

He stopped and whirled about, pointing the rabbit at Allegra. "What about Valerian? Where does Fitzhugh come into this? Won't Uncle Denny just send him out to drag you back here, like some damned hound faithfully retrieving a stick?"

Allegra shook her head. "Valerian is finished with me. I am a graceless disgrace in his eyes. He will be too busy rejoicing over my absence to follow me. But that does not mean that he will like it even a little bit if he discovers that I am leaving, for he went to a great deal of trouble to deliver me here in the first place. Gideon—I must be on my way at once. It has been two days since Valerian was last here, and I know he will be back soon, when he thinks I am done with throwing things.''

"You throw things?"

She hopped to her feet, wishing Gideon would keep his mind on the subject at hand. "Never mind, *cugino.* Are you going to help me or not? I would go to Isobel, who would dearly like to see the back of me, except that she believes herself so in love with Bernardo that she would perish before allowing him to return to Italy.'' She made a face. "Isobel is so nice to me now. She is so nice to me that I have lost all my appetite and cannot eat. When I think of Valerian and the fool I made of myself with him, I cannot eat. *Cugino,* you must help me, before I fade into a small nothingness!''

Gideon stood in the middle of the room, hugging the velvet rabbit to himself in glee. "Help you, cousin? If you grow faint from hunger, why, I shall carry you aboard ship myself!''

MAX, ACTING AS Bernardo's interpreter, had been haunting the Dugdale house for the past two days, trying for a word alone with Allegra, but she had proved so elusive that he had nothing to report to an anxious Valerian when he and Bernardo returned that night to the Fitzhugh estate.

"Playing least in sight, that's what the little darlin' is doing,'' Max told Valerian when the two of them were finally alone, Bernardo having been tucked up in bed with a bowl of the sugarplums he favored (to be joined, unbeknownst to Valerian, not five minutes later by the Fitzhugh upstairs maidservant, who did not find her unfamiliarity with Italian to be an insurmountable barrier to a most intimate relationship with the handsome shoemaker).

"I don't like this, Max," Valerian said, downing the last of his brandy before refilling his glass from the decanter. "She refuses to see me. She sends back my notes, unread. I can't get within ten feet of her. And Duggy—he's no help at all. Says Allegra is devoting herself to him. She's hiding from me, that's what she's doing!"

Max sat at his ease in the oak-paneled, study, his shrewd gaze concentrated on Valerian's face. "And why would she be doin' that, I want to know. You wouldn't be tryin' anythin' nasty with the girl, would you? I had the two of you as good as wed."

"And we would be, if I could only get the little imp to stay in one place long enough for me to propose to her properly!" Valerian exploded, collapsing into the leather high-backed chair facing Max's. "Do you have any idea how difficult it is to propose marriage to a young lady who has already told you—at least twice—that you love her and wish to marry her? I feel as if I've been thrust headlong into a farce and Allegra has stolen all my lines!"

"Took the teeth right out of your saw, did she?" Max took a deep drink of brandy. "Ah! Wonderful cellar you have, Valerian. Just like a torchlight procession going down my throat, don't you know. Now, to get back to your problem, boyo. The colleen has told you all about *you*. Has she told you all about *her*, I'm wonderin'?"

Valerian's head came up. "You mean, has she told me she loves me?" He frowned, considering the question. "She allowed me to kiss her. She kissed me back." He shook his head, dismissing what he'd just said. "She also told me, while we were still in Italy, that she would never forgive me for sending her to the back door of my hotel—but that seems so long ago. Surely she didn't mean that.''

He looked worriedly at Max. ''She wouldn't still be holding a grudge, and trying to pay me out the same way she tricked Gideon into asking Dugdale for her hand. And she couldn't really be angry with me for teasing her for all but asking me to propose to her. Could she?''

Max shrugged. ''I'm not the one wearin' this slipper, boyo. Don't ask *me* where it pinches.''

''You want me to ask Allegra if she loves me—*after* she let me kiss her? I can't do that. I might just as well accuse her of being a loose woman!'' Valerian collapsed against the back of the chair. ''You know, Max, I used to be considered a very intelligent, well-ordered man. Now my life is a shambles, and I cannot add two and two with any real hope of ending up with four. Is it love itself that causes this condition, or is it Allegra in particular? I vow, my life has been complete chaos since I met her. I cut short my travels, have dined with Prinny—which I vowed never to do—have a shoemaker turned Conte living under my roof, and am contemplating marriage to a woman who may either love me or be working some sort of bizarre Italian *vendetta* against me for rescuing her from poverty and that same shoemaker.''

Max lifted his glass in an impromptu toast ''To love! What a delightful muddle!'' He downed his drink, shivering as the brandy licked hotly at the back of his throat. ''Drink up, boyo, for it's a dry bed and a wet bottle you're needin' tonight, don't you know. Drink until you lose the will to think. It'll be time and enough tomorrow to go after that little colleen—and then don't take no for an answer!''

It wasn't a very original idea—and probably not even a

very good one—but it was the only suggestion that appealed to Valerian at that moment. He raised his own glass and drank deep.

ALLEGRA HAD SPENT a sleepless night—or a "white night," as she described it to Betty—and refused her breakfast tray, unable to summon an appetite. The maid, who seemed to have developed a very real attachment to her unconventional mistress, clucked and scolded for the entire length of time it took Allegra to bathe and dress in one of her new morning gowns, and then, thankfully, left her alone.

Allegra desperately needed to be alone. She desperately needed to think. Not that she hadn't spent the entire night thinking, but this time she knew she had to apply herself to subjects other than how wonderful it felt to be in Valerian's arms, how thrilling his kisses were, how dear his angel wings were to her, and how she adored it when he smiled at her in that special way and called her his imp.

That sort of thinking had served only to make her cry into her pillow, and the time for tears had passed. She had put Gideon in charge of securing passage for her on a ship—and for the ridiculous Bernardo as well—and she must be ready to leave at a moment's notice. Somehow she must convey this news to the shoemaker, and then convince him that he had no future in Brighton.

"Which will be about as simple as threading a needle at midnight," she told her reflection as she peered into the mirror, noticing that she was developing the slightest smudging of bruised purple beneath her eyes. She pinched her cheeks, bringing color into them, knowing that Valerian would pick up very quickly on her wan appearance.

Valerian. She had to be gone before he arrived. He had put up with her nonsense for more than two days, but she knew he would not be put off much longer, and she would rather die than have to listen while he explained yet again that politely brought-up young ladies do *not* ask gentlemen to propose to them.

If only she hadn't run from the room, unable to control the tears that had threatened to destroy her completely. If only she had stayed, challenging him to explain why a gentleman may kiss a young lady and then *not* propose to her!

Except then, of course, Valerian might have pointed out—as he had done in Italy when he had sent her around to the servants' entrance of the hotel—that she was not a politely brought-up young lady. Perhaps, in his eyes, she was still the barefoot, none-too-clean girl he had met in Florence, a desperate, out-of-work opera singer who had taken to stealing sausages.

No! He loved her! He had to love her! She was Allegra Crispino, singer. She had even sung before the next King of England—and everyone had loved her! She must never forget that night. She must take it to her heart and treasure it always!

Allegra reluctantly quit her room, to wander aimlessly through the house and out into the back garden, where she had promised to meet with Gideon as soon as he returned from booking passage on a ship to Italy.

She took up a seat beneath a tree that was just beginning to bud and deliberately began humming snatches from the aria she had sung at the Pavilion, in the hope that it would improve her mood.

"That sounds familiar," Valerian said, walking up behind her so quietly that she was startled into silence. "Listen, imp. Even the birds in the trees cannot help but sing along with you."

"Valerian!" Allegra's eyes widened in panic. "I didn't expect...well, I guess I did expect...although I had hoped to be...but you are early.'' She deliberately avoided meeting his eyes, looking past him toward the door to the drawing room. ''Is—is Bernardo with you?''

''Well, now, imp, thereby hangs a tale.'' Valerian sat down beside her on the bench, his lips twitching in amusement. ''No, Bernardo is not with me. You see, the Conte Timoteo is aboard *The Valiant Lady,* already bound for Naples, several thousand pounds richer than he was upon his arrival in Brighton, and very happy to be seeing the last of England.''

Allegra knew her eyes had grown wide as saucers. ''He is? But why? He seemed to be enjoying himself most mightily.''

''Not entirely. Did you know, dearest girl, that Isobel tried to corner him yesterday in the Baron's morning room? Oh, yes, she did, and quite a sight that must have been. Bernardo was highly insulted—saying something about not being stuck twice by a large-toothed, chicken-breasted Englishwoman who wanted only to keep him on a leash. I believe he is planning to return to Milan and his family, with plans to enlarge their shop. It seems he has some new idea for boots with colored linings. Max went with him, eager to get back to Naples, but he leaves you his love and the wish that you may visit him soon.''

Allegra couldn't help herself. She looked up, straight into Valerian's eyes, and burst into delighted laughter. Totally forgetting herself, she then fell against Valerian's shoulder, mirth mingled with relief all but overcoming her, and it wasn't until several moments had passed that she realized he had put his arms around her and was holding her close against his chest.

''Valerian?'' she questioned, reluctantly pushing herself free of his embrace. ''I am correct in thinking that well-brought-up young ladies do not laugh quite so heartily—or do not do so in a gentleman's arms—yes? I am yet again a disgrace to you."

He pulled her to him once more, lifting her chin with the tip of one finger. "A nuisance, yes. A maddening, confusing, adorable bundle of hot emotions, yes. But a disgrace, Allegra? When have you ever been a disgrace?"

Allegra could have begun listing the times she had behaved badly, counting them off on her fingers for him—beginning with her outrageous behavior in Italy and ending with her overweening arrogance in assuming that he loved her and then telling him so—but she decided against it.

After all, Valerian was with her now, and he was looking at her in that special way, a look that had once confused but now thrilled her. She was in his arms, Bernardo was gone from the scene, and it appeared that, yet again, she had landed on her toes.

This was not the time to tempt fate by reminding him of things best placed in *dimenticatoio*—that lovely, wholly imaginary place in which to put forgotten things.

And to think she had planned to leave England without ever seeing him again, while still harboring the desperate hope that he would posthaste come chasing after her once more, begging her to love him. But then he wasn't to know that, was he? Nobody was to know that except for her—she with her temperamental Crispino and devious Dugdale blood running hot in her veins—and *she* certainly wasn't going to tell him!

Valerian tipped Allegra's head to one side and began nibbling very delicately at the base of her throat, sending a shiver delicately through her. Was this the reaction of a man who did not love her? Was this the reaction of a man who wanted nothing more than to be a good friend to her grandfather by keeping her out of mischief, while at the same time wishing that he could be shed of her once and for all?

This was wonderful. This was everything she had ever hoped for, and she hadn't had to run all the way back to Italy to know once and for all that Valerian loved her. She had only to sit in the back garden of Number 23, and love had come to her.

She raised a hand to cup his cheek, her head thrown back as his lips traced a path from her throat to the corner of her mouth. "You were going to say something to me the other day, Valerian, something I did not think I wished to hear. Now I wonder if I made yet another mistake. Perhaps you will tell me now, while I am so very much interested in listening."

But now Valerian wasn't listening. The feel of her, the scent of her, the taste of her, had driven all rational thought from his mind. Talk? Who wished to talk when there were so many more delightful things they could be doing? There was plenty of time for talk. They had a lifetime to talk.

She was here. She was in his arms, willingly, happily, in his arms. She wasn't the mercurial Allegra now, the one-moment hot, one-moment cold bundle of conflicting emotions that so excited him, yet so confused him.

How could he ever have thought she had only been boasting that he loved her—much in the way she had boasted about her voice, and how she *had* sung for the Bishop of Bologna? She *did* have the most glorious, pure voice he had ever heard. She had sung for the Bishop—for the next King of England as well! Allegra didn't boast. Allegra merely told the truth—except for those times when she bent it a little to suit her own purpose. But then, bless her, what woman didn't?

"Valerian? You will tell me—"

He silenced her with his mouth, his kiss shattering all thought as they melted together on the bench in the back garden of Number 23, oblivious to the world around them…the birds singing above them in the budding branches of the tree…the sound of the door to the drawing room opening…the footfalls that should have alerted them to the fact that they were no longer alone.

"Excuse me, Fitzhugh," Gideon announced with obvious glee. "I hate to be the one to throw a damper on what appears to be a touching moment, but—"

Valerian pushed Allegra's face protectively against his chest, not ready to relinquish his hold on her, and looked daggers at the younger man, who was standing directly in front of them, grinning like the cat that has cornered the mouse. "Nonsense, Kittredge. Don't hold back—not when you do it so very well."

Allegra stiffened, feeling the animosity sparkling between the two men, then began to tremble as she realized that, just when she thought her world had turned rosy, all her carelessly loosed pigeons were about to come home to roost. Allegra had never underestimated Gideon—not when she had first met him in the Dugdale drawing room, and not now. He had seen her and Valerian together, and had instantly understood everything. She struggled to get free, anxious to keep Gideon from speaking, but Valerian continued to hold her close.

Gideon knew now that he had *never* had a chance with Allegra. She had most definitely been leading him on, just as he had told her, so that he could debase himself in front of his uncle, who would then ring a mighty peal over his head. He was still not too clear on why she had come to him for help—perhaps she'd also at some point taken a pet against Fitzhugh that had now been resolved—but it was definitely clear to him that he had been made a cat's paw of yet again.

She had roused him from his bed of pain, sending him off to procure passage for her and that Italian popinjay, only to snuggle up with Fitzhugh, who, unless he missed his guess, would soon be the possessor of both the promised plum and Allegra's eventual inheritance.

Gone was his hope of regaining his share of the Dugdale fortune. Equally fled were his chances of paying his debts and buying part of Georgie's racehorse. And, to put the capper on it, that insufferable Conte would remain underfoot, to blight him with his beauty.

Gideon realized that he was beginning to breathe very quickly, his shallow breaths causing him to feel slightly light-headed. Perhaps he should seek out his mother, and have her monitor his racing pulse. But no! First he would destroy his cousin, this maddening Italian interloper in his once well-cushioned life, for now and for all time!

He stepped forward another pace and smiled down at Allegra, who was, he noticed, looking decidedly pale. "I have the tickets and passports you asked me to procure for you, dearest cousin. You and the Conte can take ship tonight and leave on the morning tide. Here," he concluded triumphantly, flinging a small packet into her lap. "*Bon voyage!*"

Allegra watched as Gideon, walking with a definite spring in his step, returned to the house, leaving her alone with Valerian, whose arms had deserted her halfway through her cousin's speech, leaving her to shiver in the sudden chill that had invaded the air.

"I—I suppose you would like to hear some sort of explanation?" she suggested at last, when the silence had become unbearable.

"Not really," Valerian answered evenly, rising to stand in front of her. "I think I'd rather work this one out for myself. You were perhaps planning to escort Bernardo back to Milan before he could father an entire generation of beautiful, dull-witted Adonises here in Brighton? Oh, yes, I may have forgotten to tell you, imp, but it seems your once devoted swain has recovered from his heartbreak with a vengeance. Max found him this morning with not one but two of my housemaids in his—well, never mind that.

"Passing over that idea," he went on, his heart growing, "I would have to believe that you were planning not to escort Bernardo but to *accompany* him back to Italy. You would do this because you are desperately unhappy here in Brighton. Now, as you have mastered the Kittredges, and as you have grown extremely fond of Duggy—though I still cannot bring myself to understand why—and you have become a great sensation here in Brighton, I can only deduce that you had felt it necessary to run away from someone or something."

"Valerian, I—"

"Hush, imp, and let me finish. Yes, you were running away. Now, whom have you been avoiding these past days? Why, I do believe it is I—am I correct? You have been avoiding me. Is this because you cannot stand the sight of me? Modesty to one side, I don't think so. Is it possibly because you feel you have made a spectacle of yourself merely by being—bless you—yourself? Ah, now this has the ring of typical Allegra Crispino logic. Max told me a woman's mind is a curious thing, but you, my love—and almost always for what you believe to be the best of reasons—have turned chaos into an art form."

"*Valerian!* I—"

He looked down at her, reaching out his hands to pull

her to her feet. "If we really work at it, imp, I suppose we could go round and round for several days—or even months—trying to explain to each other all that has transpired since first we met. But that would be very fatiguing, and not at all sensible, don't you agree?"

He was actually asking for her opinion? He had finally done with spouting absurdities, his handsome, adorable face split in an unholy grin. Allegra opened her mouth to speak. "Valerian, I—"

But he cut her off once again. "Don't say another word, my darling. Just listen. I don't care why you thought you had to flee, since you aren't going anywhere ever again without me by your side. You don't have to say anything because you have already said it all. I love you. Everyone loves you. It's impossible not to, imp. And yes, I want to marry you. *Now* you may speak. Are you going to become my wife, Allegra, or am I going to spend the rest of my life chasing after you with twice the perseverance and determination of a dozen Bernardo Timoteos?"

She smiled at him, her heart and her love shining in her tear-bright sapphire eyes, then said cheekily, "I will give you my answer very soon, dearest Valerian, but first, I think I should like for us to adjourn to the kitchens for something to eat. Suddenly I find myself *very* hungry!"

EPILOGUE

THE CHARITY PERFORMANCE at the Theatre Royal, complete with the Prince Regent in attendance, had been a triumph, although Allegra Crispino Fitzhugh got no closer to the stage than her seat of honor beside Prinny in his private box.

Isobel, the original architect of the scheme, who had conceived such a performance as the scene of Allegra's ultimate disgrace, had not been present as several very talented singers gathered by Valerian performed to raise funds for the widows and orphans of soldiers who had died in the war. Isobel, along with her mother and brother, had removed to Wolverhampton the previous week on a "repairing lease" that was to last as long as Baron Dugdale desired—since it was he who, only when he was good and ready, would ultimately pay his nephew's gaming debts so that the Kittredges could again show their faces in Brighton without the danger of Gideon being set upon by his angry creditors.

"Best stretch of peace and quiet I've had since Aggie and her brats moved in," he had told Valerian happily as he waved the newly wed couple on their way after the performance and made to join the Prince Regent for a late supper at the Pavilion.

Allegra was still singing snatches from one of the arias that had been performed as Valerian entered their bedchamber an hour later, already dressed in his nightclothes, a burgundy banyan tied about his trim waist.

He looked at his wife of three weeks, happy to see that she was still clothed in the pearled-petal-strewn gown that would always be a reminder of the day he had completely and totally lost his heart to her. How he would delight in divesting her of it.

"Imp?" he prompted, interrupting her as she whirled about the room, holding up her skirts delicately while she sang another verse in lilting Italian.

"Valerian!" Allegra immediately broke off her song to launch herself into his outstretched arms. "Ah, *caro mio,* what a night! You did not mind that Prinny pinched me, yes? It was only the once, and he was so good to allow the performance. And you did once say that you felt sorry for him."

Valerian frowned as he steered her toward the wide bed, for he had missed the pinch. "Not *that* sorry, imp. Now sit down, my darling, for I have something to tell you."

"A surprise? Oh, how lovely!" Allegra's sapphire eyes shone brightly as she scrambled to the very center of the bed, her ivory taffeta skirts billowing around her. She patted the space next to her, inviting him to join her. "But you must be careful not to muss my gown. I have told Betty you would act as my maid tonight, and she would not like it if this pretty thing were to become a mass of wrinkles."

Valerian ignored the warning, watching, entranced, as Allegra contradicted herself by collapsing against the pillows, then lay close against her on his side, his head propped on his hand. It was difficult to keep his mind on what he wished to say when Allegra began running her fingertips up and down his bare forearm, but he did his best. "How would you like to go back to Italy, imp?" he asked, observing the pearled petals flutter invitingly with her every breath.

"Italia?" Allegra's smooth brow furrowed in confusion. "I thought you wished to open the London house for what you called the Season. You have changed your mind? Why?"

Valerian's left hand reached out to begin idly playing with one of the pearled petals on her bodice. "I had a dream last night, imp," he said, his voice slightly husky. "In my dream we were installed in a villa on Capri, just the two of us, spending lazy days visiting Roman ruins and the grottoes and long, wonderful nights lying in a glorious, gauze-hung bedchamber, visiting the stars."

"Visiting the stars?" Allegra's smile was of wonder. "I think you must show me how we did that, *caro mio,* for I am not sure if I know what you mean."

He leaned across her body, pushing himself up on his elbows, his face mere inches from hers. "I think you know, imp. You know very well." His lips teasingly brushed hers. "*Amerò* my darling. I will love."

She reached up a hand to brush at his beloved angel wings, then traced the line of his cheek. "Ah, Valerian. *Amerai*—you will love. I like that. And then?"

He briefly turned his lips into her palm, then looked deeply into her eyes and whispered, "And then, my dearest imp, *ameremo*—we will love."

"*Amiamo, caro mio*—we love!" Allegra agreed, willingly surrendering her lips to his.

And then there was no more need for words.

MILLS & BOON®

Live the emotion

Look out for next month's
Super Historical Romance

THE COLONEL'S DAUGHTER

by Merline Lovelace

She wasn't afraid to fight...
Beneath the polish of an Eastern finishing school
lies a soldier's daughter who can ride, shoot,
and deal cards with the best.

For the man...
Jack Sloan is a hard, handsome gunslinger who exudes
the kind of danger wise men avoid. And when he saves
Suzanne's life, she decides to ride with him through the
Dakota Badlands, with or without his say-so.

Or for his love
Jack wants nothing more than to put this upstart
female in her place – and in his bed. But he's riding a
tough trail, and there's no place for a woman in his life.
He's never met anyone like Suzanne, though, and
now he has to choose between avenging his past – or
finding a future in her arms!

On sale 6th October 2006

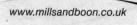